SELECTION OF REVIEWS ON AMAZON

'This is one of the most absorbing novels I have read in a long time. Modern history has been very cleverly intertwined with the present to bring a plot that is refreshingly original and frighteningly plausible but all the more gripping for that.'

'A must for those who continue to believe in humanity, in this crazy world, and are able to think for themselves. Definitely recommended.'

'The author carries us from the ugliness of the Nazi era to a turbulent present, and alludes to an unpredictable future. The journey is at times violent and jarring as we encounter troubled and sadistic characters and realise that this is just the beginning of a long descent.'

'The writer crafts his characters with skill and in doing so evokes a myriad of emotions: disgust, pity, sadness, fear and doubt. But the heroes in the story cast light and deliver hope with their goodness and faith.'

'The story left me wanting more ... A thoroughly enjoyable read.'

BLOOD RELATIONSHIPS

BOOK ONE OF RESURRECTIONS

Philip Oldfield was born in England. As a young child, he lived in New York and Connecticut for two years and still sees America as his second home. His alma mater is the University of Exeter where he read an honours degree in Geography. He is currently reading for a Masters in Fine Arts – Creative Writing at Manchester Metropolitan University.

—

Modern history breathes deeply across all of our lives. Most are unaware of its impact long after we have fooled ourselves the past is gone and buried. Caught in history's cross hairs, Claire Yohanus and Tom Abimelech come face-to-face with an ugliness of evil that tests their faith, trust and unbreakable bonds of love. Yet, this is just the beginning. Across these pages unfolds their true story – one previously unknown to the world – a battle for humanity against one of history's darkest secrets created by one of the world's greatest powers ever seen. It is a secret raised from the grave. The past is not dead. It has a heartbeat.

ALSO BY PHILIP A. OLDFIELD

The Devil in Me

The Lying Truth

My Dream Mother

Flash Fiction 25

BLOOD RELATIONSHIPS

Book One of Resurrections

Philip A. Oldfield

This book would not have been possible without the courage and testimony of Claire Yohanus and Tom Abimelech.

ISBN-13: 978-1493611485
ISBN-10: 1493611488

Grateful acknowledgment is made to all of the poets whose extracts appear within this novel and to the researchers whose work is mentioned herein. The story blends history with fiction. I will leave it within the capable hands of the Reader to discern, if they wish, which is which. For those who prefer a more relaxed option, I have included at the end of the book, a synopsis of the history used.

DEDICATION

For Tegen, Elestren, Ust and Trystan, I thank God for your love
and belief in me.
And to Helen, thank you for your love and steadfast support.

'National Socialism ... the interest of our people undoubtedly lies in the rigorous establishment of a German order ... without paying any attention to the claims [of people living there.]'

Josef Goebbels, Reich Minister of Propaganda, Diary Entry - March 16, 1942

TRUTH

By Ethel Bedford (1892-1979)

Truth is the zenith for our lives.

It brings peace within when we reach its height.

Never descend from its peak

And give deceit and illusion a place in the light.

PROLOGUE

'It's nearly twenty past nine,' said Tom, 'shall we start?'

Claire looked up from the large table where she had just wrapped the last item of documentation. She nodded and gave Tom a weak, exhausted smile. He walked over and kissed her on the forehead.

'We're nearly there,' he said. 'We've done our best. God couldn't have asked more of us, could he?'

Claire wrapped her arms around Tom's waist and held him close. 'No Tom, he couldn't.'

She looked up into his eyes and squeezed him three times.

'I love you too,' he said and they kissed.

Claire settled herself onto the chair behind the desk. Tom turned on the camcorder.

'Ready?' He asked.

She nodded and took a deep breath.

'My name is Claire Juliette Yohanus. I read English at the University of Exeter. I formerly lived in Iverna Gardens, London. Up until the summer of 2012, I was a lead reporter for one of the surviving broadsheets in the United Kingdom. I was responsible for the North American Continent. Since 2008, I have covered the presidential race for the White House. The nature of events that unfolded in 2012 prevented me from returning to the USA for the 57th presidential election on November 6 2012 … What you are about to find out is true. It is a foretaste of things to come.'

She stood up went out of camera shot and operated the camcorder. Tom walked into view and took up the seat.

'My name is Tom Peter Abimelech. I read Computer Science at the University of Exeter. I formerly lived in Banbury Road, Oxford. Up until the summer of 2012, I lived in Spain, where I attended a Roman Catholic Seminary to prepare me for the priesthood. The nature of events that unfolded in 2012 prevented me from resuming my vocation … What you are about to learn is the truth...' He paused before allowing his eyes to bore deep into the camera's lens, trying desperately to reach those who might see. 'God help us all.'

Claire switched the camcorder off.

They looked at one another. It was over.

PART ONE – SEEING IS BELIEVING

THE ARMY SURGEON

By Sydney Dobell (1824-1874)

He labours thro' the red and groaning day.
The fearful moorland where the myriads lay
Moved as a moving field of mangled worms.
And as a raw brood, orphaned in the storms,
Thrust up their heads if the wind bend a spray
Above them, but when the bare branch performs
No sweet parental office, sink away
With hopeless chirp of woe, so as he goes
Around his feet in dangerous agony
They rise and fall; and all the seething plain
Bubbles a cauldron vast of many-coloured pain

ONE

And so it begins.

Mengele boarded Bremerhaven Süd's general cargo ship *Joanney* in the early hours, its destination was Tilbury Docks on the south-east coast of England. He was its only passenger. It was to be a round trip of nearly fifty days. He was travelling, as far as the Captain and crew were concerned, as a grandfather seeking solitude in order to complete his memoirs for posterity and to visit some very old friends in England for the last time.

On March 16, he would reach his 65th birthday. The moment he had dreamed of and which the Führer had wished for, for the future of the Thousand Year Reich had arrived. When it was over, he would gladly bow out of history and leave the planning of the future to other generations loyal to the Network.

The crew busied themselves with the routines of departure. Mengele took a last look at the port's vast and silent array of yellow painted cargo cranes. These magnificent giants reminded him of the dead and dying aliens from *War of the Worlds*. A new kind of alien was coming, he thought. This time the war for the world would be won.

His eyes drifted along a row of resting seagulls adorning one of the crane's outstretched arms. They were draped like the white pearls of a necklace around a woman's neck.

A memory surfaced and he smiled to himself recalling a fertile Jewish woman, Keziah, whom he and Clauberg had experimented on during the war. Mengele remembered her saying, so fiercely before she died, "My name means polished and refined; how dare you do these things to me?"

Like pearls, she had lasted a long time.

For one member of the crew this journey would not be routine. He was the ship's steward, Willi Scheinbeck. In a former life, he was SS-Unterscharführer Adolf Säzner, a sanitary orderly at Auschwitz concentration camp. The man leaning over the ship's railings had allowed him alone to live. As a twin, he was grateful for that. How his sister would have lived without him had he died, well, it wasn't worth thinking about, he thought.

SS-Hauptsturmführer Mengele turned around as the ship's steward approached, Säzner warmly welcomed aboard the most special and treasured of guests the ship had ever carried. The day ahead, indeed the journey and the future looked bright. The former SS wartime orderly proudly carried his commanding officer's luggage and typewriter to his slavishly prepared cabin.

The ship's room was spartan, but Mengele over the years had seen worse and had lived, if he could call it that, in more confined spaces on occasions, and had been forced to share his food and company with a range of bugs that squeezed through crevices he could not.

Nearly twenty-nine years had passed since his negotiated release from incarceration by the Americans in June 1945. Despite continuous efforts to hunt him down, his evasion was always assured. He was amongst many others on the run, the occasional bone that was thrown by the Network for the media to gnaw on for a while to distract the world and, as they had found over the years, was necessary from time to time to generate myths and uncertainties. This left him free to continue the funding of ever-progressive research and each year since, he had remained focused.

Painstakingly slow coded postcards and letters had been exchanged with Professor Aguilulfo Eisenberg. Clauberg's theories had been right. Perhaps he would have been chosen by the Führer had it not been for his age and his reputation for boasting of his achievements and experiments on guinea pigs. The man did not know how to keep a low profile. He lacked the self-discipline of a soldier. Whereas he, Mengele, who had distinguished himself in combat during the war and won the Iron Cross twice, was a man who could be trusted. The Führer had recognised a like-minded soul.

Over the years, Mengele had occupied himself in South America and had been able, in fragmented bursts, to continue his own work to reproduce twins. However, being next to the operating table, trying out new human experiments, these were the activities he had thrived on. At times, it had been frustrating living on the edges of research. At least he had the satisfaction though, that the artificial breeding programme at Auschwitz – his and Clauberg's heady but haphazard days – had all those years ago, paid off and served its purpose. Professor Eisenberg and his fellow geneticists had taken their research forward in the sanatoriums and were now far beyond the rather limited vein of activity being tried and fumbled over by poorly resourced scientists from around the world.

The transformational breakthrough borne out of over forty years of combined research had come about when Eisenberg's team had extracted healthy DNA from embryonic cells and replaced them with the transgenes MAO-A, DAT1-A1 and COMT.

As each embryo grew, the research team had become increasingly confident that the genetic modification would switch on in adulthood. The actual age was still an open debate, which combined with the high rate of miscarriages, had been

14

the weaknesses the research teams had wrestled with over the decades. Nevertheless, the petri dish production line was taking shape. German's manufacturing prowess once again was being resurrected.

He felt so very proud. Oh yes, Mengele remembered, importantly one more genetic modification had had to be engineered into each male zygote. Each had to be rendered sterile by the introduction of the NR5-A1 gene. Eisenberg had assured him this last and most vital of ingredient, which would prevent the ensuing creations of the Fourth Reich from reproducing…

A knock on Mengele's cabin door drew a conclusion to his reverie.

'Enter,' he commanded. The firmness of Mengele's voice had never left him.

Scheinbeck entered carrying a pot of English tea. It was a quaint tradition that Mengele had grown a liking for over the years.

'Just as you instructed mein Kapitan,' said Säzner falling back into his old ways with his commanding officer.

'Thank-you Adolf, this is so very kind of you. How is your sister these days?'

The ship's steward stood proudly to attention, SS-Hauptsturmführer Mengele remembered his first name after all of these years.

She is very well mein Kapitan, and the medicine you gave me for her at Auschwitz is still working, she no longer has any fits.'

'Ah, that is good Adolf. I am so very pleased to hear that. It is a pleasure to see you again.'

'And you mein Kapitan.'

15

LONDON – 1974

TWO

Saturday, March 16, 1974 – London, England

Just off Kenton Street, passers-by see a privately owned psychiatric clinic, called Osprey Lodge. The five-storey building is home for fifty private patients. The home also contains an operating theatre and several private care rooms. These are located in the sound proof basement, accessible only by the lift and by use of the access key, individual copies of which, are carried by two orderlies, selected nurses and the Lodge's two private medical doctors.

Mengele, speaking in German described the pre-operational and post-operational procedures. He wanted the legacy from this room, on this day, his birthday, to be captured on camera for the future inspiration of the Fourth Reich's loyal followers.

'I plan to use prostaglandins to ripen the opening of the cervical canal and induce labour.'

As he spoke, he became conscious that the young woman before him understood every word he said. That was good. He wanted her to feel more fear, if that was possible.

'I will administer the prostaglandins intra-cervically as opposed to intra-vaginally. I want to ensure the patient feels a degree of discomfort. And that is good.' He laughed. The perverse fed his humour.

A short while later Mengele introduced the drug slowly and deeply into the woman. She was the first who had had a successful IVF transplantation that had gone to full term. The others had miscarried and for that, the mothers had paid the ultimate price.

The young woman before them had been trafficked into their safekeeping. Her wrists were strapped to the bed. She had been prepared for operation. Her mouth was entirely sealed apart from the feeding tube sewn permanently in place. Her legs were spread apart, each one restrained in metal stirrups. She lay on her back in a conventional birth position. Whilst the cycle of labour continued on its inexorable way, Mengele continued to dictate the procedures he had planned and which lay ahead.

Later, he gently eased the male, non-identical twins into the world. They were valuable commodities, the Fourth Reich's first newborn foot soldiers.

He stopped for a while then to enjoy a cup of tea and biscuits and leant over his patient's face from time to time to give her one of his renowned reassuring smiles. The young woman's eyes bulged and tears streamed down the sides of her face. Her muffled groans reverberated in the metal feeding tube. He patted her forearm.

Once the wet nursing had run its natural course, medical couriers would transfer the twins into the care and waiting arms of two sets of parents in the heart of the UK's capital city. He could have kept the mother alive and dispensed with wet nursing, but it had been so long since his last *real* operations in Gross Rosen … besides, birthdays are all about self-indulgence aren't they, he thought.

Now,' said Mengele, 'the post operative and disposal procedure for the patient. I will make use of a blood transfusion tube and run it from the patient's radial artery into her lungs. By severing the radial artery, I anticipate cardiac arrhythmia, severe hypovolaemia, shock, cardiac arrest and death to follow in that order within 2 minutes and 30 seconds. I estimate loss of consciousness will occur in 30 seconds. Let's see how accurate I am, shall we?'

Following dinner and when the time in the evening had arrived Mengele rose to give his final speech to the invited multi-national guests, consisting of investors, industrialists, politicians, bankers, armed forces officers, civil servants, medical personnel and media moguls.

'Today my sacrifice is a legacy for history. We have arrived at the dawn of a new Reich. As the momentum towards worldwide use of IVF grows, as surely it will, so too will the opportunities arise for us to seed genetically engineered zygotes into desperate mothers around the globe ...'

Monday, March 18, 1974 – Tilbury Docks, England

In the early hours, the captain of the Joanney welcomed aboard his unassuming passenger.

'How was your visit? Did you find your friends well?'

Mengele replied, 'It was a very satisfactory gathering, thank you. Seeing everyone again made me feel we were almost blood relatives. It was good, yes.'

'Good. The ship's steward will escort you to your cabin whilst we make preparations to be underway. Sleep well.'

Mengele took to his bed with a deep sense of satisfaction. He had fulfilled his duty to the Führer and to the Fatherland. The Fourth Reich was on the rise. He closed his eyes and breathed in the raft of recent memories. His chest had filled with pride when he had turned to face the Nazi flag and had gazed upon the picture of their leader hanging from ceiling to floor. That had been his time, his only time. And when he had faced his audience once more, he knew then how much he would have relished real power; no wonder the Führer thrived on it.

In time, waves of untroubled sleep swept over him.

Wednesday, February 7, 1979 – Bertioga, Brazil

Following a light lunch Wolfgang Gerhard, also known as Dr. Josef Mengele, went for his usual afternoon swim in the Atlantic.

He was found later, floating, unmoving, face down. Would-be rescuers dragged his lifeless body to the shore. Despite their best efforts, they could not revive him. His work for the Reich was indeed, now over.

LONDON — 2012

THE MASK OF ANARCHY

By Percy Bysshe Shelley (1792-1822)

Written on the occasion of the Peterloo Massacre, Manchester

And he wore a kingly crown;
And in his grasp a sceptre shone;
On his brow this mark I saw -
'I AM GOD, AND KING, AND LAW!

THREE

Wednesday, July 4, 2012 – Friars Mead, Tower Hamlets, London

The itch in the killer's mind had become insane. He could not resist it. He did not, in the end, want to. He scratched at the scab and felt the venom rush as the floodgates collapsed and the poison within him invaded his brain and entered the sinews of his body. The rush was raw and visceral. He was awash with it.

The angry stream of vengeance had been fermenting, until the hidden serpent waiting to spit, to urge him, to drive him, to force him to kill, struck. And when he did, the first killing had felt so good, so right. God's justice.

The power he felt over the final moments of death was an intoxicating drug when the last fragments of life convulsed as his victim fought back with one last surge to survive, until the grip of death twisted the final juices of life out of its prey. The man's tongue had turned blue, then black. Froth, spittle and then blood oozed from his mouth. The dark brown hairs across the murderer's forearms formed an ebony river coursing over his tattoos. Try as they might, the hairs were unable to cover the images.

On his left forearm, the words, 'I am God and King and Law' encircled a scale of justice icon. On his right, in blood red ink the following words had been scored, 'The Mask of Anarchy'. Underneath, a gruesome smiling face of death was wrapped in the grip of a hissing serpent.

Death had beaten its drum in the early hours of the morning. Beat the life out of the man who wore a scarf to highlight his face, but in reality was worn to hide the wrinkles of age around his neck. The scarf had been a gift from his lover. A lover he had no more. There was no one to miss him. The unfortunate, as he was now, had been walking along Manchester Road. He had been in the wrong place. His sentence, deliverance to the Almighty sooner than he would have wished.

In the pub, the victim had seen the coarse and muscular man in fleeting glimpses across the several bars inside. Once or twice, they had caught each other's eye. His build had made him acutely conscious of needing to be wanted again. And when finally he had drunk enough courage, the man had dematerialised and was gone; despondent, he had left.

He had been making his way home on foot. It was quiet, just him, his thoughts, the pavement and an empty road. Had he known his fate, he would have preferred it to have stayed that way or at least to have a passing witness or two, another car on the road even, to see the steps he took that would end his life. If only.

When a solitary car had pulled up alongside of him, there smiling was Eros reborn resting one of his strong tattooed arms on the car's open window, he had not hesitated. The decision to say yes had been easy. He had warmed to the sight of a dog, with gorgeously sleek black fur, lying on the back seat. He had leant over and patted him. The dog had wagged his tail and licked his hand, which probably tasted old and salty.

Back home, his cat had watched him and the much taller, bigger man, trailing the warning scent of a dog on his clothes, enter the hallway and make their way deeper into the house. Lust had rapidly turned to fear when the powerful – now unstoppable – killer tightened not loosened his scarf. He was forced to the floor. He wanted to scream. He wanted so desperately to shout. His eyes bulged. His tongue lolled. A knife slit cleanly across his throat.

The only sounds he could make, none other than his killer could hear. In the final convulsions of death, his heart had been removed. The beat of death had drummed loudly in his house. An insane justice had been done.

In the shower as the killer's rage subsided, and the itch had been sated for now, he had watched with dwindling curiosity as the remnants of death disappeared in a swirl down the plughole. Silently, unobserved he had had left. In the car, his dog, waiting patiently, enjoyed a new form of meat that night. One he would take a liking for. His master had not forgotten him; it was a dog's life after all.

FOUR

On impulse, Tom made the phone call. The one he had been vacillating over all day. Truth be told, he had been wavering over this call for years. How do you face the truth when life offers so many alternatives, so many other callings to pursue? There had been no answer. When her recorded voice invited him to say something, leave a message, he had hesitated before saying what he had planned to say. Serendipity would do the rest. Her warmth brought out the best in him. It always had. Maybe, he had done the same for her ... until that was...

With the hotel phone at rest in its cradle, Tom looked around the desolate room. It reflected his feelings. His mind was distracted. It had been mirroring his heart of late. The beat sometimes drowned out God's voice.

He took a shower instead of a bath. The cubicle was small, but utilitarian. The towels, a tad shabby, though clean, dried his body well. Water had a habit of reviving him, but not this evening. Tom felt the disconnections from the seminary and the first jolts of being back in England return. His reflective mood deepened. It was not the direction of depression he was heading in. It was about him escaping the demands of daily office, a prerequisite of commitment to religious life. Nor too, was this a pinch-crunch moment, in as much as Tom was not about to leap off the bridge of faith into the swollen river of the material world.

25

In the last five years, Tom's religious preparation had compressed him, like a spring under constant load. Having stepped away from the burden of commitment, his mind was now filled with chaotic thoughts, jostling and colliding and fogging his brain to such an extent, he could not see a way forward. His life was full of dichotomies, each luring him this way and that. He had choices to make.

Yet even in this reflective mood, his desire for meditation, to feel the flow of agape within him was abandoned. It was almost as if in this bone weary, dog tired state, that doing what he would normally do, became not so much a solution, or a remedy to engender calmness, but conjured instead, feelings of confinement. Of claustrophobia, even. He had to escape.

He needed a city-break from God. It had to be long enough to taste, but not one where the material world consumed him. Good intentions are just that though. Initially, he settled for drinks in the hotel's bar. That alone was enough to kill the dead. So dressed in his crumpled linen suit and open neck shirt Tom strolled along the streets away from the hotel. The urban effects that warmed the evenings in London, coupled with a gentle breeze, freed his mind.

His journey led to a warren of small restaurants and local distilleries fronted by pubs. They reminded him of his undergraduate days sampling the varied delights of Devon. The inviting flicker of candlelight enhanced the welcoming mood of restaurants, whilst chic, minimalist and bold bars were filled with animated raucous customers. Wherever his eyes roamed, people avidly talked, ate, gesticulated, smiled, laughed and drank. All was a joyous orchestra of sights, sounds and scents; memories of Claire warmed his senses and he smiled.

As he wandered further into Camden, Tom was drawn to a quirky pub, The Fiddlers Rest. Looking through its windows, he could see people packed, not quite to the gunwales, or in commuter tube closeness, but still, despite occupying small intimate spaces, all seemed happy, amidst the heaving throng of joyful humanity.

What drew Tom's eye in particular were two plaques above the bar. They were easily visible for passers-by to see. The first one read, *'The measure of love is when you love without measure.'* How true, how challenging and how so very rewarding, he thought. Provided of course, you have the energy to scale those peaks and breathe in the pure oxygen of love. Not so good though when you come down or worse still, fall foul of unsure footing and with flailing arms plummet to the ground, dragged down by the gravity of your own personal issues. In those times, one can only hope love is returned without measure. He had done his best. Sometimes he had got it right. But that one time: the most important time, he hadn't.

The adjacent plaque made him smile. It lightened his mood. It read, *'Laundry, drop your pants here.'* He wondered if the two phrases when combined as one reading were for customers: when you enter this pub everyone should get on with one another at all times and leave any dirty linen or personal issues behind the bar and basically have a bloody good time. Just the place he needed. The atmosphere beckoned.

FIVE

Tom entered the good-natured crowd and wove his way left and right, turning sideways on many occasions in order to, almost crab like, arrive at the bar. Along with other contenders, he rested his elbows on the counter and waved some notes in his hands, hoping to catch the eyes of bar staff.

He was at the far end and at the right-hand side of the bar. To his left there appeared to stretch an unending line of expectant customers. A man next to him, a similar age to Tom, was dressed in a checked shirt and jeans.

Tom asked, 'Are you being served or next in line by any chance?'

'No idea mate. We're at the wrong end. I've been here for ages; the bar staff keep focusing on that wedge of people in the middle.'

'I see,' said Tom, 'I'll assume I'm after you. If not, I'm sure someone will say. Think I'll stand up tall to see if I can draw some attention and get us served.'

'Are you a local then?' he asked.

'Me? No, I'm just in the city for a long weekend; needed a change of scenery,' replied Tom. 'What about you?' he added.

'Yeah, I'm down for a long weekend too. My girlfriend's over there.' He pointed to a woman wearing a snug fitting white dress; she had shoulder length dark hair and, thought Tom, was in her early to mid 20s. The man continued speaking,

'I'm thinking of moving down here to live with her, but I'm not sure.'

The need to queue for a drink took second place for a while and Tom asked 'Why is that?'

The man hesitated for a moment before replying, 'I live on the coast near Hastings. I've got two boats moored there. The thing is, if I moved here, I'll never get near the boats and will have to give them up. But I'm not sure I want to do that.'

'It's a lot to give up a passion, I know. I made a decision five years ago not to. And now…' Tom went on, 'Is there any way you could berth your boats on the Thames somewhere? Or could you make sure that you diary in regular visits to Hastings? Better still, perhaps, could your girlfriend move to Hastings instead?'

'That's not possible,' he said, his voice sounding resigned, 'I can't afford the mooring fees on the Thames and besides there's a huge waiting list. More importantly, Anne has a good job in the East End and has her young child to bring up. I'm a freelance graphic designer. So I'm mobile, you see.'

'Your problem reminds me of a line from a book for people seeking focus and direction in their lives. It's written by Stephen Covey. In it, he says, the main thing is to keep the main thing, the main thing.'

The man repeated the phrase over to himself several times. He looked across at Anne. Her eyes broke into a radiant smile and she waved at him.

The man looked at Tom and said, 'Do you know something, you have really helped me to see what I want to do. It was obvious. Staring me in the face and I couldn't see it, was frightened of what it might mean I guess. Strewth, a decision's easy when you see things clearly.'

The man extended his right hand and said 'I'm glad I've met you. My name's Mark.'

'Mine's Tom,' and they shook hands.

Mark said, 'Tell you what, as you're here by yourself, why don't you come and join us? We're meeting up with a gang of others later and going to a nightclub. The crowd we'll be with are a great bunch.'

It was settled then. The crowd of friends arrived later. Tom was immediately part of the throng. It was great, just what he needed. It was good to be reminded of what life is like, in the good times, within the material world. The good times continued at the nightclub. Buoyed by the company, one drink led to another and another; the mood and the alcohol just flowed, and Tom went with it.

The nightclub, the 201, in Camden Lock Place, was cavernous, noisy and heaving. As the night wore on Tom couldn't recall how many drinks he'd consumed. His body and his alacrity of thought knew otherwise. At midnight, Mark and Anne said their goodbyes, leaving Tom to carry on with the party of newfound friends. An hour or so later they gradually said their goodbyes too, until at last, Tom realised, he was the last one left.

The beat of the music grew faster and louder,

SIX

Harry had sourced burundanga, known as devil's breath, a Scopolamine drug from Colombia. Tasteless and odourless, it made people forget and highly open to suggestion. The thought of someone being under his total control, throbbed strongly in his veins and made his smile difficult to contain.

The drug had arrived in the form of chocolate and powder, some of which he had transformed into his own very special brew of soda. He would use more of it when his guests decided to stay with him and only then, if they played up.

As he approached his nightclub, Harry watched the canal's water gently lapping against the wall; it was almost in time to the steady pulsating beat of the music within. Through the warm summer night time drizzle, the lights from the mock Victorian gas lanterns, which stood sentinel guarding the water's edge, shimmered across the glistening cobbles of the street. Steam ferociously pumped from the club's air vents. Voluminous clouds opposed gravity and dispersed themselves into the warm July night air.

Harry paused in the alley between the club and an adjacent old dockside warehouse, which by day was a maritime museum. He could feel the power, the ascendency of his omnipotence tonight. The urge to do it had been growing for months now. It had reached fever pitch. The itch was irresistible.

He smiled lewdly allowing his mind's eye to mingle closely among the dress-hugging, trouser thudding gyration of his clients, imagining them soon to be merged together in a tumult of humanity bursting at the seams on the dance floor. Harry grinned. He could hardly wait.

His real colours hidden, Harry strolled through the entrance lobby. At the bottom of the brassy red-carpeted stairs, he nodded in his baronial fashion, condescending to thank the door attendants as they opened the wrought iron doors to reveal the bars and dancehall areas. Several customers greeted the eccentric owner of the club.

Surrounding the main polished wooden floor was a balcony set aside for the more sophisticated revellers who were drinking lager, vodka, and coke. Girls sat upon boys knees and in turn, many a boy sat gregariously on their girl's lap too. Cohorts of glasses stood in retching command on the tables. The shout filled limited conversation was consistently drowned by the searing beat of the speakers.

From the panorama of the balcony, up in the gods, the sophisticates gazed and on many occasions glazed their eyes onto the glorious kingdom of humanity below. Through his opera glasses, Harry watched the masses swaying, heaving, hugging and snogging the night away. Like a screw in a prison, he was searching for the new inmate. Scanning the livery from this watchtower, he spotted his first likely looking candidate, a miserable looking drunken wretch, and one who seemed at odds in the room, on the outside. Not part of the dance scene, definitely – don't worry my son, Harry will save you.

He studied him, twenties, possibly early thirties, almost not part of this world, thought Harry. The man's face was wan, made to look worse by the way his skin stretched across the cheekbones. I hope this boy has been through something and some, he thought, I think I might like it that way, strong within, maybe, but on the brink, a little on the edge.

Sweat across Tom's forehead was the product of alcohol and the re-emergence of an old fear. Swirling lights from the chandelier overhead reflected his agony. He was caught between the crowd and one of the main columns on the vast dance floor. The fingers on his left hand tapped a tattoo in his trouser pocket. His right hand repeatedly flexed open and closed as he tried to release the tension in his muscles, rid himself of the arthritic effect of toxin building up in his body.

Harry smiled and gloated like a cobra over its victim before the strike. He slowly and deeply filled his lungs and simultaneously felt his chest expand and fall, stretch against his shirt. He pleasured over the rush of mounting anticipation. His muscles gorged themselves with blood, ready for the hunt. He felt powerful. He felt omnipotent. He was the Alpha and the Omega.

Tom stood near the column of the Colossus' leg, trying to ignore the looming pendulum that acted as a huge anchor for the twirling chandelier. It flashed a sensual rhythm to the music's beat. The lights were mesmerising, galling him. He tried to merge unnoticed into the crowd at the bar. It was useless. His senses were overwhelmed by the intoxicating array of drinks that slung their smells at him like a winter gale forcing its way into his clothing, his hair, his skin and his nostrils.

He fumbled for his beer – was it his beer, he did not know, he did not care – and attempted to drink without spilling it. However, the trembling in his arms would not stop and the elbows of the 'happy crowd' made him look senile, shaken and stirred with Parkinson's. In the midst of his sabbatical from the Church, in the chaos of this club, the alcohol he was drowning now gave him clarity over how much he was out of touch with the secular world. For the first time since, when was it? It was when he had moved from primary to secondary school. That fear of fear, when his outsider feelings had erupted into a great huge tidal wave of numbness, was rising to the surface.

The alcohol surged within him. Nausea edged itself closer. Tom felt the tension expanding his brain from within as if it was about to burst and pound against the inner surfaces of his skull. The neurological network connecting millions of internal pathways was malfunctioning. He knew then that the switch between freethinking and thought stammering was being inexorably and firmly, pulled downwards. He panicked. He had to get out, but stumbled into the maleness of the crowd at the bar spilling drinks onto himself and, as he could see from the ugliness on the faces of the group, on them too.

'Hey! For fuck sake, what you doing, you dick?'

A man mountain with seemingly bulging six pack eyes thrust his face into Tom's – whose urge to vomit increased when the Neanderthal kept his forehead, head to head with his. The breath from the man's mouth contained an unholy concoction of food and drink. Tom felt his body temperature rise and the increasing sweat now smeared across his face only served to accentuate the minute side-to-side movement of his adversary's skin against his.

'Leave it Mick, he's pissed himself,' shouted another of the group who pulled the would-be aggressor away.

They all looked down at Tom's beer sodden trousers and as one, hyena laughed. Tom staggered into the crowds and headed for the exit. All who saw him thought he was dancing out of step with the music.

'Too much to drink, then, me old son; good to see you're leaving quietly.' One of the bouncers closed the wrought iron doors and shared a comical exchange with his counterpart.

Tom's eyes passed unfocused as he ascended from the seething pit. His nostrils flared and his chest heaved. He gasped for air and emerged out into the night like a floundering fish. He stood on the cobblestones shaking. He arched his back against the wall, and weakly felt the drizzle, its droplets sparkling in the nightlights like falling chakras, flow over him. His eyebrows acted as temporary shields protecting his eyes from the water, but eventually, they too retired and were overwhelmed as memories flooded into his consciousness.

Sunday, August 14, 1994 – Ruddington, near Nottingham, England

'Come on Tom, double, double dare you; I'll go first even.'

The two of them ran along Ruddington's footbridge, which passed over the railway line to the City of Nottingham. Just south of the railway embankment lay the town's cemetery. It acted as a silent cutting in the earth in contrast to the criss-crossing of the track, which severed its way across the Midland countryside.

Jim careered onto the ledge of the Iron Bridge first. He was faster and eager to show off his stamina and skill. He did not have time to speak again, but Jim's eyes spoke to him as he fell, until the tearing of gravity ceased all communication. Tom came to remember Jim's screams and his own – again, and again.

SEVEN

Friday, July 6, 2012 – The 201 Club, Camden Lock Place, London

'Goodnight Guv, have a good evening', said one of the bouncers as Harry passed by up the stairs.

'I will. Make sure you both set the alarm properly tonight. Remember, I don't want a repeat of last week's fiasco,' commanded Harry.

'No problem,' they both replied in unison. Like two bloody parrots, thought Harry.

They in turn mouthed silently to one another, 'You bastard, you self-preening bastard.'

As Harry mounted the stairs, he did as he always did; he preened his hair and adored his physique in the angled ceiling mirror that ran from the bottom to the top of the stairwell and reflected the entrance carpet in the lobby. He knew as he left the nightclub that the street outside was deserted, all save that is, for one individual, Harry's inmate. His mobile monitor allowed him to see the entrance as viewed by the camera positioned in the eaves.

Harry walked past Tom and dropped the 1.5-ounce GPS tracking device into his victim's jacket pocket. It was such an easy task aided and abetted by Tom's near insensibility to the world outside. He was lost in his own nightmare. From his phone, Harry could now watch the progress of his inmate's journey into the night. The device allowed him to see the distance between him and Tom and also his speed and direction over the streets he moved along.

If he had wanted Harry could take his time, for the battery life of the tracker lasted five days. But Harry was in no mood for delayed gratification. Besides, he did not want to risk the discovery of it or for that matter to find the next day his would-be victim had changed his clothes. No, tonight was Harry's night. That was all there was to it.

The drizzle turned into a short downpour and when it subsided, Tom, subdued, weaved his inebriated way along streets unknown to him. Seeing he was a potential target for a laugh, he was picked up by some youths in their car masquerading as a multi passenger cab service – share and save. He even thanked them, when they dropped him off at his hotel, handing over the remainder of his money for the fare, including a tip, which he proffered for the driver. He watched bemused as the cab drove off, the occupants laughing.

Tom found himself somewhere in the abandoned back streets of London's Docklands. In this drunken state, he had been parachuted into an area rich in detritus: home to a homeless mosaic of people confused by dementia or drugs, populated as the dumping ground of seagulls and scented by the stench of faeces from waste ground used by cats and humans alike.

The humid night air, magnified by a breeze, fanned the intensity of the fetid smell into his lungs. Nausea hit him. Doubling over, Tom vomited, splattering his shoes in the process. The sound of his retching echoed against the dark walls of warehouses. Rats feasting on their rotting supply of food scurried into hiding.

Tom dried his mouth with a handkerchief from his trouser pocket and blearily surveyed his surroundings. He was lost. The streetlights were out. He zigzagged across the road in search of a street sign. He was in the East End docklands and the territory of abandoned derelict warehouses, which were popular with urban photographers and apocalyptic filmmakers.

It was a location full of industrial history, perhaps, too, riddled, and contaminated with asbestos.

A red child's bicycle, a stolen ride from a distant off-licence, lay discarded on its side. The back wheel eerily revolved and the constant click, click, click, of the ball bearings touched ears in the shadows not seen by Tom, one of whom was a homeless vagrant nesting down for the night. The man's long drawn out hacking cough rung out in the night. To Tom it sounded like the tolls of death stalking victims with an asbestos filled bell, dusting particulates on all who passed by disturbing the floor and walls of the abandoned buildings.

From behind a solitary shrub stumbled an old man, looking like a throwback from General Custer's last stand, longhaired and long bearded. He was dressed in a worn greatcoat, beneath which could be seen his stomach, swollen with undigested bad food.

Gradual awareness of the surroundings ricocheted off Tom's chest as nervousness and anxiety solidified and dragged him away from his lingering stupor and into the bleak reality of the night. In the distance, he could see car headlights coming towards him. They illuminated the extent of urban decay he had walked into. Not knowing how to walk out of here, or remembering from which direction he had come, Tom hailed the driver and hoped the car would stop.

'What's the matter?' asked Harry, enjoying the comforting sound of the electric motor lowering the front passenger window. A warm, friendly smile was painted on his face.

Tom was careful to steady his sway and keep his body under some semblance of control as he crouched down by the open window. Doing his best not to slur his words, he said, 'Thank you slo much for stopping.' He swallowed the urge to retch again. 'I'm lost; any idea where the nearest bus stop or tube is?'

'Sorry mate, I don't,' Harry replied.

The hope in Tom's eyes faded, 'Oh.' His mind still floating on a sea of alcohol was unable to process another solution.

'Hold on,' exclaimed Harry. 'I've got a street map in my side pocket ... hop in. I'll put the interior light on. We can check the locations of the nearest stops.'

Tom opened the door and slumped into the passenger seat as Harry turned off the car's engine. Tom, lopsided, turned to face Harry, who was opening up a map. Harry suggested he leaned closer to get a better look. Tom nodded, his head bobbing like a toy dog on the parcel shelf. With the help of gravity, he moved closer. Swiftly, Harry blew the burundanga dust into Tom's face. He waited a few moments before saying, 'Let's go to my place, I have a few things I want to talk to you about.'

'Sure,' slurred Tom, 'I'd like that,' idly wondering why his mouth felt full and his tongue swollen.

EIGHT

It was nearly three in the morning. The polished tiled surface reflected Tom's body – a discarded puppet in the corner of the cell. Masking tape covered his mouth. His arms were tied at the wrists behind his back by a plastic strap. Two steel rings around his ankles, shackled his legs. A metre long rubber bungee attached between them gave him what little movement he was allowed.

A large fan, flush against the wall in the uppermost part of the cell provided ventilation. Harry had made sure the fan was large enough to force air in or alternatively, force it out – all of it.

Harry had also installed, purely for the comfort of his prisoners – his humour was rarely funny – heating from under floor pipes that ran the length and breadth of the cell.

Harry was a big man. Tumbling Tom, his first inmate, unconscious out of the car had been easy. He had carried Tom easily over his shoulder and into his converted home, a warehouse.

In comparison to Harry, Tom had nothing physically to admire. However, his mental attributes intrigued Harry. His wallet had revealed that one, Tom Abimelech, 29 years of age, was on the verge of becoming a Catholic priest. Harry needed to think how he was going to dismantle this man's character, unravel his mind.

40

In the meantime, the monitors showed him Tom was alive. His body had settled into a heavy sleep. Everything was as it should be. Perfect, thought Harry.

He left for Tom's hotel, confident that his systems would record his victim's movements and any sounds he made, whilst the restraints would prevent any harm coming to him, yet.

The distant hum of the mosquito whirled overhead. If only Tom had remembered to draw the net around the bed. He awoke as he fought to swat the blood-sucking insect away. It was then he realised he could not speak. He was trussed up, ready for the slaughter.

Tom's eyes opened a fraction as light entered under the dark veil of his eyelashes. A wall fan hummed – the mosquito of his dream. His brain thumped; hell's head twisted inside his skull.

To his right face down, mirror like tiles stretched away from him. Against one side of the glass room stood ominously a polished stainless steel adjustable height mortuary table, above which, flush against a wall, hung surgical instruments.

Next to this was a counter, sunk within it was a white ceramic sink; the ugly base bulged out underneath. Rearing their sinister heads above the sink, loomed large stainless steel long armed taps, idling, and waiting. A flexible wall mounted hose with a spray attachment lay curled, as if half-asleep in a foetal position.

Tom twisted his body and rolled onto his back – this is not happening; this is a mistake, his thoughts pleaded for a welcome reality to replace this clinical cage.

He was trapped – a fly in a spider's web. He looked at himself, naked, a klaxon warning sounded in his head.

Tom whispered his prayers fervently.

'Holy Michael, Archangel, defend me in the day of battle, be my safeguard against the wickedness and snares of the Devil and by the power of God, thrust down to hell Satan and all

wicked spirits that wander the earth for the ruin of souls ...
Hail Mary, full of grace, the Lord is with thee, blessed art thou
amongst women and blessed is the fruit of thy womb, Jesus.
Holy Mary, Mother of God, pray for us sinners, now and at the
hour of our death. Amen.'

He needed to move. The weight on his arms from his body
had become unbearable. Through cramping agony and with
Herculean effort, he writhed and struggled upwards, using the
wall as a prop, until at last, he sat back, almost upright against
it.

He looked up. Embedded near the edges of the ceiling were
several thick steel rings, much like the ones used to hold bulls
in a market before the slaughter. Fear breathed its cold spell
into the room. His bladder was uncontrollably full. He hung on,
until the residue of the drug overwhelmed him and he slept.

'If I can just climb out of bed, I can grab a few more hours of
sleep before Rutenga's cockerel crows and awakes the village
heralding the start of another day.' Tom found what he was
looking for. 'Ah, there it is. What bliss.'

Urine gushed over his legs and flooded the floor around him.
In a sweeping torrent it flowed, then spluttered and ebbed, like
a river losing its source. Tom awoke and found himself lying in
the warm waters of his humiliation, and sobbed – a man losing
hope.

PART TWO – FRAGMENTED HISTORIES

NINE

Two in the morning, it was nearly home time. Well, for most of the staff that is – another hour or so cleaning away most of the mess and then he would leave the rest to the fag ash cleaners in the morning. Besides, he had needs he wanted met and he was getting impatient – get these fucking wankers, tarts and airheads off the premises – to please the Guv – and then find someone.

Outside a police car drifted idly past. The officer in the front passenger seat used the spotlight to flash the powerful light along the alleys and dark passages surrounding the nightclub zone. The officer called out to a couple of lads who were emptying their bladders in a shop doorway.

'If you don't put your dicks away, I'll use my karaoke stick to give them a stinging lesson.'

One nervous unfortunate caught in the light's spots, flipped his away with a hurried splash. The two officers laughed and drove on. A short time later, they caught a young couple in the spotlight's cross hairs who were locked in a passionate embrace up against a wall behind the back of a well-known takeaway. The man actually paused momentarily, his trousers and boxers around his ankles, as he blurted out, 'For fuck sake!'

All of these glimpses and more made up the concoction of street nightlife, the diurnal dichotomy to the family activities so prevalent by day.

Before going their separate ways, they both made sure, absolutely, that Harry's Club was shut down properly and the security systems in place were switched on. The system, which, if tripped, flashed by landline to the nearest police control room, 'Intruder alert' giving the address in a feminine robotic voice common to so much communication technology. Electronics and synthesisers – not wages and livelihoods were the things that mattered nowadays.

Once in the comforting environment of his vehicle, he drove down Farrington and eased along into Kings Cross Road. Just past the Interline Hotel on the right, the road swings to the left and away from Penton Rise. He passed by a stocky man dressed in a hefty 80s style blue duffle coat and pointed his car further along Kings Cross.

He slowed his vehicle to a crawl, allowing time pressured drivers to slip past him. His focus was on the kerb or more precisely, the women vying for his attention. And one of them could have it all.

He always took his car to the bays at the end of Tolpuddle Street. He liked to imagine he had an affinity with the martyrs from Dorset who staked their claim, their right, to be part of a Grand National Union. Their transportation in the 1830s created a unique sense of identity between city dwellers and agricultural workers, the rural urban divide, temporarily broken.

Only he was not brave enough to face Harry. Harry the Bastard. His insistence, "If you want a fucking job here, then no union membership – full, fucking, stop." He could still almost feel the spittle that had landed on his face as Harry hammered his voice into him.

He pulled in next to a long legged woman, his favourite. In her early thirties, she was wearing a tight short skirt tonight. It rode keenly up her hips when she leant into his window and slid her hand along the inside of his legs. He was the protector of women and provider of income for King Cross's own.

Life was okay, not bad at all. How easy it was to lie when there was no one to challenge him.

All was quiet. The girl had been gone for some time now. He had stayed in the car. No movement, just stationary in blissful solitude. Somehow, it was comforting, time alone, untouched by anyone. He let his head tilt backwards onto the headrest and allowed sleep to seep into him. For the time being, an unseen hand absorbed the swathes of anger that cursed his waking days.

LONDON – 1988

TEN

The first day heralds nothing fresh. It had never been the start of a good New Year. It was always just a rollover of misery from one to the next. Pinch, drunk, first to the bottle, the only race, his dad ever won.

He never went to school. He was not allowed. The education authorities never knew he existed. His father treated him as if he did not want him to exist either. The constant rant he would hear coming from the lips of his dad whenever he argued with his mum, which was often, was "I never wanted him anyway; he's a bleedin' pain in the arse!"

Despite the haranguing from him and the beatings, his mother would stand up for her son and shout back, "Count yourself lucky he's kept us going this long!"

When he was 10 years old, he asked his mum why she never ran away.

"You'll be happy Mum; I'll look after you." His voice had risen to its full boyish strength added, "You know I will. I'm big enough!"

She smiled. But his mum would have nothing of it. She told him she had her reasons for staying with his father, that it was always good to look after women, that he should never ever be like him, and asked him to promise not to ever mention it again, no matter what happened. Reluctantly, he had promised. She was his friend, teacher and mentor. He adored her.

48

Her escape was poetry, writing it sometimes, although she never showed him. Yet she would readily share readings from her favourite poetry or from a wide array of choices of much loved stanzas. She found beauty in words and revelled in the imagery of creations from a wide range of poets, Shakespeare, Donne, Shelley, Browning, and many more besides.

Poetry was their bedtime ritual. Poetry became his comfort blanket. The visions and ideas would transport them both into other times, faraway places and the lives of so many unmet people. He experienced escapism at the touch of every page, the whisper of every word and the beat of every stanza. It became his escape pod too.

19:59 hours, Friday, January 8, 1988 – London

The time and the date to him are like skin stuck on a hot plate melted and seared into the painful hands of memory.

Nearing the end of his 13th year, he had nursed his mother since last Sunday morning. He had noticed she'd been feeling breathless since the Friday before. When she sat down on the edge of his bed to read him some poetry on the Saturday night her breath was still strained. And yet she reassured him that she wasn't ill, just a cold. He awoke once in the night and heard her in the bedroom next door coughing loudly. Dad was away on one of his usual long driving trips, so if mum needed caring for, it was down to her son, him, to look after her.

Late on the Sunday morning, he had woken up. Normally, as a treat on this day she would bring him breakfast in bed, yet no mum and no breakfast. He emerged from under the bedclothes and immediately felt the cold and the dampness in the house cling to his skin as he trotted to the toilet to empty his full bladder.

He did not hear any of the normal noises of pottering coming from downstairs. Odd he thought. He then heard coughing, spluttering, and other sounds from his mum as she cleared her throat and spat out phlegm. She was in the bedroom still. He knocked on her bedroom door.

'Mum. Mum, are you alright?' She did not answer.

He hesitated to go into his parents' bedroom. To do so without his father's permission was dangerous. His dad would fly into a rage if he ever broke that rule. He would beat him into tears ranting, "Next time, mind your fucking manners son." Such was the fear he felt, that like a slave freed from his chains, his master gone away, he felt paralysed, unable to decide and act with initiative. The years of oppression he had suffered, despite his father's temporary absence, still ensured the psychology of bondage was the overseer of his behaviour in the home.

'Mum?' His unbroken voice cracked with fear for her welfare.

He heard her vomiting. The sound seemed to come from somewhere ungodly deep within her throat. It truly terrified him.

'Mum,' he wailed and burst into his parents' room.

Bloodstained tissues littered the bedspread; some of them had fallen to the floor by the bedside table. His mother was lent over a bucket. Her hair hung loose, not elegantly tied up as it always was whenever he saw her. The stench of vomit clung in his nostrils.

'What's the matter Mum?'

She looked up at him, her breath, wheezing, her fringe wet from sweat. Strands of hair clinging to the side of her face were matted with vomit. She seemed confused for a moment, as if she did not recognise him or know where she was. She was about to speak when a sharp stabbing pain nailed into her head. She winced and breathed in sharply, holding a hand to her brow.

He rushed to her, tears streaming down his face; he could hardly breathe himself such was the panic he felt inside. The bucket was about to topple over and he grabbed the side and saved it. In so doing, his hand slid around the rim and his skin came into contact with saliva and slime. He wanted to retch himself then, but somehow kept his nerve. He had to be strong.

For the first time in his life, he found the roles reversed. Caring for his mother came naturally to him. She did not want him to call the doctor. Luckily, they could not get hold of dad. On the road, he had no access to a phone. In fact, it was heaven without him around. There were no arguments between his parents. There were no beatings of him or his mother. He did not have to hear the abusive words that came so easily into his dad's mouth, which crushed his confidence and flattened any emergent self-belief.

It was lovely to be able to move around the house and be the master of his own surroundings without fear of getting something wrong or crossing over some unseen boundary that seemed to hover daily in his dad's head. He imagined that his dad had an alternating current in his brain. One day, such and such was okay, the next, not. It forced him to tread warily around his father. However, try as he might, he lacked the soft paws of a cat and was daily unable to avoid making the wrong sound.

He found he was getting good at making food for his mum in those five sweet days they had together – sweet because he had the full responsibility to be the carer. With her guidance, he had been able to string together edible meals as long as they were populated with tomato or brown sauce to mask some of the blandness of his cooking.

To him, though, his mum seemed very weak. Her chest was full of phlegm, although blood no longer appeared on the tissue and thankfully, she had not been sick anymore. Washing the bucket out had been horrendous. He wanted to avoid looking at the vomit as it slurped out, but even when he turned his eyes away, they somehow were drawn back; curse his curiosity, he thought.

Normally he disliked the smell of bleach, but he had never been as grateful to its medicinal aroma as he was when he washed out the clinging liquid film and stench with warm water from the bath's shower hose attached to the taps.

His mum reassured him that despite her temperature, it was "coming down" she said, that she was "getting better." That cheered him up and put a smile on his face. Seeing her so ill on the Sunday had made him appreciate, for the first time, how fragile life was and how very difficult he would find it if she died. The thought of him alone with just his dad had haunted him in the early days of her recovery.

For the first two, his mum, more or less, wanted peace and quiet, this allowed him do his own thing, which he filled avidly with poetry and drawing. The drawings were mainly about him with his sword and shield fighting and then slaying monsters; some of them, he thought, were pretty scary looking, the last one with drooling lips and grinning yellowed teeth was his father, and he knew that.

When he had finished it, he sat back in his bed against the wall, the picture propped up against a pillow at the other end. His mood darkened. He could feel his upper lip curling. He grabbed a black pencil and scribbled manically to obliterate everything. But that wasn't enough.

He sneaked downstairs and took a large kitchen knife from the drawer. Stealthily, he knew not why, a sixth sense, perhaps, he crept quietly and slowly back upstairs towards his bedroom door.

He saw the door opening. No squeak. No hinge whined. Silently the man stepped through the doorway. Standing, amid the doorjamb, towered his father. Light from the bedroom window, squeezed itself out – "excuse me," it said, as it touched his dad's shoulders, whose girth virtually filled the void.

The son watched hidden behind the banister and waited to pounce on the monster before him. His father's shadow moved slowly across the room, inch by inch he approached his son's drawing on the bed. He stopped and cocked his head to one side, like a dog. He seemed frozen there as if in a sudden narcoleptic stupor. This was his son's moment. Slowly, slowly he moved. He was the cat now. He padded across the landing, silent as the night, whilst his mum lay resting; she'll not be sad at her husband's parting, he thought.

Step by step, with knife aloft, he edged closer to hatch the dreaded plot, long held within and to be vented now, to kill his father, to kill him, now. Swiftly he moved – a hunter at full pelt. He lunged and plunged the blade deep within his father's back, and then as his victim fell, again and again in the monster's face; first the eyes and then the mouth, the blood splattered everywhere. Despite the gore, he was a thrilled assassin. Eventually, the monster was slain. His father vanquished, he was now the hero.

Breathing heavily from the exertion, he let his body fall backwards onto the bed and laughed out loud. Yes. That's how to do it, he thought.

As he recovered his senses, he sat up and looked around at the mess he had made. Fear walked back into the room again. The drawing was slashed to shreds. That in itself was not the problem. The pillow behind it was. It was almost disintegrated. Its foam stuffing was scattered over the bedclothes; smaller fragments were dotted here and there across the carpet, for with each stroke of the blade tiny fragments had been torn out and flung backwards into the air landing wherever the trajectory slew them. If his father ever found out, and how he had caused such damage, he'd be in the biggest trouble, ever, of his life.

After much searching, he found the dustpan and brush in one of the kitchen sink lower cupboards, not under the stairs where mum stored the hoover. He dare not use that, she would ask why he was cleaning his room, and he could not think of a ready answer. After half an hour of meticulous brushing, every bit of foam was swept up and put into a bin bag along with the decimated pillow and its case.

He couldn't risk leaving it in the dustbin, dad would wonder why more than one bag had been used and he'd be bound to peer inside. Eventually, he hit on an idea, to burn it all in the back garden, right at the back, on top of the rubble by the trees and then scatter all of the ash in the small copse beyond their garden fence. It was just over the small brook that barely trickled past the houses.

Relieved when the evidence was disposed of, he had a quick drink of squash to quench his thirst and then popped up to see how his mum was. She seemed to have a bit more colour in her face. She must be getting better, he thought. This was confirmed, as far as he was concerned, when on the Wednesday of that week she asked him to read her some poetry. And she said, of his choosing. He was ecstatic.

As he thumbed through the pages of her favourite anthologies and then flicked back and forth between some that he was vacillating over, she watched him. She didn't ever quite feel like his mother, but in these thirteen years she had grown to like him, almost love him, despite what would eventually happen to him, and in this moment, right now and as a child, he was a good lad.

He obviously felt the world for her. If only she could have reciprocated wholeheartedly, but you cannot force feelings can you, no matter how much you can fool others along the way? He looked up and smiled and she warmly smiled back. She had made her choice all those years ago.

'So tell me my handsome recitalist, what have you decided upon?'

'To a Haggis, by Robert Burns;' he cleared his throat and began.

'Fair fa' your honest, sonsie face, Great Chieftan o' the Puddin-race! ... '

Throughout, she laughed, he laughed, she applauded, and at the end, he bowed.

'Excellent darling!' she said, 'I've not laughed so much in… ah I forget; it was wonderful. And the way you moved your mouth around the words, admirable. Aye, my wee master, you've got a pretty good Scots accent too; not bad, not bad at all'

He leant over and hugged her tightly. 'I love you Mum, with all my heart.'

Her heart tore when she heard him say this.

'I love you too darling. I truly do,' she replied.

ELEVEN

Friday, January 15, 1988 – London

Bubbles do not last forever.

Their small universe imploded when his father returned home earlier than expected. As the key turned in the lock of the front door, the sound shook them both into silence. Even the door hinges moaned as he pushed open and then slammed the door once inside.

'I'm home, what's for dinner?' his dad's rough booming voice plastered the walls of the house with fear once more.

With his imaginary sword in hand, the son came downstairs and told his father that mum was ill in bed. 'Mum's got pneumonia, she thinks.'

'New what? It's a bloody cold I bet, the lazy cow,' said his father. His voice stretched the last word out like over chewed gum.

It left a bad taste in his son's mouth.

His dad went storming upstairs, his body charged, prepared to brook no obstacle. The son heard them row as he sat on the stairs. Mum lost the fight. She always did. With her dressing gown half on, she moved past her son and dragged herself downstairs, the colour in her face turning pastel again. He looked up as she passed him.

'Don't do it Mum, you're not well enough. You know you're not. Let me cook. I'm good at it now.'

She put her fingers to her lips, urging him silently to be silent. He mutely obeyed. He heard his dad fart loudly and then

56

turn on the TV in the bedroom. Later, his dad shouted down for him to bring up a bottle of beer from the fridge. Quick as a flash he obeyed.

In the kitchen, he watched his mother prepare food, wiping globules of sweat from her forehead, the colour now drained completely from her face. Her breathing was laboured. She moved her arms as if she was carrying tree trunks.

She smiled wanly at him and said, 'I'll be fine love. Why don't you go in the lounge and watch some TV whilst your dad is upstairs hey?'

And off he went; nervous about his mother, but assured by her she'd be alright. The western on the 'box' wasn't much good, but it distracted him from his thoughts for a while. During a gunfight, he heard a clatter in the kitchen.

'You alright Mum?' he called out.

No reply. He sprang from his chair, ran into the kitchen, and found her lying on her side, shaking and shivering, a plate of peas smashed over the floor. Her eyes were rolling upwards. Quickly he dashed upstairs to his dad. The bedroom door was shut. He knocked. No answer. He knocked again, this time more loudly, incessantly. Still no answer and his dad and the house phone were in the bedroom.

He had to go inside, 'Just have to.' He mouthed the words and girded himself with courage.

He drove himself onwards. The bedroom door creaked open. His dad, mercifully, was asleep on his back. The phone was on the bedside table. He picked up the handset, put his small index finger into the dial at number 9, and moved it round clockwise, once, twice and... His father woke up. He froze. His finger stuck to the spot, half way round, nearly there, but ...

'What are you doing?' his father growled.

He shrank back. The ogre was awake. He would have his way. Nervously, he explained that mum was collapsed on the kitchen floor. His father barely listened as he put on his trousers and slung a jumper over his vest.

His dad strode past his son, forcing his body up against the wall and glowered at him, 'Later,' he said.

A cold arrow of fear pierced the son's heart.

In the kitchen, mum was still lying on the floor. Dad was pushing her back and forth with a 'slippered' foot, as if he was rolling a river log.

'Come on, get up, stop playing for sympathy, you'll not get it here.'

Mum's eyes rolled from side to side with every partial rotational tilt of her body. She did not stir. Her lips released an involuntary and unconscious groan. Dad turned the cooker off and whatever was boiling continued to vent steam into the cold kitchen air. Dad grabbed a cold pie from the fridge along with another beer and went to go back upstairs. He turned towards the son.

'You! Stay with her; I'm going back to bed.'

The kitchen floor was like a larder. He got the blankets from his bed. The kitchen lino stuck to his skin. He nuzzled and snuggled into his mum as best he could. He hoped that his body warmth, for as long as it lasted, would help her in some way.

He awoke shivering. She had stopped moving. She was asleep, he thought, that is, until he looked into her open lifeless eyes and knew she was not. The digital clock reflected the inverted time in her eyes. He swivelled around to see what it said; it was just before 8 pm.

It was a time and a night to remember.

Mum's funeral was a cold affair in all ways. She was buried in Nunhead Cemetery, Southwark. At least her resting place was beautiful. Somehow, he knew not how, his dad had persuaded the authorities that he had come home and found her dead with their son lying next to her. Following a post mortem, her death was recorded as natural causes. Her son knew the real cause. No authorities picked up on the fact that he was not at school. Their only interest was foul play. Having found none, they moved on to the next case.

Until he turned 16 years of age, the next 3 years or so were a mixture of hell when his father was home and relative calm when not. His education stopped the day his mum died. Well, his formal education anyway. Almost every night dad would come back with one of his newfound mates and they'd watch TV upstairs.

Food was mostly from cans and white bread. Somehow, the bread had an uncanny knack of absorbing damp from the house. Each mouthful felt like he was swallowing glue. He survived, just, and without turning feral. He had his mum to thank for that. Her love of poetry gave him pictures of better worlds.

Thankfully and without objection, his dad let him have all of her anthologies. He lovingly stored them in a regimented fashion on his bedroom windowsill. He kept his favourite one at any one time, opened by his bed on the side table. He would look at the gradually blurring text each time he drifted off to sleep imagining her lying cosily next to him and his pillow.

On his 16th birthday, dad came into the room; he never knocked, and threw a manila folder onto his bed.

'Here. Have these. They're yours.'

Without another word, his father left him alone.

Perplexed he picked up the folder and opened the flap. Inside was an adoption certificate along with a letter. His name he had grown up with was not the one on the certificate. He slowly peeled open the envelope which only had his name on it. It was from his mum, who he now knew was not his real mother. What else was false he wondered? And why did she stick with a man who wasn't his real dad? Anger and tears surged together. He screwed the letter up, unable to read it, and threw it headlong into the centre of the room. Grabbing his jacket, he went out for the night. And this time, he wasn't going to ask for permission.

At gone past two in the morning he returned home. Home, he thought, hardly. The door was on the latch. All of the house lights were out apart from a glow coming from beneath his dad's bedroom door. Dad was often out late on a Saturday night and his parent's room was the only place with anything valuable in it.

Going upstairs, carefully now, he heard something crash to the floor, followed by grunting sounds. His dad was being attacked, he thought. Despite the venom he felt towards his father, his instinct to protect stepped in. He pushed open his parent's bedroom door and stood aghast at the scene ahead of him.

The bedside lamp had fallen to the floor, its glass shade and bulb cracked and broken. A naked man stood with his legs apart, another was knelt on the bed. The man standing was his father, who shouted, 'Shut the fucking door and get out.'

In the room next door, the son quickly filled his rucksack with clothes and his walkman. Despite the hurt, he also packed two of his mum's favourite anthologies together with the birth certificate and her crumpled and yet unread letter.

He would never step back in this house again.

LONDON – 2000

COMPOSED UPON WESTMINSTER BRIDGE

By William Wordsworth (1770-1850)

Never did the sun more beautifully steep
In his first splendour valley, rock, or hill;
Ne'er saw I, never felt, a calm so deep!
The river glideth at his own sweet will:
Dear God! The very houses seem asleep;
And all that might heart is lying still!

TWELVE

Twelve years had nearly passed since his mother's death and ten years since he had left home. He was on his way to Westminster Bridge via the underground from Farringdon tube station. He, Wordsworth and his mum would be there to remember and enjoy the sights of the river, the lights reflecting on the water and Parliament ablaze with spotlights.

The lines were busy, but trains were running on time. He arrived with many other alighting passengers at Westminster tube station at 19:57 hours. He was running close to the wind, but he would get there if he sprinted. Boxing and running had made him very fit and strong.

As he moved swiftly towards the exit, he saw the unmistakeable profile of his dad. Once experienced, never to be forgotten. He was waiting for a train. The next one was due in two minutes. It was his time and night to remember.

On impulse, his anger snaking around his intestines, he walked several yards past his dad and stood by the wall vaguely watching him and other would-be passengers. It was busy on the platform. His dad, as ignorant as ever, shoved his way to the front and stood beyond the safety zone, the tips of his shoes close to the platform's edge and in front of the yellow painted line.

Was this to be the moment? Was it now or never? Surely, everything in the universe had colluded to provide him with this chance to put the demon to rest, for good. Smoothly and slowly, he eased his way through the crowd, his hoodie already pulled up to keep his neck and head warm against the cold.

The almost unmoving air was transformed by the approaching train, which created a strong breeze as it announced its near arrival. Its lights were blazing. A woman's broad brimmed hat was blown off and wafted high into the air, drawing the looks of waiting passengers. The digital clock slowly, but surely, peeled back number 8 and the time changed to 19:59 hours.

This was the time to remember. It was now, as he gently pushed his father in the small of the back. His dad's feet stumbled and with all the subtlety of a dancing fighter, the avenging son hooked the demon's right foot from under him and the monster fell forwards. People screamed and so did he, but his was in celebration.

Gradually he backed unobtrusively away from the onlookers and made his way to the centre of Westminster Bridge. He was late for his rendezvous with his mum and her favourite poet, but tonight, he knew, she would not mind at all.

LONDON – 2012

THIRTEEN

Friday, July 6, 2012 – Hotel Petunia, Bedford Place, London

At just after four in the morning Harry drove to Tom's hotel. He parked in a side street, several roads away. The keys to Tom's room nestled in the pocket of the linen jacket. It was definitely on the tight side, but in the shadows cast, it might help to convey a passing impression that Harry was Tom. The thrill of potentially being caught stimulated Harry. He liked the feeling. It was energising, inspiring, motivating. Harry was on a roll.

He placed the key in the hotel's front door and entered the lobby. Thoughtfully, the reception was unmanned at this hour, he thought. The floral crimson carpet of the foyer conveyed a moss like quietness to his footsteps. The well-worn tramline towards the stairs showed the journey many guests made to their beds – yea, and how many slept, the seedy bastards, he said to himself. The stairs were opposite the reception desk, which was partially cluttered at one end. Tourist guides and business cards for taxi firms and nightclubs were on display, including the 201. Good boy, Colin's been around and left some.

The stairs' curling banisters gently spiralled upwards. He decided against the stairs. Ahead of Harry, the smooth stainless steel doors of the lift stood quietly waiting to open for the next guest.

He entered the lift and pressed button 2. After a seemingly unending pause, enough time for yet one more drop of sweat to slide down his back, the doors slid silently across and the lift rose to the second floor. Harry stepped out. Room number 25 was opposite. Tom's room was number 29. To the right, in 27, Harry could hear the muffled conversations of a couple arguing. The rising tempo of their voices sounded like they might end up battling all night he thought.

Entering Tom's room, Harry allowed his eyes to adjust to the subdued street lighting that filtered in through the window. Working quickly now, he went to the bathroom and grabbed two discarded towels, still damp from its occupant's use. Harry smiled and then placed them along the bedroom door. No one passing outside would see a light coming on. Crossing to the crimson and cream curtains Harry tested the draw on them. Thankfully, they moved silently and smoothly across. He could not risk being seen by anyone from the Maxwell Hotel opposite.

The curtains would not meet in the middle no matter how hard he stretched them. Harry cursed and hissed under his breath. Time was pressing and sweat was oozing through his clothes. He felt bloody uncomfortable. He was already starting to blame Tom for his predicament.

Harry could not mess around or afford to hang about, but he wanted an insight into his prey. The inquisitive side of his motivation overcame his impulse to take flight. He went to the light switch, paused and then turned it on. A few seconds passed whilst he remained pinned like a rabbit to the wall.

In those same seconds, Ms. Kerveen looked up from her writing desk, her attention drawn like a moth to the sudden flickering of unexpected light. Her most creative hours were often late into the night and early hours of the next day, when life in the city was more subdued. Memories from her life interwoven with her imagination could return and flourish unimpeded by the distractions of the day.

She had not yet spotted the occupant in the opposite hotel room. She could just make out the stature through the curtain's material. He was a man, and a solid one at that. She picked up her binoculars, a useful item over the years. She mostly used them to observe people from afar. Individuals often revealed more of their character when moving and talking unfettered by thoughts of being observed by interested eyes. It helped stimulate ideas for her characters. There was an unending supply of them in London.

Searching for a suitcase, Harry found a holdall under the bed. He swung it onto the mattress. Methodically searching all parts of the room, he found amongst several items, clothes, a radio, several books, a diary and a framed photograph. Harry resisted the temptation to dwell on each of Tom's possessions. He would have time for that later. Closing the bag was a bit of a problem, but with his weight bearing down on the top, he managed to zip the infuriating irritation together. Tom had a lot to answer for. Turning off the lights Harry crossed to the door, grabbed the towels, folded them neatly over the side of the bath and left.

Across the street, Ms. Kerveen saw the lights go out in 29 and imagined the thickset man undressing and where he might have been that night. She made a small character note and posted it onto the cork-covered notice board hanging on the wall to her left.

KNOW THYSELF

By Alexander Pope (1688-1744)

Chaos of thought and passion, all confused;
Still by himself abused, or disabused;
Created half to rise and half to fall;
Great lord of all things, yet a prey to all;
Sole judge of truth, in endless error hurled;
The glory, jest, and riddle of the world!

FOURTEEN

Friday, July 6, 2012 – Harry's Place, Thames Path, London

The mug of coffee smelt good. Time to relax, his prey could wait, was out of it anyway. Harry was excited. He clutched Tom's diary tightly in his right hand. He was about to enter the private world of his prisoner. An honour bestowed on him by the gods, he thought, oh, blessed be those that deal the cards of my fate.

He settled into his well-worn leather and favourite rocking chair. He liked the familiar, the routine. Turning the first page, he stepped through the portal into Tom's mind.

Wednesday, 7 September, 1994 – Nottingham Coroner's Court, England

I was sat in an oversized adult chair. I felt like a male version of Goldilocks intruding on the hardness of Big Bear's chair. It dwarfed me. I was dressed in my iron creased school shorts – mum insisted – wearing my white shirt and meticulously knotted tie. The usher pushed the large wooden double doors slowly together. My ears focussed unwillingly on the swish arising from the carpet as the draft excluders swept everyone and all sound away.

The closed airless world of the courtroom came to abrupt life. The wooden gammel was struck down three times in rapid succession, formally announcing the end of Jim Cohen's life. Dad squeezed my hand. I glanced into his eyes and felt the barriers of our years fall apart, and out of the ashes grew – I'm

69

certain of it – an unspoken understanding – a bond that life, nor death could or would break. Jim still lived and this process, this hearing, this inquest only sought to draw a line in the sand of our small human histories, unrecorded for the most part. Of our physical lives, Jim's timeline had stopped. Stopped dead on the railway line traversing Ruddington. And whilst his death, the manner of it, that is, still haunts me, I know he lives and together at Jim's inquest, Dad's eyes told me.

I looked up, not at the Coroner, but at Jim's dad. He was holding Jim inside of himself. His eyes were angled downward across his face, slanting from left to right. Just like Jim's. His dad's eyes were intent on the face of the Coroner, whose voice sedately rambled on, recording the sadness of the incident, the accident wrought out of boyish exuberance and bravado.

I wondered if Jim's dad ever heard those words. Did they echo into the empty chamber of his head? Did he wish me dead and not his son? Consumed by grief, was his mind closed down, unable to process the Coroner's words? Throughout the hearing, he sat poised, exemplifying a statue of marbled stillness. An aura rested on his shoulders and was reflected in his countenance that day.

The days that followed were tough. As a child, I had no real control over whom I saw. What child does? And despite Jim's house and his parents having been a second home and family to me, I lost contact with them. I heard in 1998 that Jim's mother had died along with many others caught up in one of Germany's worst train disasters of all time, a high-speed crash. I thought that I would never see Jim's dad again.

Monday, 1 October, 2001 – Exeter, England

I arrived at the University of Exeter's student union building, a nervous but excited survivor of 'A' levels. Initially I felt shipwrecked – all at sea, surrounded as I was, by an eclectic bunch of students and a cacophony of voices whilst waiting

70

with one other new student for a guided tour and introduction into university life.

My sense of being a castaway onto a strange new island of adventure was mirrored by the internal architecture. White painted struts angled themselves as columns to support the ceiling. On one of the upper levels, the room was bounded by a balcony, around which the 'old lags' sprawled themselves on chairs or on the floor, surrounded by empty sandwich cartons, crisp packets and plastic throw-a-way cups and surprisingly – files and paperwork.

The hubbub of conversation and the mixture of accents, nationalities and cultures spread amongst the breeze of studying life as the students flexed their intellectual muscles. How I love debate. Some wrestled with tutorial assignments that were occasionally interrupted with side conversations: on the previous night out, the problem with the occasional local non-student beating them up; or the TV vogue for soaps everyone was so into.

Across from the balcony and the void of space, below which ran the reception, stood curved bay windows, which faced inwards and sentinel like marines on the bridge of a ship attending to the security of the captain, but on this occasion, protecting seminar rooms.

Our tour guide Lucy arrived. I left behind my musings and followed her avidly. She took us on a warts and all tour of the campus and filled us in on life in the city of Exeter and its surrounding environs – Dartmoor, the Exe Estuary and the sea.

I called mum and dad with a cleansed update of the weekend, the day after the day and night on the razz. Dad was engrossed up to his nose in a newspaper. No doubt he and I would talk later about some political scandal or sophistry conjured up by the plethora of spin-doctors that seemed to multiply exponentially leading up to a general election. The next one was not until 2005, but dad was a horizon scanner.

Sometimes I wondered if mum ever got exasperated with him. Yet the truth was, as far as I could tell, they both revelled in the melting pot of discussion. Besides, it was not all politics and geopolitical agendas; they did make joint decisions over all aspects of domestic life. When I think back now, they were probably closet Catholic Marxists, if there is such a description, well if not, there is now.

I know mum was enthused by his effervescent personality and intellectual rigour. She used to draw on his musings and their discussions and develop themes arising from them into wall hangings and murals. Her work was in demand from amongst the corporate entities that walled the square miles of some large cities around the world. Each piece of art made an awe-inspiring statement, not just because of the sheer size and magnitude of them, but because of the layers of messages and meanings, each one, interwoven, conveyed.

She used to plough any money she made into the Catholic charity that supports the poor in the developing world. So in a small way, my mum's statements of art were fitting checks and balances in the foyers of these global giants. Come to think of it, the wall hanging around the Student Union balcony was a rag and bone version of her mural – *Living in the air*.

Tuesday, 14 August, 2007 – Ruddington Nottingham

In the week before I left to join the English College, Catholic seminary, Valladolid in Spain, I returned to say good-bye to Jim. I was resting my forearm on the railway bridge, drinking in the memories. Time seemed like a full circle and I had just crossed the diameter to the other side. I was ten again. I spoke freely to Jim as we stood together and embraced within the void of time. Feeling, knowing he was there with me, I took him through the journey of my life: from his death, from my withdrawal, then aggression, then wretchedness, then eventually, as I came through the tunnel of my emotions, to a more accepting view of myself. Forgiveness had been the way forward.

I told him of my roller coaster of friendships that I went through towards the tail end of 'A' levels. And all along how my dad, like the rock of St. Peter, stood beside me, then beneath me, as I stood on his shoulders and climbed into young adulthood and threw myself into university.

I told Jim of my Claire, my dear sweet Claire, and my love for her. How we met, our many walks across Dartmoor and around the rugged coastline of Sidmouth, of our debates about the serious issues affecting our contemporary world and how history, theology and present and past literary giants viewed similar circumstances from contrasting angles in different times. And I told Jim of my parting with her. Was I right? I don't know, I'm still not sure. I love her deeply and miss her and yet I feel the yearning of God calling me deeper, ever deeper.

I responded, but Claire, parting from her was … and then I saw Jim walking towards me. But he was no longer ten, he was old, but those eyes of his, those eyes, I could not speak. At 24 years of age, I, upon seeing Jim's father coming out of the shadows from behind the closed door of time, was for once lost for words. My vocal dexterity from university debates evaporated as I sought to wrest control of my emotions.

The stones on the bridge crunched under his boots and abruptly, when he stopped, the sounds they gave life to, were snuffed out. And then he spoke. As he did, Jim's face came alive in his father's smiles and in his mannerisms – the way he tugged on his left ear, whether for comfort or to focus on the subject he was pondering on as we talked and talked. We covered fourteen years and how the impact of Jim's death had affected our lives. Such bonds are the treasures of life.

He saw me off with a hearty handshake and a bear hug. We parted company. We never met again. I heard that he had died a year later on his way to his rendezvous on the railway bridge. I was the arrow of the future. A future I shared ethereally with Jim. And Jim's father and my dad, they were the bows upon which we were both propelled in the spiritual and physical planes of existence.

1 January to 31 May, 2011

From my early childhood, I remember my island – Maranatha. An island beckoned me to simple adoration of Christ. Looking back now, I realise that the place is blessed in my heart. I remember how in the stillness on the beach, amidst the shadows cast from shore trees gently bending in the soft heavenly breeze, I would lie on the warmth-shrouded sand. Footprints lay behind me; a trail of tiny faltering steps had indented themselves along the beach, my footsteps. To my left, in the dunes, I could hear the sound of laughter as children played and raced to the central tree of life.

In my dreams I would find myself arising out of my bed and floating through the window, alighting a cloud, not knowing where I would be borne, yet feeling draped by His presence. Utter peace would fill me, none that I would ever find on my waking. His cloud would bear me over rooftops and dew covered street lamps and a wooded copse before setting me down by the side of the central tree – my lifeline. I would cling to its trunk, praying for glimpses of His presence.

Each time at the cusp of waking, He would come to me. He would always say the same words.

'Be still and know that I am God.'

I was reminded then, as now, that I was hungering for the solace of His presence. Rarely did I give Him the time to spend with me, let alone allow myself to walk with Him during the day. Yet in that dawn light, the only time for me, perhaps, at the cusp of my awakening, I would be still and alone with God. On one miraculous occasion, I had a vision. In Christ's presence, I travelled a journey. It was a life's journey in the blinking of an eye. It was Christ's journey. And this is a calendar of His...

Tom's written meditation had stopped. No journey with Christ. Nothing. Harry's breathing was released from the impulse to be still and silent. For the briefest of moments, he felt like a latecomer at an important speech. Everyone was sat transfixed by the speaker's vision. The speaker had stopped and fixed his eyes on Harry as he entered the room. He was an intrusion. No matter how hard Harry tried, he could not meet the power of the man's gaze. One by one, all eyes in the room joined those of the great visionary, swivelled, and directed their gaze onto Harry. The silence, like a monster in a nightmare, grew bigger and bigger. Harry felt he was about to be consumed.

Irritated with his reaction to Tom's thoughts, Harry flicked roughly through the well-worn pages of the diary; no more entries or further reference to the meditation and reflections were recorded. He felt frustrated.

He switched on the digital recording and fast-forwarded the timeline of Tom's movements and lapses of consciousness. He played it right through up until the point where his victim sobbed and the muffled sounds of his anguish echoed in the speakers. Harry smiled. Yawning and stretching he retired to bed. Tom was not going anywhere.

FIFTEEN

Friday, July 6, 2012 – Harry's Place, Thames Path, London

When Harry awoke, he pulled on another coffee caffeine hit and let it warm his insides as he read a further extract from Tom's diary.

July 2011

Deep calls to deep across the oceans of time, until at last God finds a way. I had made my way up into the garden. The noise of the traffic had lessened to a background rumble. The bouncing balls and the playful sounds of children echoed gently around the houses on the hilltop. The birds chirped and twittered to one another. They set the surrounding landscape alight with the variety of their songs.

The early evening breeze scooted and skirted from branch to branch and flitted quickly off the grass blades. Carrier bags tied to sticks over the finely tilled earth crunched and crinkled away the would-be rustlers of the seedlings. Yet try as I might, my thoughts at the time would not take on wings to be near you. I was unable to recall the lines from our shared poem, if only I could remember the name, then I could share it with you again. The distance, like the mortar, has hardened. And we … we have long since sauntered on our separate journeys…

Harry entered Tom's cell. The wretch, lying in a pool of urine, was unconscious. Harry slowly winched Tom into an upright position, until his arms were stretched and tied up to the heights of Harry's bullrings. Tom swung to and fro. Placing a stool underneath him, Harry lowered Tom's buttocks onto the seat, might as well make him feel comfortable. Harry smiled at the thought.

He gently peeled the silver masking tape away from Tom's mouth, admiring how the skin almost clung to the tape's closeness, a friend it did not want to let go. Better, the devil you know. He struck Tom hard across the face; this forced his head sideways until with a sweaty splat it was stopped by the armpits of his upper arms. Tom surfaced slowly like a submerged and wary submarine. His eyes struggled to open. His lids had weights of drug and alcohol induced sleep dragging them down. His eyes flickered open and shut, open then shut.

'Wake up priest. Wake up.' Harry's voice was brutal.

Tom's eyes zeroed in on Harry in alarm. His head was thumping.

'You're a priest, isn't that right Tom? Perhaps I should say, Father Tom.'

'What? Where am I, who are you?' Memories fragmented; words stumbled out of Tom's swollen mouth.

'Answer the question. You're a priest. Isn't that right?' barked Harry.

'No, no, I'm not a priest, I'm... '

Tom's voice trailed off. His senses were slow to boot up. The absurd reality of his surroundings was re-emerging. People of the hope stood mutely in the ether.

'In training are we then?'

'I'm in training, as you put it.' Tom's defiance swelled. 'You mentioned we, you are too, I guess, and holding me here prisoner is preparation for your ministry is it?'

'No. It's preparation for you Tom. Have you got faith in Christ Almighty? When hope is almost gone, will you still have a glimmer of it, no matter how small, to keep you close to Jesus? Or in my language, will you have the fucking balls to persevere?'

Harry punched Tom this time and hard too, now that his prey was awake and could feel the impact. Yes, a solid bludgeon with his fist smashed across the right cheek. Blood spurted miraculously from his prey's lips. Harry loved it. His signet ring had branded a wheal on Tom's face.

Skin close, Harry brought his face uncomfortably close to Tom's gaping eyes, which darted, much like the enlarged white eyes of a horse, bolting from a predator.

'And don't fuck me around again mate! And don't fucking forget that Tom – Father fucking Tom!'

Spittle spluttered out of Harry's mouth spraying Tom's face. Harry grabbed Tom's hair and forcibly nodded his head back and forth.

'Good.'

Harry's chest heaved in and out, as he sucked in the calming effects of huge quantities of air.

'That's good, very good Tom, very good indeed.'

As if the one-sided altercation had never occurred, Harry continued. The un-nailed Christ hung limp. Through swollen lips, Tom replied to the inquisition. Interiorly, he held onto the consoling memories of his journey in Spain – the 'road to Santiago.'

LINES WRITTEN IN KENSINGTON GARDENS

By Mathew Arnold (1822-1888)

Calm soul of all things! Make it mine
To feel, amid the city's jar,
That there abides a peace of thine,
Man did not make, and cannot mar.

The will to neither strive or cry,
The power to feel with others give!
Calm, calm me more! Nor let me die
Before I have begun to live.

SIXTEEN

Friday, July 6, 2012 – Clare's Place, Iverna Gardens, London

Claire returned home to her High Street Kensington house a day later than planned, having arrived at Heathrow Terminal 5 around 7 pm. She was exhausted and felt sick with it. All caused from the shoving, hustling frenetic activity of traversing the United States following the primaries from January through to the end of June. She would be back in November to cover the results of the presidential elections.

She paid the cab driver after he placed her luggage on the pavement. Back home she was relieved, but something was bothering her the moment she arrived, a nagging feeling, not all was right. She shrugged her shoulders, putting any dark thoughts down to extreme tiredness. She hoisted herself and her bags up the steep terraced steps and into the voluminous hall of the town house within which she lived.

As always, thanks to Maria, her post was stacked in piles along the marble shelving that jutted elegantly out into the hallway. A leaf-framed mirror stretched the entire length along one wall above the shelf and added to the sense of space and grace of the house. Travel weary shadows stared back from underneath Claire's eyes as she quickly took in her reflection – bills, an assignment, more bills and a parcel.

Hurling her bags onto the bed, Claire collected her post and, after making herself a camomile and spearmint tea, eased herself into a reclining chair. She looked at the red light on the home phone indicating a number of voice messages had been left. She decided to listen to them in the morning. If anything had been urgent, then people would have called her on her mobile. She skimmed through the mobile, electric, gas bills, and scanned the bank statement for income and expenditure anomalies. The letter was from a woman, Claire had never heard of. She was called Mary Yohanus and was trying to trace her family history. Claire cast her eye over the enclosed family tree.

The parcel contained a book and a short letter from her father. The book was by Joanne Harris, entitled, *Chocolat*, one that Claire had often thought about, but never got around to buying. Life being so hectic her mind was constantly cluttered with ideas and investigative assignments. She opened the front cover and read the enclosed letter.

To my darling C,

As I was passing through Zurich Airport on my way to a medical conference, I thought about you working in Washington. Chance would have it that I saw this book. And I know you haven't read it, despite it being out for years and years now!

Thought you would like it. It's one investigative read, you will not have to think about. I expect it may bring back some bitter, but I feel more sweet memories. Forgive me. Besides, being in Switzerland, how could I resist the title?

Love you lots and may God Bless you – always.

Dad xxx

Furrowing her brow, she breathed away some tears forming on her scrunched eyelashes and held the novel close to her chest drinking in the memories of her mother. Claire spoke aloud to herself.

'My poor sweet dad.'

Sometimes memories cannot wait to be heard. Heaving a forlorn and heavy sigh, she shuffled the rest of the post together and put it all to one side.

SEVENTEEN

Saturday, July 7, 2012 – Clare's Place, Iverna Gardens, London

It was just after nine in the morning when Claire awoke. She arched her body and stretched her arms and legs to ease away the muscle contractions and elongate her spine. Tired after a punishing tour of America and still suffering from the effects of jet lag, she yawned. Her lower jaw clicked as tension was relieved. She laughed then, almost hysterically, imagining what her colleagues would think of the hyper efficient professional Claire in such a laid back relaxed state.

She was going to have a lazy morning. Claire slid into her silk dressing gown and her sloppy slippers and shuffled slowly into the kitchen. Efficient as ever, Maria had bought some provisions, the essentials in Claire's book, ground coffee, fresh milk, croissants and marmalade. Not only that, Maria had very sweetly provided Claire with a whole stack of Guardian G2 crosswords.

Claire made a mental note to wrap up Maria's present she had bought for her when in Washington DC, a small statue of the White House together with a guidebook to this magnificent building. She would leave it out for Maria along with the money for the food items when she came over on Wednesday to sort out Claire's laundry.

Later, when the cafetière was charged with a full contingent of coffee, the aroma was magnificent. Such bliss, Claire could not have wished for a more pleasurable start to the day. It was much needed too, after the almost endless schedule of events, speeches and interviews she had witnessed or conducted, and then written about and filed with her editor. With a mouthful of delicious croissant drenched in exquisite marmalade, and primed with her pen and crossword, heaven had just arrived.

Stretching again after breakfast as she sat at the table, Claire's arms reached out wide and high to the ceiling; she imagined herself holding a broom handle as she twisted slowly from side to side enjoying the pleasure of moving the muscles in her back and in particular, releasing the tension from her shoulder blades. Boy that was good, she thought. She yawned again when standing up. They were unstoppable.

A shower was the summons she gave herself. Even that felt like an effort, but she was getting restless and needed to secure momentum to wake up from the hovering soporific and exhausted state that occupied her mind and body. In the shower room, she let her dressing gown slide to the floor and stood sideways examining the profile and contours of her body in the mirror. Despite the long hours, eating out and absolutely no time to fit in exercise in America, Claire looked good she felt – I just wish I had someone to share it with. The thought made her part sad and part happy. The latter because of a fond memory that had popped into her mind regarding a passionate encounter she had had one surprising weekend, and totally out of character, last year.

The shower proved to be sublime. The large sunflower showerhead stormed water over her body. It was if Victoria Falls was pounding on her skin. It felt so invigorating. She stood there for a while with her palms flush against the shower tiles and allowed the pleasure of the warming liquid heat to refresh her spirit and ooze away the pervasive aches. Feeling refreshed, she dressed and felt ready for the day.

Remembering the three unheard messages on her answering machine Claire went into the living room and pressed the play button.

2:30 pm, Wednesday, May 9:

'Good afternoon, Ms Yohanus, it's Jack Brown here, I've finished making the desk you commissioned and look forward to hearing from you so I can arrange to set it up in your home when it's convenient. Bye for now.'

Excellent, she thought, wonderful news, I know exactly where that's going.

8:30 am, Saturday, June 23:

'Hello, er, um, it's Mary Yohanus here. I'm sorry I'm not used to this. I don't like speaking to a machine. I posted a letter to you three weeks ago. It's about my family tree you see. As I'd not heard from you, I thought I'd give you a call to see if you had received it. Hope you don't mind me calling. Hope to hear from you soon, many thanks, Mary.'

Clare spoke out loud. 'What the ... How'd she get my number and bloody hell, 8.30 in the morning? That bloody woman.'

7:23 pm, Thursday, July 5:

'Hi. Claire it's me, Tom ...' Claire's heart jumped. 'I know. A bit of a shock after five years hey? Anyway, I'll explain when we meet. Sorry, I should say *if* we meet. I came down today for a long weekend in the city, needed a break.

'I'm staying at this cheap looking hotel, the Petunia. If you're free and of course, naturally, if you want to meet me, I'm here until Monday or Tuesday. I'm not sure how long after that really.

85

'My mobile number is the same, hope you've still got it. I know how organised you used to be. I should have written my number down to read out. I'm so useless at remembering numbers. I haven't changed in that respect, apart from also losing a bit of weight.

'So, if you want to meet me and haven't got my mobile, you can reach me at the hotel and leave a message; and hey, Claire … whatever you decide, that's fine, take care, love, Tom.'

Claire's thoughts rushed and gushed ahead of her. Oh my gosh … Tom … of course I want to see you, you stupid, silly bugger.

It was 12.15 pm. Claire left a warm message on Tom's mobile. She could kick herself now for spending the whole morning in such a fashion. Nevertheless, she was where she was. After finding the telephone number of the Hotel Petunia, Claire got through to a male receptionist.

'Good afternoon would you put me through please to a Mr Tom Abimelech, who is staying at your hotel?'

'Yes Madam, hold the line, please, whilst I check to see if he's in his room.'

The line went silent for a few moments, Claire waited excitedly with barely contained patience.

'Hello Madam,' the receptionist was back on the line, 'Mr Abimelech is no longer at the hotel. He left on Friday.'

'What? Friday did you say? That cannot be. Tom, Mr Abimelech left me a voicemail on Thursday night saying he was staying at your hotel until at least Monday or Tuesday next week. Would you please check again?'

Claire could hear the audible hiss of frustration as the man breathed out.

'There is no point Madam. When I checked, I asked the manager if we had a guest by that name. She informed me that Mr Abimelech came back to his room, she thinks probably in the early hours of Friday morning, and took all of his belongings.'

Claire retorted, 'No! What's going on? Tom isn't like that. Have you called the police to report him missing?'

'I am sorry, Madam, I really have to go; there is nothing else I can add. I wasn't on duty when Mr Abimelech registered.' And with that, the receptionist said goodbye, and hung up.

Claire felt in a state of shock. What on earth had happened to Tom? His supposed behaviour made no sense and did not ring true about him. She was worried but tried desperately to maintain her composure and calm her racing thoughts.

EIGHTEEN

Saturday, July 7, 2012 – Hotel Petunia, London

Tom had obviously underplayed how cheap the hotel really was. It was like walking back into the 1970s: formica tables, drinks trolleys, even a serving hatch between the reception and the back office. The place contained all the hallmarks of an era bygone, and good riddance, thought Claire.

The manager, Alison White, was not keen to talk. In fact, she had gruffly told Claire to mind her own bloody business and that it was a police matter. The manager had reported him as a guest who had left without paying. Something she was particularly annoyed about, as that was the third guest to do so in the past month.

Claire realised protestations and challenging the manager would not get her anywhere.

'I'm sorry that you've had three guests run off without paying the bill, dreadful behaviour. But I wonder if I could really call on your good nature to help me. You see, Tom is an old boyfriend and a good friend; it just isn't like him to run away ... As I mentioned to your receptionist on the phone earlier, Tom said he would be staying at your hotel until Monday or Tuesday as he was in the city for a surprise long weekend. He wasn't too sure whether I would be back or not as I'm a reporter. He knew that I'd been covering the US presidential elections, hence, why he wasn't staying at my place.'

Claire showed the manager her press card, which displayed her position in a well-known broadsheet. This and, probably the offer to pay Tom's outstanding bill was enough for Miss White to relax and open up. Thank God, thought Claire.

'Your receptionist mentioned Tom left in the early hours. May I ask,' said Claire, 'why you think that might be the case?'

Miss White replied, 'As you can see, we're a cosy compact hotel. Some of our guests virtually live here, as do others in the hotel opposite, the Maxwell. I'm the owner manager of both; they used to belong to my parents.' She added, by way of explanation before continuing, 'So I'm familiar with the coming and goings and, the goings on ... Your boyfriend,' Claire's heart missed a beat at the thought, 'sorry, your ex,' she misinterpreted Claire's reaction, 'was in the hotel bar until around 9.30 on Thursday night. He had a few drinks with a bar snack, before saying to the staff he was going out for a walk and would be back later.'

'Only he didn't, did he? Didn't that raise any concerns with you at all?' asked Claire leaning forward as she spoke.

The manager fidgeted decisively in her seat.

'Well, no actually, it didn't. The reception is staffed until 11.30 pm. All guests have an external key in case they come back to their rooms late. From 7 am, the reception is staffed again. Mr Abimelech didn't come for breakfast; the last serving is at 9 am.'

'And you weren't concerned that Tom may well have left without paying?' asked Claire.

'Well, it crossed my mind, yes, but only slightly at that time. It did remind me of the other two men that had done a bunk, but I said to myself, not three times, surely,' replied the manager, 'and besides some guests don't take breakfast. And as he had gone out the night before, I just assumed he was still asleep or resting in his bedroom or something.'

'So what happened next?' asked Claire.

'Normal routines continued. We're busy here, so his absence slipped my mind until the chambermaid came to see me at 12.30 pm to say that Mr Abimelech's room was empty. When I asked what she meant, she told me that he wasn't there and his belongings had vanished.'

Exactly, thought Claire, into thin air, but people generally don't, do they? Despite her growing sense of uneasiness, Claire maintained her outward composure.

The manager had continued speaking. 'I immediately went up to his room to see for myself. There was nothing, no sign of him. The bed had not been slept in, his bag was gone. He hadn't at least taken the towels. The last two buggers had.'

'This may seem like an odd question Miss White, but had the towels been used? And if so how had they been left?'

'I'm not sure what you mean, sorry,' said the manager.

'Had the towels been left scrunched up on the bathroom floor perhaps?' Claire elaborated. 'I ask, as I've never known Tom to be tidy, unlike me, and, despite my constant reminders to be so.'

To lend credence and create, she hoped, a bond of camaraderie between herself and the manager, she added, 'It's a bit exasperating at times; do you know what I mean?'

'Yes, I know exactly what you mean. Threw my last man out; couldn't take it anymore. Yes, come to think of it, didn't see it as anything of note at the time. Of course, why would I? The towels had been used, they were still damp. I'd noticed that … yes, I do remember now, the towels were neatly folded on the side of the bath. Perhaps he's tidier when he's not with you? Men!'

'Quite' said Claire pensively.

Unless Tom had radically changed during his training for the priesthood, and she doubted that, something was seriously amiss. Her thoughts magnified her fears. She had a few more questions for the manager.

'Did anyone of your staff see Tom in his room before he went out? And if so, were his things unpacked in any way?'

The manager was starting to understand the way Claire was seeing things. Perhaps he had gone missing or something worse. Her spine shivered. People do disappear, sometimes without trace, she thought. And sometimes they're never found. Or if they are located, they're not always alive, though, are they? Either way, having met Ms Yohanus and finding out she was a highflying journalist, it was difficult to believe she would be a friend of someone who was a fraudster. Then again, she wondered what job, Mr Abimelech really did. Surely, he must be in a similar economic class to Ms Yohanus. That being the case, would he really choose to stay at my hotel? Unlikely she thought. Of course, he could be in-between jobs. Yes, that might explain it. She would love to find out more.

'Actually, I did go to his room at just after 6 pm that Thursday night. He'd come down to ask how to get an outside line to call someone. The instruction leaflet had gone from the room. I was still on duty. So leaving the reception staff in the lobby, I went to his room with him to explain and also to put a spare copy of the leaflet back. It contains a digital code, which has to be typed in to get an outside line. Anyway, by the phone was a picture frame and I noticed it contained a lovely picture of a young woman. Of course, when you came here this afternoon, I knew it was you straight away.'

Claire's heart jolted, but despite her anxiety she smiled, and for the present she couldn't stop herself – dare she think of him, as her Tom again. He still held her close to him wherever he went. There was still hope, she thought.

'One more thing,' said Claire, 'Do you mind if I have a look in Tom's room? It will help me get a feel for things.'

The manager checked, a new guest for the room was due at 4 pm, so there was time. As they went in the lift to the second floor, the manager spoke. 'I'm beginning to share your thoughts that Mr Abimelech could be missing. Before you go, I'll give you the police incident reference number for the crime I reported and also the station who dealt with my call. They said they'd pass it on to CID, but no one's been around yet or telephoned back.'

It felt strange to be in a room where Tom had so recently been. Worryingly, as her thoughts edged closer to his presence, she imagined him calling out to her for help.

'Now we're in his room, is there anything else that springs to mind Miss White?' asked Claire.

The manager cast her eyes around, 'No, I don't think so ... wait a minute, that's right. The curtains were drawn when I came up here with the chambermaid. I remember now, the blasted things don't meet in the middle and I'd thought the handyman had fixed them.'

'Do you mind if ...?'

'No, go ahead.'

As Claire drew the curtains, she saw the Hotel Maxwell. A room opposite also had its curtains drawn. That room had a good view of Tom's.

'Hope you don't mind me asking, but who might be staying in that room over there?' asked Claire.

The manager hesitated before speaking. 'You know I shouldn't tell you, but I can see how important it is for you to find your Mr Abimelech. One of our permanent guests lives there, Ms Kerveen. She keeps herself to herself. Never lets the chambermaid change the linen, likes to do it all herself. She's a bit of a night owl, so may have seen something, although she's probably asleep right now.'

On the way out Claire picked up a nightclub card, 201. 'Just one more thing,' she said to the manager, 'are there any pubs, restaurants, hidden away nooks and cranny type streets in the area? They're the sort of things Tom's drawn to.'

NINETEEN

Saturday, July 7, 2012 – Metropolitan Police Service, London

It was nearly a quarter to four in the afternoon. Claire felt she was making some, but so very little progress. She jostled her way through crowds either in the underground or out on the streets. It was heaving virtually wherever she went on this Saturday in London. The heat did not help either.

She arrived at the entrance to the police station ten minutes earlier than she had arranged with DS Raven. She was lucky he was working a shift this weekend. At the reception, a female civilian member of staff dressed in a white blouse with blue epaulets, mirroring the style of the police uniform, saw Claire arrive and slid back the glass partition located above the counter. Greeting Claire with a model smile, she spoke in a singsong voice reminiscent of her Welsh valley roots.

'Good Morning Ma'am, how may I help you?'

When Claire explained whom she was here to see, the receptionist asked her to take a seat whilst she called the officer down. The ambient sound of the back office faded into silent oblivion when the glass partition was closed. Claire took up a seat in one of the orange coloured foam filled chairs and rested her arm on the light pine replica arms. She toyed with the idea of skimming through the police community newsletter, but decided against it and meditated in the brief few minutes she had. The mushroom painted walls and the surprisingly quiet surroundings of the reception had a calming, soporific effect on her.

The detective who came down to the counter flirted with Julie the receptionist, before looking out and checking on his appointment. Julie was forgotten.

His mouth moistened, then went dry and he swallowed deeply. He took in her femininity immediately. Her long dark bob hair rested on her shoulders. He thought she was around 5' 10" and curvaceously slim in all the right places. With her eyes closed, he could see the extent of her long dark eyelashes and the image of an ebony Cleopatra came readily to his mind's eye. Her long slender fingers curled gently around the end of the arms of the chair. She was stunning, beautiful. No doubt about it. He imagined she had the ability to unconsciously ease her femininity through a crowd, and pull all thoughts and desire from both men and women after her, as if her whole aura and sensuality possessed some thought fragrant perfume that left a trail of envious eyes behind her.

Pressing the door release button, DS Raven entered the reception foyer and walked eagerly towards her.

Claire heard the click of the door and opened her eyes. She was calm and centred.

His mouth became desert bone dry and he found it difficult to swallow. His Adam's apple swelled.

Her head turned towards him and her bob moved in unison and rested on the nape of her neck and shoulders. She floated off the chair to greet him.

As one, they both extended their arms and shook hands; her smile and the spark in her eyes were immediate and embraced him wholly.

'DS Raven, it's good to meet you Miss Yohanus.'

He was so formal, when every nerve in his body strained at the leash to hold her, to be absorbed by her.

'Shall we go into this meeting room where we can talk more easily?'

More easily, who was he kidding; he had to focus, but oh, those eyes.

He slid the panel on the door across to reveal the red emboldened words – meeting in progress – and closed the door behind him. She was seated behind the table. He took up a seat opposite her and placed the file between them both, she waited patiently. He rallied his thoughts and pulled himself away from those eyes and focused on the green coloured file in front of him.

'Thank-you for seeing me, I'm very concerned about Tom, his whereabouts. We're old friends, a close friend actually. His disappearance is out of character. I know he's not a thief. I would very much appreciate it officer, if you could perhaps give me a bit more background to what's going on?'

DS Raven recounted the facts and the recent spate of deceptions in the area, not one mention that Tom might be a missing person. As the officer droned on, Claire's mind drifted onto Tom.

Tom supported her through the tragic death and the loss of her mother. Claire had been suicidal in her anger and her anguish.

'Suicide may seem like the only option sometimes, but it isn't Claire, give yourself time,' he had said.

Easy for him to say she had screamed. He was not the one who had been lied to by both his parents. No one had told her that mum was dying. It was going to happen, there was nothing she could do about it, and her degree would have been adversely affected if she had known. That was the story she had been told.

Her mum did not want her to know and dad had kept his word that he would not tell Claire.

Dead, just like that. No time for Claire to say farewell, no chance to hug her mum or chance to hold her one last time. She could not stop her body shaking.

'Oh, I miss her so much Tom. I can't live without her; she was my mantra that carried me through my childhood and into university. Dad was always in the office or abroad on business trips, mum, and I, well, we were closer together as a result. I know it sounds incredible, but I feel if I've had my umbilical cord severed for the first time now. Up until now, it seemed that it was still somehow connecting the both of us. My lifeline is gone Tom. It's gone.'

She wailed. 'I want to be with her.'

She sobbed and shook and rivers of tears broke over her face and dripped from her nose and chin. Tom had held her closer that night; closer than she had been held by him before. As her crying subsided, she whispered.

'I wish I had your faith Tom. I wish I had your faith.'

'You do Claire. You just don't realise that you have. One day you'll be aware and you *will* see. In my dark moments, my shadows raise up fears and anxieties that I know are not from God. The difficult part is putting my wholehearted trust in Him. When I'm able, I centre myself and reflect on God. All things become calm for me. He is the mantra of life and you and I, everyone; we are stewards of our lives, not victims of mechanistic events. God has given us the responsibility to nurture, protect and uphold our lives, they are not our own to dispose of. Killing ourselves goes against our innate desire to preserve life, to persevere, and to meet life; to embrace it, not to end it, but to respect its integrity and hence our own integrity and that of others.'

'So Miss Yohanus, that's it. We haven't found him yet. It's recorded as a theft so to speak. One of several that I gather from the hotel manager when she phoned me, you are aware about.'

DS Raven did his best; he really did try to listen to her theory that Tom was in fact a missing person or even worse, had been kidnapped. He wanted to say you are right, if only to see the warm spark of radiance in her eyes that he just knew was waiting to ignite him with their joy, but he could not, tied, as he was to view it as theft, pure and simple.

Her protestations gave him more time in her heavenly company, but he knew he could not meet her halfway on this one. In the end he pointed her towards the organisation Missing People, perhaps they could give her the comfort he so longed to provide.

TWENTY

It was 7.15 pm. Time had entwined its slow tock around the speed of Claire's heart. It had been over six hours since her meeting with the hotel manager and the police. She was losing energy. Adrenaline had long since shot its bolt, and her reserves were almost depleted.

She had taken on board the police's almost inane advice. However, she had at first, started a tour of the accident and emergency units across London. It had been fruitless and foolish; she knew in her heart that would be the case before she started. Yet, probably like so many people, when faced with the sudden disappearance of a loved one, hope, no matter how delusional, gave her the strength to hold onto the edge of the cliff and stop herself falling into the pitiless chasm of despair.

In the end, though, the chaos of crowds, the queues and the mind numbing boredom of waiting to be seen had got to her. The battle to get staff to look through the blank screen of the reception and see her with humanity in their hearts was lost. Getting staff to respond kindly to her simple request of help in finding a loved one had been futile. Her attitude and low blood sugar levels no doubt had played their part. She had heard, so often, the voices of staff falling back onto the Data Protection Act as the reason not to tell her anything, or harbouring under the umbrella of bureaucratic procrastination, or that they were busy dealing with real emergencies to avoid looking to see if Tom was or wasn't in their hospital. It had taken its toll on her patience. In one unit, she had forgotten by now, which, Mount Etna had blown. She had screamed loudly. It was a loudness displayed by those possessed by fear of time snuffing out hope of their loved ones being found alive. The bare walls of indifference had been dehumanising.

'Just tell me for fuck sake. Have you or have you not had a man of this name, fitting this description, wearing a bloody linen suit?'

A security guard ushered her off the premises and she had beat a hasty retreat. In the end, she placed the hospital search in the bin of wasted effort. Panic had caused her to follow a barren path. But action had felt at the time better than nothing. She had been a busy fool and she knew it. She was sick with exhaustion and hunger and was not thinking clearly. All a result of the stressful demands she had imposed on herself in a frantic search to unravel the fog that blocked a vision to Tom's whereabouts. She had not been to the other hotel, yet, or been in touch with Tom's parents. Seeing them could result in a tricky reception.

Meanwhile, though, she needed food and drinks badly in order to refresh and collect her senses. The Cantonese 'fast-food' restaurant with its rows of seats and benches was the quickest solution she so desperately needed. It was heaving with the lower-middle chattering classes, ideal for Claire to hide herself amidst the crowd. The waiting staff were as industrious as ants. The top 'Mama' sharply deployed orders that guided her workers effectively in seating customers and serving them with alacrity.

Claire was guided to the end of the last table at the rear of the dining area, the one nearest the open plan kitchen. The clutter of utensils, the spitting of heated food in sizzling oil and the singed scents of spices assailed Claire's senses. She sat facing onto the street. Her eyes were temporarily magnetised by the pavement hustlers vying for attention from their market stalls, the wild gesticulation of stallholders and hagglers alike were all visible to Claire, but their words were as soundless as a silent movie playing out through the rectangular expanse of the window.

She ordered chicken noodle soup and green tea. Enough to sustain and restore her body and mind she thought. Customers vied with one another to be heard. Some sat idly fiddling with their chopsticks, lost in thought or trying to hide their discomfort that they were not engaged in the circle of stories 'waggoned' around them. The Mama was instructing a new server on her expectations.

'Stand to the side of the room, not intrusive, but looking round to respond to or guess the needs of customers. Greet them quickly. Keep them happy. That way they come back. Clear?'

All these exchanges sank into Claire's consciousness. People's lives were happening now; their worries, all hidden behind the public masks on display. How many though were in the force of a personal tsunami like hers she imagined? Perhaps they were in the eye of the storm. On the other hand, maybe they were unaware, blessedly so, of the rage about to collide into their lives.

The waves of noise ebbed and flowed and crashed against the tables as an increasing number of people were fed, their food filled mouths swallowing oratory into silent undulating wavelets.

Claire's spiced warming soup arrived, fortified with ginger, chunks of chicken, thick worm-like noodles and meaty vegetables. Eating the yang food served its purpose and this coupled with the drinking of green tea had injected energy and balance into her veins. Frantic feelings, for a while at least, had been mellowed, but the search had to go on.

TWENTY-ONE

Saturday, July 7, 2012 – Hotel Maxwell, Bedford Place, London

Time had slipped quietly past nine in the evening. The sun was beginning to set across London. Nature was slowing down. The lights of the city were taking over its role. It was getting late, but the owner/manager had said Ms Kerveen was usually awake well into the night. Claire tentatively knocked on Ms Kerveen's door. No response.

Claire knocked louder, more confidently, calling out, 'Hello.'

Seconds passed.

The chatter of a woman's voice saying 'Stay,' several times could be heard from within.

Eventually the door was opened a fraction and Ms Kerveen's face peered out. It was difficult to tell, but Claire thought she was possibly in her late 50s. She had long honey blonde hair that was seemingly swept back under a black wide brimmed hat made of velvet. Her striking dark eyebrows curved around high above her eyes, giving her oval face an expectant look. A black chiffon scarf encircled her neck and rested lightly on the shoulders of a long black trouser suit.

She simply said, 'Yes?'

Claire smiled and said, 'I'm sorry to disturb you. The owner/manager of the hotel said you might be able to help me. My name is Claire, Claire Yohanus. I'm trying to find a close friend who stayed at the hotel opposite last Thursday night. His room windows are opposite yours and he seems to have gone missing. I was wondering if you might have seen anything.'

Expectant eyes looked upwards, the irises half-hidden underneath her lids as she poked here and there in her memories.

'Yes, I do recall seeing some movement that night. It gave me an idea for a character. Please, do come in and I can tell you more.'

In the narrow hallway, Claire eased herself along the opposing brim of the woman's hat, the edge of which brushed her clothing as she passed into the room. The heavy, deep scent of Ms Kerveen's perfume crept as an unwanted guest into her nostrils. In the close confines of the room, the initial impact of the aroma was overpowering.

As if Claire had spoken, Ms Kerveen said 'Oh, forgive the powerful scent. I've just put it on. It'll fade soon.'

'I'm sorry,' said Claire, 'I've called when you are just going out haven't I?'

'Yes, but don't worry, I'm going to late night house party in Southgate. My taxi isn't due for another hour. I like to get ready early. It saves me from the flustering of last minute preparations. Such distractions bedevilled my life in my younger days. The hard earned wisdom of age, I'm afraid.'

As Claire entered the main living room, she saw a timid looking sausage dog quivering behind the back of the settee; it reminded her of a childhood friend and the sight of rolled up newspapers that were positioned at the base of the internal doors in Kate's house to block out drafts.

'Don't mind Kevin as you go through, he's timid, but he's very friendly when you get to know him ... Take a seat, Kevin will soon come out once he knows you won't hurt him.'

Claire sat down on the rose tinted, cloth-covered settee and Ms Kerveen joined her. As predicted, Kevin waddled out and stood snugly next to his mistress's ankle, wiggling the stump of his tail. His polished swollen eyes seemed to be almost smiling into Claire's.

'Now my dear, I'm Sam, short for Samantha. Tell me more and let's see if I can help.'

Her calm, reassuring voice softened the hard feelings of anxiety bubbling within Claire.

As Clare breathed deeply in to speak, she noticed a large framed photograph hung on the wall opposite. It was a picture of a young woman, Sam, she guessed, dressed in light leathers sat astride a motorbike next to a young biker, almost a Che Guevara look alike. The backdrop behind them both was breathtaking; the Sierra Nevada Mountains seemed to stretch endlessly into the distant horizon.

Claire shared a synopsis of what she thought may have happened to Tom, of the conversation that she had had with the hotel owner/manager, including the detail about the curtains not drawing properly in Tom's room, and what she had done since then.

Sam listened intently, gazing into the depths of Claire's eyes and studied the rich character within her face. It was evident that Claire was so very much in love. Sam had known that depth of feeling too a long while ago.

When Claire had finished describing the course of events, the emotions it had resurrected were apparent in the subtle trembling of her body. Sam leant forward, placed a hand on one of Claire's forearms, and rubbed her skin soothingly. At this display of humanity, Claire no longer felt alone within the nightmare that now occupied her thoughts. She fought to hold it in, but could not help herself. She burst into tears and sobbed. Her charade was broken. Her shoulders shook.

Sam moved closer and embraced Claire who rested her body against Sam's. In her time of need, in these intimate moments, this bubble of space, Claire felt the touch of an angel. In between sobs, Claire talked about how much she missed the touch and the scent of Tom, and above all how the hurt ached from the gulf inside of her. She was so distant from the feel of his love, which he had given so generously in all the ways she had needed. No other man she had met matched him.

Sam cried too. Years of grief were unlocked. Both gave and received. It was the intangible gift when hearts are truly open. How long had it been since anyone had held Sam or shared such an intimate moment with her? In truth, friends were not always enough. It had been thirty long barren untouched years.

Jonathon had been his name. Jonathon Charles Chambers. She could still smell the sweet scent of the honeysuckle from the hedgerow as they lay entwined as lovers, in love, so often do, and rested in heaven amidst the comforting bed of soft warmed grass and the soporific warmth of a cosy summer's day. And then, on the way home, they had come off his motorbike. Just like that, skidding on gravel. Jonathon colliding with a telegraph pole had had the life crushed out of him. She had been thrown free, but scarred across her face, for life. Makeup hid the blemishes, but nothing had eroded the loss of him.

Tonight these memories and more surfaced between them. Sam cancelled the taxi and returned with a freshly brewed pot of tea. For a while, she became Claire's missing mother. The soft touch of good spirits flowed freely, given easy access by receptive minds. They chatted about things from their pasts and the present. They became two kindred companions: mother and child, friend with friend, human being seeing another human being. Fears of sharing the deepest of hurts had been abandoned. Trust blossomed. The best that we humans can be was revealed.

When they discussed last Thursday night, Sam's memory of the early hours of Friday morning was vivid. One thing for certain in Claire's mind was this. The stocky man that Sam saw that night definitely wasn't Tom.

When it was time for Claire to leave, they both stood up. Confident Kevin faced with the height of two adults scampered to safety and harbour behind the furniture. As she and Sam were parting, Claire spoke.

'Thank-you so very much; tonight, was so unexpected, but so needed.'

'My dear Claire please, there's no need. You've helped me in more ways that writing closeted here has ever done. I've been crazy. I allowed myself to be imprisoned in my emotions when Jonathon died, well, you know it all now; I died too. Lost myself in the waves of emotion and never let go. Tonight you saved me when I hadn't fully realised how much I needed to change and break free.'

Sam's eyes welled up. She quickly gulped a breath of air to steady herself...

'Anyway, suffice to say, I've been a bloody fool. Not anymore, I can tell you.'

Both she and Claire laughed uncontrollably and loud then. Hysteria broke out. It came from the birth of exhaustions played out. Above all though, it came from the shared recognition of the madness and the absurdity of being human. They were both experts at making a hash of their lives. They held each other tightly once more, the closest of friends in these final moments together.

FALLEN ANGEL

By Harold Denmart (1974-2012)

If I was a butterfly without wings,
Would children sing in wonder as I plummet to earth?
With fragile delicacy, would their windward eyes, like me,
show no mercy?
Or would the airflow carry me away so I could breathe life for
yet another day?
But I have no wings;
I'm attached to the Earth,
I am a fallen angel with unkind hands,
And woe betides to those who fall onto my land.

TWENTY-TWO

I touched her forehead with my forefinger and lightly traced a gentle line above her eyebrows and down around her jaw line until I had fully traversed the circumference of her face, and then gently, as a breeze whispers to a butterfly, I floated my fingers over her eyes. How beautiful she was. I leant closer and felt the pull of her lips draw me closer still. As one we kissed.

And then the dream stopped abruptly. Tom awoke to his cellular reality. The memories of Claire faded swiftly as if the sun had risen with bright intensity to burn off the early morning mist hovering over the lawn. It had never ceased to amaze him how often he dreamt of her – the shadows of his sub-conscious tap-tap tapping away at his dedication to the priesthood.

Harry had beaten him again and again until he had lost consciousness. Tom had not given the answers in the way that Harry had wanted them. He wanted the truth, the whole truth and nothing else. If he felt Tom kept anything back or erased elements of his story, Harry had been like a sledgehammer and repeatedly beaten him.

A speaker somewhere in the room shook Tom's ears into listening.

'Tom, good morning, how are we today? I've just listened to the weather report. It's another sunny day. No news about any missing priest I'm afraid … Sorry Tom. Let me know what you want for breakfast eh? I've left a menu by your head, just turn to the left – that's it, see it now? Call back in five minutes for your order. Okay?'

Silence over the airwaves then. Only Tom's thoughts clashed like symbols in his brain, over and over again – bizarre, surreal, a living nightmare. Was this real, a dream? Real – dream? Lights flashed on and off across the room.

Harry laughed. This was fun.

Darkness, brilliant whiteness, pitch black, then stunning, intrusive light and dark abysmal gloom. Square cubes of flashing light danced chaotically around the room, jumping out from behind the blackness, the darkness – flash and flash again. A dark void, then waves and stars of light undulated and danced in a swirling galaxy above Tom's head. Pain drilled into its centre. Was he in between reality or dream, dream or reality?

Then silence. Unconsciousness brought sweet oblivion.

When Tom awoke, gentle light pervaded the room, his room, and his cell. No menu and no food, what a futile but immediate thought it was, prompted by the ache in his stomach. Tom prayed for patience. Out of such a gift from God would come eventually hope, he hoped. His left forefinger traced the cross, repeatedly, frenetically at first, but at last – at last, became a slow rhythmic calming meditation.

The silent eyes wired into the ceiling conveyed the black-and-white images to the monitor in Harry's control centre. Hardly any movement and yet, the camera zoomed in on Tom's fingers of his right and left hands.

Filling the screen, the Stations of the Cross were splayed out on the floor. Mind you, you needed a lover's imagination to see it, visualise it, you know what I mean, but hey, Harry-the King, Harry-the oppressor, nay Lord, God-if you please, could read

Tom's mind. The diary helped, to be sure. It was an almost live art performance, street theatre.

Was Harry entertained? Entertainment to Harry involved primeval thoughts. As a child, Harry's entertainment, amongst several infantile vices, was capturing butterflies. Not collecting, just the idle dismantling and removal of their wings. He would leave them to stumble, to crawl and fall into the nearest scavenging ant. Imagine being dragged away mercilessly by the cohort into the black heaving cavernous and carnivorous pit.

What drives such a mentality to behold such destruction, to rest on his childlike elbows and smile as the beautiful butterfly is dismissed from this earth? Why could not Harry the child behold the butterfly with love in his eyes? What events, treatment, abuse, disturbed him? Adult Harry did not give a shit. In fact, Harry was a 'fuck-em' philosopher. He existed. He knew what he knew. Moreover, what he did not know did not matter.

TWENTY-THREE

10:08 hours, Saturday, July 7, 2012 – Harry's Place, Thames Path, London

As St Ignatius of Antioch, said of priests: "they are like the living image of God the Father."

After the beating, the bleeding and the bruises, Tom faced what he saw as the fact. If Harry felt in any way that he was lying, or holding the slightest thought or feeling back, the punishment would become ever more severe. Tom was in little doubt that at some stage in this process within the confines of this room, this cell, he would meet his death. Therefore, when Harry asked him what drew him to the priesthood and what temptations teased him to want to leave, Tom answered honestly. In fact, from this moment onwards, Tom obeyed his tormentor.

'No matter how much I strived to fit the mantle of priesthood or how much I talked the talk, I felt deep down within me an incessant pull back to the material world. And that world for me started and ended with Claire. However, idealism excited me. The excitement and the exhilaration, which pumped through me as I entered training, were real.

My intuition told me this was the right path for me. But, I've come to realise that I, perhaps many others do too sometimes, mistake our subconscious wants for intuition and allow the fabrication of truth to be the truth as we commit to a course of action. I fooled myself and believed that the priesthood was the right thing for me. I felt it was divine inspiration. This inner and outward display of conviction persuaded all before me, no matter how much I loved them... or, how much they loved me.'

Tom paused. His mind awash with the moment he had told Claire. He allowed the pain of her abandonment to bubble on his insides. He had blocked real feelings. He had been the log in his own eyes. He had refused to see.

His head bowed. He continued speaking slowly as thoughts melded with emotions and the memories were relived. Tears dripped to the floor as they ran down his face. The dripping tap would not stop this time. Tom immersed himself in the facing of his final confession. It was the only real one he had ever held back. He recounted the painful memory. Every moment of guilt wallowed in his gut.

'Claire lay next to me, her head resting on my chest, her arms and legs entwined over me. I breathed in the fresh smell of her, like the aroma from freshly dried clothes that had been hung out to air in the breeze. Her rich, thick, long raven hair splayed out over my shoulder. The fingers of my left hand gently played with the strands of Claire's hair as if I was playing Heaven's harp over her. She breathed out a sigh of contentment and spoke.'

"Tom that feels wonderful, don't stop will you?"

'It felt like heaven. It was. Yet in that moment of intimacy I felt the whispering of God calling me to speak. I resisted the call. But the whispering was incessant. The next words I spoke brought an abrupt end to heaven.'

"Claire; you know that retreat I was on last weekend? ... Well, I was speaking to one of the sisters and the priest there and I decided ... "

"Decided what?"

'I hesitated. I could not voice the words. I lacked the courage. Claire twisted her body in my arms and raised herself up enough to look into my eyes. She looked deeply into them.

A perimeter of tears formed in the lower part of them as rivulets streamed down over her cheeks. Her face took on the mantle of a Madonna statue. She closed her eyes and the outpouring of her grief continued.'

Oh, Tom, please. Please don't. I love you so, so much. My heart will break without you."

'Her body shook. Sobs erupted from her opened mouth as she panted out the pain of loss.

"Tom. I love you. Please don't do it, I beg you."

'Yet in my dogmatic way, then, I was determined. I set my face towards God's goal for me. I, with the mantle of Christ upon me, stood by my choice. I told her I felt it was the irrevocable calling of God. That no matter how much I loved her, and I did love her so very, very, much, the calling of God beat like a drum in my heart willing me to say yes to being his servant.'

Harry brought his hands together to beat out a slow and harsh applaud. His loud laugh engulfed the room.

'So you're a fucking pussy! When push came to shove, when faced with the one you love, you didn't have the guts, did you? And you thought God fucking called you? You are a fucking dick! Can't you see? It was the devil! Stone me! Here's me without any education and I can read right between your lifelines. All the time you thought, you were following God's calling and there's the devil sat on your shoulder, pretending to be God. He called you away from the one you love; I reckon your one true love as well. That way the devil killed two birds with one stone. Boy that makes me laugh. What a fucking dick you are!'

Tom slowly raised his head and looked at his tormentor. This brutish and uneducated man had seen Tom for what he had been. He truly felt naked upon the cross.

Harry went on, 'Come on now, now you're in the flow, and I don't mean your pussy tears, tell me a bit more about why you're God's man? One of his foot soldiers I reckon.'

The nails just beat harder into the cross as Tom bared his self to more humiliation. He knew it would come, truth and torment. Whatever Tom did, Harry would have his way.

'It was several events on and around one Easter. I was walking on Burgh Island ...'

Harry looked confused.

'It's a short way off the coast of South Devon. When the tide is low, you can walk across the sand to get to it.'

Harry nodded for Tom to continue. He did.

'It was a cold, windswept day and I was heading up to the top. When I was half way up the slopes, I stopped and looked down at the sea and the rocks below. The rocks seemed to be moving forward whilst the sea stood still. It felt like I was in a portal between kairos and kronos.'

'For fuck sake.' said Harry, 'You gotta explain some of the words you use; I'm not a fucking academic. Jesus.'

'Yes, sorry,' said Tom, and immediately thought how stupid he was for responding as if he was in a pub having a normal conversation over a pint of beer.

'Both words originate I think from ancient Greece. Kronos refers to chronological time; you know the 24-hour clock, seven days a week, 12 months a year.'

Harry nodded. Tom carried on speaking. He was becoming like Pavlov's dog.

'Kairos refers to those moments in life when something special happens to you. It almost feels as if time is standing still. In those moments, you feel you are living only in the present. That is the only thing that exists. The past has gone; the future has yet to happen. Your life has pressed the pause button. You become aware of everything. That's when you truly live.'

Harry knew that feeling well. Harry ordered Tom to continue. He obeyed.

'The earth had slowed down. Every nook and cranny, each feather and blade of grass, the crease in the leather of my boots, the soles tipped with dampened winter soil – all became magnified in slow motion. The sea and the rocks, acting as a butt to the waves, overtook me. It was surreal. As I walked forward, the moment was gone. I experienced Kronos again.

Later I went into a supermarket to buy Easter eggs for my nephews and nieces. I walked in another aisle that day to others. People were switched off to the spiritual dawning of Easter. They were alive only to the endless shelves of chocolate eggs. The oversupply was grotesque. Row upon row of shoppers were overweight. The tragedy was – for tragedy it was – they seemed to be part of the shelves.

They had allowed themselves to be overwhelmed by the brands available. This despite the fact it was all, just chocolate. The god of choice had consumed them. They were like cattle, chewing the cud, but not really living.

I mulled things over. I saw it then. This was their Easter. They never saw, felt, knew about, or believed in the resurrection. God was calling me. He was inviting me to speak on his behalf, to tell his lost sheep that the pastures of heaven gave life to all who were dead.'

Harry cut in harshly across Tom's words. Harry's patience was exhausted. 'For crying out loud you did keep falling for Old Nick's tricks didn't you? The rocks and the water moment, that was just some quirk of the angle you were seeing I bet; and bang there goes you falling to your knees halleluiah like. You're a fucking joke ... And all that bollocks you talked about the shoppers. They were probably knackered grafting and trying to make ends meet on low incomes. How many people do you think earn a living wage in this country? Not fucking many, I can tell you. They were probably stressed out knowing neither of them could afford to get an egg for their kids. As for them being overweight, that's because they can only afford, and were brought up on, junk food. What world do you live in? Jesus.'

Tom involuntarily looked up at Harry.

'Yes fucking Jesus. You're a middle-class twat stuck up his own arse.' Menacingly, Harry added, 'I'll see you later.'

With that threat hanging in the air, he broke wind and left Tom alone with his thoughts and the foul stench.

It was still and silent in the room. The aloneness was oppressive. He had never quite secured a constant touch from God. Not felt his sacredness, touched his stillness, and let his God in, so he could live in him and reflect him fully. He thought he had, but he hadn't. It had been his choice. He hadn't chosen to be constant.

In this moment, a kairos moment, Christ stepped through the door and sat with him. Tom broke into hysterical laughter. He was encased in this prison. This was his material world. In the spiritual world, he was now alive. He was free when he chose to soar into the heavens. Like an eagle, Tom spread his wings and flew.

TWENTY-FOUR

14:30 hours, Saturday, July 7, 2012 – Harry's Place, Thames Path, London

'What, of death Monsignor?' Tom asked.

'What of it? Death is about life. Our time on earth is precious. But how many people do you see who spend the currency of their time, their moments alive, not really living? Countless people I have met over the years live what I call plutonium half lives.'

Tom looked puzzled.

'Plutonium is used to measure geological time and the vastness of epochs. When I imagine the slowness of time covered by the thousands and millions of years they embrace, it seems to me that so many people drift through life in a slow plutonium fashion. These people may very well live long lives, but of what profit to themselves and to the world do they bring? Many of the people in the Western and developing worlds live their life without meaning. They dully accept their circumstances, their work, and their fabricated desire to consume material things as if this is life. They are enslaved to their perception, blinded to the multiple universes they could explore if they chose to *live* their life. And in the living, better still that people spend their currency being prepared for death.'

'Prepared?'

'When I was a young priest, I had the honour of walking for a while in the company of a young soldier. He taught me something precious. It transformed me. He moved me from living a life full of theory to a life full of meaning. He was fully conscious that every day death could take him. In that consciousness he brought such life with him into everything and into the people, he met. He possessed such energy – powered by the sun I'm sure. He was energising of others purely because of the aura surrounding him. God most surely walked in his heart. His eyes were ablaze with the spark of the spirit. The world was truly blessed with the power he had to live.'

'How would you have me prepare for death?'

'I've learnt over the years that one of God's greatest gifts is to give us the power of choice. The freedom to choose what we can do in any circumstance, no matter how disabled we might be, how constrained we are or how poor or uneducated we are. In other words, whilst sometimes our options to choose may be limited, we have the responsibility to make the right choice, as best we are able, to live.

In preparing for death, we have to prepare for life. Every thought, every feeling, every word and action we take, we are responsible. Time will pass. Our lives will pass. How we live our life through this pass is our responsibility.

As we grow from childhood to adulthood, all of us cloak ourselves willingly, even if we think it could be unconsciously, with habits. These habits over the years can become so strong that over time they become like the thick vines of ivy and slowly but inexorably tighten their grip on how we choose to live our lives.

Shattering the shackles of habits requires people to possess themselves with the strength of Hercules. We acquire that strength simply by starting and choosing to embrace a new habit, one that embraces life.

So in the morning, let your first thought always be this:

"I may not live to see the night."

If you embrace this thought as your mantra throughout the day, I guarantee that over time this habit will grow strong. You will live every moment in the present moment and live life to the fullest as if each moment was to be your last, and then you will see, feel and know how precious the currency of time is.

Each night as you go to sleep, let your last thought be this:

"I may not live till tomorrow."

Contrary to what some, sadly, quickly conclude, this habit teaches all who adopt it, optimism. They discover how joyful life should be and in living this new way, they learn how to unwrap the gift that God gave them – the choice to live.'

It was just after two pm. Harry had had a good lunch. It was time to get down to it. He was looking forward to this.

Tom looked up and saw through the thick soundproof glass of his cell that Harry was walking towards him pushing a large metal box. The door slowly opened with the edge of the trolley being used as a lever by Harry to push his way in. The metal box was a coffin.

Tom's mind trembled with shock. He could feel his whole body from the top of his head to the bottom of his toes heating up. His palms felt damp. His heart felt like he had a nail or stake against his chest that was starting to be hammered slowly inwards – so finally this is it. I may not live until tomorrow. I may never see Claire again and seek forgiveness. I may never have the opportunity to tell mum and dad how much I have appreciated them loving me the best way they knew. I may never...

Harry – the confident, spoke. 'I've brought along your bed for tonight. I thought you might like to know where you'll be sleeping. Or perhaps, I ought to say, where some of you will be.'

Harry chortled at his own sick humour. He pushed the trolley and the coffin against one of the walls and in the line of sight of the mortuary bench. Harry strode quickly to the counter by the sink, whistling as he went. There he donned a heavy black plastic apron and very neatly looped the straps around his waist and tied it precisely with an even length bow. He looked up and smiled in a friendly fashion towards Tom.

'You like music Tom? What kind I wonder? I like music, especially when I'm learning a new hobby. And Tom, guess what, you are my new hobby. You're my first. In fact, I think you should thank me for doing you the honour of putting you first amongst everybody else I could have selected. What do you think? Are you going to give me thanks then?'

Tom propped against the wall and constrained said nothing. Tom's chest rose in shallow breaths. That pleased Harry, it really pleased him. Along the counter was a micro CD hi-fi system. To the right of it was a case that contained a selection of Harry's favourite music. The sounds would provide background white noise to help Harry focus his mind on the task in hand.

Harry selected a CD and prised open the case. Taking the disc out, he slowly looked at the back, blew ever so gently on its surface and then placed it into the drive. With the remote control in hand, he pointed it at the machine and pressed play.

Welcome to hell.

TWENTY-FIVE

'You'll love this music Tom,' shouted Harry above the sound of the heavy rock music, 'it's Black Sabbath's volume 4. I love it. You'll love the tracks *Tomorrow's Dream*, and *Changes*. They'll have special meaning for you on this day.'

Harry walked over to Tom and grabbed hold of his wrists and dragged him up to and onto the mortuary table. Despite Tom's violent struggle, his desire for survival, he was powerless to stop whatever was to come next. Lying prone on the cold metal surface, with drainage holes for liquid running around its perimeter, Tom stared up at the ceiling as his limbs, one by one, were separated and tied individually to each corner of the table.

Bizarrely, in the midst of the pounding heavy rock music the song by David Bowie, *Starman,* sprung into his mind as he pictured himself spread-eagled about to enter a universe he had no control of. Then Tom moved quickly into a bout of hysteria when the Back Sabbath song, *Changes*, was played. His mind was on David Bowie's song-title of the same name, and insanely, Tom laughed and cried as Harry sung along to the heavy rock band's lyrics.

'See Tom, I told you, you'd like it. It's good isn't it?' His voice was barely audible above the din.

Harry took hold of a broad black felt tip by the sink, and moving his body in time with the music, he danced around the table with his eyes closed. He had a broad grin on his face. His arms were raised as his body moved to the rhythm. As one track finished Harry pressed the pause button.

'When I was a child Tom, I used to play with butterflies. They are such fragile insects. When bored, I'd cut their wings off, one at a time, just to see the effect. With only one wing, they would spiral down to the ground in helter-skelter fashion until they collided with the ground. Their legs wiggled as they fell. God, it was fascinating.

But I grew up, put away my childish ways and led, what many might see, a pretty normal life. No violence or thoughts of it, apart from the odd fight outside a club or pub. No desire to dismember anything or anyone.

Then this craving started. Last year I had inklings in my head to hurt people, to kill them. The hurting part gained supremacy. I would fantasise about having people under my complete control, totally powerless. I wanted to be able to do anything with them. The sense of power I felt in my chest was potent, irresistible. It was an adrenaline rush. Seeing you here, naked, vulnerable, frightened and confused Tom, it's a really powerful feeling.'

Harry breathed in a satisfying lungful of air. 'My childhood roots have returned. I've wondered what a human being would behave like if they had each one of their wings removed one by one. My initial thoughts were to cut off one arm followed by the other, then each leg in turn.'

Harry moved the black felt tip pen as if that was doing the thinking.

'But then I thought, nah, the pleasure would be over too quickly. Besides, I wondered if the helpless victim would go and die before I had had time to possess them, if you know what I mean. So now, I think of all the attachments to the human body as wings. Now, where do I start with you? When I stood on the balcony at my nightclub...'

121

Tom's eyes flickered with surprise.

'That's right Tom; that's when I first saw you. I watched you closely. You're left-handed. I noticed you had a nervous habit. You kept putting your hand up towards the left hand side of your face and scratching, or perhaps stroking was it, in a downward fashion towards your cheekbone. So Tom which part of your body do you think I am going to remove first?'

Tom focused on his mantra silently.

'Well, Tom?'

Tom focused on his …

Harry put his right hand between Tom's legs and squeezed the exposed testicles hard.

Tom let out a high-pitched scream.

Harry released his grip and stood there waiting patiently. He was in no hurry.

With tears running from the side of his eyes, his face flushed, Tom hoarsely replied, 'My left index finger.'

'Good,' Harry replied in a sickly warm voice, 'Now that's agreed, I have dice I want to roll. Even numbers I will remove this finger slowly; this will allow you to feel every tear of your skin, muscle and bone. If odds, then quickly by using a chisel and hammer. If that's the case, my advice Tom, keep your hand still. You don't want me to miss or hit more than one finger now do you?'

Almost as if it was an afterthought, Harry added. 'One last thing, you'll have to trust me on this. I won't cheat on odds or evens. After all, I've got to start somewhere, haven't I?'

Once again, Harry's alter ego smiled reassuringly.

Tom listened against his will as the dice rattled from side to side in a small metal container. It felt like a dark Kairos moment. Time moved painfully in slow motion. As the dice tumbled onto the mortuary table, Tom's heightened senses felt the vibrations in the metal surface as with each bounce the dice rebounded before coming to a standstill. He lifted his head up and watched as Harry leaned slowly forward, examined the result, before picking up the dice nested in the shelter of the shadow cast by Tom's right leg.

'It's a six,' rejoiced Harry.

His voice sounded almost childlike in his excitement. Harry wheeled a tabletop trolley up to the mortuary table. It was the same height. He placed Tom's left-hand upon it. Harry then picked up Tom's left index finger and drew a neat black circle around its circumference, about half a centimetre from the palm.

'Now Tom, I need you to stay very still as I start sawing through using this little hacksaw here.'

Harry was at his best when he focused entirely on one specific task until it had been completed. Life was good, simple and uncomplicated that way. He turned Black Sabbath back on and got stuck into his new habit.

For Tom, the first tearing cut was the end of his inauguration into Harry's universe.

PART THREE – NO TURNING BACK

AULD LANG SYNE

By Robert Burns (1759-1796)

Should auld acquaintances be forgot,
And never brought to min?
Should auld acquaintances be forgot,
And auld lang syne?

For auld lang syne, my dear,
For auld lang syne,
We'll tak a cup o' kindness yet,
For auld lang syne.

TWENTY-SIX

02:13 hours, Sunday, July 8, 2012 – a London all-night café

Claire took her warm chocolate croissant and americano to a side table by the front window. A couple of young lovers ate each other in mouthfuls, which despite her woes, made Claire smile at the energy and the joy of youth.

The chocolate from the sweet pastry smudged partly across her lips. She pushed sticky fragments of the crumbling flakes into her mouth and finger-licked her tips to savour the last teasing remnants of her early breakfast as she reflected on her encounter with Sam. Claire had been so uplifted by the humanity she had experienced with her. At the same time, she was grateful not only for Sam in seeing the interloper in Tom's hotel room, but also, for painting in stark relief, how people, so easily, can give their lives over to time and let time decide for them how they live their lives. For, live their lives they might. But they might not be alive to the living.

Claire, she had to admit it to herself, face it for what it was, had been tiptoeing inexorably along that path. Now she and Sam had been set free of that path for good, no matter what. In fact, they had been brought together, she now realised by the fate that may have stripped Tom of his freedom, or God forbid, his life. How the world twists and turns for good and for ill.

In the events that ensue, do the ends justify the means? Or are the endless battles, which each side may seek to win or lose all part of the collateral losses and setbacks in the war of ethereal worlds, she wondered. Perhaps the views of ancient history, the beliefs of the Greeks were right after all. Humans may well be mere pawns on a massive global chessboard, with parts sacrificed for the ultimate victory, with all aspects of people's lives under the control of the gods. But Claire wasn't ready to be a victim yet, a mere bit player in her life. Neither now was Sam Kerveen. Good on her, thought Claire. Perhaps we humans should all fight back.

The surrounding banter of other late nighters, the rush of steam heating drinks, even the reassuring clinks of cups touching saucers, all and more combined into a swirling sleeping pill of sounds. In her exhaustion, Claire leant forward on the table and fell asleep.

A leafy suburban street off Banbury Road, Oxford, England

The car radio told her it was 6.23 am. At just over a stretched hour from Kensington, London, Claire was driving into Oxford. It would not be easy calling on Tom's parents. However, it had to be done. Five years ago, she had been wretched to them. Blaming and screaming at them for her loss. Not thinking they might have felt the pain too. She blocked them out of her life, completely, refusing to open letters they had written and barring their number on her phone. Any contact. Talk to the hand.

They must have known she had surmised and yet they had not told her. The truth is and the truth hurt: Tom had not told her. Tom had kept it secret. She almost felt as if she was reliving the episode of her mother's death and the secrecy that had shrouded her final months. That's why she had exploded when her emotions had been triggered. What a fool's errand of love she had flown with Tom. She should have been volcanic with him. Yet she was not. Why did she protect him so from her anger? She took it all out on his parents, and oh, how she did.

They were fellow conspirators against the enemy of the state, her. Following the shock of his announcement Claire had flown into an uncontrolled frenzy when she saw them. Her behaviour was at odds with herself; she had forgiven her father over her mother's death, perhaps better to say, understood why and knew it was out of love.

She and Tom had been so close, so in love. They were tied in mutual commitment, like a vine, strong and vibrant together, hadn't they been? Then all of a sudden, they withered. The pain, the sense of betrayal, the grief, and the jealousy she felt towards the Catholic church all curdled and blended together in her head, heart and emotions. Her life had been liquidised.

Claire turned her Volvo into Tom's parent's driveway. Gravel was crunched mercilessly underneath, until her car pulled effortlessly to a halt. Hydrangeas welcomed her arrival. Early morning, she thought, what timing. It can't be helped and it was too late now. She glanced upward towards the streak-clouded sky and marvelled at the beauty of the azure heavens. She stood in-between the twin pillars of the front archway and rang the doorbell a few chimes. A tired voice could faintly be heard grumbling from an upstairs open window.

'Who the devil is that for goodness sake?'

A few minutes later and the front door unlatched. Tom's father peered out from the half-opened doorway. A mop of hair pointing every which way from a head fight with his pillow swamped George's head. Attired in a silk gown and dark slippers, his face did not greet Claire in a chorus of applause.

'What on earth? Claire. What the … What are you? … For heaven's sake, Claire.' He looked at his watch, 'What time do you think it is?'

'It's Tom. He's missing.' She blurted out before George's angry eyes scythed her words away.

'Tom. What do you mean Tom? He's in Spain, in training. Surely you of all people haven't forgotten that.'

'No, of course not, but George, he's back in England, staying in London.'

'Back in England? Don't be so daft. We'd know. He'd tell Monica and me.'

His response was pure exasperation; he looked ready to close the door in her face.

'George. Please. Don't. Can I come in? Give me a chance to speak; I'll explain.'

George mumbled into obstinate silence and listened to Claire's explanation. The front door nevertheless, as if it had a life of its own, refused to move. When she had finished, his response was immediate and bitter.

'Oh, I see now. Of course. Early in the morning, before the other vultures arrive on our doorstep. That's it, isn't it?' He sneered, 'You're after a scoop.'

Claire's voice notched an octave higher. 'Can't you just listen?' It wasn't going at all well. 'It's got nothing to do with my work. I've just come back from America. Heard the voice message and followed my nose on Tom's trail ever since. I'm exhausted. I haven't slept properly since Friday night, only grabbing a few scrap hours in the early hours of today slunk over a café table in London. Please, I need to talk. I want to share my thoughts with you both, what I've found out. You know three heads better than one ... Besides,' she hesitated, should she say more, enter into the reality of her intimacy with Tom, conscious if she did, that the stonewall face before her and the look of disbelief that crisscrossed his features would solidify? 'I had a dream last night. I know he's in trouble somehow, scared but alive.'

With her palm against the door's panels, she rapidly continued and forced her words to roll over his scepticism and his attempts to interrupt. When pushed, she was a fierce storm to be reckoned with.

'You see, when Tom and I were going out,' she watched George's face frown in despair, 'yes, I know it was a long time ago, but when we were away from one another, and when we both had something of a monumental nature on our mind, somehow, by telepathy I suppose, in our dreams, the one worrying about something would communicate the nub of the problem to the other.

'It was nothing planned. It just happened. When we separated, it stopped. I guess his voicemail to me resurrected the connection. It is like a radio wave. I've tuned myself back into him again. George, you know Tom and I were so close, how much I loved him. I still care for him. It's real, believe me. Can I come in? Come on, George. Please.'

He melted. George the snowman was back.

Five years of not talking were pushed ajar as he opened the door to welcome the prodigal daughter home. He gave her an enormous hug – sixty months worth in fact. He then held her gaze for a few moments and spoke.

'It's good to see you again Claire. My nearly daughter in law, eh. And you're back from the wilderness. I'm sure Tom is fine, absolutely fine. You know me. Keep calm and carry on. You do the same.'

He watched her face break into a half smile and a slight sparkle twinkled in her eyes.

'Yes, that's the spirit. Besides, you're just in time to help Monica and I celebrate our 30th wedding anniversary today. I'll get the kettle on.'

'Oh, George, I'm so sorry, what timing, well, here's your second celebratory kiss.' Claire kissed him affectionately on both cheeks.

'First actually,' he winked, 'and don't tell Monica now, will you?' His eyes twinkled and the mock request for secrecy was assured.

George placed the freshly filtered coffee on the coaster next to Claire.

'I'll just go and help Monica get up and catch my first kiss.'

He smiled then, it was as if Tom's radiant eyes were in the room. Off he went, allowing Claire a chance to familiarise herself with the surroundings. Tom's picture stood framed on the wall to one small side over the fireplace. The rocky outcrop of Haytor on Dartmoor stood to one side of him as he perched on a plateau rock, posing for the photographer. Claire remembered it well, for she had been behind the camera.

TWENTY-SEVEN

Sunday, September 21, 2003 – Dartmoor, England

The sun had risen just over half an hour ago. The wind was already up, tousling his hair with feisty passion. Tom was starting to doubt the wisdom of the early morning trek, even if it had been his idea.

'Come on Claire, hurry up! My smile's freezing to my face.'

'Patience, Dear Heart! Patience,' she teased, 'a virtue you must learn one day and how about now.'

She changed the aperture down a few 'F' stops, wanting to capture his presence in stark sharpness and reflect that with the distant water laden dark cloud behind him.

'Beautiful,' she said and clicked.

The trouble with memories they can be like a swarm of mosquitoes sometimes, attacking you from all sides, until one gets you, and you feel the pain, too late to catch the one that got away.

Saturday, December 26, 2009 – Sidmouth, England

Some of the large boulders dotted along the beach beneath the sandstone cliffs were scored with horizontal lines traversing their surface, as if a Giant's boots had embedded its tread into the rock face. The waves sloshed and pounded the rocks, finding air pockets to burst amongst their number. The turbulent water spun particles of sand into frenzy and turned the sea around the Sidmouth coastline into an angry and sullen brown mass. It matched her mood. The rock islands and groynes standing a few hundred metres into the bay might be an effective protection for the seafront, but their presence did nothing to hold back her tears.

From the cliff top pathway, near Jacob's ladder, a winter tourist put 20p into the telescope and initially swept the horizon. As the telescope swung back and forth, the solitary figure of a woman filled the screen. The tourist paused, observed the woman and then followed her gaze out to sea.

The sun's rays had broken through the cloud canopy spreading two spotlight beams onto the sea's surface. The resulting reflection unveiled a platinum phosphorous glow across the skyline. As the wind gusted, the gaps in the clouds shifted and the spotlights beamed over the water as if the coast guard were searching for a person lost at sea.

Claire hailed them, but the light pulled away in the other direction

'Oh Tom, how could you let me go?'

Claire stood with her back against the seafront railings and gazed almost hypnotised by the endless expanse of water. She cast a lonely figure possessed by many internal shadows, no eye could see. Claire dwelt upon the last time she was here with Tom. Moving away from the railings, Claire came to the pathway, which here and there expands into weather beaten alcoves that run along the bottom of the sandstone cliffs. In one, she stopped and searched the names and messages left by numerous passers-by, past and present. Many inscriptions were worn down by the elements, but there, yes, still visible, she found theirs, 'Tom and Claire, 2005 – true love, our souls know it.'

The gentle mutterings of George and Monica in their bedroom upstairs hummed lightly into Claire's ears, bringing her back

132

into herself once more. Despite her worries about Tom, she realised his parents had not yet taken in the possibility that he might be missing or worse. That notion in her mind was reinforced when she heard Monica speaking effusively.

'Oh, George, you shouldn't have. It's so lovely.'

Claire smiled for them both, but tiredness was pulling at her heels still. The furniture around her looked inviting. She took her coat off and snuggled up on the deep blue velvet chaise longue, which overlooked the main window. This gave way to a rich panoramic view into their garden, which was filled with an array of mature trees and shrubs and a large luxurious looking swathe of emerald green grass.

The distant sound of a storm bubbling fed into Claire's senses. It was the kettle boiling in the kitchen. The aroma of toast wafted and summoned her like a snake charmer's punji as she uncoiled herself out of the basket of sleep. She stretched her body as a cat does along the length of the chaise longue. Her legs extended, her toes curling, she yawned uncommonly loud for her whilst simultaneously raising her arms high in the air and twirling her wrists like a baton swirled by a majorette.

'Good dear, you're awake now I see. You looked so tired when George and I came downstairs, we didn't have the heart to wake you. Now let's have some toast and marmalade and find out what's been going on … George. Put the kettle on again, dear. I want to make sure the water is at tiptop boiling before you put it in the pot. Okay?'

'But it's… Yes, darling,' George called back. 'It's nearly ready, be with you both in a jiffy.'

Monica wheeled herself over to the dining room table and finished the laying of it for breakfast. Claire watched her, remembering how fiercely Monica guarded her independence. She confessed to herself how much she loved to see Monica again. She was such a lovely woman. And Claire had always felt she was, yes, it had to be acknowledged, almost a second mother to her.

Despite Monica's disability, or maybe because of it, she made more of an effort to look so elegant. Her long thick hair spiralled upwards and blossomed like a half opened leafed fan, an ebony wooden hair stick, whose head was shaped like a butterfly, held her locks in place. She was clothed in a cherry red full-length silk dressing gown, the lapels of which were embroidered with an array of indigo, gold and red winged butterflies.

'Your dressing gown Monica, it's exquisite' effused Claire.

'Why thank-you my dear, George gave it to me this morning as our wedding anniversary gift.' Monica's lightly blushed pink cheeks complemented the colours perfectly.

'What a beautiful present. It's absolutely lovely,' Claire replied.

George's theatrical entrance and tray full of goodies to consume expedited the start of a far ranging discussion, which touched on the past, what might have been, this part Claire found difficult, for she still longed for Tom, before covering the immediate issues and the impact of the present situation regarding his whereabouts.

'Well, I think the best course of action at this stage is to report him as missing to that London based organisation you mentioned Claire,' concluded George. He went on to say, 'And of course for you to use your research skills to see if you can track him down. It's obvious the police are not interested. This seven day malarkey about most missing persons doesn't help us one bit does it?'

'I agree,' said Monica. 'You keep us posted. Here are both our mobile numbers and email addresses. If you need any on-line research doing, just give us the orders, and we'll be on it. And whilst I need George around for certain things in and around the house, I can manage for several hours or more if needs be. So don't hesitate to summon him, will you? And you will keep us posted, won't you? I mean, as often as possible,' she added, her attempt at stoicism undone by the escape of her last words.

'Of course I will,' promised Claire, 'and thank-you for being so loving to me. I know I was wretched to you both in the past and...'

Monica put the tips of three of her right fingers gently onto Claire's lips. 'Shush, my dear. You're a fine woman. Now be gone with you. You've a man to find, my son.'

TWENTY-EIGHT

The alarm music from August Kilterton's mobile – Wagner's Ride of the Valkyries woke him up as usual. Like clockwork, he stretched and yawned. He glanced over at the empty and neat side of his king-sized bed. He needed a new bedmate soon. Maybe tonight was his night.

When Kilterton was outside of his front door, he looked around at all of the drawn curtains hanging miserably up and down the street. His unexciting neighbours slept, wasting time, not him. He slipped on his blue tooth headphones and pressed repeat play on his mobile. The Ride of the Valkyries just had to be one of the best running inspirational sounds out there. Energised, spirits high, off he went pounding down the streets that in times gone by had once been known as Twickenham Park Gardens. By mid morning he'd be in his favourite pub along the Riverside by the Thames with a glass of wine and the Saturday paper to ease himself into a relaxing afternoon. By night, the world would change. Kilterton would be out with friends. Things would be so much better: it was Rick's birthday and Pride Day. They could have a joint celebration. As a mark of the day, there was a buy one, get one free at The Wray Inn. This was a date with destiny, too good to be missed, he thought.

It was twenty past ten at night. He had done his reconnoitre in the morning. It had been a pleasantly warm day, lots of visitors. It was a big draw for the people he was after. The front and one side of the pub faced onto the Thames. The riverboats dropped off and collected fun dwellers at regular intervals ensuring a good turnover of people. There would be lots to choose from.

Around 4 pm, he had returned, this time in a non-descriptive small tradesmen van he had seen earlier and borrowed from a nearby building site that was closed for the weekend. Parking in the shaded part of the pub's car park he slipped on a lightweight zip up worker's jacket emblazoned with the word maintenance on the back. Donning a baseball cap to hide his eyes, ostensibly for the shade, he knelt down by the frosted window of a male cubicle which he had earlier identified would be his lair for the evening. Using a cutting tool, he removed the glass and replaced it with sticky back plastic frosted glass previously measured to fit and adhere to the surface. Job done, he returned the van, no one the wiser and went for a pleasant stroll along the river. It was going to be a productive day.

That night, he sat in the empty men's cubicle, the one nearest the outside wall and furthest from the door, and waited. The garrotte rested easily in his palms. The non-metallic wire was attached to easy grip handles at either end. The cubicles squatted pregnant, as if in anticipation of new life coming their way opposite the urinals.

The footsteps, splashes and flushes crowded out the silence as customers dashed back and forth from their drinks and companions. Then the sound came, which made him smile. Silence, then the echo of solitary footsteps cascading across the tiles coming to a stop near his lair and he like a hungry spider pulled his web tight between his hands.

Sounds of normality were essential. He flushed the toilet and pulled up his zip. Comforting manly sounds were accompanied by a clearing of his throat and a sliding back of the door's bolt. No one else entered the eye of the storm, just him alone with the next victim. Good. The risk of discovery was intoxicating.

He strode forward quickly and with all of his considerable strength, muscles bulging, he pulled the wire tightly around the victim's neck. The garrotte's handles were rotated quickly, the noose without mercy tightened; at the same time the murderer, his tattooed arms and hands swollen with colour, overlapped the handles around the victim's neck and pulled sharply back, forcing his victim off balance, squeezing his trachea and cutting off the supply of oxygenated blood to the man's brain. Kilterton's windpipe had been crushed. His eyes bulged. With his penis still lying unzipped, he was dragged efficiently backwards and propped effortlessly onto the toilet seat.

All was quiet in the car park. Like a gymnast on the rings, the assailant hoisted himself first and then his victim through the window. Laying the body prone, he drew out his knife and cut a neat deep slice across Kilterton's exposed neck line, the garrotte ligature acting as a guide for his work. The bloodied blade cut Kilterton's shirt open. Other tools worked their way through his sternum. Powerful hands ripped open a cavity into the chest and his still warm heart was extracted, placed neatly in a clear plastic bag and slid into the murderer's jacket pocket. On impulse, the murderer attacked Kilterton's lifeless body further. That will show them, he thought.

He left quietly and confidently. He felt so very relaxed. Soon enough now, the news would break. Fear would be walking the streets of London and he was the willing pedestrian carrying death.

All was good in his world. He glanced over at the well-worn book on the front passenger seat and smiled. His dog gamely ate his supper on the back seat. He leant over and gently ruffled his pet's head.

'Good boy. You like that, don't you?'

The murderer drove off then and on impulse turned right rather than left and headed towards Richmond Park. It should be quiet at this time of night. He was looking for this newfound sense of peace to stay with him on this, his journey, now that his crossing into the annals of infamy had truly commenced. He drove along Sawyers Hill and turned off into a side road. He was fascinated by the chasms created by minute potholes, which were revealed one by one by his car's headlights. He imagined that if each was filled with fresh and clear rain water, then on a moonlit night, hundreds would reflect a galaxy of earthly stars along this humble road.

His musings were interrupted. He saw the unmistakable shape of a woman's body lying discarded on the grass verge. One of her arms and legs were tangled awkwardly in some shrubs. She hung there like a puppet snagged in nature's barbed wire fence. He brought his vehicle to a standstill, his mood, sombre. It looked as if someone had thrown her away – detritus for a local council worker to pick up in the morning. Anger bubbled.

Nearby buildings watched from the shadows, the lights far and wide were turned off. An eight-foot high wall encircled the curtilage. No one was around. It was only him that approached. With the car engine quietened, silence draped itself around them both and cloaked the two strangers together. Dropping to his knees, he sobbed uncontrollably.

'I'm so sorry. I was too late to save you. I would have come if I'd known. You should have called me. You know I would have come.'

She was still warm, still soft, and not long from being alive, from breathing her fresh life in this world. He gently unravelled her from the snare and pulled the edge of her dress down to cover her nakedness and the scratches over her thighs and buttocks.

'If only you had called.'

He held her in his arms, her head and shoulders resting on his chest. Her hair smelt so fresh. By torchlight, which faintly glowed across the pages, he softly read out his favourite poem, *Remember, by Christina Rossetti.*

'Remember me when I am gone away,
Gone far away into the silent land;
When you can no more hold me by the hand,
Nor I half turn to go yet turning stay.
Remember me when no more day by day
You tell me of our future that you planned:
Only remember me; you understand
It will be too late to counsel then or pray.
Yet if you should forget me for a while
And afterwards remember, do not grieve:
For if the darkness and corruption leave
A vestige of the thoughts that I once had,
Better by far you should forget and smile
Than that you should remember and be sad.'

The adult in him was no longer sad. The child within however, shook his body with rage.

He knew who to blame, he always did. Would his father's ghost never stop inhabiting others? Enough was enough. He knew. Yes, he definitely knew now and how. He would make fear cling to them all like tar in the sand. Great clumps of fear would never be washed away from their memory. He would shock the world.

TWENTY-NINE

00:08 hours, Sunday, July 8, 2012 – The Wray Inn, Riverside, Twickenham, London

Popular as he was, Kilterton was not missed. It was not that his mates did not miss his company, they just all agreed among themselves, when he cropped up in conversation, that good ol' August had probably found a tight mini to ride home in, and in their inebriated state, they all laughed at their flat and rather tired humour.

Outside in the shadows by the toilets Trevor was with his boyfriend for the night, Toni. Both were intent on a lightening embrace. However, Trevor's eyes were drawn instead to an object a few metres away. It was the outline of a body, motionless. Someone had had too much to drink, he thought. Still, the guy wasn't moving at all.

He abruptly pulled away from Toni, leaving him confused and walked towards the drunken man. As he did so, his shoes kept sticking to the car park's surface. A car engine started and almost simultaneously, the headlight beams were turned on. In one surreal and statuesque movement Trevor, caught in shock relief against the annex called out in a mixture of hoarse whispers and shouts.

'Oh no ... Oh my God. Quick, quick, someone ... call the police.'

He looked down at the pool of thick dark liquid that ran from the dead man's body, the gaping hole in his chest, and then he looked down at his own shoes.

'Oh my God,' he whispered.

Friars Mead, Manchester Road, London

She had just finished tidying away the dishes after tea and biscuits following the eleven o'clock Mass. The readings in church had not affected her mood. Daisy Maypinder was feeling annoyed. She had told Mr Courtish that she would collect his order for her catalogue on Thursday last week. She called around then, and Friday and Saturday, and still he had not been home. He could have, no he should have, left her a note or better still, as they've arranged before, put the order in the recycling bin. Now, because she had delayed the sending off the whole order for everyone, she would have twenty unhappy customers on her neck next weekend, all moaning at her.

"Why hadn't their orders arrived?"

Just wait till she gave Mr Courtish a piece of mind. She could wring his bloody neck.

'Mr Courtish,' she called his name through the letterbox. Her nose reeled, as the distinctive smell of rotten eggs from within the house invaded her nostrils.

'It's Daisy. I've come to get your order.'

There was no reply. Instead, his cat came running up to the letterbox whining constantly and standing on its hind legs, pawing at the door, its feet pushing on the unopened post, which was slowly, so very slowly, sliding apart. It was then that Daisy noticed the dark stains around the cat's face, the blood red streaks over its whiskers and Mr Courtish's Saturday delivery of a solitary bottle of milk standing obediently on the doorstep, the milk looking distinctively curdled in the heat.

'Oh my Gawd.'

Her body started to tremble. She fumbled nervously for her mobile phone, mis-dialling 999 several times.

142

'Hello, yes … the police…'

It was not the discovery of the first horrific murder that transformed the gay community. It was the realisation that two had occurred in quick succession. There was an unseen threat out there. Emergency planning swung almost immediately into action promoting the availability of psychosocial and mental health services support. Extra police were drafted in. And yet… and yet, no matter how much support was available, no matter how much care was given, or how long telephone listening continued, each potential victim knew that they alone were ultimately, by themselves. No one else was in the sights of the killer.

It was their turn to wear a pink star sewn onto their clothes. Wherever they went they imagined individuals could see who they were and people could feel the fear haunting them; the scent of it filled the public's nostrils. The media morbidly thrived on it. The pub gossip writhed in it. It was as if the pit of hell had been opened and flames from the abyss deliriously licked the fat off conversation and salivated over the polarisation hidden but bubbling away in the cauldrons of some Londoners' hearts.

The predatory white shark that lurks and waits in the shallow feeding waters for unsuspecting swimmers had now evolved onto land and swam amongst the gay community. It was a threat that focused not on heterosexuals, nor on lesbians or children. The threat was entirely focused on gay men. It was their lives at stake. It was their very hearts at risk.

Yet in the face of this and later events, their adversity, the gay community and many other communities would, in time, bind together. The immediate response was to hide away, to become reclusive, but quietly through the close affection of their family and friends, the superglue of love would grow stronger and widen. The community victims of fear would accept and draw upon social support above and beyond that offered by the State.

As the latent impact of the traumas sank deeply in, it eventually would tap into the reservoir of informal networks; the water table of contact, a listening ear, a hand on the shoulder, a hug in despair; all these things and more would help.

The big society is as it ever was, not a political creation, but born, self evidently at the dawn of civilisation. Sometimes, to the world's loss, it slumbers, bad deeds connect and multiply, and at other times, even if temporal, it stands up as one voice and does not fail the forsaken.

Even local religious communities stripped away any thoughts and feelings of prejudice and reached out with one voice. This was a voice, which recognised common heritage – a forgotten aphorism – humanity should always communicate with and offer support with humanity. In the immediate aftermath, Pride became the platform upon which a collective voice was heard. Bonded together by their common desire for harmony, the seed of celebrating life, not being frightened by death, or kowtowed by fear, was sown.

THIRTY

09:15 hours, Monday, July 9, 2012 – Metropolitan Police Service, London

Despite her protestations and threats to make a complaint, DS Raven refused to budge. He would not expend time and police resources going to see Ms Kerveen on the basis that she saw a man in the early hours on Friday, which Claire claimed couldn't have been Tom. This, despite the obvious fact, she had not been the witness or seen him for several years.

DS Raven reminded Claire of his advice to make contact with the missing person service he had mentioned previously. His heartbeat was in turmoil – ignited by the flush of passion that blushed across her face when she argued her case and saddened that her interest was drawn to another. Any chance, the foolish man thought he might have had of taking Claire out on a date was most definitely extinguished by his resolute refusal to look into things further.

Her confidence in British policing ebbed further. Before doing anything else, Claire searched the internet to find out for herself the facts about missing people. DS Raven had not filled her with any optimism. The simple advisory leaflet, *Understanding Missing Persons* he had given her as she left was so simply written, it was almost derisory. She scanned the web for pages and reports. The statistics did not really help at all. So what if 97% of missing people are found within seven days and the majority within the first 16 hours. Tom might be one in the 3% category.

The hard numbers of people missing in the Metropolitan Police Service area every year were even less comfort. Forty nine thousand went missing, of which around one hundred and thirty are found dead. She hoped to God that Tom was not one of them. As she read on, her heart sank that little bit further into negative territory. London records showed an inability to identify a number of individuals who had been found, of which nearly three hundred were dead bodies, twelve consisted of just body parts and nearly thirty, although alive had some form of memory loss, dementia or amnesia and the like.

Claire reluctantly re-read the advisory leaflet. The police record an alleged missing person into one of three categories. High risk means individuals who might be in immediate danger of harm because of their age and/or vulnerability or if they pose a threat to the public. A person defined as medium risk means they might be a danger to themselves or others, whilst an individual who is in no apparent danger or a threat to the public is classified as low risk. That, insisted DS Raven was Tom. Claire had hit the buffers.

The Missing Person Bureau did list Tom on their website on Tuesday, July 10 2012 – it all felt too little and too late, but hope mixed with the heavy cocktail of love is a powerful drug that drives people on against the odds when others would give up the fight. So from that Tuesday onwards, if anyone searched for missing people in London, a thumbnail picture of Tom would appear. This was set within a rectangular box, which contained an eight-digit reference number, his name and the date since he had been missing, or last seen. Visitors to the website could click on Tom's name, which took them to a single page providing more detail surrounding his disappearance. A range of buttons on the website enabled visitors to get involved, inviting them for example to let the

Missing Person Bureau know if they had seen him, or if they wanted to, they could download a poster of Tom.

However, no hits on the web page were ever recorded. Then again, why would it ever be? The only people looking for Tom were Claire and the limited support that his parents could give. Yet the life jacket of hope kept them above the water, although at times it was difficult to know if the leak in it had grown bigger. Meanwhile, the world continued on its journey. We all did, oblivious to the planned future ahead of us. Freedom, as it ever was, an illusion.

THIRTY-ONE

Monday, July 9, 2012 – Bedford Place, Camden Town, London

It was mid morning, but Claire had learnt her lessons of the previous days. There was no point in depleting her reserves. If she fell ill, what good would that do Tom? Taking her frothy white coffee over to the bar counter window Claire sat on one of the stools facing out on Bedford Place. To external observers she idly scooped up some of the overflow and allowed the seductive, chocolate sprinkled, white cloud to melt in her mouth.

She was adjacent to the Hotel Maxwell and almost immediately opposite the Hotel Petunia. Tom had left its front door in the early evening last Thursday. She reviewed the notes in her diary about the pubs, clubs and restaurants suggested by Miss White, the owner/manager of the hotels. Claire needed somehow to get in touch with Tom's heart.

Which way would you have turned, left or right, that night? She knew it would be easier to enter inside of him if it was on a Thursday night and she could idly walk out of the hotel front door, as he must have done, relaxed, and followed her nose. However, Thursday was an age away. She looked through her bag for her pencil and came across the 201 Club card, but left it there as a discarded thought.

Whilst the chatter of customers reverberated in the room and the clatter and clink of cutlery on china played offbeat tunes in her head, Claire rotated her fingertips over her temples, gently massaging them, and allowed her thoughts, her memories, her emotions to weave their way along the waves and currents of the past leading her into the Tom she knew.

Tom smiled easily at her. His eyes often twinkled and sparkled. She could not but help smile back. He made eye contact with strangers easily. She blushed. People warmed to him. She did. She did still. He struck up conversations with strangers easily. She felt safe and magnetised in his company. Tom was open. His openness encouraged reciprocity from the people he met. She was so very open with him, more than with anyone, ever before, she paused in her mulling … more than with anyone else, ever since. Was she that hurt still?

He was eccentric. How she loved him for that. Tom liked to walk. He liked quirky places. Together with those habits would lead him anywhere. Her heart sank at the thought. He had not taken a taxi as far as she knew, but he could have hopped on a bus and… his wanderings could have led him … it was almost useless to try, almost.

She skimmed through countless pages about places to eat and drink within Camden. She circled several. Yet, the trouble was, the problem for her was, almost every place in the guide could draw Tom's eye. It would be the evening atmosphere and the tempo that would tease him to enter. This could turn out to be an exhausting systematic slog, notwithstanding that some might not be open during the day for her to speak with staff. It was also equally possible that the people she asked may not have been working last Thursday. It would be she knew, a long day; at the end of which, she resolved in herself to accept, could be one empty of any progress.

Crossing the road, she stood on the entrance steps of Hotel Petunia, smiled warmly as she glanced upwards to where Sam used to sit at her desk writing. The text she had sent Claire on Sunday was from a woman who had got back behind the driving wheel of her life – she was just about to start a week's retreat in Florence, Italy entitled, *Love Serves*, all about how to find oneself and grow outwards to others. Well done you, thought Claire. Sam's spirit and thirst for life would come back, she knew that. Poor Kevin would have to learn new tricks and walk faster to keep up with his mistress's new vitality for life, that's for sure.

Shoulders back, feeling the sun on her body – which way would Tom go, she thought; no, she had to feel which way he would go. The sun warmed her, her mind drifted into thoughtlessness as if enwrapped in a sumptuous spiral of brain waves swirling around her mind as if it too had been soothed into silence by the wondrous beauty of classical music in her head. Instinctively her body, as if stood on a slowly moving turntable pivoted around to increase the sun's aspect on her. She was drawn to its warmth. She headed west away from the morning sun. Tom would have headed towards it as it apparently curves downwards towards sunset. The Earth would be spinning reassuringly on its axis. It was comforting to know some things continue.

THIRTY-TWO

Monday, July 9, 2012 - Camden Town, London

Camden Town is festooned with bars, pubs, cafés, restaurants and clubs. Any other time Claire would have relished spending time here. The many temptations to wander could so easily have had her veering off in search of new and interesting nooks. There is a buzz about Camden, an array of colour that feeds the eyes and a concoction of food aromas in the air when venturing into certain parts that can tease one's mouth to distraction. How Tom must have revelled in his wanderings here last Thursday night.

Right now, though, Claire needed to rest her weary body on the empty bus stop bench. It was, for all shoppers, nearly the footsore end of a Monday shopping marathon. The retail store staff forced yet another budget grin to let the customers know that their presence and purchases were deeply valued. The bustle and the hustle of shoppers snaking their way, British bulldog fashion across Camden High Street gave way inexorably to the windblown rustle of human litter.

The gusting of the wind picked up and swirled with increasing frequency the discarded rubbish – papers and carrier bags – into the air, grotesquely but elegantly dancing as they hitched a ride on the warm flows as the cooler evening breeze bore in. These too, were joined in a staccato of ragged sounds as a crumpled fizzy soft drink can waltzed in chaotic circles across the pavement slabs.

Claire looked at her reflection in the window of a closed shop on the opposite side of the street – permanently by the look of its insides. A closing down sale hung at angles within. Display shelves begged to be filled again – not to be. A solitary woven orange sunset coloured handbag – unsold, had taken up the role of rearguard for forgotten shoulders.

This blighted store displayed an unintended empathy to Claire. Abandoned, disarrayed, and broken up. Her lungs heaved in the air and then sighed out the sense of lost hope she so easily felt. It was the not knowing of how to find Tom. She felt he was alive, sensed it, but no pathways opened up before her.

Some young boys – just past the cusp of teenage hood rolled their skateboards over the pavement slabs, which were populated with long since flattened chewing gum now firmly dug into their foxholes. The skateboard wheels produced rhythmic sounds as the sometimes airborne vehicles passed fleetingly over concrete grooves and mortar joints – how well versed these boys are, capable, unknowingly, of creating poetic sounds in their cityscape playground.

It was nearing 6 pm and Claire had virtually carried out transects of Camden Town. Despite her best efforts, all avenues by road and by conversation had run their course. Showing pictures of Tom, chatting to staff in shops and even in her desperation to random shoppers had thus far revealed no sightings of him. Of course, what did she really expect? She knew the impossible scale of the task. Nevertheless, how could she stop? She almost felt insane inside, numbed by the separation of herself from the everyday activity of people that had thronged and bustled in Camden all day long.

She'd learnt a great deal about the night-time life in the area, but each time when it came down to her purpose, finding Tom she drew blank after blank and the shaking of heads. If she saw one more head shaking, one more blank expression, by god, her whole body was itching to scream in frustration and anger at people, anyone, and it almost did not matter anymore, she was at that stage of exhaustion and stress when civilities to one's fellow human beings can sink beneath norms. She wanted to stamp her feet on the pavement, raise her arms in anger in the air and shout.

'Someone. Anyone. Help me. No more excuses. Tom's life is at risk. Is there no one here that can help?'

Like all of us, mostly, when faced with the insane desire to display our angst, we somehow hold it in and maintain a vice like grip on our chest and vocal chords. Gripping her determination with both hands Claire stood up. She walked crisply, confidently down the High Street, time to get a drink and bit of bar staff banter; never lose hope she thought, never lose hope.

Her fast pace required her to move in a swift chicane action as she strode past a gaggle of mothers pausing by the entrance to Boots considering the merits of one more dose of retail therapy versus mundanely acquiring evening household provisions.

Ahead of Claire, some twenty metres away, a young and excessively skinny bowlegged man ambled. His stature was one she associated with a drug taker. The man's thick matted hair sprayed out over the turned down hood of his hoodie.

When Claire was some five metres away, the man's back seemed to resonate a palpable feeling of uneasiness, almost fear within her. For some unfathomable reason she felt a loathing and a hatred for him. Simultaneously, as that feeling became evident to her, the man suddenly stopped and turned himself bodily towards her.

A dishevelled beard darkened his face, which was a shocking contrast to the white chaos in his eyes. In those moments, she tried to avoid looking at him, but their eyes remained locked.

Claire picked up the pace, to navigate a swift path past him. His eyes seemed eager to hurt her. A cold unwholesome feeling emanated from him. She carried herself forward. No sooner had she passed him when the man started to walk again. He was following her.

Claire resolutely refused to allow the fear to grow bigger. She was, after all, in the busy High Street. She was nearing a crossing onto and off a roadside island, traffic was busy commuting, there were people nearby stood waiting for a bus. She would be safe.

All too well, though, she recalled the random attacks by strangers.

She headed towards a nearby pub and its welcoming protective doors. Customers were socialising within. Behind her, she heard the man ooze a chilling chuckle.

She looked behind. His face twisted like a bent plastic loaf tie into a deranged smile. He stopped. He abruptly turned around and crossed the road, ignoring traffic lights, and the drivers who thumped their car horns.

Claire's breath escaped rapidly. Her chest heaved and deflated. She thanked her guardian angel for watching over her. Irrational it may be, but it gave her peace of mind and helped to slow the beating of her heart. Once inside the pub, the step change in the atmosphere almost immediately relaxed her.

The long bar straddled almost the width of the place, beer pump handles stood waiting whilst others were in use as the busy bar staff served. She had been in here before, earlier in the day, but in the early evening, the ambience seemed different, warmer, perhaps because more customers were here, the chatter humming was comforting to her ears, reassuring her that the world was indeed normal, life is as it is, not her reality. Perhaps it was because workers were unwinding from a hard Monday and wanted to wash away the blues of a life in a shop or office, especially on a hot day like this.

She ordered a bar meal and a double Jack Daniels Tennessee Honey and Coke and took up a seat by the window facing onto the street. She felt good here, relaxed. The whisky was sublime. It had the sweet effect she needed to slow down. As she crunched on an ice cube, shifting it from one side of her mouth to the other she knew her evening was not over yet. New bar staff were arriving for the evening shift. As she ate her meal, she watched how people came in. When the pub was less busy they would walk further into and along the room, finding a table and seat first and then going to the bar; this would almost inevitably be at the point furthest from the entrance. As the bar became busier, more crowded, new customers, almost to a person, approached the bar nearest the entrance first, aiming to join the queue of customers, although some sent a scout off in search of seats and a table. Each of the bar staff seemed to have their own territory and a Caribbean looking man in his twenties seemed to occupy the bar turf facing the entrance.

Claire joined the third row of customers and some seven minutes later arrived at the bar. He was over six feet tall, an imposing presence, wearing a pristine white short-sleeved tee shirt neatly aligned around the contours of his torso.

'My name is Damien.' He had a Jamaican accent and a broad infectious smile; Claire warmed to him, 'How may I help you?'

To her great relief, he had seen Tom last Thursday night, had served him in fact, pointing out that Tom had gone off with a crowd of people, one of whom he knew was a regular, a woman. He did not know her name, but she came in for a drink on a Wednesday or sometimes, a Thursday night. It was potluck for Claire which night.

She left Damien with her mobile number asking him to show this woman Tom's photograph if she came him. He promised Claire he would and pinned Tom's picture to the wall behind the bar, scribbling a note across the front, 'Leave up here, Damien.'

Hopefully the woman, when she came in would stay long enough for Claire to come and meet her or if not, at least call the mobile.

A GARDEN BY THE SEA

By William Morris (1834-1896)

I know a little garden-close,
Set thick with lily and red rose,
Where I would wander if I might
From dewy morn to dewy night,
And have one with me wandering...

Yet tottering as I am and weak,
Still have I left a little breath
To seek within the jaws of death
An entrance to that happy place,
To seek the unforgotten face,
Once seen, once kissed, once reft from me
Anigh the murmuring of the sea.

Journey to Broadstairs, South-East coast of England

At last, a day and evening of enquiries had borne some tentative fruit. After all paths had been concluded, there was literally nothing else that Claire could think of to do between now and Wednesday evening that would take her any further forward in finding Tom. Feeling overwhelmed, she knew a break from the emotional pressures and brick walls she had been smashing into would help.

Her flat in Broadstairs called out to her. She was too tired to drive. She would travel by train, which meant underground as well as a mainline over-ground journey. She allowed her mind to be almost vacant as she sucked in and welcomed the random conversations of fellow travellers along the way.

Waiting on the tube platform she heard one woman say to another, '… and he was made redundant yesterday.' The response was brief but quick, 'Oh dear; quick, here's the Circle Line train.' And so ended the interest in someone called Dave; apparently he had been made redundant after 15 years of loyal service in some call centre, sadly missed by all, so it seemed.

In a carriage on the tube, Claire listened to an American family, a mother, father, son and daughter, all having random and sometimes unfinished conversations with one another, almost as if they were talking to the train carriage on occasions, such were the inconsistency of responses.

The father said, 'Perhaps we should take in Shakespeare?'

'I don't understand what Shakespeare's about,' said the son.

'It's complicated,' said the mother.

'Well, there's Richard Five, that's about the battle of Agincourt,' said the daughter.

There was silence.

'Shall we visit Harrods too?' The father said.

Again, silence.

'It's on two floors. Lots to see; whadaya think?' he asked.

Talking was not reciprocated.

Automated tube announcement, doors open, 'Mind the gap, mind the gap.'

'I don't get it, what's the gap to mind?' asked the daughter. 'It doesn't mean much to me.'

If silence was a journey, the family had not tired of it.

'It's light!' said the son whose voice was cut off by the sharp injection of his father's voice.

'One more stop and we change. Hey, look up. Daylight,' exclaimed the father

'I could see the sun. I knew we were on the outside,' said the son.

'Yeah, that's right,' responded the father. His voice was avoidably petulant. He disliked coming second.

Gratefully, on the train en route to Broadstairs, Claire listened with mounting humour at the virtual monologues between mother and daughter.

The mother spoke first, 'I'm really annoyed with the train company; I'm going to write them a letter.'

'I can't get through,' the daughter exclaimed.

'It really is not on. You reserve seats and find they're not reserved. Really,' the exasperated mother expressed.

'Where's Joni gone? She could have waited!'

The daughter's voice trailed into silence, 'Hazel. Hazel. Hazel! I'm talking to you,' railed the mother.

Claire looked out of the carriage window and wondered if she would do any better being a mother of a teenage daughter, she smiled – probably not.

The sea glistened in the distance. She was nearly there.

THIRTY-THREE

09:30 hours, Tuesday, July 10, 2012 – Harry's Place, Thames Path, London

Saturday night at the 201 Club had been busier than Harry had wanted, keen as he was to see his house guest. However, one of the bouncers was off for a week. He had forgotten. Harry's itch to kill had dominated his thinking and blotted his memory. The fucking tosser sent by the temping agency had been a right twat and useless when a fight broke out. Harry had had to mix it, been awhile since he had, but when he stepped in, he soon realised he hadn't lost any of his old touch, knocked the geezer clear off his legs – boy he could still pack a punch, not bad, not bad at all. The customer who'd been bottled wanted the police involved, people nowadays – such bloody pussies; that meant a long time wasted giving a witness statement. He could do without court appearances. That was not now though, so he forgot about it. It was easy for him to switch attention. He liked the new Harry. He was keen to get back to Tom. It was not fair to keep the poor boy waiting.

The trouble with Tom was this: Harry thought the sound of Tom's screams and the physical pleasure that he would get from slowly cutting through layers of skin and bone would have been satisfying – it wasn't. The result was not at all neat. And that had increased Harry's irritation with Tom for not keeping his bloody hand still. Harry's botched initial attempts to stem the bleeding, which had been trickier than he had anticipated, made him feel really pissed off. So, he had changed

159

his method. Bit of burundanga and Tom was up for anything and keeping his limbs still for Harry – no problem, the silly bastard. Harry was even more pleased with the results when he progressed onto using a rechargeable surgical saw. It gave a neat cut and was straightforward to use. Harry liked neatness, was obsessed by it, an oversight he had made when he removed Tom's first body part. He had forgotten the pleasure of seeing the fine straight slice across butterfly wings from his childhood. Precision severance, that is what Harry craved.

Thus far, one finger, one ear and four toes placed in the shape of a question mark. They all looked rather pleasing laid out on the velvet in the steel coffin. So much so, that Harry had taken a photograph. He had decided to take more each time the number of body parts increased and the design took shape. In fact, Harry hit on the idea of producing an A1 poster when the layout within the coffin was completed. He would hang it in the basement, the first of many. It would be a good memory. Yes, his own private gallery. Tom would be his first amongst equals. Death is a great equaliser. Harry could almost visualise his masterpiece now, entitled, *Tom Abimelech – I do not know who I am*. Pity the world would not see it until Harry was dead.

What Harry had read in the Sunday paper from the weekend inspired him. It was Nikola Tesla's birthday today. The man who brought to the world alternating current had given Harry cause for celebration. Tom needed a few more shocks in his last days. Besides, it would give Tom a rest from amputations before Harry moved onto his larger limbs and internal organs.

He flushed cold air into Tom's cell lowering the temperature rapidly until goose pimples were popping like fizz candy all over his naked body. Harry watched on his remote screen as Tom still unconscious from yesterday, gradually moved into to a somewhat constrained foetal position. The remote camera zoomed in on Tom's exposed testicles. As the coldness seeped into the room, Harry watched fascinated as each testicle moved independently, the skin tightening and retracting, each in its own way, away from the arctic blast and closer to the inner comfort of Tom's body.

When Harry entered the cell, he dragged Tom towards the mortuary table. The blood from yesterday was gone, sluiced away, and ready for today. He flung Tom, a rag doll, face down with his hips and genitals rolled over a convex tube. The tube had a hole drilled all the way through, into which Harry hung Tom's flaccid penis. As always, he tied Tom's arms and legs to the four corners of the table. Next, he slid a cable into Tom's urethra and attached the other end to a manual dynamo. It was similar to a technique used in the Vietnam War and, as Harry had heard, was probably still in extensive use all over the world, especially in South America.

He turned the music on and pushed the volume up. Black Sabbath thudded base heavy against the walls. Harry had to work surrounded by music. He cranked the dynamo in time to the beat. Harry loved it, especially, when Tom's face grimaced as each electrical current shot up his penis. When Tom eventually came round, his screams were blood curdling, as bad as, if not worse than, the pain of amputation. Harry shouted with exhilaration, the screams, the music, the body convulsions and contortions against the straps, what more could he ask for, this was what man was on earth for.

'So where is your God now Tom? Hey? Gone walkabout again has he? You're abandoned me old cock; ain't no one gonna save you; ain't no one gonna be there when you're dead.'

Harry double cranked the dynamo.

'Now how does that feel? Come on Tom, speak up!'

Tom screamed.

'That's it Tom. You're doing good son.'

Despite the cold in the cell, beads of sweat dripped from Tom's forehead. Force-fed food and drink; washed down with a hose, subjected to unspeakable pain, he wanted to die. The voice of his grandmother and visions of her slow death came back to haunt him. The memories and her words written in his diary tested his resilience for life and yet paradoxically gave him comfort. How long was he to live? He longed for death to come quickly.

THIRTY-FOUR

Mid-morning, Tuesday, July 10, 2012 – Harry's Place, Thames Path, London

'I want my time to come. I want my time to come.'

My grandmother's voice had lost its strength. It was feeble and pleading. She repeated the phrase laying there immobilised, bedridden and skeletal in the nursing home. She squeezed my hand and I reciprocated. I broke down in tears. As I sobbed, my grandmother, who so often was trapped in the frightening world of dementia became aware of my presence.

'Don't you worry Ducky. Don't you worry Tom; I'm so sorry darling, but I want to go.'

She gripped my hand tightly – strength beyond her feeble looks – and gently rubbed my hand with her fingers.

'Don't you worry Ducky.'

It was then that my grandmother asked me about Claire, not having done so for five years or more, ever since her demons had taken over.

'How's Claire Ducky?' Her question unwittingly probed my pain further.

'We're not together Nan; I'm training to be a priest.'

'Oh,' she replied in surprise, 'I didn't know, you didn't tell me. Why didn't you tell me Ducky?' Her voice was gentle, loving.

'You've been ill – not at all well Nan …' I added a small white lie, was it not right to do so? '… For over a year now. It didn't feel right for me to tell you, to upset you.'

My grandmother accepted the explanation and asked, 'Why did you and Claire separate?'

I told her how it had all come about, adding, 'I miss her in so many ways.'

'You're a good-looking man, Tom. Have you met anyone else?'

I talked about the priesthood as if the vocation was another woman. How beautiful she was and how much colour she had brought into my life. I knew the more I chatted, the more I realised I was really talking about Claire, not the priesthood, not the Catholic Church, not God.

My grandmother listened as I talked. A smile shone in her eyes. It was a bright, radiant light. Then as I paused to gather my thoughts – her eyes faded. The light, snuffed out. She moved her eyes away from me, looked around the room, and lifted her head off the pillow. Her grip on my hand loosened and then she turned to me and spoke, but not to me.

'This is not my room. Where am I?'

From that moment on her vascular dementia re-asserted control. She was gone forever. My tears and my prayers flowed freely. Thirteen days later she died.

For Tom, the moments, the hours spent with Harry became a dark nightmare that gutted his soul and tried every which way to pull out the spirit. He wanted to go, but something in him, his life force resisted. Pain became his new way of life. Surreally, he felt his threshold rose to counter the levels of increasing pain, almost as if the heavier the weight of responsibility one carries, the greater one's strength can grow to meet it.

What had Tom become? Whatever he was, he lived outside of himself. He found himself floating high above Harry's head as Harry brought out a whip that had three leather strands and was beaded with jagged shards of glass and serrated pieces of metal. When Harry's muscles bunched as he drew back the whip to strike, Tom, as if he was in a lift, slowly descended to eye level and found himself looking deep into Harry's eyes. The pupils were dilated, a universe of impenetrable black. No light was reflected from them. They were as a bottomless pit where no goodness was left to come out.

Black Sabbath's *Iron Man* stomped with thuds into the cell.

Tom counted.

One: the whip fell harshly upon the back of the body trussed across the table. The body convulsed as the whip tore clumps of skin loose and flicked blood across the body and over Harry's face.

Harry licked his lips.

Two: red jagged wheals crisscrossed and protruded like tramlines uprooted by melting tarmac in the boiling heat of the sun.

Three: the body moved less; only skin, sinew and blood flicked and flowed freely.

By the count of ten Harry stopped. Tom's back ran with blood. Star shaped flaps of skin and swellings had erupted into ugly molehills. A fascinating pattern had formed across Tom's shoulders and lower back. Harry felt sated.

With Tom now unconscious, Harry hosed his body down and watched as loose fragments of skin tried to stay loyal to Tom, but eventually they too gave up the fight and flowed into the sieve. Harry had to capture everything. The flotsam and jetsam, when dried, might be useful as a light dusting once all of the other body parts had been laid out. His evolving abstract was coming together nicely, he thought.

THIRTY-FIVE

Tuesday, July 10, 2012 - Viking Bay, Broadstairs

The rain fell from the sky like a fine garden spray and adults and young children alike ran about and through the rainbow speckled water as the sun's rays gave them each their own individual display of kaleidoscopic colours. Yet, as quickly, almost as swiftly as the mist of rain had come, it was gone. The sky returned to an arid equilibrium. Claire watched, detached from the joviality.

The laughter and squeals subsided. The veil of modesty and reservation – the status quo – gradually returned to the strangers, a collection of families and young couples brought temporarily to communion by the consequence of nature and the unleashing of spontaneous, feckless and excitement filled activity. The time limited community, disintegrated.

Can we never go beyond our limitations, our social norms, she thought. Are we always to be constrained by the chain gang mentality of being islands, separated minds, locked away in our own realities? She picked up her picnic and strolled wearily along the seafront to her third-floor flat.

The flat, purchased with the money from her grandfather's will, overlooked Viking Bay and the vast seascape beyond. Sometimes, with her binoculars, like a mariner's wife ashore, she would watch the Ramsgate to Oostende ferry forge its bow waves away from the coast of England. The tidal cycle of waves and currents had always been constants. And yet, as the spectre of climate change and its physical impact begins to filter into the everyday lives of the masses, perhaps they'll come to realise, she thought, that continuity is not a given. Perhaps wellington boots and Siberian clothing will become de rigueur.

Back in the flat, Claire tried to relax into the low-slung chair she had moved to the bay window, anything, to allow her body to unwind in the sun's warmth. Yet she could not avoid the ominous feelings that rent her insides. She dwelt upon the tumultuous waters ahead. What storms would rage? How would she respond should she find out Tom had died and worse still, had been brutally murdered?

The news reporting of the three murders in London had unsettled her to say the least. Talking to colleagues at Head Office had re-assured her that maybe Tom had not been caught up in the disturbing spate of killings. Besides, just because Tom was missing, did not mean he was at the mercy of a killer. Although, as time moved on, it was difficult to run away from the thoughts and feelings that he had met his doom. Such thoughts clouded her judgment and started to snuff out what little hope she held onto.

The breeze through the open window nudged her into wakefulness. She had slept after all. Yawning, stretching, her eyes widening, alighted on an eclectic anthology of poems. Flicking through the pages, she allowed the book to fall open naturally and read a poem. It reminded her of how she felt without Tom – orphaned without a home. The poem, written across time, was crying out to be heard, like her now, she felt. She breathed out a short, sharp mirthless silent laugh, like a horse clearing its nostrils.

She had tried to move on. Claire had had several relationships, but none touched her deeply enough to connect the triangle: the need to feel love of the heart, of the mind and of the body. Only Tom had managed that. Despite her failed attempts, she was not eager to sacrifice the search for the man that was capable of all three. She had found that Tom had been a rare species indeed. Claire was not yet willing, as some she knew, never her, to compromise on just one or two sides of the triangle. After all, her interest in basic maths was one of her strong points.

The Orphaned Asked Equation
By George Henry Smedley (1888-1917)

Sequences follow mathematical rules,
Yet the laws of physics dissolve us fools
Until we – social amoebas that we are
Divine our intentions from the stars.
We gaze forlorn at shooting arrays
Mindless that in endless ways
Our imaginings are such mortal things;
They lack long half-lives to heaven's wings.
We idle like four-stroke engines.
Absurd, we know we'll get no mention
In life's dispatches or recognition,
And that what we gave was sound rendition.
Inarticulate, mocked - we cry,
This kills our heart and makes us die.
We try to fly and soar like birds,
But social equations give us merde.
Logarithms, algebra, hold your breath and pause,
Wait now, be English, wait! You'll hear no applause.
No, the only sound you'll ever hear
Are death's dark footsteps dragging fear.
To the has-beens, 'never-was's', or 'try-to-be's:'
They're flotsam – toss them in the seas.
Let tidal waves break their bones
For lonesome wanderers have no homes.

Claire abandoned all thoughts for a while and literally stared into the spaces around her, seeing all but taking nothing in. In that silent void, a cruel whisper spoke to her. It was a dark verse, which leapt out, seized her thoughts, and shook her senses awake. My God! A cold shiver ran down her spine. Seemingly random locations, savage, brutal murders; they were connected by poems. She felt certain. The killer was striking victims and selecting them in locations chosen by stanzas.

She rapidly flicked through the anthology and with darkening thoughts turned to a poem by Gilbert Parker, *In Camden Town*. The last two stanzas haunted her.

> I sing this song, borne all along
> A space of wasted breath;
> And build me on from room to room
> Unto the House of Death,
> Where portals swing forever in
> To weary pilgrim guest,
> And hearts that here were inly dear
> Shall find a Room of Rest.

It was folly to allow her mind to make such erroneous connections. Still, her gut told her it was true. The poems were linked to locations where men had recently been murdered. Her heart plummeted and mind raced all in one blundering cycle in her chest. Maybe, probably, who knows, God knows. Her spirits sank. Her feelings held sway. She concluded, despite herself, that Tom was most likely dead and his tortured body was yet to be found. Her hopes had been false. Her determination to prove he was alive was to be to no avail. Her folly had been to believe she was right and to convince others she was. She had given Tom's parents false hope.

Now she stared honestly into the pot of hope. It was empty. Delusion had swept in and compelled her to see it had been full when it was not. Aye, love blinds us all to hope and even the slightest tenuous thread keeps us yearning to be right. Now, what was she when she stared into its dark depths. The only reflection, she saw was a woman wearing a jester's hat. She had been a fool, too much in love with a memory, a reminiscence that had chosen to erase his life from hers. Why had she not let him go? She had hoped for more.

Darkness prevailed. Hope died.

She wandered aimlessly outside. Shadows of people long gone walked past the broken woman sobbing into her hands, each one touching her head with love.

Time passed.

No one else approached her to provide comfort. When the opportunity came, when she passed by along the promenade in a state of shock, which was plainly evident on her face, live passers-by did exactly that. The opportunity to love in that moment was gone. The balance against them weighed heavily then.

Drained of hope, beaten down by grief, Claire found herself on the beach. She breathed heavily, heaved sighs, slid down, and slouched against the seaside wall. Her feet rested numbly in the sand. Families played around her, children and grandparents paddled in the sea and jumped over the small trickle of waves on the shore. Laughter, giggles and fun provided surround sounds.

How alien to life Claire felt right then, right there. Her anger returned. How could these people carry on living life as if nothing bad was happening in the world? My God, it was nearly right on their doorstep and yet, they blinked at the news items of London murders with indifference.

She could see so easily now, so clearly, how people can go wild and live chaotically from relationship to relationship or want to hide away under a quilt, retreat into their homes and themselves. Life does go on and seeing it so, only serves to remind how different your reality is to the experience of others. That is until the seeds of destruction touch their neural pathways too, and batter down the mirage that life was liveable. Sometimes it was not. Tom had been wrong.

An hour or more passed unnoticed. The sun, normally so kind, had reddened her legs in her darkness. Even nature was against her.

A brightly coloured beach ball bounced her way and landed on her lap. Instinctively she grasped it with both hands. She was like Atlas holding the world in her hands. A little girl, perhaps three or so, ran giggling up to her and then hesitated to come closer. Claire's moody face acting as a barrier to her coming closer.

Had Claire already lost herself so far, so quickly, that delight in the pure presence of an innocent child left her untouched? The girl rubbed her nose; it was itching with tickly sand. She smiled broadly. A wobbly tooth was proudly on display. Her eyes twinkled in expectant hope that the adult would bounce her ball back to her.

Claire held onto it with one hand, rubbed her nose too, and winked and smiled back. The girl, with her name printed on a brightly coloured badge swinging in motion – she had got lost before – hopped from side to side. Her anticipation mounted. She was the greatest catcher in the world.

With an almighty oomph, Claire threw the ball into the air and as it floated earthwards, Rose-Mary Tobias caught it. Indeed, she was the best catcher as her parents naturally told her. She ran off towards her mother dwarfed by the world she now carried on her shoulders; one day, who knows, she might carry a bigger burden and her face might mirror the scars left by the ball's soft indentations against her cheek.

Claire rubbed her face until her senses were back. What had she been doing? Where had she been? Down, but not broken, wrong about Tom, maybe; but she was damned right about that bloody serial killer, she thought. How evil walks into people who swallow its poisonous pill and wreak other lives on a whim.

Her phone rang. The barman from Camden Town she hoped. It was Dan; one of the sub-editors … no she was not anytime soon going to submit her analysis. 'Well, sometimes life is more important than the news.' She abruptly hung up – 'bloody people.'

The last line of that poem played in her mind. She too was a lonesome wanderer without a home. Claire's thoughts batted conversations back and forth across her hemispheres. Where on earth could I in all circumstances, in all ways be myself – without fronts, sides, charades; good and bad tempered, hysterical, excited, wild and wicked?

Poems, if she let them, drew Claire in. They are like a painting crafted on bare canvas: the layers of letters and word strokes and the explicit and implicit meanings of light, darkness and shadows, are for her, all framed for the writer and the reader. Poems pull her forever inwards into another world, life and reality. These dynamics drive the relationship between her and the poet. Like two mirrors placed face to face, the reflections between them could be infinite.

She sat forward and hugged herself. Her seated body moved in slow minute circles. Claire was like a needle suspended from thread. Tick tock pendulum motion. Emotions and thoughts swung either way sideways in graceful arcs up and down. Each one stretching out into the void beyond her body attached to an invisible strand. It was as if her blood and neurological cells were connecting to hidden others and multiplying the powers of intuition.

In a micro-cusp pause between ascent and descent, much like the edge of a river against the bank, where all motion is zero, the awesome, unrelenting, unmistakeable magnetic pull drew Claire inexorably – but oh so willingly to her territory, her mansion, her palace and all its treasures, its panoply of rooms and its infinite grounds. He was alive, she knew it.

'Oh Tom, how I miss you...'

THE TYGER

By William Blake (1757-1827)

What the hammer? What the chain?
In what furnace was thy brain?
What the anvil? What dead grasp
Dare its deadly terrors clasp?

When the stars threw down their spears,
And water'd heaven with their tears,
Did he smile his work to see?
Did he who made the Lamb make thee?

Tyger Tyger burning bright
In the forests of the night,
What immortal hand or eye
Dare frame thy fearful symmetry?

THIRTY-SIX

09:00 hours, Wednesday, July 11, 2012 – Metropolitan Police Service

Home office pathologist, Dr. Jacob Rogers presented the following at a closed meeting with Commander Bulrush and Detective Sergeant Raven.

Summary report: post-mortem on Eric Courtish; aged 63, a white male

'The body was lying on its back on the deceased's living room carpet, the shoulders flat. The head was turned upwards, stretching the neck. Both arms were lying extended from the shoulders above the head. The left and right leg had been placed full-length and adjacent to each other.

'The body was fully dressed. A pink cotton fibrous scarf was around the neck; the torso was dressed in a black cotton shirt, the trousers were also black cotton, the socks were pink cotton and the shoes were black lace up brogues.

'The body has a number of perimortem injuries to the neck and chest which are directly associated with the manner of the victim's death. Electro-microscopy scanning revealed the heart had been removed perimortem.

'There are a number of post-mortem wounds to the face, neck and internal organs, the latter accessible via the open chest cavity. The injuries consist of puncture marks together with signs of the skin being chewed. Examining the size of the puncture wounds indicates they are consistent with those capable of being inflicted by a domestic cat. A cat was found in the deceased's home at the time the body was discovered.

'There are blunt force injuries to the tissues of the throat consisting of patterned abrasions and contusions to the skin of the arterial neck, indicative of strangulation. The patterned injuries matched the cloth pattern of the deceased's scarf; the injuries form a horizontal circumscription around the neck, which suggest it was used as a ligature. The pressure from the ligature fractured the hyoid bone and this would have resulted in the obstruction of the carotid arteries preventing blood flow to the brain. Depending on how long the force was applied, this would have led to the victim losing consciousness.

'There are fingernail marks above the ligature abrasion; these were caused by the deceased's own fingers, most likely as he struggled to prise the tightening scarf away from his own throat.

'Two centimetres beneath the ligature abrasion is a wound to the throat which is deep and produced by a sweeping movement of a sharp implement. The jagged abrasions on the victims left-hand side of his throat is the entry point and a smoother abrasion is apparent upon termination of the wound. There are no hesitation marks on the skin along the line of the incision. The flow of the incision from left to right indicates someone from behind the victim cut the throat; it may also indicate the assailant is right-handed. The implement is likely to be a double bladed knife. The upper part of which is serrated, the lower side, smooth. It is possible the knife used was a hunting knife. It is not possible to say how long the blade of the knife is.

'The chest cavity had a vertical in-line incision that had been made along the sternum; the width and depth of the incision is similar to that used by a battery operated orthopaedic sternum saw for thoracic surgery. The sternum was subsequently snapped apart, giving access to the median sternum and the heart. The pericardium membrane was cut open and the heart removed.

'The body showed signs of putrefaction, indications of this include substantial amounts of green staining around the abdomen and brown-black discolouration of the veins. Taking into consideration the ambient temperature within the house and the weight of the victim's body, the death occurred sometime around Wednesday, 4 July to Thursday, 5 July, 2012...'

'In other words gentlemen, the deceased's heart was removed whilst he was still alive.'

'Thank-you, Doctor Rodgers. I'm interested in the sternum saw. How loud is it?' asked Commander Bulrush.

'Yes, the saw; I've actually brought along the type we use. It'll help as an illustrative example.'

Removing it from its small metal case, he pressed the on button.

'As you can see, it's compact, and as you now hear, it has a quiet operation, about 63 decibels, like the sound of normal conversation if you were say, one metre or so away.'

'I see and would I be right in assuming that each saw blade might leave its own cutting mark?'

'You know, I hadn't thought about that, but now you mention it, that's possible. I'll re-examine the groove in the bone, and photograph them. If you like, I'll email the images across to you.'

'Yes, good idea. Send them to DS Raven though. He'll be acting on my authority when undertaking further enquiries. What of the other two post-mortems doctor?'

'You'll find them underneath the first. In summary, the cause of death and modus operandi for the killing of August Kilterton was similar to that inflicted on Courtish, although he had contusions and abrasion along the underside of his body. This was most likely caused when his body was dragged through the toilet window. His body was also laid out in the same manner. The only real difference was that the victim's penis had been severed and placed in the deceased's open mouth.

'The unknown female victim, whilst found lying in a similar position to the other two victims, had no injuries that were consistent with theirs. We have yet to determine the cause of her death and are awaiting toxicology results. Blood found on her clothing matches that of Kilterton. So it is possible that he murdered her or that his murderer had contact with her following Kilterton's death. I'm not clear on this aspect; although it's unlikely that Kilterton was the assailant.

'I would add that one fact binds all three victims together. The DNA belonging to a fourth person was found on all three deceased.'

'Thank-you doctor, let me know the outcome of toxicology as soon as you have it.'

Commander Bulrush turned his attention to his subordinate, DS Raven.

'I want you to put in motion two actions: contact all UK on-line outlets for hunting knives and also suppliers that sell sternum saws. We need to find out who sold any of these items to London based addresses.'

Commander Bulrush paused before speaking further.

'Doctor Rogers, when we've finished here, would you mind making sure Raven has the right terminology to describe the sternum saws, that'll reduce any confusion.

'Raven, I expect all of the results from the investigation to be reported directly to me by Friday morning 06:30 hours.'

'By Friday Sir? That may not be possible.'

'Just change one word, from 'may' to 'will'; that'll keep me satisfied. We haven't got time to mess around, the Pride protest is almost upon us, things can so easily spiral out of control. We've got to get a grip; so, sort it

''Oh, and doctor, one last question, how long would it take to cut through the sternum using a saw such as yours?'

'About 30 seconds. After which the bone would need to be levered, braced or snapped apart to secure open access to the heart.'

When Dr. Rogers had left, Commander Bulrush turned to Raven.

'Remind me when I retire, not to keep a pet cat.'

They both laughed. Gallows humour was the guts that helped staff in emergency services to stay sane.

THIRTY-SEVEN

One pm, Wednesday, July 11, 2012 – London

National News

'Two men's bodies found in separate locations in London on Sunday morning have been named by the police.

'August Kilterton, 39, a computer-programming manager from the borough of Richmond was found with a garrote around his neck in the early hours on Sunday 8 July in the car park of the Wray Inn, Riverside.

'Eric Courtish, 63, a retired civil servant from the borough of Tower Hamlets, was found at his home address, Friars Mead, mid morning last Sunday. Details of his death have yet to be confirmed by the police, but they are believed to be similar to that of Mr. Kilterton.

'The Metropolitan Police said post-mortem examinations gave the cause of death as strangulation brought about by use of a ligature around their necks. They refused to comment on reports from eyewitnesses at the time the body of Mr Kilterton was discovered, which suggest his chest cavity was open and that his heart may have been removed.

'Enquiries made at the Wray Inn, a popular destination for people interested in the gay scene, suggest that Mr Kilterton was a regular customer and a well known face in the local community. One customer spoke to our reporter on the condition he remained anonymous for fear of becoming the next victim.'

'We're all in shock; deep shock. I knew August. We all did. He was a popular guy. Very fit, a runner. We're all wondering who'll be next. I mean, we heard on Monday that an elderly gay man was found murdered in his home. I didn't know him personally, but two people, both gay, both murdered, what's not to fear. Of course we're all frightened.'

'Pride has published a press release. They are holding a rally on Friday 13th walking from the Wray Inn and ending in Manchester Road, Millwall, near the home of Mr Courtish. Pride wish to show the world that fear will not stop them from being proud of who they are and to combat prejudice wherever it lies. Pride also views the rally as a protest about police conduct arising from these murders, which they claim is evidence of a blatant lack of communication and disregard for the protection of the gay community.

'The Metropolitan Police have refused to comment on Pride's press release other than to issue the following statement: 'We will deploy resources appropriate for the maintenance of peace as the situation demands.'

'In a separate Metropolitan Police statement issued earlier today, they have said the body of the woman who was found in Richmond Park just after noon on Sunday by a couple out walking their dog, is in her early 20s. Her identity and the cause of death have yet to be identified. However, the police are not connecting her murder to those of the two male victims.'

THIRTY-EIGHT

12:15 hours, Wednesday, July 11, 2012 - Harry's Place, Thames Path, London

'Come on you skinny bastard.'

Harry gave an encouraging kick to Tom's left kidney. Tom grunted in pain, his eyes flickering, as if the shutter on an SLR camera had a stutter.

'Come on!' The last word stretched out in an angry irritable tone.

'Not long now, nearly done with you.'

Was Tom listening, even aware enough to take things in? Harry carried on regardless.

'Look, I've got to go to the nightclub later, so won't have time to finish up here and clean up. Don't want to rush the final bits of the jigsaw.'

This meant nothing to Tom. More burble droning in his ears like a mosquito searching for blood.

'Been some epic news on two murders announced today. Just heard it, some fucking killer has ripped his victim's hearts out. Is that juicy or what?'

Tom with half opened eyes stared at Harry's animated features and wished he had the strength to ...

'But enough of that, there isn't time now. I want to leave you with some passing thoughts whilst I'm out. Interesting sentence in your diary, I hadn't realised how much so, until I looked it up on Google last night. Psalm 139, your favourite, your diary says. I guess line 19 is right up your street now. If only it would happen to Harry. I bet that's what you're thinking: "God, if only you would kill the wicked bastard," well here I am God. Give us your best shot. Come on!'

Silence. Harry looked around the cell.

'Kill me!' roared Harry as he spread his arms out wide and looked up to the ceiling.

Silence. Harry stood motionless.

Harry's breathing. Tom's coughing.

Silence. Harry swivelled his head towards Tom's face.

'You see, Tom, the reality is this. This is it. There is nothing. There is nothing out there, no God, no heavenly being floating through the cosmos. Nothing!

'You know, and this thought came to me last night. One day I reckon, they'll invent an intergalactic spaceship, yea, that's right, *Star-Trek* for real, and the human race will reach the edge of the Universe. There's got to be a fucking edge ain't there? Do you know what they'll find? Not God. No, they'll see themselves looking out into another world full of humans, but fucking giants.

'Then it'll dawn on mankind, we're in this geezer's fucking eye! The human race just one of the trillions of organisms, good and bad, that jostle for life in its body. And in the other eye, there'll be a parallel universe, where I'm good and you're bad. Now wouldn't that be rich Tom?'

Tom gave him a derisory look.

'Yea, I know, my ideas are absurd. And as you're finding out, so is your fucking faith.'

Silence. Harry hung his head as if deep in thought.

'Tom, you're forsaken, but not by me. Right, I'm off now. I'll be turning the lights off. It'll be dark. No light reaches down here. There is nothing. There is no God. That's right Tom. No God, just me. As for me, I'll be back tomorrow, just you wait mate. Just you wait.'

Tom heard in the distance a heavy clunking sound, the lights went out. Absolute darkness bounced around his eyes. He had no idea when tomorrow was or indeed what day it was today. He felt broken. The darkness created imaginary flashing lights in his cell as if lightning flashes were dancing in the corners and the edges of the room or photographers were flashing light bulbs. In his exhaustion, it was all strangely soporific. He was weak. Being awake used up energy, thinking hurt his brain. Some wounds were crusted and some so terribly sore, others continued to ooze blood, whilst some wept pus.

He slept.

'You'll be alright Ducky.'

The fleeting voice of his grandmother faded as a memory like a morning mist of consciousness giving way to a daybreak of pain. It was still dark. Pitch-blackness. All around him was silence. It prevailed. Enough was enough. Was this Harry's new device?

God would not come. Tom hated him for that. And he hated himself for wanting God's company. He was not real. He was an imagination given reality by billions of delusory believers. We have believed for over two thousand years, how could we turn our back on belief now? I can, he thought.

Tom could hear himself think, it hurt, pause, place a comma there, a semi-colon here; a large exclamation mark there. Anger, rejection and despair – there was no God. Tom was flotsam, forgotten by something, some entity that did not exist. He almost laughed at the thought, the absurdity of it all, but instead coughed up congealed blood sucked up from his nostrils and spat it feebly out into space; cloying strands stuck to his chin. His dried lips were cracked. He was thirsty and yet he did not want water to live.

Tom in his sense of betrayal felt the tightening tendrils of bitterness wrap their sight around his mind and fever fed on his thoughts. Pick me up, why don't you? Squeeze me with your hands. Why don't you? Mould me. Feeling better now you bastard. I am a good man. Am I? Am I the Pharisee and he the sinner? Without God, does sin exist? I am nothing now. I am no thing. Sleep. When it's needed, it's better than sex so I've read.

A trickle of blood oozed from Tom's gaping mouth as he lay on his side unbuckled from his shackles on the cell floor. So Harry had unbound him. Why not? He was broken. He would not be leaving the cell alive. His head was arched awkwardly at an angle, for no pillow was afforded for last rites.

He slept. It was easier that way.

Dreams took him back in time. He was in a Canadian canoe with Claire on the River Dart, near Stoke Gabriel. It was early autumn. They had let the canoe drift along the fishing net rippled water and allowed themselves to drink in the awesomeness of the sky.

'What artist,' asked Tom 'would come even close to capturing this on canvas? The hues of blue, indigo and cerise, aren't they breathtaking?'

Claire resting her head and back into Tom's chest gave an affirmative sigh. Behind them, to the north, the setting sun had pinpointed its golden light into an angelic shaped cloud, which moved as if marching into battle towards darker foreboding clouds.

'Peace, perfect peace,' said Claire.

Their thoughts merged with the sky, the hills and the surrounding fields. Then the peculiar sound of a rabbit squealing pierced their harmony. On a sloping pasture to their right, a buzzard crouched over its dying prey, ensnared in its sharp talons. A rook harried in a vain attempt to secure a share of the furry feast. Life and death are such close companions, they mused, even on a day such as theirs.

THIRTY-NINE

Wednesday, July 11, 2012 – Prime Minister's Question Time, Houses of Parliament

The Speaker rose from the chair amidst the hubbub of banter within the crowded chamber; lines of Ministers and Shadow Ministers sat trailed along the benches opposite one another.

'Order, questions to the Prime Minister, Mr Herbert Thomas.'

With a speed belying his age, he stood up, spoke and sat down, 'Number one Mr Speaker.'

'Prime Minister…'

'Thank-you, Mr Speaker, I have had meetings in this House with ministerial colleagues and others, subject to some alterations in arrangements, I shall have further such meetings later today.'

'Mr Herbert Thomas.' The Speaker summoned the MP to ask a further question.

'My constituent Eric Courtish, who was found brutally murdered on Sunday 8th July, is to be buried in two week's time. I am sure the whole House will want to join me in expressing our deepest sympathy to his family and friends... '

Sounds of agreement echoed around the Chamber.

'… and also to acknowledge the great fear this heinous crime has instilled in the gay community within not only my constituency, but across the whole of London. Can the Prime Minister assure me that the Government will be relentless in the pursuit of the culprit, in taking all courses of action, to do whatever is necessary to put the murderer behind bars and to ensure the gay community, who are rightfully terrified, are given additional police protection until this crime and one of a similar nature in the Richmond Park constituency are solved?'

The Prime Minister rose to speak.

'I fully support what the honourable gentleman has just said. I wish to offer my deepest condolences to the loved ones and friends of Mr Eric Courtish and also to the other victim of these barbaric crimes, Mr August Kilterton. I'm sure everyone in the house will share my sentiments ... Let me just say to the House that there was also a third person found murdered in Richmond Park on Sunday, a woman. The police inform me this crime appears to be unrelated. They have yet to trace her identity. However, there is likely to be a family, most likely in London, very soon in abject grief at her loss, and I'm sure the whole house will wish, along with me, to pray for them.'

The Prime Minister paused with his head bowed in a moment of silence. The House, surprised, followed suit.

The Prime Minister continued.

'I have had meetings with my ministerial colleagues from the Home Office and also, the Metropolitan Police Service. The Home Secretary will brief the House in more detail later today. However, let me assure the House, that this Government will do all that is possible to ensure the safety of the communities in which they live and moreover, the police will be tenacious in running to ground the criminal responsible and putting that person behind bars. I for one hope, for a very long time, a life time.'

The House cheered and several members rose to secure the Speaker's attention.

The problem was the safety of communities was not assured. How could it, in truth, ever possibly be?

FORTY

Wednesday, July 11, 2012 – Office of the Home Secretary

Following the so-called lone wolf massacre in Norway in 2011 and the threat from right wing extremists, the UK's Home Secretary injected extra resources to counter and combat the rise of anarchy. A briefing report by the secret intelligence services lay open on her desk. She took a sip from her coffee and read on.

> The underlying menace from extremist groups lies in their everyday ability to spread violence like wildfire through mobile and social media networks. These groups constantly develop, evolve and change their communication channels.
>
> The growth of anarchic groups has increased as a direct result from 9/11, the West's response, the global economic meltdown in 2008, low or minus economic growth, the Euro crisis, austerity measures, the Arab Spring and the growing sectarian unrest and violence that is spreading, almost as a contagion, beyond national borders.
>
> In addition, the rise of mass unemployment across the Euro zone and difficulties in securing real ethnic and cultural integration have become launch pads for large swathes of the population to become alienated.
>
> Those seeking to distil and harbour anarchy in the masses have found that change in the status quo can be

achieved when they act together with one voice, with one aim – the overthrow of the State.

To spread anarchy, sectarian or right wing groups may endeavour to spark unrest by disseminating rumours against minority groups and capitalise on popular sentiment, imagined fears and emotions. Half-truths spread further and faster. Divisions are easy to split open.

Investigations, summarised on page 15, reveal that in the very near future, one to three years at best, lone-wolf individuals are likely to join together if the right vehicle is offered to them and holds out the prospect of being able to voice their principles and vent their anger in violent confrontations. This will be unlike the Nordic massacre. It will be on a far bigger scale.

The tinder is waiting for the spark. This may in turn ignite widespread riots and disruption across the UK as the population springs forth to retaliate.

The long-term scenario presented to previous administrations of low risk but high impact series of events culminating in a sequence of unstoppable revolutions in western countries could now become a reality.

In response to this increased level of threat, the Government's police and secret intelligence services have magnified their search for sectarian and right wing fanatics that conceivably pose a threat to national security. The focus has been on individuals with the capability and charisma to ignite the spark.

A hitherto unknown group has been identified, recently formed; it is called 'The 600 Brigade.' Its leader is Anderson Bernhard Collins of Anglo-French descent. He moved to London from France in September 2008 to read Geography at the LSE.

Contact has been made with our security service counterparts in France, the Direction Centrale du Renseignement Intérieur.

Investigations are also underway into the background of Collins' maternal grandparents who lived in Davos, Switzerland. Reports indicate they were refugees from Germany when the Third Reich was nearing collapse at the end of World War Two. It appears the Grandfather may have been a high ranking Nazi official. We have requested assistance from the German Intelligent Services, the Bundesamt für Verfassungsschutz.

Collins' grandparents died in 1951 during what was known as the *Winter of Terror*, when a series of avalanches killed over 265 people in Austria and Switzerland. Police reports on their deaths indicate that a skier off piste may have started an avalanche which swept Collins' grandparents to their deaths whilst out walking. Reports from witnesses at the time indicate the skier survived. However, despite police investigations, search and rescue, the individual did not come forward and was never traced.

There is no evidence at this stage to connect Collins to the neo-Nazi movements in Germany. However, the Minister will be aware of recent press coverage (29 June, 2012) – seemingly, German agents within their domestic intelligence service destroyed crucial information about one neo-Nazi terrorist group literally hours before it was due to be delivered to government prosecutors investigating widespread far right violence and crime across the Federal Republic. This incident highlights our concern that foreign government officers and right wing groups may be acting in concert. The risk is that groups such as the 600 Brigade will act as magnets for lone wolves and encourage their migration into the UK.

FORTY-ONE

Wednesday, July 11, 2012 – Camden Town, London

Around about this time of day, five-thirty, workers draw near to their favourite watering hole in Camden Town – The Fiddlers Rest. Today, the heat from the sun had been blistering. The pub is even more inviting for those seeking the pleasures of subtle air conditioning – ceiling fans and the cool shadows that can be found within the inner bars. These give refreshing hope to wilting customers. For the sun worshippers, who live and visit in their thousands in Camden, the pub's part-shaded pergola courtyard allows those not so fond of cave dwelling, to continue their vitamin D top-ups.

Claire greeted Damien and the large welcome smile when he arrived for his evening shift behind the bar. She ordered a double gin and tonic and strolled outside to wait for the woman that had been in a group with Tom last Thursday night. Damien promised to send her outside. About twenty minutes later, a young woman, of mixed race in her late twenties, with gorgeous round and large eyes, which were shadowed with bold Cleopatra eyebrows and make-up, approached Claire with a broad cheerful and open smile.

'Hi. Claire? Damien sent me out here, said it would be easy to find you. My name is Denise. How can I help you?'

Claire learned from Denise about Mark and Anne. They had introduced Tom to her and the rest of the group before moving off to the 201 Club down at Camden Lock Place.

'It's massive. A balcony encircles the main dance floor. Watch yourself if you go there, the owner's often looking down from on high. If someone takes his fancy, he will let them know and offer them free drinks for the night and a taxi home. A bit dodgy, but some girls shrug their shoulders and go for it.'

Claire managed to glean a vague memory from Denise about the clothing Tom was wearing. It confirmed what she already knew. Denise also gave her Anne's mobile number in case she wanted to find out more. But as she and her boyfriend Mark had left before, there seemed little point. Other than that, all Denise could add was that they had all left the club before Tom, so where he went from then on, she had no idea.

'Oh, one more thing,' added Denise, 'hasn't he got a real soft spot for you?'

'Really?' Claire's heart soared, 'Why do you think that?'

'Well, it became a kind of in joke between us girls in the end. At first we'd correct him, but the more Tom drank that night, and he had a skin full I can tell you … well, every time he spoke to me or one of the other girls in the group, your name was on his lips, he'd always call us Claire – seems he can't get you out of his head.'

Denise smiled that cheerful smile of hers. But somehow, Claire's on this night was bigger, much bigger.

FORTY-TWO

20:30 hours, Wednesday, July 11, 2012 – the 201 Club, Camden Lock Place, London

Three hours after leaving Denise, Claire was heading for her next destination, buoyed by the help she had had and the news she had been given. When the light shines, people seem so willing to share their trust and joy. Damien and Denise were just two small examples in the pond of life. Yet without such water to drink, life would surely stagnate. With renewed hope injected into her, Claire's step possessed more energy.

The evening was still warm, but thankfully without the disembowelling heat of humidity that sapped her legs and weighed her down with deep-sea-diver's boots on each foot. She moved with enthusiasm as she walked over the bridge to Camden Lock. Halfway across, infectious laughter could be caught by passers-by – a gang of rugby-sized blokes were sharing pints and bonhomie in a pub's outside seating area. Couples and friends were sat on the edge of the canal wall – kicking time together and allowing the calm waters to pace their conversation. Behind them, there was a bubbling cauldron of mid-week revellers enjoying Wednesday, the best day – more than half way and, as they all knew, it was downhill skiing to the weekend. In another life, she would be part of the buzz and enjoying the rich array of food available from the eclectic ethnic offerings in the market.

Camden Lock has its own natural community energy. It seems to bubble up from the pavements and ooze out of the buildings. Even the mural on the side of the railway bridge shows workers more interested in the hubbub than work – two men were sat on wooden swings dangling by ropes from the top of the bridge. They held onto paint pots and brushes, but they were far too busy for that. Comings and goings came first.

As Claire turned left onto Camden Lock Place, the cobbled road and pavement lent itself to an ambling pace. Part way down was a jewellery shop. On display were radiant gemstones and jewels nesting in necklaces, rings and bangles. In another life, a different time… a dream away. Ahead of her at the end of the road stood the imposing and incongruous sight of the four-storey 201 Club. Running from top to bottom on the left hand side of the building was a massive banner stained with the image of a man's smiling face 'welcoming guests inside.' As if the banner was not enough, floodlights pitched their illumination onto the façade of the building, painted as it was in garish gold coloured paint. It was tempting to ask herself as she approached the building, in what way would Tom have enjoyed being in a place such as this. However, as swiftly as the thought arose, it was swept aside. He would have been enjoying the company and probably been oblivious to the space around him.

The doorman watched Claire as she approached. He had spotted her almost the moment she had turned the corner. So used to being the man in control of women, he found himself uncomfortably, almost uncontrollably so, out of his depth. He was not a good swimmer.

Claire asked to see the owner. The boss had warned them all, "We're short of staff tonight, so use your fucking initiative for once, and don't hassle me over anything that can't wait till next week."

The doorman emboldened by the goddess before him, clicked on the two way radio, blotted out Harry's words and forgot the swinging Sword of Damocles over his neck.

'Mr Denmart –' he started to say.

'What the fuck is it now?' Harry's voice held nothing back and belted into the doorman's earpiece.

'I've got a reporter to – '

'A fucking reporter, tell him to piss the right off. For fucksake, I said we're stretched and you fucking call me about this.'

The doorman nodded and smiled. Claire was watching him.

'Yes, that's right, Mr Denmart, her name is –'

'Do you want your nuts screwed or something? Stop being a wanker and leave me to get on with more important things. See me later, you got that?' Harry was going to bust this guy's balls.

'Ms Yohanus – a Ms Claire Yohanus, she's standing next to me. Can you see us both?'

The only time in his life he would be next to someone who was so gifted and so beautiful. She was an intoxicating and heady combination for this male amoeba. She was close too, he could feel her soft, welcoming and warm, rounded hip touching his as together they stared up and into the camera lens.

Instantaneously, Harry switched from anger to joy, as if the other had never existed. The veil of contorted features that had erupted on his face out of frustration was now awash with the welcoming visage of a tarantula. Prey had arrived. Timing is everything.

The doorman directed Claire down to Harry's office. He felt smug. He was not the only one overawed by her presence, was he now?

'Ms Yohanus. Come in; come in, 'Mi casa es tu'casa.'

Claire wanted to laugh at the obsequious welcome. The man was odd, no doubt about it.

'How may I help you?' Harry asked with enough smarm to coat the room's walls in it.

Harry listened intently. He was hungry to get to know her. He was pleased to learn she had been looking for him and was ecstatic when he heard the police had not listed Tom as missing. No, he couldn't say that he'd seen Tom last week.

'Thursday wasn't it?' he asked and carried on talking, 'Tell you what though, I will have one of my staff go through the archived video file to see if they can spot Tom from the photograph you've given me.'

The photo was taken a while ago, thought Harry. Tom had lost a bit of fleshiness around his face when Harry had picked him up; then he smiled to himself, and a bit more since.

Claire wondered why Harry – he had insisted on using first names – smiled then, perhaps he was having an internal tête-à-tête, as she often had, and so intensely, of late.

'Thanks for your number, I'll give you a call Claire, one way or the other,' Harry had said after he had shown her around the club and as he was seeing her off at the entrance. Both were blind to the other doorman who passed by behind them.

'Yes, please call soonest; even it's in the early hours' said Claire.

She breezed off into the night, homeward bound, satisfied at least for the day, that she had done her best to find Tom. If she could place a time when he left the club from the recordings on the in-house CCTV, it might provide her with some leads. Claire knew too that if she saw him on the video, well, even that might help her to be closer to him than she had been for a very long time. There would be more hope then. She might be able to tap into his thoughts.

Harry's face looked happy, almost serene, a cat with its face stuck in a bowl of cream. He turned and slapped the amoebic doorman on the back.

'You did the right thing tonight son, the right thing.'

He placed a £50 pound note in his employee's breast pocket.

'One more thing, don't mention to anyone she came here, will you now?'

Harry placed his somewhat enormous club of a hand on the back of the guy's neck and patted his skin slowly. The doorman got the message. More than his life was worth, he thought.

As Harry moved downstairs to his office, he met the off-duty doorman on the way up; he was carrying several sets of car keys.

Harry snarled, 'You're on leave. What are you doing here tonight?'

Then it clicked.

'Have you been leaving your clients car keys here then? Silly boy, you'll get into trouble with your other boss if he finds out.'

Harry's pace of words slowed deliberately, the implication laced with menace. 'But he won't find out will he?'

Harry's eyes narrowed. Power, even over such little things as his staff, he loved it. Inside, the doorman railed with anger.

'Tell you what,' said Harry, 'you can pick up and clean my car tomorrow and drop it back to my house all nicely cleaned and polished, inside and out, and he'll never know, will he? It'll be our secret ... '

Harry would give Claire a call in the early hours, just as she had asked. He liked playing Cupid. It was almost as fun as ... no; don't be stupid, nothing was as much fun as that.

LONDON – 2002

FORTY-THREE

Summer 2002 – The Wray Inn, Riverside, Twickenham, London Borough of Richmond

How quaint everything was back then. The boats nestled on the opposite bank were tied together, like horses waiting for their cowboys to have one more shot of whiskey in the saloon. By the look of the paintwork, some of the cowboys had stayed inside for too long.

The racing green water idled along just like the many visitors and residents living in and around the Riverside. Often, the weather was just a bit too warm, the air just a bit too humid to encourage any sudden desire for fast movement. In fact, having a laminar flow was the order of life, of nature and people living in harmony together. The vast array of mature trees burnished in rich green foliage provided shade and temporary respite from the sometimes cutting rays of the sun. All in all, life carried on in a steady and predictable fashion. It was just the way residents liked it.

Yet change happens. New ideas, new people migrate into the most sheltered and protected corners of the world. The summer of 2002 saw new owners acquiring the Wray Inn. The new owners were known to their customers as Abe and Luther. Indeed, that is who they were. They had been together for 28 years. Life had been good to them. Their careers pursued independently, whilst sharing their domestic life together, had been successful. And for those people who possess the assets and acumen, as they did, the call to pursue other lifestyles is sometimes like a small branch on a tree tapping on the window pane of wherewithal, gently prompting a decision to move on and enjoy the winds of change. So Abe and Luther moved from their fast paced career paved lifestyle, and swapped it for the quaintness of the Wray Inn and its environs. Of course, they had a vast network of contacts and friendships which they enjoyed and had nurtured through the decades of their life together. Naturally, everyone wanted to taste their little corner of heaven. As the years rolled on and social media blossomed, the reputation of the Inn grew and grew.

Unfortunately, the hands of fate can sometimes deal surprising cards. In the fourth year of their new life, Abe showed the unmistakable signs of dementia. The loving soul that he was withered on the vine, wearing down the fortitude of Luther's stoic character. However, sometimes cruel accidents are nature's way of giving a blessing in disguise.

One autumn day, as the dawn began to rise, and mist and fog shrouded the river, its banks and the footpaths, everything appeared as one. Abe, dressed in his royal blue cotton dressing gown, his claret coloured pinstripe pyjamas and with one slipper on and one foot uncovered, opened the front door of the Inn, breathed in the white mist and took a walk along the clouds to heaven.

As the sun rose, the mist gradually cleared and Luther, following a frantic search, found his soul-mate floating face down in the waters on the opposite side of the riverbanks. His body was partly entangled in a boat's mooning line; her name was 'The Gabriel.' Abe had always been a faithful Roman Catholic, up until dementia had taken hold that is. Although a non-believer himself, Luther took comfort in this one small omen. For a few years thereafter, Luther gave life, his last hurrah.

Business prospered and friends still visited, but sometimes, when the stuffing is gone, the stuffing is gone. Outwardly, Luther was his jovial self and even inside his head, he pretended that life was still good. Indeed, it was, but try as he might he knew his heartbeats were wedded to his mate. With each passing moment, with each busy day, the beat of Luther's heart became slower and slower, until, like the dying flow of a river robbed of its source, his heart stopped. He had no relatives, but his friends were to him stronger than family. His close ones rallied and gave him the radiant send off that he most deservedly, deserved.

LONDON – 2012

FORTY-FOUR

*Late evening, Wednesday, July 11, 2012 – The Wray Inn,
Riverside, Twickenham, London Borough of Richmond*

Some people say don't they, that buildings absorb the feelings
and the love of all those that pass by and dwell within them. It
has to be said that if this is the case, then the Wray Inn was the
epitome of that aphorism. The new owners rejoiced in their
good fortune and prospered. That is until the discovery of
August Kilterton's body in the car park. Business
understandably had been quiet since, although a handful of
loyal long-term customers continued to prop up some of the
bars inside. Then things took a turn for the worse. It was not
nature's branch tapping on their windowpane; it was the
hammer of anarchy coming to smash up their lives.

It was ten that Wednesday night when they descended. The
timing of the assault was carried out as police shifts changed
and new ones came onto the beat. In this window of
opportunity, they surmised police cover would be minimal and
escape more likely. Having watched the news about the
murders and the planned march on Friday, some quarters of
London city didn't much care for the likes of the community
that were happily communing down by the river. So through
their own biased and prejudiced networks they hatched an
impromptu plot to tool themselves up and bring a bit of their
man love to the Riverside. That was their only planning. What

happened that night was utter chaos amidst the blood lust of thirty short minutes of Blitzkrieg at the Wray Inn.

The two police officers on duty guarding the white tent in the car park by the toilets were overwhelmed. The silently moving crowd knocked them to the floor. Quick moving hands ripped off their radios and bound the officers' wrists and ankles together with plastic ties. Then, as one, almost like Godzilla rising from the waters, they smashed into the pub. Every single windowpane throughout the building was shattered. The crowd moved like storm trooping army ants. Doors were ripped off their hinges, bottles and glasses were hit in a frenzy of home runs. Furniture was slashed. Sinks and cisterns were ripped from their fittings. Fleeing customers and staff were beaten without mercy in the garden. Petrol was spewed across the entrances and when the last ant stood outside the pub, it was torched.

At 10.30 pm, the 110-decibel air horn heralded the hooded army's tactical withdrawal. The storm troopers melted away into the night.

As the fire crews battled to contain the inferno, as the smoke billowed like a dozen steam engines at full throttle into the night air, the TV cameras on the opposite riverbank took in and pumped out the news and the scene of devastation. When the morning light broke, the smouldering skeleton of the Inn was revealed. It almost appeared to shake in the gathering breeze.

As one fire tender drove off, the TV cameras zoomed in on the now visible welcome sign in the Inn's trampled garden. Daubed in large red letters were the words: 'Stay out of Millwall!'

FORTY-FIVE

02:30 hours, Thursday, July 12, 2012 – Claire's Place, Iverna Gardens, London

As they lay entwined and she was idly playing with his chest hair, he started making ringing sounds in her ear.

'Stop it Tom, you're ruining the moment.'

He started laughing. Yet his voice continued to ring incessantly.

'Tom, stop. I've had enough.'

She threw him off abruptly and sat up.

The room was dark apart from the red glow of the bedside clock. Still drunk from sleep, she picked up her mobile phone, two missed calls, unknown number. The phone rang again, its vibration made her jump. It was that man Harry, the owner of the 201 Club. He had found footage of Tom leaving.

'Wonderful. Thank-you so much, I can be at your Club in forty-five minutes or so.'

'Okay. That's a good idea. But, as it's late, gone two-thirty in the morning and I'm already up, why don't I pop a copy over to yours? That'll save you having to come out. I can put it through the letterbox. Twenty minutes sound good?'

'Why sure, and, thanks … Harry,' she replied, still feeling awkward using his first name.

Claire threw some water on her face in the bathroom, wrapped her nightgown around her waist and shoved her note diary into one of its pockets. She left a voice message on George and Monica's phone, saying she'd made progress at the

206

Fiddlers Rest, explained that all was well and that a chap called Harry from the ...

The phone recorder had timed her out, 'Blast it.'

The kettle boiled. The doorbell rang. No sound of the letterbox opening. She left the coffee pot unfilled, pushed her hair back behind her ears and took a deep breath before marching boldly to the front door.

Harry stood there, almost on the top step, smiling. He had a fixed grin on his face. Seconds passed between them. She looked at him as he did at her. He was wearing thin gloves. Should she slam the door in his face?

He looked down at his hands, and as if answering her look of puzzlement, said, 'I get eczema sometimes; it flared up bad tonight, been a stressful day and night. Anyway, here's the video footage I promised.'

He held out the CD case in his left hand. He smiled, relaxed. Perhaps he felt as awkward as she did. Claire hesitated, and then came forward. As she did so and as her fingertips were just barely touching the case, Harry, in one rapid movement, hit her brutally hard in the face knocking her unconscious. He dragged her back into the hallway and taped a piece of cloth that he had soaked in chloroform over her nose and mouth. He carried her to his car and slung her roughly on the back seat. He had decided against using burundanga. He did not want her to be out for hours. More importantly, he wanted Tom to be back together with the one he loved. A final get together. Harry was a heartless romantic and he knew it.

Harry's Place, Thames Path, London

A half hour drive along the A4 and A3211 and Harry was home with a new butterfly. With the garage door safely closed, he rolled Claire onto her back, took hold of her ankles and pulled her body slowly out of the car. Her nightgown became caught on the rear seat's fabric. Acting in a way not dissimilar to Velcro, tugging the material backwards, the cloth on her pyjama bottoms rode up into the creases between her thighs. He breathed in deeply and felt the bulk of his chest stretch the shirt he was wearing. He wanted her.

He carried her as if she was a lifeless mannequin doll. Her body lolled loosely as he mounted the stairs and entered the kitchen. He walked swiftly along the hallway and the combined open plan living and dining room and into the passageway beyond to the lift, which would, once inside its snug confines take them safely down to the basement to see Tom.

Tom's naked body lay in a curled up foetal position facing away from the door. He stirred slightly as Harry entered the room with Claire draped like a dead fox around his shoulders. Tom remained oblivious. Semiconscious and confused, reality had lost its meaning.

Harry lay Claire on the mortuary table and outstretched her body across the length of it. He took his time undressing her. The operation whetted him. Naked she was irresistible. Her skin was soft and clear. His eyes followed the contours of the body until they reached its zenith. The dark, richly covered soft and inviting mound loomed closely into view. Harry had to fuck it.

He roughly pulled Claire's legs apart. Her labia majora stretched and opened. Harry could hold back no more. He grabbed hold of Claire's ankles and dragged her body towards him. Using one of his forearms to prop up her flopping legs, he forced his way into Claire's dry resistant flesh. Her breasts moved against his thrusts. As his surge arrived, Harry savagely rammed her body several last times before collapsing, sated, across it. Harry the Bastard, was done.

FORTY-SIX

Through swollen blackened eyes, between the jagged edges of a headache that scratched her skull, Claire struggled to escape the murky vision and make sense of events. Tom. Door. Dream. Harry. Phone. CD. Kettle. Nothing was in order. Her brain felt mashed up. Each time she tried to lift her head from the tiled floor, the stabbing pain, like a nail penetrating her head, would expand and explode. Tiled floor? Kitchen? Bathroom? Ahead of her, she could make out the hazy smudgy outline of a body. It was naked. Man or woman, she was not sure. She struggled to un-stick her eyelids. She must be in the half world of dreams and consciousness. Whistling arose and fell in undulating sounds around the room and from somewhere behind her. Sounds of light skipping footsteps echoed flatly across the room; someone appeared happy, she thought.

The light in the room was intense, intrusive. A deep cavernous headache in her brain screamed for it to stop, to go out. Nothing changed. She could not move. She was in a dream that prevents movement. That's it. The fuzzy image of the body crystallised as her eyes adjusted to the harsh light. It was a man. Why was he there and ...?

A radio was turned on, a softly spoken woman's voice, soothing and reassuring, seeped into Claire's consciousness.

The whistling danced above the woman's comforting timbre. The pitch was twisting this way and that, like discordant jazz musicians playing their instruments in an argumentative jamming session.

She wrenched her attention back to the man again. His back, her mind reeled. His back was in uproar. It was covered in bruises and swollen wheals that looked like crisscrossing railway lines set upon a chaotic urban transport network. Chunks of skin were missing. Great gapes, literally torn, bloodied potholes were scattered over the surface. Small pools of blood edged the line of his body. Some of the wounds oozed. Others were crusted over, dried blood had crisped and clotted on their surface. The man was lying on his side. He was thin. His legs were curled upwards. His hair was dark, short.

She took account of herself. She was naked. Her left arm was extended behind her head. It was aching. She could feel a numbness creeping down from her fingers, as if her arm had been dipped in an ice-hole on an Alaskan lake; the cold was edging closer to her shoulder. She tried moving it down to drape the weight across her chest and stomach, but her wrist was constrained. Yet her right arm was free, as was the rest of her body. She twisted around, looked upwards, and saw that her wrist was manacled. There was no other word for it, manacled. A tight leather strap was wrapped tightly around her wrist. A stainless steel loop protruding from its surface was shackled to a thick leather chord and metal ring sunk into the surface of the wall. Wake up.

She struggled to sit up and gain a seating position on her haunches. Grit and determination saw her through. She had a better view of the shredded man. His right ear was gone. Oh my God. A deep convulsing groan erupted from her. This was no dream. This was Tom.

The 8 am beeps sounded from the radio heralding the arrival of the news. The stark reality of her imprisonment blared siren sounds in her head. She swivelled her head around to the right. Her eyes absorbed the reflections from the large metal coffin resting, waiting, on a trolley. Her heart rate quickened. Tight shallow breathing gathered pace and constrained the movements in her chest. Her eyes fell upon the whistling man. She had finally found the answer. It was him.

Harry the Bastard called out as if he was a radio jock in Vietnam.

'Good Morning Claire ... Good to see you're awake now.' He winked.

Her body shrank away.

'That's right love. You should have trusted your intuition. I gave you a chance now didn't I? To tell you the truth, though, poor old Tom here, well, he's been kind of missing you. But he'll be happier now coz you're here. Do you know, he's cried about you? He's talked endlessly about you. How much he regrets splitting up from you, and the memories he has of you, what a fool he'd been.

'I told him so. Straight out with it I was. I felt almost sorry for him. But, now with you here, Bingo, I've got a full house, plus I get to play match-maker, makes my heart sing.'

'You fucking bastard. What have you done to Tom?' she screamed.

Harry laughed. This was fun. 'That's me. I'm a right fucking bastard. And I gave you a right good fucking this morning.'

Claire's features paled and sunk down the plughole of shock as she became aware of the bruising and soreness inside. Then anger and hatred resurrected and her cheeks flashed red.

'You sadistic fucking bastard,' she shouted, kicking out towards him with her legs.

Harry the hyena laughed. 'Well, you certainly got spirit. I'll give you that. Almost makes me wish I'd waited till you were conscious, likes a fight me.'

Tom stirred into consciousness, and started to roll over onto his back. Hollering in agony, he gave up.

'Tom. It's me, Claire.'

'Good Morning Thomas, it's a big day today.'

Tom's mind swirled in confusion.

'Oh my God Tom, what has he done to you?'

Claire's voice appeared like an angel on wings. Death must be calling.

Harry leant over and close to Tom.

Tom implored her. 'I want my time to come,' he whispered hoarsely, for the strength was out of him.

'What's that, Tom? ... Good. Good to hear that. Not long now. Was going to be today, but a chance meeting changed all of that. I've brought Claire here to be with you … that's right. I'm giving you two love birds a chance to take back some lost time. Am I not a god Tom? That's more than He's done. He is the God that isn't.'

Harry's bulbous ballooning head turned towards Claire and he continued.

'Now call me a heartless old romantic, but in a moment I'm going to release you from your restraint.'

Claire looked at this sick man's face and wanted him, body and soul, to suffer and die.

Harry had continued speaking. 'I've taken all of my tools out of the cell whilst you slept. I'm going to leave you a bowl, cloth and a towel and some food and water, even a blanket too. You can nurse Tom, if you want, in his final hours. As for you, I've not decided how or when yet. But to put you in no doubt,' Claire wasn't, 'you'll be joining Tom on his journey soon enough.'

Tom groaned in agony. With herculean effort, he had finally rolled over. His head lolled to one side and he found himself looking at Claire. The sight was almost impossible to take in. She swung her face towards his, tears streamed from her eyes and mucus ran from her nose, but she managed a smile.

'Hi Tom, it's me. Sorry I'm late.'

Tom's battered features broke into a crooked smile. He touched a distant memory of their shared joke. Hysteria creates humour in the darkest of places. She was a welcome sight. At the same time not, for she would share his fate, see his agony, and like him, die without hope in her heart. Or was her being here a blessing? For if they were both to die at this mad man's hands and tools of torture, was it better to do so in the company of each other's love? His heart swelled, no matter how weakly.

Harry stood over Claire.

'Now if you try anything, one punch, kick or any act of violence, I promise you, I'll stick Tom on that table and end his life here and now before you've even had time to say goodbye. Do you understand?'

She nodded in acquiescence.

When Harry released her and had left, Claire crawled over to where Tom lay. She now took in the horrifying facts that he also had some fingers and toes missing. She lay as closely to him as possible and held his right hand that was splayed across the floor. He gently squeezed hers three times. She responded to their shared memory.

'I love you too,' she whispered.

Through chapped and cracked lips, his voice rasping against the dryness in his throat, he whispered, 'Forgive me.' Tears trickled down his cheeks.

They lay there, looking at each other for some time. The enormity of what had been and what was yet to happen put to one side, unimportant in these moments of being together. Yes, they were mad. Had been ever since they had met, mad for each other, madly in love. Through swelling and bruises, through torture and pain, through life and the hell of events itself, they were mad. There was no denying that now. It was Tom's epiphany. And Tom, he no longer fought to resist being with this woman, this lovely feisty, independent, beautiful woman.

He had stepped, finally, onto the right path for him. And God smiled. From this moment, the memory would be timeless.

Then Tom coughed. His body hurt the more so as it shook in response to the jarring physical force. Tom needed water, yet he also needed to drink in the presence of Claire. He had five years to quench.

She touched his ragged and drawn face. 'Oh my darling, my poor sweet darling.'

FORTY-SEVEN

Thursday, July 12, 2012 – Harry's Place, Thames Path, London

The camera zoomed in. Harry watched his very own big lover house reality TV show. He was enthralled, a bit of light relief before the busy day that lay ahead. Not least of which the stage wiring to sort out at the Club before it opened at eight tonight, and perhaps, one more tool to buy. Yes a busy day indeed. He might leave them be until tomorrow, or maybe Saturday. He might do them then. With her, now he had got to know his little concubine, he didn't feel quite the need to end things so quickly.

Then again, and this was his conundrum. He was working on an idea. Perhaps his first A1 poster should be the two of them, both sliced in half by their length ways and then sewn or glued together, with the question mark from Tom's body parts placed above their joined up head. And the title: 'Co-joined twins?' No; 'Joined at the hip – co dependent lovers?' Maybe that or better still he pondered, 'Inseparable.' As was his way, he was obsessive; Harry got stuck into this distracting habit, playing with ideas, like a cat with a mouse, until exhaustion squeezed the fear of death out of the prey. Finally, he hit on the idea of joining parts of their two names together as the title for the image. Yes, that was it, unending love, 'Erotical – with something missing.' With that piece of his mental jigsaw in place, Harry downed the last dregs of his coffee and left.

Harry's barbarism had disassociated Tom's mind from himself. His body rejoiced at being touched. The closeness of Claire was energising. He felt like a battery on charge, could feel the trickle of electricity flowing into him. Little by little, Tom began to return. He noticed how swollen Claire's eyes and nose were. Harry had given no quarter.

'You're beautiful,' Tom said, his voice barely a whisper.

Claire, gently holding Tom cradled in her arms as she dripped water from the cloth into his mouth, smiled and brushed away tears from his and her own cheeks. The five-year gap between them in the end was no divide. When love is let in willingly, love comes easily. She laid Tom softly on his back before putting fresher, warm water into the bowl. Squeezing away the excess, Claire gently, lightly, lovingly, gave him a flannel bath. Verdant spring voices arose from heaven's chemistry and touched Tom, stimulating a swirl of his inner colours that radiated indigo and azure in his mind's eye. He could now see clearly.

When she had finished, he whispered her name. With one hand resting on his leg, the other gently on his hip, she looked up.

'Claire, will you marry me?'

'You silly bugger, of course I will.' She leant over him and they kissed with the gentlest of passion and the stirrings of long ago. Their lips parted. Their mouths were fuelled with the richness of such a delicate and tender touch. Love, the most powerful force in the universe girded Tom with the strength of angels enabling him to raise his right arm until his fingers were able to rest on the back of Claire's head, and as a feather touches, he stroked her hair, caressed the nape of her neck and let his fingers drift slowly down her back. How welcome was the lightness of his embrace. Claire's heart sung. She nestled down along the side of him and nuzzled her nose into the side of his neck.

The simple tenderness of her breath and the closeness and warmth of her body were comforting, reassuring, relaxing. Whatever may lie ahead, they were drawn to living in this present moment together and the light blanket and the love covering them nurtured their bodies into sleep.

FORTY-EIGHT

Thursday, July 12, 2012 – Outside of Claire's Place, Iverna Gardens, London

It was noon. Had they already left things too late? George and Monica had rung Claire's home and mobile phone several times. Leaving a series of voice messages, but hearing her disembodied voice and the lack of real contact had only increased their fears. The shadows of doubt had grown.

If they had called the police, what would they have said: that Claire had left a message in the early hours and had gone out, and yes, they were worried? The police's response to Tom's disappearance gave them no belief in the prospect that any action would be taken.

No, it was up to them.

Although neither had said it, they both knew Monica would slow George down. Earlier that morning, she had girded her loins to be by herself, knowing that possibly, she might have to go beyond the time she could easily cope with, and had told George to "Just go! I'm made of stern stuff you know that. I've got plenty of metal within me to keep me going for a lifetime yet, so don't you worry now. I'll be fine."

Claire's car was parked nearby. George knocked on the door, pressed the bell several times, still no answer. He bent his body almost double to call through the letterbox in ever-increasing decibels. Still there was nothing and, no sounds of life from within. She could be at the nearby shops. George decided to give it another half hour and sat on the front steps. A cat strolled up and tried to curl itself around his legs. George was having none of that and shoved it away. Thirty slow minutes anxiously passed. No return. A traffic warden walked by and eyed George suspiciously.

'I'm waiting for someone to come back,' said George somewhat irritably. He was more annoyed with his in-built guilt than the gawking of the warden doing an added value job for the neighbourhood.

He called Monica, nothing from Claire either. He stood up, shook the blood back into his hips and went back up to the letterbox. Moving his head like an American quarterback, he looked from one end of the street to the next, all was clear. He stuck his arm through the gap in the door and spent several backbreaking moments moving his hand and fingers in a circular arc trying to find a key.

The cleaner from across the street in the second floor bedroom looked down on George and had the same response as the warden. He did not look like he was a burglar. Who would be that obvious? Then again, maybe that was his art; perhaps he was capable of blending into the background of non-threatening normality like an unnoticed beige cardigan.

George finally managed to extricate his arm from the aperture, his faced flushed red, the veins on his forehead prominent and pulsating a raised supply of blood. He felt slightly giddy for a few moments. Little stars twinkled in space before his eyes. The in bit had been easy, but getting out was like removing a ship from a bottle. Frustrated, hot, and bothered, his blood was up. He walked down the side of the house and down a small number of steps to the basement window. Peering inside, he could see it was a utility room. Standing in the shade from overhanging eaves, George gave the pane a sharp jab with his elbow. The glass smashed, the handle moved down easily, he would soon be in.

FORTY-NINE

Thursday, July 12, 2012 – The 201 Club, Camden Lock Place, London

One pm. On the dot, he arrived to collect the car – good boy. Throwing the keys for Colin to catch, Harry goaded him, 'Now do a good job you fucking twat.'

Catching them smoothly in one hand, Colin started to walk off; Harry's ringing endorsement prodding him at his back.

'And don't you fuck it up or you'll be out of both jobs. Oh yeah, one more thing, and don't forget it, I want it back tomorrow afternoon at my place. I'll get a taxi back tonight.'

Colin turned and nodded as he said, 'Right boss. Will do,' before quickly making his way out of the office. He had a lot to fit in before tomorrow dawned, and wanted to avoid any confrontation with Harry the Bastard.

He drove Harry's Mercedes to his mate's valeting service near the Elephant and Castle. Going to his work would cause hassle, create questions and he could do without that. As he was turning into the wash, dry and clean service spaces, he watched a police car drive past with an old guy slumped in the back, the drunken face of a forgotten father, he thought, half pressed up against the passenger window.

Pulling the car to a stop in one of the parking, washing bays, he got out. 'Hiya Pete, how's it going cock?'

The mid-twenties aged man with ginger Ivy League cropped hair who was dressed in overalls looked up and dropped the sponge in the bucket of soapy water.

'Hey-ay! How goes it geezer? Good to see you Col. Like your motor.'

'S'not mine mate,' said Colin. 'Don't ask neither. It's complicated. D'you mind if I gives this one a thorough? I'll give you some cash in hand, if I can use all your gear. Alright?'

'You are keen Col ain't you. Help yourself. I'm stopping for some scoff soon, fancy a cuppa?'

'No ta mate. I'm up to the gunnels as it is. Gonna crack on with this baby and get it sorted, soon as.'

The outside washed and polished up well. Harry would be able to see his ugly mug in it now. Inside the car, the sweltering heat got to Colin. Leaning underneath the front seats, he caught sight of a diary. Looking inside, he soon realised it was not Harry's. No, it definitely was not his at all. His face darkened. There was not time right now, no, he had set his sails, this was his destiny and besides it was all too late anyway – 'Fuck it.' He could not deal with his mum's expectations, right now. 'Sorry mum, I did my best always, didn't I?' She answered him, as she always had: *Of course you have my darling boy. You've always done your best for me. I know that.*

When he had finished, his mate told him not to bother with cash. 'You can get me a few jars next time I bump into you when I'm out on the razz.'

'Cheers mate,' Colin responded. All the same, he left twenty quid in Pete's office after using the toilets. It was unlikely he would ever see him again.

Honking the horn, he drove off. Forty minutes later, through heavy traffic, he left the car in a 24 hour parking bay, grabbed his bag and the diary and made his way to a nearby café. Inside, it was a poor person's place. You could tell. The décor was unattractive, pale pink emulsion was plastered over the bumps and lumps and potholes of the walls' uneven surfaces. Tacky art hung at awkward angles, some optimistically for sale and produced, by the look of it, from within the local community.

Customers had the 'choice' of sitting on an array of uneven legged chairs at rickety wooden tables adorned with plastic floral patterned covers, topped with vases of plastic flowers, some of which, had petals missing. All had a light coating of dust. Grease was smeared across the eating surface spread by a cleaning cloth that had been hastily dipped and squeezed out from the sink that morning. This, combined with the distant underlying basal smell of stale sweat embedded deeply within customers' clothes, added to an atmosphere, where he could walk in and out unnoticed by staff and clientele alike.

Thinking people would pass promptly on by and he would be left undisturbed to ponder over his recent discovery. Not one of the dull-eyed pasty-skinned people within took much notice of the muscular short haired man carrying a rucksack. That is, not beyond the interested gaze given by cattle as they chew the cud and stare almost blankly at humans who come and go in their uncomprehending lives.

Colin ordered food. The mug of tea and three rounds of bacon sandwiches was fuel enough. The mix slid down his throat and sated his hunger. Another mug of char later, sunk with a battleship dose of sugar perked his brain into making the decision. He took out a pen and wrote in capitals on the last page of Claire's diary: 'OS HELM PRE-JUDGE FELON.'

If she survived, then maybe she would find the ins and outs of why or perhaps not of the why, he had chosen his path. Was it really ever his path? It was a path, but had he chosen it or it him? Part of him did not care, but the other part did, the part which was him when he was an innocent 13 years of age and too when he became an angry, very angry 16 year old. Yes, those parts did. Was it his mother's influence or that man, his non-father, who had come back to haunt him this year? He had no choice. The itch had to be scratched. The more he responded, the greater he felt affirmed. This was his mission. They were a different species and one to be rid of. The campaign of mayhem and fear he was causing had made the itch slightly more bearable.

By underground, he made his way to King's Cross Station. Peeling back the tape from the sealed clear plastic A4 envelope, he held the contents down with his forefinger and placed inside a blank card, inscribed with a personal note from him. Sealing the envelope afresh, he put it a newly purchased holdall and had it stored safely at the left luggage counter.

FIFTY

6.13 pm, Thursday, July 12, 2012 – the awakening was coming.

He caught the tube to Richmond. Seventeen stations and two lines later, he arrived. As he walked along the pavement running alongside the A307, the ambling pedestrians, many of which were face down and absorbed by the mesmerising glow of their phones, adeptly, intuitively perhaps, dodged the detritus of the day: two expertly placed chips projecting a 'V' sign from some drying dog shit and a greasy burger wrapper adhering itself around the peeling green railings and discarded chewed gum. ATM cash receipts, carelessly discarded, waited on the slabs to be kicked in their face by the brushing breeze of passing footsteps.

Passing a pizzeria Colin purchased two pizzas, just small enough to fit in his rucksack and continued on his short journey to the bed and breakfast he had booked previously. It was located on one of the side streets off Richmond Road. The shop facades, he thought, did little to inspire people to make purchases, and some with 'FOR SALE/LEASE' signs suggested several businesses had gone bust. Times were hard for shopkeepers and shoppers alike. Businesses needed something to boost their profile.

In his own way, Colin's presence boosted income for traders in the area, all keen to secure coinage in the guise of plastic to fill their dried out water table of depleted coffers. Some thought that they were greedily jumping on the 'ghoul' rush ride, profiteering as a result of the distasteful infamy the locality gained that summer by servicing the unfettered hunger of visitors drawn to the macabre. Others thought it was just good old-fashioned community spirit. Wasn't that what England was famed for?

Slinging his bag in the armchair and grabbing a bottle from the room's fridge, Colin sat on the windowsill and ate his fill of pizza before tossing the boxes and their remnants of burnt hardened edges to the floor. The beer tasted good. Another went down equally well. He leaned back against the wall and brought his knees up to his chin.

Daylight gradually gave way to twilight. Shoppers hurriedly gave way to the gathering noise of youth. He took out his newly bought clothes and laid them neatly on the dressing table adjacent to the en suite. Undressing, he retired early to bed. He welcomed warm memories and that of poetry, and ignored the dark night and day ahead that was scrambling desperately to climb up and clamber into bed with him.

Time had been well spent. All was planned. All was in motion. He had no family. He had done what he had done for good reasons. He gave thanks for what he was about to do. He did not imagine anyone else would thank him or forgive him. It was all too late anyway.

Ben, his dog, was asleep in the rear garden of his home. He was at peace now. Obediently, he had lain down on his side in the warm grass. His tail had beaten a soft continuous and happy thud onto the earth when Colin had nuzzled into his neck and whispered in his ear, 'Good boy. You've been a good boy.'

Yes, Ben had been happy in his last moments, blissfully unaware before his master had quickly and silently cut open his neck. Colin had held Ben whilst his warm body drifted slowly into oblivion. Yes, Ben's last day had been good. Colin's last night had been too. He did not expect to see another one. He had done his best for his mother and that after all, was all that mattered now.

FIFTY-ONE

The home phone rang. It made her jump. It was nearly 11 pm. Picking up the handset from the side pocket in her wheelchair, Monica answered, despite the display showing an unknown number was calling.

'Hello.'

Silence, apart from shallow breathing in the handset.

'Hello, George? George is that you?'

More breathing … the phone went dead.

It was quiet in the house. George had been gone for twelve hours or so. She had heard nothing more from him since his call. He had not answered when she had phoned earlier. He'd probably left his mobile on silent mode, forgetting he wasn't at home and therefore wouldn't disturb her when she took one of her many frequent naps during the day.

The house was warm. Monica shivered.

The phone rang again.

She jumped.

The ring was insistent. She did not want to answer it. Eventually the ringing stopped. The answering machine kicked in. The volume was turned to zero. The red light blinked, a message had been left. She did not want to pick it up.

Her hands felt clammy as she wheeled over to the answering machine, the light's steady and slow pulse was far behind the pace in her heart. She pressed play. Silence interspersed by

226

breathing and then a voice spoke. It was from a man's muffled voice talking on a speakerphone. He had a coarse London twang. Monica's heart was pushing itself to escape from her chest.

'Good evening, Mrs Abimelech. Perhaps you would prefer if I used your first name, Monica. Yes, Monica, I like that name.'

The man's voice slimed across her nerves.

'I have Tom. In case you're wondering, and you are, aren't you now, I can tell, I also have Claire. The game is almost up for them, my little game. I'll give you a clue. It's a puzzle. Say a prayer or two. I would if I were you.'

Pop music could be heard playing in the background.

The cold male voice continued. 'I had this premonition tonight. Let's just say I'll be seeing you and George soon, very soon.'

The man laughed. It was the kind of laugh that infects the youngest child when they find themselves winning a board game against their older siblings. Yet, this man's laugh was hollow and forced. It was as if the light of all life had been snuffed out and only darkness from the void emerged. The message stopped and the machine's electronic automated voice concluded.

'There are no more messages.'

A fuse blew and the entire house was pitched into blackness. Shadows darted like demons around Monica. Her hearing heightened. Her senses adapted. She fumbled with sweaty palms and fingers for her mobile phone, desperate for the safe haven of its glow. The casing slipped in her hand and fell to the floor. The front door handle whined slowly as it was pushed downwards. She pulled on the home phone. It was stuck in the side pocket. With a heave, it came out at speed and her clammy fingers lost traction on the plastic. It somersaulted off into the darkness clattering against something hard.

Darkness skewed the distance of space and confused her spatial memory of furniture in the room. Moving frantically forward, Monica's wheelchair collided with a standard lamp. The light bulb exploded when it made contact with the wooden floor. Monica's fear overcame her control and she let out a primordial scream before shouting long, high and loud, her voice piercing the night air.

'Help! Help me … Call the police!'

'Monica. Monica, it's me, George. Where are you? What's going on?'

'George. Thank-God it's you.' Her sobs echoed across the house. 'I thought … I thought it was him.'

The mini fob torch on George's key ring did for once, come in handy after all these years of redundancy. He found Monica sobbing uncontrollably halfway from the living room into the hall leading to the under stairs cupboard. She had not made it and would not have done if…

George got down on his knees, ignoring the broken glass cutting through the cloth of his trousers and hugged his wife deeply.

'It's alright darling.'

George's soothing guttural reassuring tone eventually eased her fear and distress. At first Monica's howls had rocketed. She was safe in George's arms and yet twisted with fear and worry hit by the hammer of that man's voice beating out his sinister message in her head. Their world was falling apart around them. Her rapid intakes of breath slowed. Her breathing took on a more regular and relieved rhythm. She was almost capable of speech now.

A loud banging on the front door and a neighbour's voice calling through the letterbox abruptly disrupted their universe; it was Jeremy from the house next door.

'Monica. George. Is everything alright?'

'I better go and answer it love. Won't be long,' George kissed her on the forehead and with stiff and bloodied knees got unsteadily to his feet.

As he opened the front door, Monica could hear the muffled words exchanged between the two men before George returned to her. She was no longer so distraught and when he came back asked George to fix the lights first. He said he would do that. Then they needed to talk. As it happened the trip switch had thrown itself and had automatically turned off all the power in the house. George would ask Measures Electrical to pop out to give the house the once over.

He hadn't liked the thought of leaving Monica alone by herself after sunset, but getting whisked off by the police for being in Claire's house had taken a long time for him to be believed, particularly as he begged them not to call Monica because of her heart condition and that plus worry about Tom missing. It had put them both on edge, he claimed. That was true. Eventually the police had gotten hold of Claire's father, who spoke to them and then to George.

"George was an old friend of the family, there was nothing to worry about," he had told them.

George agreed to pay the call out fees for the emergency window repairs and this final bit of negotiation satisfied the police that a burglary had not been underway and that he was for all his ineptness, guilty of only being an anxious father. Unfortunately, when George tried to persuade the police to take seriously the disappearance of Tom and now of Claire, they did not quite see it the way he did. So eventually in the face of exasperated officers, George, like Claire before him, gave up the attempts, albeit feeling extremely frustrated. As he took a taxi back to Iverna Gardens to collect his car, the mobile phone had rung. Claire's father, Andrew had called him back.

'George. It's Andrew here.'

'Andrew, thank God you've called. I didn't have your number and the police wouldn't give it to me.'

'They found me via a conference I'm attending, rather a long one, been here for over a week now. I'm thoroughly exhausted. I'll be glad to be back home. The conference ends tomorrow. Now tell me, what *is* going on?'

George brought in a pot of tea laced heavily with sugar into the living room. George's thinking was that the sugar content and some biscuits would help Monica get over her shock, so he tempted her with a small plate of her favourites. The steam rose from the tea as George poured the brew into two cups, the gurgling bubbling sound playing out comforting, reassuring, everyday noises. She looked pale and drawn. The cup shook in her trembling hands as she lifted it to her mouth, rippling the tea's surface and reflecting windblown sand dunes.

As directed by Monica, George listened to the voice message on the answering machine and as he did so, his face was sombre. His blood ran cold. The hairs on the back of his neck stood up. His back shivered. He did not move. No wonder Monica was in a state of shock.

Unsurprisingly, a call back was not possible. The number had been withheld. However, together they could reassure themselves. They could feel stronger. Two against one and strengthen the odds. Bravado perhaps, but they had to find courage from somewhere when faced with such an adversary. Neither of them were about to don a woolly jumper that's for sure. They were not ones to become lambs waiting for the predator. But their lives had been lived and whilst they had, they felt, several more decades before daisies took root in them both, Tom and Claire had yet to fully live theirs.

'What was the name of the detective that Claire saw last week? Was it Ethan? Devon? Bevan?' asked Monica.

George looked at her, his face blank. He was not one for remembering names, faces yes, but not names. She knew that, he was merely a white board for her memory to brainstorm.

'No those names don't sound right. What was it? Come on Monica!' she chided herself. 'Avon. Graven. Craven. Shaven. Got it!' she said triumphantly, 'It's Raven. Sure of it. Detective Sergeant Raven, CID, Metropolitan Police Service.

'Are you absolutely sure?' asked George.

'Absolutely!'

'We'd better give him a call then, see if he's interested in a missing person report this time. I'll try calling him now' said George.

'No George. I will,' said Monica asserting her independence. 'I was here when the call came through. I experienced the terror first hand. I think I'm best placed to convey the urgency of the situation don't you?'

'Well, but...'

'No I am best placed for this one George. Now, please pass me the phone.'

FIFTY-TWO

23:57 hours, Thursday, July 12, 2012 – Metropolitan Police Service

Three minutes to bloody midnight, thought Raven, and the report was still unfinished. Pastry flakes lay discarded across the plate. Some lay scattered on the carpet under the wheels of the office chair. The report had to be on Bulrush's desk early tomorrow morning. The results, if you could call them that, were frugal crumbs that probably would not have helped Hansel and Gretel find their way home. That said the work had pulled up a number of leads. Uniform had been sent out to probe further and report back to him. Surprisingly, or maybe not, given the sub-culture of gangs and youths in some places in London, about fifty-odd hunting knives had been bought, but only three sternum saws purchased. Of the latter, all three had been secured by obvious medical practices. Naturally, that did not preclude the possibility that the killer was in the medical profession, but if that was the case, a wider net had to be cast and there had not been time for that yet.

He had also been waiting to hear back from a chase on burglaries to see if any sternum saws had been stolen. He had asked Johnston, in records, to run the check and get back to him. In the end, by 21:30 hours, not having heard anything, Raven went down and collared Johnston before he slunk off for the night. The bastard was going to do the work tomorrow morning. So Raven had 'sat on him' there and then until he had finished off the search. It had not taken that long to do anyway, which made Raven even more irritated with Johnston's attitude. Some people like to sabotage for their own ends, careless of the consequences.

It was a good job that a check had been made too. There had been a burglary reported overnight on Tuesday, 8 May this year from a private hospital in the City of London, and a sternum saw had been taken. Interestingly, nothing else had been removed. No hunting knives reported stolen, but then again, would the people that owned them, want the police to know they were the 'proud owners' of one? Probably not, so Raven had sorted the list of who had brought what, when and where.

He was working on the assumption that the 'would be murderer' was also the sternum saw burglar. He looked for purchases made shortly before or after the theft. This gave him a list of five possible suspects, three of which had been seen by uniform and for the time being ruled out and two, had not been in when their homes had been visited. Raven had instructed the uniform night shift to call at their homes again. He had just taken a call to say one of the two, a guy called Davis had been seen and no leads there. He was a keen fisherman, had loads of rods and tackle in his shed, and at this stage, he did not give uniform or for that matter, Raven, any cause to doubt the veracity of his claims. That left one person to track down. He was not at his house. Raven told the patrol sergeant to have his bobbies 'stake' the place out overnight and stay there in case the suspect came back.

All of these points and steps taken were set out in the Bulrush report. Raven was exhausted. He had been clocking up the overtime hours, good for his bank balance, lousy for his love life, or lack of it. Frustrations abounded. Then there was Claire Yohanus. What he would give to ... boy, he shook his head, back to work, or he'd never get home and back again with some kip grabbed in-between.

The phone rang. 'DS Raven here.'

A woman's voice on the other end, 'Sergeant Raven, my name is Monica Abimelech.'

Jesus, I'll give it to Ms Claire bloody Yohanus, she'll try any angle at any time to get me to listen.

'I'm calling about my son, Tom – '

Raven cut abruptly across her. 'Look, Mrs Abimelech, I am sorry that you haven't seen your son for a while, but I really do not think there is cause for concern. I'm sure he'll turn up soon and everything will be okay.'

Monica continued as if Raven had not said a word, only pausing to let him finish his excuses. '… and about Ms Claire Yohanus, you see they are both missing now.'

Was this another tactic to secure police interest, Raven wondered. 'What do you mean she is missing as well?' Raven's voice was politely irritable. He was tired and stressed. Bloody games he could do without.

She had his interest now, almost. Perhaps he would listen properly. 'Sergeant, this evening I was at home by myself when I received a phone call at nearly eleven pm. A man left a message on the answering machine. The message was about Tom and Claire. If you wait on the phone just a moment, I'll play the message back to you. I think then you might agree that they are in trouble, serious danger I fear, and they need your help.'

The dark side and coldness of a man's voice reverberated down the phone line and into Raven's ear. He sat there listening intently. All trace of exhaustion left him as adrenaline kicked in.

'You see Sergeant, that's why my husband and I are worried. Now do you understand?'

'Indeed, I do Mrs Abimelech. Let me have your home phone number, the name of your telephone company and I'll see if we can trace who made the call and where from.'

'Our home number is 01865 125 521. Our phone company is a local provider, Oxford Telephone Company.'

Raven also wrote down Monica's address, promising he'd arrange via the local police force to have a marked car sent around to their house and that he would look to sort out round the clock cover for them. Before finishing the call, he started his apology.

'Mrs Abimelech? Just one more thing before I go. I am sorry that we did not take your son's disappearance seriously. I hope you understand that with so many people allegedly missing every year, and most turning up again pretty soon thereafter then – '

It was Monica's turn to cut across the conversation, not something she would ordinarily do, but these were, after all, extraordinary circumstances. 'I understand Sergeant. Let's hope you can make up for lost time and make one mother happy by finding my son and Ms Yohanus alive.'

When he replaced the receiver, he paused for several moments, his left palm still on the handset before picking it up to make another call. The first one was across an internal government network outside of the organisation he worked for.

'It's me. I think it has started. The great days are arising...'

Ten minutes later, he hung up and dialled another internal number, the Metropolitan Police Service switchboard. 'Raven here, number 2486; may I have Commander Bulrush's home number please? Thank-you.'

Raven made the call to Bulrush's home within the first hour of Friday, July 13, 2012. It was going to be a long bloody day he thought.

There are times when one might wonder if thoughts cause the outcome, act as premonitions or are merely a perverse collision of coincidences where individuals and their pathways meet. Sometimes, though, there are bigger things afoot.

DAVOS – SWITZERLAND

THE FLEA

By John Donne (1572-1631)

… Cruel and sudden, hast thou since
Purpled thy nail, in blood of innocence?
In what could this flea guilty be,
Except in that drop which it sucked from thee?
Yet thou triumph'st, and say'st that thou
Find'st not thyself, nor me the weaker now;
'Tis true, then learn how false, fears can be;
Just so much honour, when thou yield'st to me,
Will waste, as this flea's death took life from thee.

FIFTY-THREE

Friday, July 13, 2012 – Davos, Switzerland

A population of just over 11,000 people live high in the Swiss Alps. Inspirational Davos is the highest city in Europe, nearly 1,600 metres above sea level. It is a small faraway city, a magnet since World War II for international medical research, specialist clinics, laboratories and private hospitals. No wonder Davos is perceived as a city of knowledge. It hosts the high profile annual conference for the World Economic Forum which brings together elite individuals in academia, business, industry, media, politics and publishing, seemingly to work together in shaping global agendas. Davos is a city of power. It has a powerful profile, and international reach. It was a reach far bigger than its size would ever suggest and thus possessed the visible camouflage of something familiar that is never noticed. Welcome to Davos, the chameleon.

Good things have opposites.

Behind the curtain of probity in Davos lies a vast global communications infrastructure built solely for the Fourth Reich's Network. Raven's internal call had been a mistake. The Network had picked up and monitored his conversation via its communications behemoth akin to the likes of GCHQ in the UK and the National Security Agency (NSA) in the United States. The Network's communication infrastructure and reach, shadows and taps into the infrastructure of other agencies, much like the linking of personal computers challenge the processing power of supercomputers. No parliamentary or senate committees act as overseers and protectors of individual privacy and liberty. Such terms as these do not exist in the Network's lexicon. This leviathan is in the hands of puppeteers. When Raven's call had finished and the recording was later played back to the senior commanding officer, a judgment was effortlessly made. A flea that breaks the skin is no lover, blood relationships must be severed.

'They have broken the silence expected of all. Eliminate them.'

LONDON

THE CHARGE OF THE LIGHT BRIGADE

By Alfred Lord Tennyson (1809-1892)

I

Half a league, half a league,
Half a league onward,
All in the valley of Death
Rode the six hundred.
'Forward, the Light Brigade!
Charge for the guns!' he said:
Into the valley of Death
Rode the six hundred.

FIFTY-FOUR

04:30 hours, Friday, July 13, 2012 – Riverside, grounds and ruins of The Wray Inn

In the early hours, the early risers, the steadfast, the fearless and those who were frightened, but courageous enough, joined the pre-dawn gathering. In the half-light, the figurehead for London Pride stood on the soapbox and said these words.

'We start this walk today together. We walk today to remember August Kilterton who was brutally murdered in the grounds of this warm and friendly Inn and Eric Courtish, who died cruelly in the same fashion at his home in Friars Mead, Manchester Road, Millwall.

'And we walk today to show the world that their deaths and the devastation wrought on this inn and the livelihoods destroyed, will not pass with indifference by us or any other decent people.

'We stand here today to recognise the right we have as gay men – in fact the right of all people who are members of the LGBT community – to live our lives free from the shackles of prejudice and fear, and to live in harmony within communities wherever we are on this earth.

'For we know this, do we not, and we say this, do we not, that each and every person on this earth shares one common humanity and for which by right, should expect, give and receive a common humanity.

'So now, I say to you this … Let us remember together. Let us walk together. Let us be proud together. For in this moment, on this day, a brighter day will dawn.'

The short speech, timed to perfection, coincided with dawn giving way to the radiance of a brand-new day at 04:59 hours. The crowd made up of women and men and numbering in their hundreds cheered and applauded the Right Honourable Bruce Catzgill MP. He looked upon everybody and acknowledged each and every one of them. As he stood there allowing the sun's rays to warm him, he bowed his head, closed his eyes, and prayed. Believers and non-believers followed suit.

Their courage was stirred and in this spirit of belief in humanity, it was difficult to accept they were quixotic. But we all have to dream. Perhaps one day, yes one day, it will be so, as it was, ever is and ever shall be. Yet in the meantime, in the quotidian nature of life, if we look for it, the silence among them and between them was a reaffirming bond. It was one which they would need ever more so, as later events assailed them.

For now, though, quietly at first, a lone woman's voice started singing *Let it Be*. Her beautiful folk singing was added to, as little by little, others joined in, until everyone together was connected physically, holding hands and arms, swaying in harmony together.

It was magnificent.

The advance guard of police outriders moved off with their lights flashing providing an advance warning to oncoming traffic. Bruce Catzgill and a small cohort of people – friends and acquaintances around him led the way. As the colourful crowd moved off with their placards and banners, they were accompanied and supported by a rousing marching band.

Little notice was taken of the Wray Inn's last survivors. Out of the seventeen daffodils dancing in the light breeze, which unlike others had miraculously survived the devastation of the pub, only one had opened. Only one was opened fully to the eyes of the world, eager to live its life and bring colour to others' days. Would this one flower, standing tall and proud, live the longest or would its bright presence be plucked away before its life was ready to end?

A five and half-hour journey on foot was ahead of them. They crossed the Thames at Richmond Bridge. As they did so, boats travelling underneath sounded their klaxons in support. The walkers' pride in what they were doing increased.

As they walked along Paradise Road, bystanders stopped to watch them, the majority breaking into spontaneous applause. As the walk progressed along its winding way to the Greenwich Foot Tunnel, some took up the unseen call, and left what they had planned for the day and joined the procession. This increased the walk's numbers, seemingly having multiplied into their thousands. The basket of generosity flourished and expanded.

Beautiful things happened. Bakeries, takeaways, and street-side cafés shared freely their offerings. It strengthened the weary and rayed smiles on the faces of the children that had joined in the journey with their families.

The merry throng mixed and talked together. Soon many realised that they came from all walks of life, embraced all aspects of sexuality, originated from a multitude of races and from many religions and none. It was difficult not to believe in those moments that harmony was indeed possible on Earth.

There were also times in the long hours of the walk when people fell silent; from the front to the back it swept over them, undulating as it moved. The silence was good. It put people back in touch with their inner selves and allowed them to reflect on the nature of their lives.

Gradually, as if some hidden voice flowed between them, as indeed often happens when people commune in a common purpose, they assimilated a veiled knowledge. The more they did this thing for love, for the good of others, the freer they became in themselves. Hope had commandeered an anchor in their lives, one that despite the trials and tribulations ahead would remain strongly within many of them always.

The band at the front struck up another rousing march and the pace for a while quickened as they passed by Clapham Common. Runners stopped and watched the colourful parade. Youths playing football came to the sidelines of the park and cheered.

'Good on you all.'

Does it take suffering, disaster, injustice and distress to bring diverse people together? The sense of well-being and well wishing increased. The police relaxed. So far so good, what could possibly go wrong that they had not already thought of?

By around 10.30 am, some five hours into their journey together, they arrived at Creek Road, which is near the Cutty Sark and the Greenwich Foot Tunnel. From there, they would follow its path as it led them underneath the Thames. In another half hour or so they would arrive at Friars Mead, their destination and which, would mark the end of their bond.

FIFTY-FIVE

Friday, July 13, 2012 – Friars Mead and Manchester Road, Millwall, London

In one, twos and threes, men and women had come, browsing idly in shops and stalls, some buying a few items here and there, a book from a charity shop, or a teapot from somewhere else; just trinkets to add to their bags they carried, a masquerade to hide their real intent.

Customers moved slowly, unhurriedly and as is often the case on such pleasant heart-warming days, individuals smiled at each other in passing – locals and strangers – all communing in consumer friendship. The retailers, and the owners of local pubs and cafés were chuffed as more visitors had been drawn to the area on this day, each seemingly happy to part with their money in return for the eclectic array of goods and services available in and around the Isle of Dogs.

Even a spontaneous game of baseball had pitched up at Mudchute Park. That was a first. And again in ones, twos and threes, the happy relaxed shoppers made their way lazily, as those in no hurry often do, across the park to watch. Eventually, if truth be told, there must have been some six hundred. Most watched, although some joined in the game playing in a slow energy releasing, conserving kind of way. It was such a hot day.

Two helicopters hovered nearby overhead in Manchester Road, the shuttering sound spilling over into the air space of the Park.

One contained the police, the other a TV camera crew. Their attention focused on the unravelling story stretching out along the road. It was almost like a division sign between two ways of seeing reality, with a police rank and file cordon providing the line which divided them.

'Here we are hovering above Manchester Road, near the junction of Friars Mead, the location where Mr Eric Courtish, a local gay man, was found brutally murdered last Sunday. As viewers will remember, another gay man, August Kilterton was found murdered in the Wray Inn car park near Richmond, in Twickenham.

'Pride announced on Wednesday that they would march the sixteen miles from Twickenham to here as a mark of remembrance of the lives of these two men. As a possible consequence of that announcement, which some commentators argue was merely a match waiting to ignite further displays of prejudice, the pub was burnt to the ground by a masked gang. Customers were savagely beaten and a message was daubed on its sign warning Pride to stay out of Millwall.

'Well clearly the explicit threat in that message has been ignored as we see people within the Pride march making their way up the road towards the line of police. The march is led by the openly gay MP, Bruce Catzgill, who has been in a long-term relationship for the past 15 years. As the camera zooms in, viewers should be able to see the band, which seems to be striking up plenty of music and by the look of things, everyone is singing their hearts out. It's a shame we cannot hear them.'

Oblivious to the unfortunate faux pas, the TV presenter continued her overview of how battle lines seemed to be shaping up.

'If you have just joined us, I can tell you now, that a significant number of people, including families with young children, parted from the main grouping of Pride marchers just after coming out of the Greenwich Foot Tunnel. My guess, from the scene below us, suggests they may have heard the noise of threatening sounds coming from the hundreds of anti-gay protesters who are being blockaded from advancing towards the march by a line of police and mounted officers.

'Now, as the helicopter's camera pans to the right, just off Manchester Road, viewers should be able to see a small park. In the midst of a potentially violent confrontation, a baseball game is being played, avidly supported by the look of things, by several hundred people. This surely must rank as one of those bizarre eccentricities of British life. Life carries on regardless of what is going on. It seems to thrive in this little pocket of the United Kingdom...'

The TV coverage switched to the studio and focused on the presenter and a newly arrived guest.

'I'm joined this morning by Commander Malcolm Bulrush of the Metropolitan Police Service ... Commander Bulrush, in the face of the widely reported views about the real and the present threat of violent disorder today, why didn't the police ban the Pride march and also use public order powers to prevent the gathering of anti-gay protesters in Millwall?'

The police helicopter filmed the large crowd of mainly white English manhood bunching together in knotted formation as they marched down Manchester Road towards Friars Mead, all seemingly intent on confrontation. A line of mounted horse police officers stood abreast the road facing them. Behind this first rank stood a three row deep wedge of riot-shielded officers, all intent on a rigid defence.

As the Pride crowd and its recent followers moved on past Millwall Park and into Manchester Road, they could hear, above the music from the band, the feral visceral chants hunting though the air to find their ears. It was difficult not to feel apprehension.

Families wished their newly met compatriots well and peeled off, safely away. The young children looked confused. Better for them that they were too young and remained too innocent to know; thus as it should be. The bonded crowd of marchers reduced now to hundreds, some six hundred in all, marched around the bend in Manchester Road, near Blythe Close. They could clearly see some 500 metres or so away the police attempting to kettle men bent on venting their hatred. They could hear the baying for their blood.

When the pit of hatred saw them, they chanted. 'You'll not get our arse, but we'll get yours, yes, we'll get yours.'

Some of the anti-gay protestors threw bottles and bricks over the heads of the police, whilst others pushed and shoved the nearby black railings until the bars came away. As spears, they were propelled through the air, some entering the chests of horses. The horses panicked and into the disarray the knotted bunch of thugs bulged forward into a charge clashing with police in a hard thud of anger and pent up hatred. Smoke grenades were thrown.

In the mayhem, the Pride music died away. Yet, they all stayed strong together, determined to stand their ground and mark the bookend of this their journey to recognise the place where Eric Courtish had died. Amidst the swaying lines of police that held firm against the onslaught, MP Bruce Catzgill once again took to his soapbox to address the crowd. This time he had a megaphone. This time he had to shout. Knowing that the TV helicopter crew would be filming it all – the riot and the gathering of their peaceful walk, he took his step towards a place in history. He must stand firm. He must stand calmly and show the world that fear and prejudice always diverts freedom down blind back alleys and the dead end streets of the past – love was here to stay.

'We've made it! ... Well done to you all.'

The crowd of followers applauded.

248

'We've come a long way, not just today in the heat, but in the arduous decades long past when men and women before us had to closet their lives, but not now, not ever again. This is a freedom we will not give up.'

Everyone cheered.

'Today we all felt, we all saw and we all heard, the genuine affection and love of complete strangers as we walked the sixteen miles to arrive here in Manchester Road to mark the time when Eric Courtish was found dead, murdered, this time last Sunday – 11.15 am. He, along with August Kilterton had a right to life and to live as they did. As we all do. Behind me you can all hear and see the blind hatred that seeks to wipe away our humanity, to take away our right to be who we are. We are part of humanity. We are here to stay.'

The Pride marchers roared their approval with rousing cheers.

'Mr Courtish and Mr Kilterton lost their lives merely for living theirs. In the face of such a bitter pill, I say to you this … we should all be prepared to lay down our lives by fighting for our rights to live freely. The murderer who carried out the heinous crimes seeks to instil fear in us all. He seeks to snuff out our existence. He may succeed with some of us, but he cannot kill all of us and nor can they that bay behind us.'

The crowd erupted with a strong, unified shout. 'No!'

'As an MP I stand for democracy. Yet, as a person of the rainbow, as you – men and women of the world and the people who walked with us today, and all of those who showed us their humanity and gave us their offerings today, we all, yes we all, stand together for democracy.

'We stand for the right of people to be heard. And yes, we stand for those behind me, baying for our blood, for their right to be heard. But what I will not stand for. What we should not stand for, is chaos, where the rule of just law, as we have now, is threatened by those blighted by their own ignorance or blinded by their own dogma. After all, as human beings, all we are asking, as I'm confident, all of you are asking, is to live and, if lucky enough, as I am, is to love and to be loved in return.'

The colourfully clothed throng hooted and cheered their agreement, with many shouting out, 'Yes. That's right.'

Bruce Catzgill was pleased. The words, the response, it had all worked perfectly. 'So come, let us sing now – loud and clear – let us sing out strong – *All we need is love*.'

The crowd cheered and applauded. On cue from Bruce, the band struck out the notes.

As the clarinet and trumpets played the penultimate ending of the song and as the crowd sung loud and clear, as laughter, smiles, and harmony grew, absurd as it was in the midst of the violence being thrown against the wall of police, an avalanche from another direction broke upon the Pride revellers. Bruce Catzgill MP saw them coming as the last notes were hit. His face broke into confusion, and then fear, as the tumultuous wave of violence broke upon them all.

The baseball game – players and crowd – metamorphosed into something ugly and evil. It struck the Pride marchers from behind. In hindsight, the testosterone-fuelled thugs tearing down railings and hurling make do spears and bricks, were mere kittens playing at violence.

A muscle bound man with tattoos across his hands grabbed Bruce Catzgill by the arms and pulled him off the soapbox. At first, Bruce instinctively tried to pull away, but as he turned to look into the eyes of his would be assailant – the valet who regularly cleans his car – a feeling of relief spread across his face.

'Quick,' roared the valet above the din, 'follow me! I'll get you out of here.'

And so, like a desperate baby elephant holding onto the tail of its parent, Bruce allowed himself to be dragged to safety. As they weaved and shoved their way through the bedlam and the quivering reed of people, blood and brains splattered onto the MP's face. A poor unfortunate had fallen victim to a baseball bat that had been swung heavily against his head and had smashed open his skull. Other marchers were screaming, shrieking, running and falling in chaotic directions, frantically trying to avoid the bloodbath, but the avalanche of violence was suffocating. Knives tore into necks and backs, slashed faces and severed arteries. Bones were broken, and faces stove in. It was like a gruesome scene being relayed from a wildlife documentary filming the culling of seal pups. People were being battered and stabbed to death.

Overhead the two helicopters were powerless observers. The shielded ranks of foot and mounted officers were themselves in danger of being overrun by the violence on top of them. For them to turn and defend the subsequent attack on the Pride march, which had flanked their lines would have exposed their own safety further. Hobson's choice faced the police operational commander on this day. Snap decisions were made by the officers on the ground and of their own accord they turned and charged into the baseball-bat wielding affray.

Through blood, spittle and screams, he was twisted and turned as they wove through the bloodshed. Bruce's mind was unable to absorb the reality that confronted his eyes. The velocity and ferocity had never been seen before on mainland Britain. And so it was with indescribable relief that he and his saviour arrived in the relative calm of upper Amsterdam Road. The distant sounds of street war seemed to inhabit another world now. The silence in this road after the battle, although it still raged, was almost deafening. Boats chugged along the Thames. Bruce became aware of the heat from the sun again.

Normality, the humdrum, was not such a bad place to be after all.

Bruce took out his mobile phone. He had only one thing in mind right now, to call his love. His love had left missed calls and a voice message. He returned the call.

'I'm safe! I just wanted you to know…' He took a lungful of air. '… to know that I'm okay.'

'I can see. The helicopter TV camera crew are filming you now. The presenters are talking about the hero that saved you.' Francis spoke in his calm and deep voice. Its sound never failed to make Bruce feel safe.

Bruce looked up and saw the helicopter high above him. He looked behind him and at the valet who was kneeling down unzipping his rucksack. They both exchanged smiles with one another. Bruce walked towards the river to take in the green serenity of the water.

Francis said, 'Wave to me.'

'Don't … I'd love to, you know that, but I can't, it would seem so frivolous to the outside world.'

'I know. I was joking!'

'Oh, of course,' said Bruce, 'I'm still in shock, I guess, can't take it all in, what's happened and …'

'I love you Bruce. You're safe. I can't believe it. I'm so … Oh my God. Bruce! Bruce!' Francis's deep voice screamed and bellowed even as the phone flew from Bruce's hand and somersaulted backwards above his head.

The garrotte around Bruce's neck was twisted sharply and savagely around his throat. And with two kills behind him, the removal of the heart by his killer was over in seconds. No finesse, there was no time. With the bloodied hands of a field surgeon, Colin thrust the MP's heart above his head and shook it insanely towards the eye of the helicopter's camera lens. The presenter had ceased to speak; the sound of someone vomiting splattered the airwaves.

Colin, with one final play to the camera – for infamy and fear – leaned back, outstretched his arm, the way of javelin throwers and launched the dripping organ in an arc. Millions of viewers watched it splash without dignity into the Thames. You Tube traffic ballooned on this day.

FIFTY-SIX

11:15 hours, Friday, July 13, 2012 – Harry's Place, Thames Path, London

How strange it was that in the past five years they had endeavoured, and indeed had, lived their lives separately and independently, and yet, the invisible beat of their hearts had always been, unbeknown to them, in rhythm together. They carried on whispering to one another, not because they were conscious of Harry's camera recording every word they said or watching every movement they made; indeed in their shock and focus on each other, they were not aware of it. In one small way, their ignorance of its presence was good as it gave them the illusion of private intimacy even though they existed in the most grotesque and bizarre of surroundings. In reality, the whispering chimed in with the energy that Tom had left in his voice. For Claire, it mirrored the closeness of her intimacy with him, and naturally, without thinking, she had matched the level of his.

The hours and days of torture had naturally taken their toll on his body and his reserves. They clung to one another physically and emotionally, absorbing the intensity of each other's presence. Tom's breath was slow and at times laboured. The bleeding had stopped and crests of scabby dried blood pockmarked his skin.

'Do you feel ready to die Tom?' she asked.

'In the moments before I knew you were here, I longed for death; yes, I was ready. And you?'

'I can't say that I feel ready,' said Claire. 'I feel oddly disassociated with this situation, as if this horrible reality isn't real. Part of me feels that I'm not really here. It almost feels as if I'm an actor holding a mask in front of her face and am looking down upon two fellow performers locked in a love and death embrace. Strangely, though, I feel quite calm, almost serene. I don't want to die, but know we soon will. Yet, I'm happy, content in the knowledge that I'm with you, that I've found you.

'It has meant so much to know that of all the times my intuition had told me you love me, it was true. Knowing that now, I can honestly say, that being here with you is the most wonderful place for me to be on Earth. I know that may sound insane, it most probably is, and yet it isn't ...'

She paused to wipe away a tear running from the corner of her eye.

'If you had died without me being here, and if we had not had the opportunity to speak honestly to each other as we have done so over the past several hours, nor had you proposed to me and for me to have said yes ... all of these things I would not have touched or known about ... but I know my heart would have missed the knowing, and the seeing, and the hearing and the being with you, for the rest of my life.'

Tom squeezed her hands and smiled.

'I understand. I no longer wish to die either. Being here with you reminds me of why I so want to live. The torture, the pain and the sheer brutality of Harry has rocked my faith. Part of me feels like Peter, I've been put to the test and been found wanting. I lost my hope and renounced God. And now I know your presence here is a gift that God has given us both. A chance, our only chance perhaps we would have taken to speak honestly, openly with no reservations, nothing held back, to tread the path of my mistakes, to hear your words of forgiveness, to feel the joy of being next to you in my last moments, I was able …'

Tears welled up and he choked back words.

Tom corrected himself. 'I am able to be fully me. And yet I wish with all the power of my heart that you were not here. That I could know you were safe and would go on to live without me. That would be the greatest gift I wish I could give you.'

'No,' she said. 'Don't. I wouldn't want such a gift. You are the gift. To die knowing you want me is the most precious offering I could ever have received.'

Claire looked deep into Tom's eyes and said these words. 'Love is always ready to excuse, to trust, to hope, and to endure whatever comes.'

'I Corinthians,' he replied, 'you are so right and so wonderful, my lovely, lovely woman.'

To hear a man say "my woman" would have under any other circumstances almost caused Claire to froth at the mouth, for she was no chattel of a man, some mere possession of his. Yet when Tom said those words, she knew by her saying a resounding yes, to be with him that she was his woman and in turn, he was her man. And that did not sound offensive, or possessive, or controlling. To give each other the gift of the other is the greatest anyone can offer. She knew that now. She was confident. It felt good, for it was good.

Claire responded, 'Yes, I am, my lovely, lovely man.'

The grace given to them in these final moments was sufficient to sustain them, to endure whatever might come next.

It was not long coming.

A movement beyond the door's window caught their eyes. Harry was walking towards the entrance carrying what ominously looked to be a circular saw. As he entered the room, twirling the plug from part of the extended cable, he looked excitedly at them both, his artwork.

'Hello you two love birds, I hope you've appreciated what I've given you, that is, time to reconcile, make it up; all lovey-dovey now are we? Good to see that you've made good use of my little love blanket.'

He smiled knowingly at Claire. Her face, this time remained impassive. She had not told Tom. What was the point of it all? It might have caused more heartache than he could bear. Why increase his suffering? And she, she had found healing in the externalisation of her feelings, in the nursing of Tom and in the reciprocity they had shared in sharing their love for one another. Had they lived, she would have told him. He would have loved her through the anger and the raw spleen of emotions she knew she would feel over the rape, if she had allowed herself to touch them. Conversely, she was relieved that apart from his version of cryptic hints, Harry had not chosen, yet anyway, to tell Tom either. And Tom was too weak to pick up the crude clues or lewdness from his voice. She prayed it would stay that way.

Harry walked over to the counter and plugged the saw in. He turned it on and then off. The blade had spun sharply into life. As its revolutions and menacing high-pitched sound ebbed slowly away, he spoke.

'I guess you both know what is going to happen now, well, not precisely, but you know enough that neither of you will be alive for too much longer. Your suffering will soon be at an end.'

Harry smiled at them expectantly, almost looking as if he had anticipated a word of thanks or round of applause. Instead, he shrugged his shoulders. Taking the fine black marker from his pocket, he walked over to them and removed the blanket covering them both. She looked juicer every time he laid eyes on her. It would be a shame to cut off the relationship, but now he had whetted his appetite for fear with Tom's mother, he had lost interest in the game with these two. He got so easily bored.

That was one of his many problems, but like the others stacked up inside of him now, did Harry bother? Did he fuck.

Turning to his friend Fear who had his arm around Harry's face and words, he explained his plans to create a poster out of them both. Harry could see that they tried to be brave, and indeed they were he thought, incredibly so, but the squeezing of each other's hand, the colour drained from their faces, told him fear was eating into them. That felt good. Harry knew then, without doubt, that he was the Alpha and he was the Omega.

He enjoyed too watching their fear turn to anger and back to fear again, when he told them about his late night phone call to Tom's parents.

'That's right Tom. When you're glued together forever with Claire, your parents will join me here too.'

'May God forgive you,' Tom hoarsely whispered.

Harry laughed.

'You bastard fucking maniac,' shouted Claire.

'And for that,' he looked at Claire, 'I'll track down your father later. He's very easy to find. As he's so keen on in-vitro, I might introduce him, bit by bit...' he always smiled at his own jokes, '... to some petri dishes so he can see for himself what it's like to be on the receiving end of a medical experiment.'

'What on God's earth created you? You sick fuck.'

Claire spat into his face. The saliva dripped off his right eyelid before he wiped it quickly away.

'You fucking bitch.'

Harry cursed again as he laid a boot into Claire's rib cage. A sharp snapping sound heralded the arrival of broken bones. Claire whelped in pain.

With a glimpse of his voice returned, Tom raised its volume before he collapsed back against the floor.

'Leave her alone Harry. For God's sake, you've won; you've got us in your complete power, just stop.'

Harry had swung his boot back to give her another one for luck. He'd won. The man, the proto-priest had admitted it. Sweet words; Harry's boot returned to the floor. What the heck. He had won.

Claire held the right-hand side of her rib cage. The pain made her body want to double up. The force of Harry's boot had lifted her up off the ground and across the floor away from Tom.

Tom tried to reach Claire, to give some hint of comfort that he was there, but he could not muster the strength to move and touch her.

When Claire's immediate pain had subsided, she meekly obeyed Harry's instructions. He told her to lay flat on her back with her arms down by her sides, her legs straight out, but slightly apart.

Tom lay there without a morsel of strength left to call upon and looked sideways at them both, his head lolling to one side. He was verging on losing consciousness. He watched as Harry straddled Claire's body, stood over the top of her and looked up and down at her nakedness. Harry's booted feet were planted either side of her waist. His eyes looked as if they were consumed by carnal thoughts. Tom had seen that look before when he had stood in front of Bishop Ferguson for confession. And like Tom, although he had done so in words, she fought back.

As Harry started to kneel down and moved to pull her legs further apart, she knew then what he intended. Despite the pain, Claire's adrenaline moved her body quickly. A feral cat strikes hard when trapped. She brought her right knee up with storm force nine velocity knocking Harry's balls into his stratosphere. His body lurched forward and he crashed headlong against the wall with a loud thwack before rolling off to one side and away from Claire.

Harry raged above his own pain.

259

'That's it you fucking bitch. I was going to chloroform you both so you'd feel no pain and I'd get a nice neat cut. Well, fuck that idea. This first poster is going to be a bit fucking abstract now.'

Harry, breathing hard, grabbed Claire by the top of the head and pulled her viciously across the room by her hair, her scalp stretched painfully to meet his grip.

Tom tried to lift himself up, but the strength to do so was never in the room.

'No Harry! Don't.'

Tom's hoarse voice was drowned out by Claire's screams. Her body kicked and thrashed wildly, but she was no match for Harry's strength and bulk. Tom collapsed to the floor powerless to intervene.

'Stop Harry, please stop. Oh God, where are you? I beg you.'

Claire's body was slapped harshly onto the cold stainless steel table. Claire struggled. She kicked out. She even managed to catch Harry's face with her fist, the connection ineffectual against his towering strength. Harry backhanded her with his knuckles thwacking into her cheekbone. She yelped in pain, the rings on his fingers tore across her face. As the back of her head jolted backwards – skull and skin smacking against metal – the will to fight on weakened in her. But she fought on.

A short sharp right jab from Harry's club of a fist, which was thrust downwards harshly into the centre of Claire's brow and nose put, paid to her struggle. This was no contest; she was the flea on his skin. She was ultimately harmless to Harry. He knew that, but oh how he enjoyed this fight, more than he realised he would.

Despite her attempts to side swipe his chin, claw at his face and even force her fingers into his eyes, Harry was able to wrench her arms, force open her legs, and tie all four of her limbs to the bloodthirsty corners of the table. With red scar lines running vividly down across his face like an unevenly ploughed field and with sweat beading on his forehead, Harry sucked in a huge lungful of air.

He was triumphant.

'Right, you bitch. Welcome to fucking hell.'

He turned around and put his apron on. Slowing down now, he restored order in himself and tied the bow neatly as he had done so before, during the many times he had worked on Tom. There was always the comfort of routine to ground him. He selected a CD by the Police and popped it in the player. This was going to be good, fucking good. The song *Roxanne* boomed across the room.

FIFTY-SEVEN

11:33 hours, Friday 13 July, 2012 – Amsterdam Road, Millwall, London

Bruce Catzgill's body lay torn open and lifeless. The garrotte scored deeply into his skin. The surgical saw lay on its side across the road near his body. An office worker had been standing at the upstairs window, her mouth agape until a silent and then piercing scream cut across her work mates' desk tops. Her mug of coffee fell from her hands and bounced across the carpet spilling its contents. It was just like the MP's blood had done, she later thought.

Grabbing his rucksack, Colin ran to Harry's parked car where he had left it the evening before. The wheels screeched as it pulled away. He had one more delivery to make. Ten minutes later across two roundabouts, and through the Limehouse Link, he arrived.

11:43 hours – Harry's Place, Thames Path, London

Harry laughed. The music blared in the room. Claire struggled like a bull with a cowboy riding her. The ties had kept her still enough for him to get the joy of drawing a long, if not straight black line down her forehead, and over the entire middle of her body, including that tasty mound of hers. He would make her suffer now. Good and proper.

Getting out of Harry's car, Colin slung the rucksack over his shoulders and slid the knife neatly in its sheaf within the small of his back.

'This one's for you Mum.'

Harry's home was impressive. It cast a shadow over Colin's face as he banged fiercely on the front door.

'Harry. It's me, Col. I've brought your car back.'

As Harry picked up the circular saw, fingered its teeth and was about to push the switch forward to on, the front door's intercom by the counter blurted out. It was a man's voice. Looking up at the screen, Harry saw his employee at the door.

'What the fuck now?'

He put the saw on the counter and turning to Claire said, 'Don't be cut up. I'll do you later.'

Harry hung up his apron. Eager now that he had remembered. He was bent on collecting his freshly valeted car, of that, he was certain. As Harry opened the front door, he was greeted by Colin wearing rainbow coloured clothes.

'What the fuck are you wearing?' Harry said, laughing and exaggerating every word.

Harry's red trammelled face told Colin enough of what he needed to know. Pulling the knife out of its sheath, he lunged forward and thrust it deep into Harry's stomach. The warm skin swamped the tattooed knuckles of his hand. Such was the force of Colin's attack that Harry staggered backwards. Colin's powerful forward footsteps pushed Harry off his balance. Colin tore the knife upwards into Harry's rib cage.

Harry collapsed on the hallway floor, the royal blue carpet turning purple as its weave blended with his gushing blood. Colin kneeled on Harry's stomach, the weight of his body and the sharpness of his kneecap squashing Harry's intestines. Harry screamed in agony.

'Where is she?' shouted Colin, his voice exploding in Harry's face. 'Where's that reporter, Claire Yohanus?'

Harry laughed as he coughed up blood. 'Fuck you.' He spat in Colin's face.

'No fuck you, you bastard!'

And with volcanic anger erupting as he avenged his mother and killed his father again and again, Colin cut savagely and deeply across Harry's throat until he had almost severed his head.

Sirens in the distance, lots of them, pierced the background silence outside. The last page had almost been turned. Quickly searching the building, it did not take Colin long to come across Harry's monitoring system. The weeping from the woman and the resistant struggles to break free would have been futile. He hadn't been too late. He had saved her. The male body on the floor was motionless, difficult to see if he was alive or dead.

The sirens drew nearer. Colin found his way to the lift. The doors slid silently open. He pressed the down symbol, the doors effortlessly closed and the lift sunk slowly to the basement as if a toy submarine was sinking to the bottom of the bath. Childhood memories surfaced.

Claire heard the footsteps running back into the cell. Harry was back, it was over.

'I hope you burn in hell you sick fucking bastard,' she shouted.

Fear and anger expressed in her expletives turned to shock as a panting muscular and flamboyantly dressed man ran towards her. Blood was soaked across his clothing and still wet blood trickled down his forearms and over his tattoos.

'Stay away from me!' Claire's voice shrieked out across the cell. Her arms and legs thrashed wildly in pointless efforts to break free.

'I'm not here to hurt you,' shouted Colin, hoping to be heard above her screams for help. 'Stay still so I'll release your right wrist. The rest you can do yourself.'

Claire's body shook violently as she looked into this bloodstained man's face. This saviour started to untie her bonds, which held her to this bloodletting table. She allowed herself to believe what was happening was true. The surreal was true.

When he had released her right wrist, Colin took hold of Claire's hand and spoke.

'Whatever else you hear about me, please remember this, not everyone has a choice.'

He then ran off, leaving Claire's palm and fingers sticky from congealing blood. She looked across at Tom, he was unconscious. Quick now, she had to be quick. She grimaced in pain, but anger and fear drove her on. Harry could yet be alive. The door was ajar. Escape was in their grasp. She panicked when she heard several heavy feet pounding towards the cell. She had to release the last tie holding her left ankle. To get this far and ... no it couldn't be over, not yet, nearly free, and by hell then she could face the new threat. She refused to waste vital seconds looking around to see who or what was heading their way.

Men's voices shouted out, 'All clear here. Wait.'

There was silence as the thudding feet froze. Claire held her breath instinctively.

'Rear exit door open. Target has left the building; he is running away towards the playing fields. I say again, the target has left the building.'

Police radio voices responded. Claire let go of the still to be untied ankle strap and collapsed backwards. She covered her eyes and face with her arms and howled. They were safe. She and Tom would live. Their nightmare was over. Shock and nausea swept into her body. The urge to be sick brought her body into a seating position and she twisted herself over the left hand side of the table and vomited across the floor.

'Sarge. In here. Two victims. One alive. One could be down. You alright, Miss? You're safe now.'

An armed officer walked towards her. Another was leaning over Tom feeling for a pulse, whilst one stood guard by the door.

'He's alive, weak pulse. Get medical assistance ASAP.'

Tom would be okay. Surely, he would be okay. After this torture chamber, after what he had been through, after what they had both suffered, they had to have a future. She willed it to be so. In that moment, that was all that really mattered.

The officer by the table released Claire from her last restraint. Another pulled out a silver foil blanket and wrapped it around her as she swung her legs off the table and stood up. With that simple human touch of kindness, Claire broke down again and rested her head on the policeman's chest. Awkwardly, but instinctively, he put his arm around her as she sobbed until she could cry no more. The comforting, gentle thud on her back from his leathered gloved hand slowed her heart till the rhythm was calm and her breathing had slowed. Claire pulled herself gently away from the officer, her eyes red from tears. She looked up at him and spoke hoarsely.

'Thank-you.'

'That's alright, Miss. Now you go easy ay.'

Claire walked unsteadily at first, but gained strength as blood resumed its flow properly into her legs. Tom was being lifted onto a stretcher, an emergency drip inserted into his arm. His head rolled slowly sideways, his eyes opened and he looked at her, weak surprise showing on his face.

'Claire,' he mouthed her name silently, but then as if the effort was all too much, which indeed it was, his eyes leadenly closed again and he slipped back into unconsciousness.

Claire followed him to the ambulance in a wheelchair. She gave no resistance. There are times when it is good to allow others to take control. Claire weakly smiled. It was bright outside. Everything dark now seemed negative white. Everything would be okay. This had to be her mantra.

They both had to cross the bridge into everyday reality again. They just had to, and then everything would be okay wouldn't it?

KING EDWARD VII – 1910

By Rudyard Kipling (1865-1936)

Who in the Realm today has a choice of the easy road or the
hard to treat?
And, much concerned for his own estate, would sell his soul to
remain in the sun?
Let him depart nor look at Our dead.
Our King asks nothing of any man more than Our King himself
has done.

FIFTY-EIGHT

Noon, Friday, July 13, 2012 – King Edward VII Memorial Park, near Thames Path, London

He felt elated. He had done right by his mum in the end. He held onto that fact. Claire Yohanus the reporter, saved. Harry the Bastard, dead. The ghost of his father, gone.

The sun was perpendicular. The park was abandoned. It was hot. The sparse trees afforded limited shade. Office workers hid in air conditioned buildings. Locals, like rabbits sensing a predator, sheltered in burrows. The roar of the helicopter's engine obliterated sound around him or so it seemed as he ran across the grass away from the tennis courts and the bowling-green heading for a spot between two trees. They dominated the park. He had chosen this spot last night. It was the perfect place. He had made it. The Rotherhithe Tunnel passed unseen underneath. He felt the sticky heat from the traffic percolating up through the soil. His feet burned. His sweat wet shirt felt uncomfortable. The skin on his back was swelling against the rucksack he still bore. Would he have time to remove it, he wondered? He hoped so. If he was lucky, he might even feel a passing breeze. It might cool him before it was all over.

He looked at the ever-inviting river. Across the green flowing water, he could see a high rise block of apartments, Regina Point. City dwellers lived within its cells and populated its inner structure. How blessed they were to live a life free from the itch. If only he had been. He might have chosen to live another life and be one of the people living in the clouds. They dwelt within another world. The building had the look of a modern medieval cathedral reaching out to heaven. But it was easy to feel bitter. He had been robbed hadn't he?

An ant was foraging beneath his feet. People lived like termites nested within towering structures overlooking the urban desert; but ultimately, they were defenceless against the likes of him. They were. He knew that. They had one defence – numbers – acting as one. Their one weakness was acting alone. Most people were self-centred. Hadn't life slapped him around long enough to testify? When it came to choices over a gasp for life, many abandoned everyone for just one more taste of the elixir. He had seen it, been poisoned by its noxious fumes.

The itch had grown like a boil bursting fragments of his sub consciousness. It had oozed and bobbed on the surface. Feelings had bubbled like sour champagne in his head. He had always resented the taste. The power of anger consumed him. Conflicts fought for supremacy in his chest. The pain of betrayal had left him little space to breathe good thoughts. He was not what his name had been. Had his mother loved him? In his doubts, which had multiplied into blistering thoughts, the reality popped the fantasy that she had. Yet he had clung onto the cliff edge of denial. There was still hope. There always was. But things change. Nothing is constant. He knew what he was now. There was no doubt. That was the meaning of life. It made you search.

Yet he had failed to find the answers. The termites were safe, for now anyway. He had made his choice. Live life free from slavery, break the itch. He would lose his life, and then, yes, he would rise again. If he lost his life, he would find it. He had read it so. He would make it so. His faith – will determine all.

The itch had taken over as overseer. He had left behind the lone termite, abandoned Jekyll. He had allowed Hyde to live.

Now he had taken back control. Whilst the masses bled out their mediocre lives and sacrificed control to others, to their partners, their employers, to time, even, he had taken off that leash at last. Spartacus. He was self aware. He was alive.

Armed police officers edged their way across the park. Their boots bent the grass, creating yet more ridges for the insects to crawl over in their ever-changing world. The target had already proved that he was armed and dangerous. He stood motionless between two trees – Hercules. His hands were clasped around each shoulder strap of the rucksack. No weapon was in sight. What was in the bag?

Twelve armed officers from CO19 were making this park their territory now. This was to be, if it had to be, a killing field. Marksmen positioned themselves to the side and to the rear of their colleagues providing protection to the advancing officers. They moved forward to a safe distance in front of the target. They went slowly, ever so slowly, two carrying in front ballistic shields for close cover to the armed officers immediately behind them. Each officer had their Glock drawn, batons hung by their sides for use to subdue the target if deadly force was not necessary. Ballistic vests cloyed in the heat. Ballistic helmets rimed their foreheads with sweat. Heat and nerves could be a deadly cocktail at high noon. The sun continued to beat down onto their dark and thick padded clothing. It was unyielding, unforgiving.

The police helicopter had been moved to a remote aerial observation point now that the target was contained by CO19. The machine's reassuring guttural engine enveloped the area in a cotton ball of noise that cocooned all who now found themselves – the willing and the unwilling in the park. The armed ball of men and women officers stopped 100 metres away. The officer commanding shouted.

'Armed police; lie face down now on the ground with your hands taken off your rucksack and your arms and hands outstretched ahead of you.'

The target's face animated as he turned his eyes onto the police and away from his gaze across the river. Colin smiled. They were here. He could see his mother standing behind them. Yes, she was his mother; why else would she come to collect him? She hadn't changed or aged a bit, such is the gift some women have. She possessed an ageless beauty. Her long ebony hair still flowed like a dark river over her shoulders. The sun reflected in the flint colour of her locks. Her eyes sparkled. She was smiling at him, her hands beckoning him to come to her. They could once again read poetry, could discuss the work each had discovered. They could enthuse, drink their fill of rich language and allow themselves to be intoxicated by the imagery of crafted words sculpted across countless pages as they uncovered the hidden meanings resting silently, waiting between lines and stanzas.

To the officers the target looked oddly happy, unnervingly so.

'I say again. Armed police; lie face down now on the ground with your hands taken off your rucksack and your arms and hands outstretched ahead of you.'

He knelt down, his palms resting on the grass to steady his balance. He looked up into the deep eyes of his mother. The Bronze commanding officer allowed herself a millimetre of relief; the target was starting to obey her commands.

His mother's face looked confused. He called out, but no words came from his mouth. Cheap cava fizzed and then went flat in his head. The itch didn't want to let go. A bubbling cauldron of anger was surfacing in his chest. It was all a lie. Everything he had known wasn't. Even he wasn't. He never had been. He was no Spartacus. The slavish chains were too strong to break. He would never escape the colosseum. There was no hiding now from Mr Hyde ... No, he is wrong. Look, mum is smiling. She is calling him.

'Robbie, come on, we'll be late.'

He smiled. He relaxed. 'Soon Mum,' he said.

The Bronze officer observed the minute movements of the target's face, which seemed to undulate back and forth from happiness to anger as if inner demons wrestled underneath the man's skin. Now he looked calm, almost serene as the gaze of his eyes looked beyond the tight ball of officers.

He would show her that he still had her book of poems and too, many more in the anthologies he carried with him. The target brought his elbows up sideways as his palms twisted around to take hold of the rucksack's straps again.

'Stop! I say stop. I say again. Armed police; lie face down now on the ground with your hands taken off your rucksack and your arms and hands outstretched ahead of you.'

He started to slide each strap off his shoulders; the shirt he was wearing was being tugged to the right and to the left as he moved to unravel his body from them.

The millimetre had been scant comfort to the officer. It was long gone now. What to do? There was no imminent threat was there? Choices crowded around shouting for action. The loneliness of leadership laughed flatly in her head.

He brought the bag around to his front; he was unaware of the crosshairs combing his head and torso. His back was free from the weight it carried. He could feel a light breeze. It was his last blessing. Thank you. His mother was closer now.

'Show me what's in the bag. Do you still have my book?'

He nodded excitedly and looked up into her comforting eyes. He was a 13-year-old child again. Moving fast, as if unwrapping a present from her, he tore into the rapidly unzipping bag, and with a quick downward thrust, reached inside with one arm plunging into its depths.

Give the fucking order, Ma'am – they all to a person thought. The target had an object. He was withdrawing it from the bag. Give the fucking order for Christ sake.

'Shoot, shoot, shoot!'

The bullets that collided with Colin's head and torso came from the side and in front of him. The impacts twisted his body. He was transformed into a cobra emerging from its casket. His arms flung backwards and the object he was holding – the officers now saw it was a book – somersaulted through the air and crashed sliding along the grass. Colin's torso curled forwards, the top of his head hitting the ground.

At first Colin's body was upended, a grotesque statue, before gravity pulled him sideways. His body tilted slowly and collapsed onto the grass. His blood gushed into the sun-baked ground. As his life force ebbed in tandem with the outgoing Thames, the foraging ant ran for his life.

In the shade under the trees, he was with her. She sat with her back against the bark. He stood glowing with pride reading aloud from a book. She was laughing at his antics. A light breeze had changed direction. She looked up. The shadow was gone. She took hold of his hand.

'Come on,' she said, 'time to go home.'

PART FOUR – BROKEN PROMISES

ON A VOLUNTEER SINGER

By Samuel Taylor Coleridge (1772-1834)

Swans sing before they die – 'twere no bad thing
Should certain persons die before they sing.

FIFTY-NINE

16:40 hours, Friday, July 13, 2012 – St Thomas' Hospital, Westminster Bridge, London

Claire's inner child had jumped wildly into the air. Both feet had lifted off the ground and her arms had flung joyfully into space as she had wrapped herself around the shoulders of the female paramedic that attended to her. It was like tasting a sherbet dab for the first time – the joy of that first dip.

It had been a short ride with blue lights flashing and siren wailing ride over Southwark Bridge and Lambeth Palace Road to the hospital's accident and emergency. Far from disturbing, the sirens had sounded melodic to Claire. From this day forward, like Pavlov's dog, she promised herself, she would rush back to this memory of safety. Tubes ran from Tom's arms, an oxygen mask covered his nose and mouth, he was breathing strongly, although he looked very weak and remained unconscious; electronic pulses of light flashed regularly on the flat screen overhead, she guessed it meant that his heart was beating well. His body, strapped onto the stretcher, was being rocked gently by the vehicle's suspension. He was alive. That was what mattered. They had made it. The inside of this ambulance, their shelter, was a safe haven. The paramedic who was holding Tom's wrist looked up and smiled at Claire. She took hold of Claire's hand too and squeezed it reassuringly. Human touch, the electricity of life, she shared it well with those that needed it most. Gentle reality came in luscious shock waves for Claire. The emotional taste of loving human contact felt divine.

When they arrived at accident and emergency, Tom, who had lost a lot of blood, was rushed inside for an immediate transfusion. Claire thanked in her heart all of the regular anonymous donors that gave their blood and time in return for a biscuit and a cup of tea, the silent minority helping the many. Claire vowed to write an article encouraging more to join their ranks.

Tom's body, what was left of it, thought a nurse when he was first brought in, would need surgery to ensure the ragged amputations would heal as aesthetically as possible. A mould would need to be taken of his remaining ear for subsequent use in reconstructive plastic surgery. It would help to restore the balance in his facial features.

His back had showed signs of infection and a course of antibiotics had been administered intravenously to bring down a raging temperature and kill off the bacteria growing greedily from his wounds. The drugs would give Tom's natural defences a chance to fight back against the overwhelming odds. His healing might take several months. He would have to learn to walk all over again, but that was all in the future. Intensive physiotherapy would prove to be more than the underestimated service Tom had hitherto attached to it. For Tom, the staff acting as mentor, motivator and fitness instructor all in one had pushed him. And as his strength had returned, he had pushed back. That was the Tom she knew. That was the Tom, Tom knew.

Following an x-ray, Claire was treated for cracked ribs. Luckily, her lungs had not been punctured. The painful bruising and swelling to her face and body would heal without the need for surgery. A course of medicine helped to alleviate the intensity of pain to a dull background throbbing ache.

She chose not to tell anyone in the immediate aftermath of the rape. What was the point? Her attacker was dead. And to speak of it then, in the hospital, well she felt strangely ashamed and embarrassed. Besides, Claire did not want the world to know the darker side of what she had suffered. She did not want some pervert getting off on one when he read about it in the press. Yes, she knew if she spoke up, it would get out. And then it would be Claire Yohanus, not the renowned investigative reporter, rising star who single-handily covered presidential elections, interviewed and challenged the candidates; no it would be, isn't she the woman who was raped? That would be her public scar and badge of humiliation for life. More importantly, there was Tom. His was the greater need right now.

Claire was sitting in a reclining chair next to Tom when he regained consciousness.

'Hello darling. We're safe,' she said. 'Can you believe it? This is a hospital and …'

He looked at her blankly.

'What is it Tom? What's the matter?'

He looked around the room. He took in the tubes going into his arm and felt the soreness of those that fed into his nose and travelled down deep into his stomach. He felt no real pain; morphine was a wonderful thing. He took in the blank TV screen on a platform above his bed and the open blinds through which he could see medical staff. He returned his attention to the woman asking questions.

'Who are you?' he said.

The look of shock and complete surprise on Claire's face quickly turned to laughter when she noticed the smile tugging at the sides of his mouth.

Relief transformed into a broad grin and a fun tinged reprimand in an instant from Claire.

'Tom. How dare you do that? You sod. Your bloody humour, it always was ill-timed.'

She got up from the chair, using its arms for support and brushed a kiss on his forehead.

'Good to have you back darling.'

He smiled and she heard his lips gently kiss the air in reciprocation. She told him of her saviour, she still did not know who he was, and of their escape and the journey to the hospital. However, it did not take long for him to flag. The strain and effort, largely of listening to her tell the story was taking its toll. She stopped then. There would be time later.

'Mum and Dad?'

'They're on their way,' Claire answered. 'I called them not long after I'd been bandaged and given painkillers. And my Dad's on his way too. They'll be a grand gathering for us.'

'Good. If I'm asleep when they come, wake me up won't you?' he asked.

'I will,' she replied.

His eyes gave up and closed. He was adrift on the currents of recovery. Claire bypassed the reclining chair and made her way to the parallel single hospital bed in the room within which they had both been placed. She had asked for and insisted on it. She had pushed home the facts. They had both been through a harrowing and traumatic series of events. They needed the reassurance of seeing one another safe. Being together was necessary for them both. That way, she ventured, recovery would be more effective. The staff saw the logic and the emotional bond, which must have soldered them both and agreed to the arrangement.

Until incapacity hits, the limitations of small things go unheeded. Claire felt certain they rejoiced when their time in the sun came and revelled as they embraced the satisfying feeling of vengeance for being ignored. Climbing onto her bed was more difficult than getting out. It required more use of her stomach muscles. The effort to reverse onto the mattress took up painful minutes. When she was able to lie down and feel the back of her head sink gratefully into the soft pillow it was bliss. She sighed. In bed, she realised how so very exhausted her body really was. She must learn to unwind and rest. Claire closed her eyes and when the conveyor belt of thoughts came to a standstill, she slept.

SIXTY

Friday, July 13, 2012 – St Thomas' Hospital, Westminster Bridge, London

It was ten minutes after five in the evening when George rejoined Monica in the waiting room. Monica sat with her hands calmly folded on her lap. She was looking at the murals on the walls. George knew they would be a topic of conversation on the way home. More than likely Monica had seen another opportunity to display her work and prosper from such entrepreneurial insights.

She caught George's eye. He shrugged his shoulders and extended his palms upwards. Tom and Claire were asleep then. They were loath to wake them up, yet desperate to hold Tom and to reassure their own eyes that he really was okay. The nurse in charge of his care, whilst helpful, had been a tad too clinical in her delivery, thought Monica. It had translated in her mind that Tom was more of a lab specimen, than a human being. His injuries sounded horrific.

'Come on,' said George, 'let's get some food and drink in the hospital cafeteria. I could do with some sustenance and distraction too. Visiting hours finish at 8 pm, so we've time yet.'

Part of Monica did not want to leave now that she was so close to seeing Tom. The umbilical cord is somehow never severed.

Hospital cafeterias rarely uplift the spirits. It is not because hospitals do not try, but the blending of medical staff, visitors and patients from diverse social and economic backgrounds does not quite lend itself to a communal atmosphere. Many places to eat in the normal world outside the climes of hospitals often, naturally, attract and create their own social hierarchy of clientele. Whereas, dining areas in hospitals, despite being divided by design and staff only signs, never escape the clutches of a library ambience and customers often remain closeted. Constrained eyes cast down in the presence of awkward and uncertain social surroundings. Even people watching feels taboo, out of place, intrusive on those in recovery – nightwear and drips into bodies mixing with uniforms and anoraks. It does not feel right, does it? It wasn't.

As George and Monica slow 'mowed' and glided down the entrance hall into the opening chamber of the cafeteria, they scanned the room for the best place to sit, taking in the food counter and drink dispensers in one gaze. Their eyes tracked from side to side. In the fourth quadrant of the divided room, they spotted him, both at the exact same time as it happened. Monica was about to twist round to grab George's attention when he spoke, or more accurately perhaps, projected his voice across the room.

'Andrew. Good God man. What a relief. It's great to see you.'

Monica and her chair were propelled as a curtain being swished across the open space towards Claire's father.

The sensation of speed transported her back to the beautiful cobbled area of the Quay in Exeter when she and George had travelled down from Oxford to see Tom and his fellow undergrad and girlfriend, Claire. As all four of them had swept down the hill from South Street and headed towards the river, the two students ran ahead to grab a table in the sun at one of the waterfront pubs. Not to be outdone, George had run after them, notwithstanding the mobile deterrent – he was pushing Monica, who was by then wheelchair bound as a result of a fall from her beloved horse – Sceptre. As some may know, the wheelchair is not renowned for its suspension qualities, especially over such uneven man made terrain. The faster George went, the more her head and mouth vibrated. She felt like a mobile ventriloquist's dummy.

'George – slow down' she had shrieked.

To which he had gamely replied, 'No lassie,' and he wasn't even Scottish, 'tiz time to show our true colours.'

In the end, Monica could not help but laugh as her teeth vibrated and her vision blurred as smudgy pedestrians, and seated and shaking customers, streaked past. Even they became lost to view when her floppy sun hat fell forward. She was too terrified to move it backwards for fear of losing her grip on the wheelchair's arms.

'You're a rat George, a positive rat.' Her raised voice was muffled by the hat's fabric across her face.

When they arrived on the veranda of the pub and its smooth surface, Monica flipped her hat off, swept her fringe from her eyes and looked up into the faces of entertained onlookers who spontaneously applauded the puffing competitors. She turned to George and mouthed expletives at him.

'You're a bugger; you know that, don't you?' A sparkle could not remain hidden in her eyes.

In response, he planted a hot kiss on her lips, a winning 'smacker' and whispered in her ear, 'An aperitif before tonight,' adding, 'I've booked the hotel room we've talked about on Cathedral Green.'

She pulled away from him and twisted her mouth to his ear 'George – the cost,' she whispered.

'But Monica – the rewards,' he replied and with that tease he sailed inside to find Tom and order drinks and some lunch;

warriors need energy for the fray. It gave her a chance to learn how delightful this Claire, they had heard about, really truly was. Tom had chosen well. She was lovely.

Andrew had looked up when he heard George call his name, as did everyone else in the room. Undoubtedly, not everyone was called Andrew, thought Monica.

Andrew rose from his table and greeted them both warmly. More than five years, time had kept close watch on them all and been kind to their physiques and faces. She compared the two men as they stood shaking each other's hands with mutual affection.

George possessed the presence of a large human bear. He was tall and had a thickset chest, a characteristic he owed from years of playing rugby. In addition, his light brown hair was, well, shaggy, a potential candidate for London Mayor, she'd often thought of late. His face was rounded, though not fat and the overriding impression you saw in it was of a man who liked to have fun and lots of it. Yes, that was her George. She smiled to herself.

Andrew on the other hand had short, sharp cut, grey hair. He was about an inch taller than George was, probably about 6' 2" she guessed. He wore penny-rimmed glasses, the kind that she had seen a forger wearing in an old 1940s black and white movie. His face was sharp looking too, and he had angular high cheekbones and the intellectual stance of a high court judge. Some might have said, at first glance, that he looked severe, but that impression swiftly dissolved as his features were neatly balanced with numerous laughter lines, especially around his eyes and mouth.

Unlike George, who lounged into suits, Andrew wore his like a coat hanger, each line falling richly to the floor defined by the clean cut of the cloth that marked him out from the rest of the people in the room.

SIXTY-ONE

Friday, July 13, 2012 – St Thomas' Hospital, Westminster Bridge, London

The now unarmed Bronze commanding officer peered through the blinds into the room. The victims were still asleep. Well, she had come up now, so she might as well deliver it.

It was difficult to imagine what they had faced in that basement torture chamber. Her back shivered at the thought of being a prisoner there, as always, the cliché struck a chord, but for the grace of God.

She slipped quietly into the room, her training second nature, honed into muscle memory. The outside window of the room faced out onto the Thames. The surface percolated bubbles of light and multiple flash bangs on her eyes and as she turned away, the officer saw lights flashing over the two sleeping bodies. An optical illusion, she thought and rubbed her eyes. It was if the two resting souls were being showered by chakras.

As her eyes and senses adjusted, the officer looked with pity on Tom and Claire. He in particular had had it rough. The bandage around his head and over his missing ear made him look like a wounded soldier, not long back from a bitter battle. Claire's face was swollen; mottled Dalmatian like bruising marbled her features.

The officer placed Claire's diary on the bedside cabinet with her police mobile number and a note explaining it had been recovered from the rucksack of the man that had released her.

The note said no more than that. Claire would find out soon enough who her saviour was and God knows what her feelings would be then.

'And you used a cable car and hiked on the footpaths in and around Davos?' asked Monica, 'How wonderful. It's difficult to visualise the views, but everyone says the Alps are lovely at any time of the year, although we've never been there, have we George?'

George looked confused. 'Claire had said you were at a medical conference in Zurich.'

'And so I was.' Andrew switched conversation smoothly and replied. 'I took a few days out, impromptu, and visited some old friends.'

'But I'm sure you said you were still at a conference when we spoke on the phone yesterday.' George pushed his point home.

'That's right I did say that. I went to Davos last weekend, it had been offered as a break away for the delegates; you see it was a two-part conference with very different themes either side of Saturday and Sunday. I'd given you a potted version of my time out there, and the detail was meshed together. Now do you believe me?' He smiled as he spoke next, 'we criminals need a break too.'

And with that Andrew shuffled his papers together as if making ready to go.

George looked unsettled and ready for more.

'Well, gentlemen,' rode Monica to the rescue, 'it's nearly 7 pm, and I for one want to see how Tom and Claire are. I'm desperate to see them. And now the supper has fuelled my tummy, I'm ready for the off. Who's with me?'

Andrew gallantly offered to push Monica, that is, if she did not mind and if George would not mind carrying his bags. George, with his nose displaced, had no other choice than to 'warmly agree' to the arrangement. As they strolled towards the lift to go down one level, Andrew spoke to them both.

There were times when you just have to suck it up. As George discovered, that time was now, the psychologist was to lecture them. George could feel it coming. How quickly he had moved away from being pleased to see Andrew. He was irritated with himself as much as he was with Andrew and what he, George, saw as a little power struggle with him. Not like the Andrew he'd known. Then again, it had been a long time since they last met. Maybe Andrew had changed or had always been like that, but George had been working full-time then and it probably would have passed him by and of course, now they were all under emotional strain. Well, enough of the jumbled thoughts and reasons for, mused George. Never pays to mix the cocktail. Better to allow this feeling to pass.

And so Andrew began his guided lecture.

'We know they've been through a lot. What that precisely is, we do not know. We may never know. They may not wish to discuss it. They may even feel ashamed, embarrassed or too angry or any mixture of emotions that may interfere with their desire to talk it out. No matter how much we might want to ask the questions and probe for the truth, we must resist the temptation. It is possible also that they will not remember. The shock of it all may have blanked their memories. They need time, space, a listening ear and above all, love. That will help them to heal.

'They may turn to us for support, although I doubt it. It may be difficult to share such experiences with us, their parents. And we must accept this. They may turn to professional counsellors who undoubtedly will be offering their support for as long as they need it. My guess is this though, they will turn to each other and that is where the healing, the real deep down bedrock of transformation back to a healthy outlook on life will take place. Our role, if we have one, is this. It is to be the parents we have always been to them. They need reassurance that the people out there, the ones they love and trust the most, are just there, good, solid, dependable parents that they can hug and cry with. In these situations, I believe, words do not bring healing, but the touch of a loved one, you and I, each other, brings people lost at sea back to the port and away from the storm of their emotions.'

'They're still asleep,' said George in hushed tones, 'shall we go in then?'

'Oh, George, enough of the hesitation, what's got into you all of a sudden?' said Monica.

'Perhaps I have,' said Andrew, 'I should have trusted your own sensibilities. I'm sorry.'

'Don't be silly Andrew,' replied Monica, cutting a subtle glance George's way.

'No, it was good that you covered the ground, just in case. And ignore my ego, it's bigger than me sometimes,' said George.

Monica motioned with her forehead towards Tom and Claire's room. 'Good. Friends again then; shall we?'

George held the door open and followed in behind Andrew and Monica. He was not used to being in third place. Yet sometimes it gives one unexpected advantage. Before even looking at his daughter or Tom, Andrew's eyes had homed in on a diary resting undisturbed on her bedside cabinet. Sometimes the little things reveal more.

'I'm okay from here now; thanks Andrew,' said Monica.

He smiled at her and she wheeled her chair alongside Tom's bed. To give her more room, George manhandled the hospital reclining chair to the other side of the room. When he turned around, Tom was waking up, Monica was holding his right hand and Andrew was leaning over Claire's bed to kiss her on the head, his right hand resting on the diary and slowly, imperceptibly to most people, moving it towards the flap of his suit, which partly covered the cabinet's surface.

'Be careful Andrew,' said George, 'you might knock that diary onto the floor.'

The diary stayed where it was thereafter and Claire awoke to the sound of his voice. She was confused at first, seeing her father's face and hearing George's voice.

'Hello darling,' her father said.

'Oh Dad,' Claire erupted, her voice rasping with emotion. She flung her arms up around his neck and pulled him towards her.

'Dad. Dad.'

Her whole body shuddered under the white brushed cotton bed cover. Claire's sobs filled the room so that no corner and no one in there were left untouched.

George moved to the parallel side of Tom's bed, opposite Monica and put his bear paw on his son's left shoulder. How he longed to hug Tom and allow the strength of his love to fill his son's body. He had never seen Tom so weak. When he was close to him, George's sense of his son's nothingness was brought home to him. Tom had plunged the depths of suffering, thank God he had returned.

Tom moved his head on the pillow first towards Monica and then to George.

'It's good to be back,' he said.

And mirroring Claire, his body shook with sobs from deep within his chest. His eyelids squeezed tightly closed and tears dripped out from under his eyelashes, the whole of his face pulled downwards, the pain being released was too much for his features to carry. He brought his left forearm up to cover his eyes and forehead and through gulps of breath whispered, 'I am … so… sorry … I'm so sorry…'

Tom's parents held him as close as his injuries would allow. The sound of grief poured out in shuddering jumps and heart wrenching sounds from his tightly closed mouth. His tongue forced itself up against the roof of his mouth as he fought against the flow of pain erupting from him. In these past days, trapped and bereft of hope, he had travelled the many pathways of grief, letting go of his mum and his dad and of Claire. The darkness had consumed him. He had plumbed the depths of tempestuous emotions and returned with an angel. Tom was overwhelmed. All of it, the grotesque reality, the beauty of seeing Claire, the hospital, his parents, a thousand thoughts and memories flashed and smashed together.

Eventually, the painful merry-go-round slowed and Tom's spinning head was able to focus. His forearm slid down onto his chest and over his parents' hands; feeling the touch of them was utter relief. He gulped the ebbing grief back several more times until his body stilled. He opened his eyes and looked at his parents, his lovely, lovely parents, 'Thank-you,' he said quietly to them both, 'thank-you.'

Aftermath, Friday 13 July, 2012 – Friars Mead and Manchester Road, Millwall, London

Mainland Britain reeled in shock. The world stood still. The blood stains. The bone fragments. Chaotic abandoned shoes. And bodies, masses of them sprawled and littered the road in obscene and awkward angles – protestors, assailants and police officers; they all shared the same bed now. A police horse lay on its side, a metal pole protruded from its chest; its eyes still flared in fear; its body coated with the rigor mortis of death.

In the end, words lost their meaning, for there were no real meaningful words to describe the depth and breadth of the chaos, the shock, the anger, the hatred, the fear and the grief.

Actions replaced words that weekend. Thuggery, mayhem, looting and riots, this was the new language. People understood the message. Birmingham, Brighton, Bristol, Manchester, Leeds and other cities copycatted.

It wasn't pretty.

CARPE DIEM FROM TWELFTH NIGHT

By William Shakespeare (1564-1631)

O mistress mine, where are you roaming?
O stay and here! your true-love's coming
    That can sing both high and low;
    Trip no further, pretty sweeting,
    Journeys end in lovers meeting –
    Every wise man's son doth know.

    What is love? 'tis not hereafter;
    Present mirth hath present laughter;
    What's to come is still unsure:
    In delay there lies no plenty, –
Then come kiss me, Sweet-and-twenty,
    Youth's a stuff will not endure.

SIXTY-TWO

Their parents, as promised, refrained from visiting them that weekend. She and much more so, Tom, needed space and rest. And friends absolutely, were banned from calling in. There would be time for catch up and support, many times over, in the weeks and months ahead.

Tom slept a lot. Claire felt fettered by hospitals. They had a strange effect on her and she fought against becoming subdued by the bustling yet clinical atmosphere that was neither home nor comforting.

Claire leaned back into the raised bed and the pile of pillows wedged behind to provide support. She re-read the last entry in her diary. It was now covered by a receipt for lost luggage at King's Cross, which had been taped on the inside of the front cover. The jumble of cryptic words underneath meant nothing to her, 'OS HELM PRE-JUDGE FELON.' She recalled the words her saviour had said: "not everyone has a choice," perhaps this is what he was referring to.

She plugged the radio earphones in and listened to the 1 pm news. Extended coverage was provided. She learnt that hospital mortuaries were most likely awash with bodies caught up in yesterday's bloodbath. The mention of both Tom and herself caught her attention and even more so, when she heard that Harry's body and that of the man who had saved her, a Colin Trahoney, had also been brought here for post-mortems. As she listened further, the horrific truths of what Colin had done,

293

forced their way into Claire's emotions. Sinner and Saviour plagued her thoughts.

She could not settle. Claire wished now that she had asked her father to bring in some clothes. Now he would not be here until Monday. She called Maria, who promised to pop some clothes over within the next hour or so and leave them in the ward's reception. Minutes dragged. Claire pulled herself off the bed and decided to go for a wander. In her heart, she knew the destination. She was being pulled there. Initially she felt comfortable walking along the corridors in pyjamas and slippers as patients like her, crisscrossed paths with staff and visitors alike. She proceeded into the bowels of the hospital heading towards the Oncology, Haematology and Cellular Pathology Department, within which, she had found out, the mortuary was located.

In the lower levels of the building, Claire's presence stuck out. She was tempted to don a short-sleeved white hospital coat that hung in full view in one of the side rooms but resisted it. She was not doing anything wrong, why complicate things. When asked by a passing porter if she was lost, he cheerily pointed her in the right direction.

The mortuary room door was locked, why wouldn't it be? She picked up the handset attached to the outside wall of the room and a pleasant sounding young woman's voice answered.

'Hello, Sonita Paneshi, anatomical pathology technologist here, how may I help you?'

'Hello, my name is Claire Yohanus; I'm a patient in this hospital.'

'Yes, I understand Ms Yohanus, but what are you doing down here? No viewings have been arranged for today.'

'I was hoping to see two of the bodies that were brought in yesterday, two men. Their names are…'

Sonita interrupted, 'I'm sorry that isn't possible. Only relatives and friends are allowed to visit.'

'Please Sonita, hear me out. I do know the two men. One is called Harry Denmart, the other is Colin Trahoney. Denmart kidnapped and held me prisoner along with...'

Sonita looked at the video intercom; the woman's face was instantly recognisable. It had been all over the news coverage this morning.

'Oh my gosh, you are Claire Yohani!'

'That's right,' said Claire, not bothering to correct her. 'I just need to make sure in my own mind that the man who kidnapped me is actually dead.'

'I *totally* understand.' Sonita readily empathised with Claire. 'I'd be having nightmares, always wondering if he was still alive and that he'd come back to get his revenge on me.'

'Exactly,' Claire agreed, 'and the other man, Trahoney, he rescued me and I want to... I feel silly saying this...'

'Go on,' said Sonita.

'Well, I just want to say goodbye and say thank-you. If it hadn't been for him, I'd be dead.' The merest touch of thoughts and feelings about how close she had come to death and tears were waiting ready to appear. Was she ready for this?

There was a pause; Sonita was moved at the sight of Claire's raw emotion. The woman's bruised face, dressed in ill-fitting hospital gowns, her eyes red, she looked so careworn. She looked around the mortuary, just bodies and her. Who would know? No cameras monitored here. She was by herself and ... Sonita pressed the door release button.

'Come inside,' she said.

The electronic door lock clicked open; Claire pulled on the metal handle and entered. It was lighter and brighter than she had feared, imagining a gloomy pall would somehow hang over the entire place. Even so, her heart trembled a little when she saw several empty mortuary tables. They were similar to the one in Harry's place. Sonita was wearing a sea green short-sleeved smock and trousers and a bright and breezy smile when she came out of her side room to greet Claire. They shook hands as Claire said thank-you for breaking protocols, and letting her come in like this. The young looking twenty something Asian who had thick dark hair, which was tied back and tucked into a surgical cap wore rectangular shaped glasses that reflected the lights from the ceiling. She responded by saying, 'Seeing you are a reporter reassures me.'

Claire looked puzzled so Sonita quickly added, 'You must be used to keeping your sources secret.'

'Oh, absolutely,' replied Claire enthusiastically, 'we reporters, never reveal our sources. You can trust me on that one.' Both broke into a conspiratorial smile – their sisterhood complete.

'If you wait here then, I'll just slide the two men out of the fridges and you can take a look at them both, say your goodbyes or rot in hell, whatever springs to mind.'

As she walked to the fridge cubicles, Sonita carried on speaking. Sonita certainly liked to talk.

'I think you're brave coming down here. You won't faint will you?'

There was not a chance for Claire to reply.

'What was it like? I bet you're pleased that Harry guy got his comeuppance.'

It seemed odd to hear that phrase coming from someone so young. Claire thought its use had dropped from existence. Perhaps it was the everyday language down here.

'Mind you,' Sonita had continued effortlessly, 'the one who saved you, he was scary wasn't he? Did you hear how he killed, what was it, three men, no four including Harry, they say. Yes, and all but Harry had their hearts cut out. Of course, I do that all the time and the other organs too. Put them all back in a yellow plastic bag when the pathologist has finished and plonk everything back into the patient's body. That way they don't leak.'

Sonita positioned the viewing trolleys parallel to one another, allowing "bags of space," as she put it, for Claire to walk around either side if she wished. The bodies were covered in grey cotton, plastic-coated cloth; their feet protruded. Each body had a label tied to a big toe on one foot, identifying who this person had been. It was all quite clinical and all so very macabre as far as Claire was concerned. She shivered, putting it down to the ambient chill in the room.

'Now, before I pull the covers back, have you seen a dead body before?'

'Yes, my mother.'

Time slowed down for Claire. Everything seemed rather intense. She was about to come face to face with Harry, her nemesis. Her heart fluttered within her chest. No, it beat staccato. She could not bring herself to feel repelled by Colin and what he had done to others. He had saved her for whatever reason, and for that, she felt utter gratitude. Perhaps that was selfish of her.

'And when you saw your mother, did she look peaceful? I ask, because these two men have not been prepared in any way yet, so you will be seeing them and their features frozen in the moment of their death. It might not be a pretty sight. I should also add something about Harry; his head is almost severed. So … are you absolutely sure, you want to go ahead with this? I can put them both away now if you like. No problem. Some people do change their mind at the last minute and that's fine. No shame in that. None at all.' She reaffirmed her point.

'Yes, my mother looked very peaceful.'

It pained Claire to bring her mother to mind, especially here and now.

'Look,' she made herself sound and appear more determined, 'I'll be alright. You go ahead. I've been through a pretty rough time of it these past several days. I think I can cope with anything now. Would you do me a favour though?'

Sonita nodded, her hands resting on both trolleys.

'Would you show me Harry first?' said Claire, 'and when I've seen him, please…just put him straight back in the fridge?'

'Of course I will. Ready?' Sonita raised her eyebrows, the bridge of her spectacles twitching upwards at the same time.

Claire nodded. Part of her felt relief that she had at least been unconscious when he had raped her and at the same time she felt anger that she'd not been conscious to fight him off, to let him and herself know that she would not have been subdued so easily. She hated feeling powerless. This man, even though he was dead, generated a shadowy disempowerment within her. The hospital shower had washed away the disgusting dirt he had left on her. She prayed that she was not pregnant. What would she do then? You fucking bastard Harry.

Sonita rolled the sheet back over Harry's upper body. Claire's hatred of Harry immediately tore up her face when she saw him. It was primeval. She did not feel repulsed by the sight. His head tilted backwards, pulling away from the rest of the body. Claire almost wanted to smile with vengeance, but she did not move closer. She just stared at this creature that had defiled her and tortured Tom. He had deserved to die. As her eyes bore into this monster, Claire's upper lip involuntarily curled upwards partially revealing her bared gums. The human animal was baying quietly in her chest. Yes, the fucker was well and truly dead.

She nodded again unable to find her voice to speak. Sonita drew the cover back over his dead, yes dead face. Claire reassured herself. Harry the Bastard was gone. He was, wasn't he?

Returning, Sonita said, 'Right, ready for the next one?'

Claire nodded and Colin's covering sheet was pulled back. His face looked peaceful, the eyes closed. He had dark short hair like Harry's, a similar age she guessed. They were not dissimilar in build, just looks. Despite the fact he had killed others, she could not bring herself to judge this man for she only felt gratitude. Claire said thank-you silently and prayed for him. She owed this man something, she knew that.

SIXTY-THREE

Saturday, July 14, 2012 – St Thomas' Hospital, Westminster Bridge, London

Tom was awake when Claire returned. He had more colour in his cheeks. His temperature was down. Maria had left her some fresh clothes in a holdall.

'I've got some more operations coming up next week,' said Tom. 'The doctor says if they go well, *and* if I make solid physiotherapy progress in terms of taking steps towards mobility, I could be released the following week, possibly Friday, 27 July. But that seems an age away.'

'That's the downside of hospitals,' Claire replied, 'time drags, stir craziness kicks in and we long for the familiarity of our lives.'

Claire felt the desire for the outside too, only she would see it before Tom, poor thing.

That's true. How are you?' he asked.

'I'm fine,' she replied. 'I had to make sure for myself that Harry was dead. I managed to see his body just now. I'll tell you how another time. Rest assured though, he's dead.'

'I had wondered. Part of me thinks I shouldn't feel glad that he is. My training knocking on my conscience, I guess, but in all honesty, I am. I've not even begun to process any of the whys. I've no idea how I ended up as his prisoner. I almost don't want to talk about it. Yet, there is so much bottled up inside of me.'

Claire walked over to his bed. 'Me too,' she said.

She kissed him full on the lips. He warmly responded. She could sense the trickle of energy flowing back into his body and between them. The nutrients he was being fed were helping. Passionate vigorous Tom would be back one day. She hoped by then that she would be in a position to respond too. There was no knowing yet how the effects of the rape would play out. For now, she felt detached. Maybe that was to do with the artificial surroundings they were in. Time, she just needed time to get over things. Didn't she?

SIXTY-FOUR

Sunday, July 15, 2012 – Kings Cross Station, London

The train station was relatively quiet when Claire arrived. The busker with her guitar would have her work cut out today. She looked young. Perhaps she was using the opportunity to hone her skills and boost confidence in performing for the public. She found it easy to empathise with the girl. Claire found it surprisingly difficult travelling in the outside world again.

The mottled colours across her face as the bruising continued to discolour her skin drew surreptitious looks from adults and innocent gazes from young children. Two young girls perched on their mother's luggage as they waited for her to purchase tickets from the machine in the tube station's entrance foyer had been unable to resist. Claire smiled at them both as she walked past on her way to the lost luggage counter. The younger one looked away, but the elder one stuck her tongue out, the surface of which was coloured cherry red, evidence of a recently devoured treat. Impulsively, Claire did the same and the cheeky one looked startled and turned away too. This was not how adults behave. Well, not in public anyway. The comforting return of their mother gave the brood respite from the weird adult encounter.

For Claire, the external bruising was, as she began to realise, a manifestation of the damage she felt inside. The casual looks of men had always been part of her attractiveness, had become a way of life for Claire. In fact, it happened so much, like many possessions in her home, they went largely unnoticed.

302

However, not so now, the looks seemed threatening. Their eyes hunted her vulnerabilities and poked them. It hurt. Her heart raced. She breathed as if strapped in a corset. The physiological response was primitive. She knew logically that the likelihood of her being kidnapped or raped had been low, less than half of one percent in her lifetime. Damn statistics. They are not real life though are they? And now it had happened. Statistics were a sham. They gave one confidence. Reality takes it away. Until now, if ever anyone had told her that her body would become leaden all because of an imagined fear from the experience, she probably would have shrugged the view off; only weak and fragile people succumbed.

The male attendant at Lost Luggage carried out his duties with customers as if they were regular everyday furniture in his flat. A like-minded soul, she thought. Claire was grateful for the small mercy offered by his indifference. After handing over the receipt she had unpeeled from her diary, Claire's eyes followed the attendant along the racking shelves until he stopped, bent down to one on the lower rung and pulled out a small holdall. When it was in her hands, the bag had the resistant feel of new material, not yet malleable and weathered by use. She resisted the temptation to unzip it there and then. The outside world had been intrusive enough for one day. Time to go home, she could not face the underground again, that had been a mistake. Claire called a women only driver taxi service and relaxed into the back, the holdall clutched tightly to her chest.

Sunday, July 15, 2012 – Iverna Gardens, London, Claire's House

When she got out of the cab, the familiar steps to her front door welcomed her home. Inanimate things gave no demand of her. Those alive often miss these qualities and whose minds are occupied by everyday tasks, for sometimes, the sight and the company of the lifeless gives unexpected succour. She was home. However, as she turned the key in the lock the memory of Harry forced his way in and hit her full on in the face. He was back.

She was going too fast. She stepped back from the door's entrance and pulled it shut. The door clicked into place. In an instant, she felt drained of energy, her body trembling as if low blood sugar levels were flashing red. Claire lowered herself unsteadily onto the steps and sat on the top rung, her calves welcoming the support the lower ones gave. Traffic flowed. Life moved. People passed by, some slow, some fast, and some middling. Some eyes here and there glanced up, but thankfully, most did not. Vehicles streamed by, they were logs on the river. Blasted flotsam, the words of that poem twisted into her consciousness. Claire's thoughts bustled busier than the road below. Distraction from emotions was the medicine she injected herself with.

After his early morning operation, Tom was expecting her back to visit him on Monday evening. She had not told anyone on the outside of her escape from the hospital. How easy it was to slip into prison jargon. She had only been on the ward for just over twenty-four hours after all.

Following the intensity of the days since she had flown back from America the lure of Broadstairs beckoned again. She mulled over the options. However, logistics railed against such a quest. What about her dad? She did not want him fussing over her right now, no matter how tempting it was to be mollycoddled in her sensitive state. She worried that if she let the crack of pain open up too wide, it would split her insides open and she would never get the entrails of her life back together again.

In the end, she plumped for George and Monica. His humour, her motherly presence, and the fact they had been part of it all from the beginning seemed the ingredients she needed right now. Her dad would understand. She called them. They both promised to come over, said they'd be just under two hours or so by the time they had fought their way past the press and grabbed a bite to eat.

With no thought of the media on her heels, Claire turned to the hunger the phone call had reminded her that she felt. She walked with head down to avoid over eager looks and found her way to the nearest mini supermarket. On the journey back, the ache from her ribs acted like a weather bell on her body. She slowed down to ease the pain.

Back on her house steps, she took out the hospital painkillers bent on using the ice cool water purchased from the shop to help her swallow them. She had never gotten used to taking pills, always needing to stir herself for the challenge, simple, as it always seemed to others.

Claire would throw the pills to the back of her mouth, take a swig of liquid, tilt her head back and sway her head from side to side. This she hoped lined the pills up over the entrance to her oesophagus before she attempted to swallow. Every time she felt compelled to shut her eyes tight and draw-pinch her features in as if sucking on a sharp lemon. The whole process was a major obstacle to overcome. Yet despite such preparation, one pill would conspire, she imagined, to lodge itself in her throat – much like photocopiers jamming when you have an urgent need for duplicates to meet a deadline – and she would find herself urging to throw it up. This time, though, 'operation pill,' was successful. And for this small victory she allowed herself to enjoy a little sigh of relief.

The squidgy BLT tasted good. The need to have some red meat to give her succour, despite the fat content, had won the day. As she browsed the Sunday paper's coverage of the events from Friday and Saturday, the breadth and depth of what had happened sank that little bit further in. Images and copy on the riots and their bloody aftermaths, the murders and fears about the rise of the far right were extensive. She also came across an article with photographs of both her and Tom. It imagined the ordeal that they had been through. She chose not to read it, but smiled at the headline: 'Was love re-ignited in the blood-ridden cell?' So who in her paper had let that one slip out?

Some two and half hours later George and Monica arrived. Claire's bladder was about to breach the dam. When she had made the call to them, they had all forgotten one salient aspect; Claire's house was not access friendly. After a brief pause and a long look up the steps to her front door, Monica piped up with her solution.

'Right George, you've always wanted to whisk me over the threshold. Well here's your chance my hunky fireman.'

With Claire holding onto the handles at the rear, Monica leant forward over George's back as he knelt down. With one bold move standing up, he raised her over and onto his shoulders. Initially, dramatically, he moved back several footsteps mirroring the landing fault of a gymnast vaulting, before twisting simultaneously around to face the steps. Monica let out a shriek and Claire held her hand to her mouth.

'Ta-da,' triumphed George.

The celebration was short lived when reminded of Claire's desperate plea in her eyes. He proceeded to instruct her on how to collapse the chair; something they all agreed should have been discussed earlier.

'Hurry up you two,' pleaded Monica, 'It's not as romantic as I imagined. The blood's rushing to my head.'

George playfully reprimanded her with a tap on the bottom.

'George, will you stop that.'

True to form, George disobeyed his wife. Eventually, though, in leaps and staggers, all three of them made it inside. It was just in time for Claire, who dashed to the toilet leaving them both to unravel themselves, but not before George had snuck his reward from Monica.

Claire thought that by having the noise and company of people she was at ease with around her, that it would help, little by little, to erase Harry, further. She placed the three mugs of coffee on the table and joined them both.

'So you broke into my house. How sweet of you George and to think that you went through so much as a result. And as for you Monica, how awful for you to hear that disturbing phone call,' said Claire.

'Hardly much stress and strain Claire relative to what you and Tom must have been through,' said George.

'I don't think it's time to go there George, is it Claire?' Monica raised her eyebrows at him. Had he forgotten Andrew's advice so quickly?

'Ah' responded George as he wrapped his big bear hands around his mug, suddenly finding the coffee held an avid interest.

'Yes er no, oh I don't know.' Claire's voice was vague, distant; she could feel herself being drawn back to Harry's room. Monica patted Claire's upper arm. The touch anchored Claire back into the room, refocusing her on familiar surroundings.

'The holdall?' prompted Monica, 'Tell us about it?'

'Of course, yes; part of the reason for us meeting here, thanks; I was lost in thought wasn't I?'

As Claire spoke, she brought them up to date with the contents of her diary including Colin's note. She removed the contents from the bag he had left behind. She assumed he meant for her to see and do with it what she thought fit. A strange lucky dip ensued. Monica made a list of the items, whilst George spread them out across the table: an adoption certificate, a letter written to someone called Robbie, a thank-you card written to Claire, a diary and an anthology of poems.

In addition, Claire reminded them of the entry in her diary – OS HELM PRE-JUDGE FELON.

Sitting back, all of them had thoughts, which collectively could be summed up as saying 'Hmmm?'

'Claire, why don't you read out what's in the card?' suggested George.

'Good idea,' agreed Monica, 'perhaps we should do that for everything on the table, apart from the anthology that is, unless anyone is particularly keen to do a recital.'

'Well … okay then, we can see where it takes us,' said Claire.

Dear Miss Yohanus,

I hope I was able to save you and this is you reading my note and not the police.

I found your diary by the way, when Harry got me to clean his car. It was me who wrote the last entry in it.

So where do I start? The stuff I've put in with this card may help. I mean, may help you, if you decide to look into things further. Not for me, but for people like me and our victims. Never thought I'd be like this. But an itch started this year. It got into my brain. Well, that's what it feels like. Like a worm eating me away. I don't know how else to describe it. And now, killing has become something I have to do. I can't stop. I won't stop. I know that now. Until I'm dead that is.

I was called Robbie as a child. That's how my adopted mum addresses me in a letter from her that I have enclosed. She mentions my step dad being interested in far-right politics. He was a cruel and horrible man. I killed him. He deserved it. Read my diary, it tells you more.

I've not been able to get hold of my birth certificate. There doesn't seem to be any record of it.

I've had my adoption certificate since I was sixteen. It wasn't until this year that I noticed anything different about it, apart from the fact that some sections have been blacked out. Also that phrase I've written in your diary had been stamped across the page. The adoption certificate has the time of my birth. I didn't know this was unusual until I read something about twins in the papers this year. The time of birth only appears if twins are born.

I went to the clinic where I'd been born, but they wouldn't let me in. They said that if I had been born there, it must have been when the place was a psychiatric clinic. I don't know what it is now. I took a photograph of the outside of the building and stuck it in my diary.

Before I go, do you know if I had had one wish to change one thing, then I would have wished for the gift of love to have permeated me from birth? So that all the things I have touched throughout my life would have shone. But some things, I now know, are not meant to be.

Robbie (AKA Colin)

'That's a lot to take on board. He packs a lot in. What does he mean by people like him? It all sounds so bloody incredible,' said George.

'It does,' Claire agreed. 'But why has he written to me? Why does he expect me to get involved?'

'But you are involved already aren't you?' asked Monica.

'Well of course. God knows now why I went to that lost luggage counter and why I just didn't hand the receipt over to the police.'

309

'Because,' said George, 'you've come this far without their real help and this chap Colin entrusted it to you. Perhaps he thought the police wouldn't do much with it. You know, the rant of a murderer trying to excuse his behaviour. Besides, why would they look any further? He was the killer and he was dead. Case closed. But with you; you just might be intrigued to look further.'

Claire looked upwards to the right, with her head tilted to one side as she thought about George's comment. 'Yes, you're right. I am.'

'Come on,' said Monica 'we've started now, and you're not alone in all of this are you? So let's see what else there is in the adoption certificate and then, tell you what, I'll read the letter from his mum, that is, after George has made a pot of tea for us all.'

Claire looked at the both of them. They were good motivators in so many ways. They had learned that Colin John Trahoney was born at 19:39 hours on 16 March 1974, England. The birth mother's forename was recorded as Ekaterina. Her surname was redacted. Her nationality was recorded as Romanian, born in Timisoara, 8 August 1953. The doctor assisting the birth of Colin was recorded only as Dr J.R.M. The name, surname and occupations of his adoptive parents were Patrick John Trahoney, lorry driver and Lillian Paula Trahoney (nee was redacted), a library assistant. The number of the entry in the Adopted Child Register was recorded, but the application number was redacted. Also redacted were details under the registration district, sub district, the date of the adoption order and description of the court by which the order was made, and also the signature and the name of the certifying officer.

George made a pot of tea and popped out for some biscuits as Claire had none stocked in her cupboards.

'So, enough of the focus on me, how are you feeling Monica?' Claire asked.

'What do you mean, about Tom, George, myself or just generally?'

'Gosh. I don't know. It's not like you to be evasive. I'm sorry. I guess my interest has unsettled you?'

No, it's not that Claire. Look, I'm so relieved about Tom. He's had it rough, but he'll pull through, of that I've no doubt.'

'And so what is it then? You've got me worried now.'

'Now it's my turn to say, gosh.' and Monica smiled. 'It's nothing really … well, my issues… It's just with George being so vibrant, you know what I mean don't you?'

Claire thought she did and nodded.

'Well, sometimes, I wonder if I'm enough and then I end up bossing him, just to feel in control of myself again. I feel so silly, but I don't know. I can't seem to stop myself.'

'Monica, if ever there was a man besotted, George is that man. I can't really appreciate what your disability is like for you, but my guess Monica, having listened to you both and watched the way you flirt with one another, that George is one very satisfied man.'

George had entered the house a few moments earlier and, as he climbed the stairs, had overheard the last part of their conversation. He rejoined them both rustling the biscuit packet as he struggled with his thick fingers to grab hold of the red tape and open it.

'Satisfied man you say Claire?' He paused for dramatic effect.

'Monica you are *the* love of my life and one hell of a mountain lion.'

'George you're just saying that,' retorted Monica as her face flushed.

'How right you are darling. But it also happens to be true. I love all of you, every inch. And no matter what, I always will … Now, who wants a biscuit?'

As promised, Monica read aloud the letter to Colin from his mother. It opened with the salutation of Dear Robbie. From then on it explained how his adoptive mother, Lillian, had named him Robbie after Robert Burns, her favourite poet. She claimed that Robbie had been given to them for adoption as his mother had died during childbirth. Apart from that the letter went on to say how sorry she was for never having told him that he was adopted and that if he was reading this letter now she must also be dead. She asked Robbie to forgive her and ended the letter by saying I love you so very much.

When later they read parts of Colin's diary, the true picture of his upbringing was laid bare. It was not difficult to see why he was so angry or how this emotion must have festered in his mind until he felt compelled to kill the images of his stepfather. But that alone didn't explain the itch Colin referred to.

When they turned the leaf in his diary, the photograph of the clinic where he had been born, which had been stuck to the next page, appeared. The breath went out of Claire. Her father worked there. She was sure of it. He had worked there since 1974. Confusion mottled her features.

'How incredible,' exclaimed Claire, 'I must give Dad a call, he'll never believe this, perhaps he can explain?'

'Ah,' remarked George.

'What's the matter?' asked Claire.

'I'm not sure calling your father just now is the best thing,' said George.

Surprised, Claire asked, 'What *do* you mean?'

'Yes, George, explain yourself,' said Monica.

'Well, I'm not sure how to put this ... '

George could feel the heat around the back of his neck. It did not feel good.

'Just bear with me and let me finish.'

George told them about the incident in the hospital on Saturday when it appeared to him that Andrew was attempting to remove Claire's diary.

'So what are you saying? My father tried to steal my diary. That's ridiculous, just plain silly. Why on earth would he do that?'

'I'm not saying he was trying to steal it. Let's just say he was trying to take it without being seen. I have no doubt he would have returned it, that is, after he had read it,' said George.

'It does all sound rather absurd,' said Monica.

Claire was lost for words. Anger towards George simmered. And yet she knew he had never been a man to make things up and of course, he had no reason to do so. It would not do any harm for the time being not to tell her father.

'Okay,' said Claire, 'I won't call my father. It all does seem an odd coincidence, but maybe it's best to let sleeping dogs lie. Tell you what though, let's get my computer going and see what we can find out about Osprey Lodge.'

The lodge, it turned out, was opened as a psychiatric clinic in 1972. Why it had been the location for the birth of Colin and his twin, as yet remained unknown. Interestingly, in 1978, when the first UK IVF baby was born, the clinic was taken over by a Swiss fertility clinic, 'New-Births GmbH.' This company is multinational and has clinics and regional offices in Zurich, Davos, Bertioga, New York, Toronto, Cairo, Jerusalem, Tokyo, New Delhi and Hong Kong. The headquarters is based in the small city of Davos. These facts in themselves would normally have passed all three of them unnoticed if it was not for the fact that Claire's father worked for the company. So presumably, he had started as a psychiatrist at Osprey Lodge and then developed his knowledge further within IVF when the private clinic was taken over. How much Claire's father had developed from the apparent start of his career in the 1970s was made apparent when they examined the web page containing company director details for New-Births. This showed that one Dr Andrew Peters Yohanus was made the Director for Global Fertility Research and Monitoring in 2007.

'I don't understand,' said Claire, 'I knew my dad was based in the fertility clinic in Osprey Lodge and from time to time he said he went travelling to various international conferences, but he never mentioned to me about being the global director for this multinational company. It's just too much to take in. I don't know why he never mentioned it.'

She paused in thought, a shadow of sadness passed over her face.

'The trouble is it reminds me of my mother's death and how my father kept that from me too.'

Monica spoke. 'It's all too easy for the small things to trigger the past. Then it's even easier to allow our imaginations to run away with fanciful truths as we spin anxieties into a complex web of possibilities. Then we're trapped and stuck amidst worry and doubts. Why don't you go off, have a shower, and freshen up? It'll help to change your mood. Trust me. George and I will do a bit more digging on the Internet and then when you're finished, how about we all order in a takeaway? We've brought along our overnight bags. So why don't we stay the night and keep you company?'

Claire looked at them both. Monica was right. The issues from her past were being triggered and giving them room to breathe would only fester and agitate her more.

'You're right. I'll wash away any blues and change into my pyjamas. Whilst I'm doing that, I'll leave it with you both to decide what kind of food you want, and then I'll place the order. You'll find some menus on the side in the kitchen. It'll be my treat.'

It was agreed. George and Monica quickly decided they would prefer an Indian takeaway that evening and circled in pencil their selections.

314

Next, they turned their attention to Osprey Lodge and the background to some of the directors who were associated with it. They discovered that the founding partners for New Birth were doctors who had practised medicine during the Second World War in Germany, Poland and Switzerland. Two of the doctors from Germany and Poland had served in the army during the war. Prior to the outbreak of conflict, they had both independently been researching gynaecology and reproductive technology as university academics.

The Davos headquarters and specialist gynaecological clinic was created in the early 1960s, built to replace outdated facilities and now claimed to offer state of the art care for pregnant women affected by asthma and other breathing disabilities who might benefit from the fresh mountain air.

As the ability to create IVF embryos grew, so did New Birth's network of fertility clinics. The multinational company made no secret of the fact that they operated the world's largest sperm bank and either owned or partnered with a large number of the five hundred and fifty plus fertility clinics around the world located in Africa, Asia, Australia and the Pacific, Central America, Europe, the Middle East, North America, Russia and Central Asia, and South America.

All in all, there appeared to have been millions of IVF births worldwide originating from 52 countries.

'Well, I'm dumbstruck,' said George, 'I just never realised how ubiquitous a practice IVF is. But why is it in places such as the Middle East and Asia? That beats me. I'd be surprised if those areas had fertility problems. More to the point, Andrew's part of a pretty large organisation isn't he? It makes my role as a retired director of social services look very backward in comparison.'

'Forget about comparisons,' said Monica. 'What concerns me is that I'm finding this all...well I don't know, unsettling to say the least; suspicious if I really put my hand on my heart.'

'How so?' said George.

'I don't know. It's just the little things. Piece them together and then they all start to look sinister somehow: the links to the Second World War army doctors, connections with Germany, one of the offices of New-Birth being located in Bertioga Brazil. That's where Mengele lived after the war.

'And look here on the screen. It's a small town of some 35,000 people. Davos is smaller still. Yet they both have fertility clinics. Just seems very odd. And so far, don't you think, we keep coming up against coincidences?'

George's face looked doubtful.

Monica continued. 'Yes, I know it's easy to find facts to fit theories. All the same, my gut tells me that something isn't right. There is a connection I can feel it. You felt something about Claire's diary. Otherwise, why mention it? We just haven't got all the dots yet. And when I think of IVF, which is, after all, experimenting with the creation of life and often the ending of it when non viable embryos are flushed down the drain or created specifically for drug research or the like, it makes the hairs on the back of my neck stand on end. It's Nazi eugenics all over again.'

'I think that's going a bit too far, but I do see your point,' said George. 'How on earth do we talk to Claire about it all; she'll think we're off our heads.'

SIXTY-FIVE

Sunday, July 15, 2012 – Iverna Gardens, London, Claire's House

Claire had been longer than planned, having fallen asleep almost immediately when she had stretched out on her bed before taking a shower. She rejoined George and Monica wearing her pyjamas. A red coloured towel turbaned her hair. Her cheeks glowed. She looked refreshed. George and Monica had stopped their conversation when the sounds of her feet pit patting in the hallway could be heard. They looked up and smiled at her. She looked restored.

Claire clapped her hands together. 'Right let me grab your choices and I'll get supper ordered,' adding, 'George, would you mind putting the kettle on and making a drink? Hopefully by the time I've dried my hair, the takeaway will be en route.'

Later, as they sat around the dining room table, George decanted three glasses of Alsace Pinot Blanc, the perfect accompaniment to the hot Tandoori chicken. When their glasses were filled, Claire invited them to reveal what they had unearthed during their afternoon research session.

Monica spoke first. Before she did so, she leant forward in her wheelchair, rested her elbows on the table, and placed her hands together with her chin lightly resting on her fingers. She gently moved her jaw across her hands, seeking to soothe away her hesitant and troubled thoughts and find a positive way to ease open what she had to say. Monica did not look at either Claire or George. Instead, she stared unfocused ahead of herself

317

for a few moments, her eyes diverted beyond the table towards the floor.

'When you were in the shower, we uncovered snippets of information about the organisation your father works for; including that is, the outline biography of its founding partners. There were several internet threads of information and discussions about these people. Some were purely factual and discussed their achievements that have led to the worldwide creation of a network that straddles the globe providing access to fertility clinics in every continent. However, some discussion threads are not so glowing. Some claimed that several of the directors had links to Nazi Germany. Numerous discussion threads talked about some form of conspiracy to perfect human beings by selection of the healthiest embryos.'

Claire sat still, her face for the time being passive.

Monica continued. 'The arguments, perhaps argument is too strong a phrase, the assertions made in these discussion threads feed into the wider swell of conspiracy theories that populate any number of internet sites. Now George and I have chatted about the sites that we've come across. And I know it's all too easy to start seeing patterns when no such things exist. However, I have ...'

Monica clenched her right fist and before continuing, moved her forearm up and down as if she were shaking some concealed die in her hand conscious she was gambling with Claire's emotions and reactions.

She looked Claire in the eyes and said, '... this deep seated feeling in the pit of my stomach. I only get that emotion when something isn't right. Now, we've not found evidence to support those feelings. But George and I agree on one thing. There does appear to be something below the surface of Osprey Lodge. What that something is, well, we don't know.'

Whilst Monica had been speaking, both Claire and George had followed suit in their body language and had leant forward on the table. However, as Monica continued speaking, Claire had changed her stance. She leant back against the chair and crossed her arms with either hand resting on the opposite wrist. George also noticed that her legs were crossed at her ankles. Claire's head hung low and her eyes stared at a knot on the pine wood table's surface.

When Monica had finished speaking, Claire hunched her shoulders up towards her ears, almost as if she was trying to block out thoughts. She breathed in deeply several times before slowly lifting up her head and looked George straight in the eyes. 'Do you have anything to add?'

George felt dreadful, stuck in a horrible situation. He spoke slowly, deliberately. His words heavy, like a lump hammer on a breeze block.

'With the links between Colin and Osprey Lodge; the possible connections, albeit tenuous, with Nazi Germany, it's difficult not to feel something sinister is at play. It does, though, I have to say, sound so very far-fetched. Probably is. But, I say this from years of experience. How often, even in social services circles, has there been uncovered, some truly wicked collusion between people intent on subjugating the powerless by manipulation? How often behind the veil of projected probity and kindness of some people – rich, famous and powerful – do we find dark secrets about their behaviour used to control others in unwholesome ways? The news is full of them: leaders of international organisations, celebrities and politicians, all have taken refuge in the world of *Secretgate*, pretending to be something when they're not.'

Before she spoke, Claire sat upright, put her hands behind the back of her head and stretched her elbows out wide.

'The times when people trust their instinct for self-preservation is often when they survive; by not boarding the aeroplane that crashed, killing all on board, by not getting into the car after a lift has been offered only to find out later that some poor unfortunate down the road did and was murdered or even when the Jews were initially gathered together, how many of them thought they were heading to their deaths? These gut reactions are there for good reason. I learnt my lesson harshly with Harry. Like you, I feel a deep sense of uneasiness. But my father, I ask you?' Claire asked rhetorically, her voice etched with incredulity.

Claire closed her eyes and continued speaking. 'I just cannot believe that. My love and my loyalty towards him naturally conflicts with all of your thoughts. I feel as if I'm betraying his love, even now, by finding reasons not to trust him. But, unless we look into this further, I know it will eat away at me.'

Opening her eyes, Claire leaned forward and took a sip of the cool refreshing wine. She allowed the taste and the aroma to seep in. She unconsciously licked her lips, wiping away, but savouring the last residue of the tastes in her mouth.

'The trouble is, how do we go about it without raising suspicions with my father, and at the same time, avoiding at all costs the exposure of him to hurt if, as is likely to be the case, and by God, I hope it is, all of our ruminations are unfounded?'

SIXTY-SIX

Monday, July 16, 2012 – Iverna Gardens, London, Claire's House

It was seven-thirty in the morning when Claire picked up her mobile and texted her father.

'Hi Dad, how are you? I was allowed out of hospital yesterday, but didn't let you know, as I wanted to have time to adjust to things by myself. I spent the night at home, but found things more difficult than I thought I would. I'm just wondering, would you mind if I came over and stayed at yours tonight? I could do with a bit of TLC. Love you lots, Claire xxx'

Twenty minutes later Claire's father replied.

'Hello darling, good to hear from you. Of course, you can stay at mine. That would be lovely! What time will you be over? Or shall I pick you up if that suits you better? Dad xxx'

'Brilliant! Thanks Dad. I'm calling in to see Tom this afternoon. Visiting hours end at 8. So I should get to yours between 8.30 and 9. That okay?'

'That works for me. As you're out of hospital now, I'll pop into the clinic today, but will leave in good time to make sure a sumptuous meal is waiting for you. Take care and give my love to Tom, Dad xxx'

'Thanks Dad. Will do re Tom. Looking forward to supper ☺ xxx'

Claire felt dreadful for deceiving her father and so found it easier to avoid direct verbal contact. She was relieved that he hadn't picked up the phone as was his way sometimes, "I just need to discuss arrangements," he'd start off and one thing would lead to another and invariably he would find out something she hadn't planned to discuss there and then. Besides, after she had been in to see Tom, Claire knew there would be lots to talk about with her dad. It could all wait until then anyway. He would actively listen to her, she in turn could ask him about his work in the clinic, and who knows where the conversation might lead them.

Claire could hear the sounds of George and Monica stirring and called through their bedroom door that she was just popping out for a short walk around the neighbourhood for some fresh air. Then she would make breakfast – hot croissants, marmalade, orange juice and lashings of coffee.

'Excellent,' boomed George.

'Thank you,' shouted Monica.

Later, when Claire headed towards the kitchen, she could smell the rich aromas of coffee and warmed croissants. George had the breakfast waiting, bless him she thought and gave him a hug by way of thanks.

By 10 am, they were more or less ready to go and be on their way. Claire assured them that having made it through the first night with their support and company, she would be all right by herself now. They all agreed it was best that they arrived at the hospital at different times, just in case they bumped into

Claire's father. They knew really, probably, he would not be there, but they wanted to make sure a belt and braces approach was in place.

'Just in case,' George had said.

It was unlikely any of them would be asked any awkward questions by Claire's father, but even so, if they were faced with even the mildest of queries, they knew their facial expressions when together would reveal a conspiracy and they would be unmasked.

The return from Claire's house to their car was made all the more easy for George by the nature of gravity in carrying her down the steps rather than up.

An hour or so later, George and Monica were pulling into their gravel driveway. The area was free of the press now. Yesterday's news in the recycling bins.

As George put his arms under Monica and eased her out of the front seat, she whispered in his ear, 'I love you George. I love you so very, very much.'

'Ditto,' he replied, and kissed her on the cheek.

A POISON TREE

By William Blake (1757-1827)

I was angry with my friend:
I told my wrath, my wrath did end.
I was angry with my foe:
I told it not, my wrath did grow.
And I watered it in fears,
Night and morning with my tears;
And I sunned it with smiles,
And with soft deceitful wiles.

And it grew both day and night,
Till it bore an apple bright.
And my foe beheld it shine.
And he knew that it was mine,
And into my garden stole
When the night had veiled the pole;
In the morning glad I see
My foe outstretched beneath the tree.

SIXTY-SEVEN

16:00 – 20:00 hours, Monday, July 16, 2012 – St. Thomas' Hospital, Westminster Bridge, London

Tom was lying on his front when Claire arrived, his head positioned to one side, allowing him to gain a glimpse of the outside. Claire made a mental note to ask the nursing staff to move Tom into the adjacent bed next to the external window. She would arrange for a mirror to be angled in such a way that he could look into it and in the reflection see the Thames and the thoroughfare of river traffic.

The nurse in charge of Tom's welfare had told Claire that the operation to his back injuries had been successful and a number of missing chunks of skin had been grafted from fleshier parts of his body. During the week, he would have one more operation, to ensure, as far as possible, that the injuries to his feet and hands would heal effectively. However, due to the complexity of plastic surgery involving ears, Tom would have to be transferred to the London Free Hospital, as they possess national expertise in the remodelling of facial features.

'Hi, how are you?' asked Claire.

'I feel like my body is taking from Peter to pay Paul.' He smiled.

'That's funny. I was thinking you were more like the basket containing five loaves and two fish.'

'Very funny,' said Tom, 'if they take anymore, there'll be nothing left of me and then if I'm still here, well that'll be the miracle!'

325

'The miracle my love is that we both found each other again.' Claire lent down and kissed him warmly on the side of his head.

'You're right. Thanks for the kiss. I'm sorry I can't reach you to reciprocate. So, how are things for you and what's happening in the outside world?'

Claire brought Tom up to speed with what had happened over the past 36 hours.

'So when you see my father, say nothing' said Claire.

'I shall think of this as a confession.' He smiled broadly. 'No one will hear about it. The secret lies between us. Just make sure you stay safe. The mere thought of you being in danger saddens my heart.'

'Come on, I hardly think my father is going to harm me, do you?'

For the next hour, before George and Monica arrived, they talked about the riots that had occurred across Britain. Neither of them had the desire just yet to go back to Harry's place in conversation. From time to time Claire treated Tom as a Roman emperor feeding him generously with succulent grapes, using a soft tissue to dab the loose juices from his lips. When his parents arrived, Claire took a step backwards to give them space with Tom. It was good to see the family reunited. It was even better knowing that this was her family too.

At 7.15 pm, Claire said her goodbyes. She wanted to grab a hot drink and collect her thoughts before she travelled over to her dad's. Claire was a Trojan horse. She felt absurd and disliked deceit, but here she was practising it. Yet in the confusion of recent events and, in the light of things so far uncovered, now was not the time to stick rigidly to black and white values or throw caution to the wind, no matter how much she loved and trusted him.

Later, with those thoughts of justification in her mind, Claire drove off in her car, calling in at a shop on the way over to her dad's. The evening was comfortably warm and the roads at this time of day flowed freely. She travelled with all of the windows wound down. The rush of the wind around her head swished her hair this way and that. It felt good. The elements fed her so much energy. She must remember to feed off them more often and not robotically travel from A to B, focused only on the destination.

20:06 hours, Monday, July 16, 2012 Eaton Mews, Knightsbridge, London

It was not long after eight-thirty in the evening when Claire parked her car near to her father's place and grabbed her overnight case from the back seat. She glanced along the balconies up and down the street containing an array of shrubs and colourful plants. All of which enhanced the elegance of the white stucco facades. The whole street was quiet. Its elegance was apparent. Quietness graced the area. It was far from the helter-skelter, the hustle and bustle and the fast brash life of London's more urban street scenes. Serenity was a watchword of the Mews. She breathed in its scent before pressing her father's gold coloured circular bell set within the black gloss painted and solid wooden front door. A few moments later and the door was swiftly opened by her father. His warm loving smile, matched by his strong embrace and fatherly kiss, gave Claire the reassurance she needed.

'Hello darling. So lovely to see you,' he said. 'Come inside, I've cooked up a delicious treat for you – flambéed chicken with asparagus and new potatoes,' one of Claire's favourites. Her dad was coming up trumps, 'and I can catch up with you about Tom when you're ready.'

Her father's house consisted of two main colours. The walls and ceilings were crisp snow white, as too were the majority of the furniture and picture frames adorning strategic visual parts of the internal space within. There was for example a poster size framed photograph at the terminus of the hallway adjacent to the glass rung of stairs. It was of her father atop some alpine ski resort dressed in ski clothes, holding onto skis and poles, accompanied by two male companions.

The shelving and edging parts of the house such as the banisters, skirting boards, and mantelpiece, were gun metal grey. The downstairs floors were natural wood, whilst upstairs they were white. The whole house possessed a spatial tranquillity that encouraged one's mind to float freely as if it was travelling through the air amidst the swirling tendrils of classical music. Furniture, although large, such as the two, four seat settees, somehow managed to be discreetly non-intrusive. Technology on the other hand, banged its drum loudly in the house, most dominant of which, was the 48-inch high, 72-inch wide flat TV screen in the living room. When asked by Claire previously what had possessed her father to acquire such a monster, he had said:

'I sometimes have to deliver conference speeches from home or participate in them remotely, so a screen of this vast size is necessary. Besides,' he had added, 'watching films on it, which yes, I occasionally do, to relax, is an adrenaline rush and cinematic experience. You really should try it sometime'

Claire had never taken the opportunity; her busy and globetrotting life had often taken first dibs on time.

'I've made the upper rear en suite bedroom ready for you. If you remember, it's the one overlooking the garden,' her father said. 'From there you'll see how far the branches have grown on the cherry blossom tree your mother planted all those years ago. Why don't you pop your things up there and freshen up, supper will be ready when you are.'

'Aw thanks Dad. You're just what I need, a bit of mollycoddling.'

Her hand trailed along the smooth banister as she went up the curving glass staircase. A picture of Claire's smiling mother looking down upon her was hung on the first landing. A reminder of her dad's soul mate each time he retired to bed, she knew. It always made her feel good too when she saw her mum's joyful face, never sad, which was wonderful. Perhaps it was because mum's eyes followed you whenever you approached an image of her. Mum loved the camera. Her smile was always quicker and longer lasting than a flash. And in this photo, it looked as if she was reaching out with all of her energies to greet the photographer, Claire's dad and to say, "I love you." Happier times; indeed they were. Now, good times were coming again. Tom and the triangle were back together once more.

Downstairs, clothed in a red halter neck dress, Claire took up a seat at the dining table. Her father poured a fridge-cooled glass of white wine for them both and raised his glass in toast.

'You look radiant this evening and so much like your mother darling. It must be the way you've pinned your hair up tonight.'

Claire's teeth flashed quicker than the camera too. She felt as if her face was splitting from the joy of being with him.

'To my beloved daughter, may your life from now on be full of love, health and happiness. You so very much deserve it darling.'

'Cheers Dad.' Their glasses clinked together. Claire added, her eyes full of love and warmth, 'Thank-you for seeing me behind the bruising. I admire your vision and how effervescent as ever you are about me. Keep it up. And don't you ever stop you hear,' she said.

'Never,' he replied, his mouth stretched into a broad happy smile.

As they each took hold of their napkins and spread the gun metal cloth on their laps, her dad spoke.

'So how's Tom today after the operation? He's been through a lot of trauma hasn't he?'

Her father had been right about one thing. Claire studiously avoided any reference to the detail of what both she and Tom had suffered. That was their private universe. It was locked away temporarily in the past, waiting for them both to tap into the security codes and gain entry to their end of life experiences.

'The surgeons were able to replace missing chunks of skin on his back today and have sewed up the gashes or used surgical tape to join the separated skin together. His back looks tortured still, but medical staff think that apart from scar tissue, the potholes that have littered his body should eventually disappear. Monica says vitamin E oil will help to reduce the scars and speed up the process, so we're going to smuggle some in and treat him ourselves.'

'It'll take a while to recover his ability to walk properly again I imagine,' said her father. 'Although, speaking this afternoon with some colleagues specialising in these fields, most patients – the ones who stick at it of course – virtually recover full mobility.'

'Good. That's a relief to hear. Tom and I hadn't discussed recovery periods.'

Claire went on to explain the forthcoming operations that Tom had still to undergo at both St Thomas' and London Free.

'Well, the NHS seems to be doing a remarkable job. If you don't mind, I'd like to send them some flowers and a donation.'

'No, of course not, that's a lovely idea.'

'And going back to your bruising again, it's good to see the swelling on your face is subsiding. I just love the colourful hue. What about your ribs?'

'Hey! I'm fine though. Really, I am.'

Claire's father looked doubtfully at her.

'Okay, I'm a tad sore around my rib cage, but I've some heavy duty painkillers from the hospital chemist that do the trick. To be honest, it's good to be in one piece.'

'Talking of one piece, I noticed your work diary had been returned by the police. The note on the top had mentioned that the chap who had saved you had it in his possession, is it still in one piece? I wonder how he got hold of it.'

'Yes me too,' she felt awful lying, 'But like me it's still together. I always keep it on my person. Although right now, it's up in my overnight bag. It must have fallen out in the car when I was ...' Claire swallowed a lump in her throat.

'More wine?' Claire's father asked.

She looked up. 'What?'

Her dad held the tilted wine bottle towards her.

'Yes, that's a good idea, thank you.'

Her father spoke as he poured the wine into Claire's waiting glass; the liquid's glug provided a soothing background echo in the room.

'The main thing is that you have your diary back. I imagine it would have been awful to have lost all of your notes.'

She white lied smoothly again. She was like an expert surfer coming in on a wave. Her footing, she felt, was assured.

'Oh gosh, yes, absolutely. I'd be finished without it. I haven't yet submitted my final report on the US election road trip. I've not touched the diary since. I've been so caught up in searching for Tom.'

Claire diverted the discussion from her diary and went on to tell her father about the meetings and events she had had in pursuit of tracing Tom. She stopped before arriving at the point when Harry had knocked on her front door.

Her father looked fascinated and impressed. Indeed, he always was with his daughter's tenacity – like a dog at a bone; just like your mother, he thought. That is what truly worried

331

him for her sake. The conversation moved on to lighter topics when her father asked about the US electoral trip, her travels and the meetings, she must have had with powerful and influential people in the Western world's premier superpower.

'Come on, tell me some stories no one has heard of. I'm dying to know some gossip. There must be more to what's published in the media. You know what I mean, things just you and the person you've interviewed are privy too. Off the record stuff,' her dad tempted and teased her.

'Dad,' she replied, her tone indicative of mock disapproval. 'You know I can't. But ... I do have a tasty story from my travels. I bumped into a fellow reporter down in Jacksonville, Florida, a chap called John Baderson. Hadn't seen him in ages, so we had a few drinks in a local bar by way of catch up, you know how it is, and when we had covered old ground, I asked him, if he had any interesting angles on the election campaign. Well, he told me an interesting story about some very senior guys in the Administration...'

SIXTY-EIGHT

21:35 hours, Monday, July 16, 2012 – Eaton Mews, Knightsbridge, London

When desert was served – strawberries frosted in dark Belgian chocolate, Claire's mouth watered.

'Mmm; this is delicious. You have gone to town for me, my favourite again. Thank you'

For a while, they sat in comfortable silence, savouring the flavours melting on their taste buds. Following desert, her father poured out some coffee for them both and they retired with mints to the voluminous settees. Claire asked for an update about his life. And so her father told her 'everything.' She learnt about his new role as a director within New-Birth and how and why it took him all over the world.

'Gosh. Where have I been? Mentally, I mean. You have done so much and I've missed so many aspects of your life. I'm so sorry. I've been wrapped up in my own world obviously.'

'That's okay darling. You've had a tumultuous time and my promotion came, I think, about the same time you and Tom split up. Since then, you've been here, there and everywhere. And so have I. It goes to show how easy it is for details to slip by unremembered in the need for telling, and then in the familiarity of one another, we forget to mention the important bits sometimes.'

All was explained. Claire relaxed. There was nothing sinister going on. All the doubts she, George and Monica and even Tom had had, and the joining up of silly conspiracy dots, had been a complete waste of their time. They were worries without foundation. Claire could go to bed tonight with a relatively clear head. The nightmares about Harry's place might come, but the ones with her father playing the bad guy; well they could go back into the box of her subconscious. She yawned. A sure sign she was more tired than she realised. Claire stood up and was joined by her father. She put her arms around his back and rested her head on his chest.

'Dad, leave the dishes where they are. I'll sort them out in the morning. You're looking tired. Why don't you go to bed too?'

He tilted his head forward and kissed the top of her head.

'I will darling. I'll rinse them and then, I promise, they'll be waiting for your attention in the morning.' He kissed her again. 'Night, night.'

Claire made her way slowly up the stairs, trailing her fingers this time along the smooth white walls. Tactile connections were important to her. The simplicity of the house, with its high ceilings, space devoid of clutter, conveyed a meditative energy that soothed her footsteps towards bed.

She ran hot water into the bathroom sink and washed away the last residue of makeup. After getting into her pyjamas, Claire looked for her light overnight cream and remembered that she had left it in the pocket of her summer coat. The cream had been a last minute purchase from the chemist on the way over. Her coat was in the hallway coatroom cupboard.

As she made her way down the first flight of stairs and onto the landing where the picture of her mother hung, she heard her father's mobile ring. He answered it. She was about to step onto the first glass rung, but instead her body froze to the spot. Her father's voice was hushed, but he spoke in sharp tones.

'Sébastien, why have you called? ... The diary? God man, why call now? My daughter's upstairs in bed ... No, she doesn't know anything ... No, she hasn't kept a written record of her investigation when looking for Abimelech...'

Hearing her Father use Tom's surname jarred in Claire's chest.

'... How do I know?' he asked rhetorically. 'She's my daughter. I trust her ... With my life? Of course! Look, everything's fine...' He lowered his voice, 'He can trust me... Yes of course! I will sacrifice anything ... What? Yes, I've seen your e-mail ... Look Sébastien, I've said there's nothing to worry about ... Good. I'm glad you are. Then, good night!'

Her father's voice had sounded angry, but it had also been laced with a heavy cocktail of fear. The fear spread and was contagious. Its tentacles had slithered up the glass stairwell where Claire stood rooted to the landing and wrapped its reach around her legs. She was imprisoned by the emotion. What was her father caught up in? If he came up the stairs now, he would know she had overheard him. If she moved, even the slightest moving of her bare feet, the skin unpeeling itself off the floor's surface might make a noise. Her bones in her knees might crack if she moved her legs, some hidden air pocket just waiting to explode and announce its presence. Whatever she did, he would hear her. She was trapped.

Every muscle in Claire's body was taut. Her tight chest barely moved as she breathed in wisps of air. Her hearing was amplified as if she had a stethoscope tethered to her father's movements. She could hear his fast, shallow breathing, sense that he was running his fingers through his hair and rubbing his temples, as he always did, when faced, as he seemed to be, with constricted choices and a conflict of interest.

It had all gotten terribly personal for him. Would the Führer expect the ultimate sacrifice, to demand that he end his own daughter's life? No, he was autonomous. He could not. He would not make such a sacrifice again. He had already made his choice. The email and the phone call had only reinforced the fact that his painful decision was right. He was committed to the journey now. The terminus was fast approaching. It was time to complete his destiny. Seeing his daughter tonight had been the one final joy and blessing he had wanted and now cherished. The time was now.

Claire's body trembled with relief when she heard her father walk away and make his way into the kitchen. Her teeth, released from the adhesion of tension, involuntarily chattered. It was over. She could escape to her bedroom.

Sleep would be an enemy tonight. She lay awake. In her bedroom, thoughts of conspiracy, betrayal, and disbelief and of the unknown tumbled back and forth in her head. Her thoughts were going nowhere. They were stuck on a dry cycle of spinning ideas. The timer of thought collisions was set though. Not until her mind was done and then, and only then, and despite herself, it would switch off and she would sleep.

SIXTY-NINE

2300 hours, Monday, July 16, 2012 Eaton Mews, Knightsbridge, London

The Network has total control over its followers. At one level, it carries out the function of a life support machine. Life or death is merely a switch. Once in, relationships are under the microscope. All can be subjected to the Network's cruel care pathway if it chooses. Claire's father knew this intimately. There was only one sure way out of the Network. It was one of life's certainties. Sébastien's contact had only hastened him to act more swiftly. He was convinced of his own decision now. There was no turning back.

Yet even now, his perpetual longing haunted him. The past, except the memories and the emotions, was forever out of touch. How he wished for the ability to travel back in time and change what he had started. His wife would be alive. All things would have been different. The tragedy of life he thought is the difference between dreams and reality. They can be painful and yet still co-exist in the same universe, acting as endless reminders throwing stones at your faults and failings.

His life had been determined for him. The choices he had made were the chains that could never be unbroken. Yet he still had choices if he chose. And he had.

Following his wife's demise, he had planned his exit strategy. It was simple, effective and natural. He would use his body's cleansing system to work against itself. To be implemented only if Claire's life hung in the Network's balance. It was now.

He had been devastated when he was made aware of her tragic contact with the Network's progeny. Dusting off his plan had been easy. He reached for it, waiting as it was, in the top drawer of his mind, and took it out.

He had injected the retrovirus C-SRC into his body. Its presence is known to cause colon, prostate and breast cancers. Gene therapy and other forms of medical treatment might have helped him to live. That was not his aim. He ignited a chain reaction by injecting a mutation of the K-Ras protein. This suppressed the efficacy of apoptosis and stopped his body from sweeping away the billions upon billions of harmful cells that were even now multiplying and spreading within him.

Protein 53 had been made to malfunction. His body would no longer fight to suppress the cancerous tumours. Indeed, it would aid and abet its own demise. His body was now an optimum environment for the resistance of therapies. His days were numbered. The post-mortem would discover this.

The pathologist would see the disease. He would visualise how the cells had scrambled to spread themselves throughout the deceased's body, infecting the lymph nodes and vital organs. He would know that it would have quickly undergone metamorphoses into high-grade lymphoma. He would know it led to one inevitable outcome, a swift pathway to painful death. All this and more would go in the final report for the coroner.

Everyone would understand the reason for the outward decision made by Claire's father. Moreover, that included the Network. More than anything, he owed Claire life – his life; he willingly gave it up for her. What parent wouldn't do the same he had reasoned?

Tonight he took the last steps of the dead. He removed the phial from the fridge, snapped the top off and ingested its contents. The powerful dose of morphine would block the pain to follow. He walked into his study, looked around for one last time, took in the pictures of Beth and Claire, swallowed rising emotions with difficulty and then took up a seat in his office to pen his final letters.

My Dearest Darling, Claire,

These are dark times. There are darker times ahead.

In my youth, I embraced a vision. I never dreamt as a callow man, what the consequences would truly be. Your mother's death was a consequence. I did my duty on behalf of the Network. She stayed silent for you. She knew what would happen to you otherwise.

You should know now that I have reached the end of my pathway. It is time for me to go. It is time for me to be silent too.

I loved your mother with all my heart. I still do, deeply. You may think me a foolish man expressing futile emotions when she can never hear them. But, if by some ethereal power her ears are opened, then... well, I shall soon know. Until then, my heart, as it has always done, bleeds and beats for her.

I do not expect you to understand why I have done what I have done, nor do I seek your forgiveness. The mistakes of history cannot be erased or raised from the dead. The pathway I have taken, I have taken. Indeed, I did so voluntarily back then or so I thought.

Innocent at first, I took each goose marching step to become part of the Network. Its vision was born out of the demise of the Third Reich; indeed my Führer had the foresight to set in motion the eventual creation of the Fourth Reich.

339

The Network coerces a global hive of followers; I am one of them. We are everywhere connected but unconnected; we are like unseen Wi-Fi, our presence is hidden, but felt.

However, seeing the terror of the creations that nearly consumed you and Tom challenged my beliefs and desire to continue my commitment to the Network and its foul progeny. The rightness of my decision, if that was possible, was reinforced tonight by a phone call and the chilling confirmation in my heart that I would be unable to neither demonstrate undying loyalty to the Network nor withstand its probing to find out what you know. I could not afford to delay death.

I am sorry. Immediately I have regrets in using such a weak word under these circumstances; the word "sorry" is, I realise, pitiful. It carries no weight when the hurt I have caused you by betraying your trust is irreparable.

What happened to you and Tom and to others is only a foretaste of the beginning. The DVD I have enclosed will shock you to the core. It dates back to a time when I had not long arrived at the clinic. It shows the birth of two boys, dizygotic twins, you know them as Harry and Colin.

I share with you the DVD and a file so you alone will know a human tsunami is coming that one day, not so very far away now, will engulf mankind. It will appear to be unstoppable. People will clamour to be saved. A saviour, already identified and nurtured by the Network will arise. The Network will prevail.

340

I say I share it with you alone for I know in this you will listen to me. You must. For you need to put aside your journalistic desire to break the biggest story a reporter will ever know. But even if you do find it impossible to resist, then the Network and its many tiered echelons across the globe will create so many alternative scenarios and half-truths, that no one will know fact from fiction. The news will fizzle out. It will end its days being kicked around the dustbowl of conspiracy groups.

It is all too late anyway. The die has been cast. The foot soldiers of the Fourth Reich, many more than Harry and Colin, have been unleashed. They are maturing. A new kind of blitzkrieg will dawn.

So, I urge you, I beg you, to think of your own life, what you have lost, what you have yet to gain with Tom. You have found in him and he in you, a powerful force of union – a love that I believe you will not willingly seek to tear asunder.

To save yourselves, you must desist from any further investigations that I know you have been making; I know, for your eyes and gestures told me so tonight. You need to ensure that George and Monica believe you when you say to them, "My Dad was innocent and our suspicions were groundless about him and New Birth GmbH." My death, yes, my death my darling, borne out by evidence of a terminal illness, will shock them into the reality you shape for them.

As for Tom, I know you will want to, need to share these dark secrets with him. The heavy burden will be easier for the both of you if you do. The close bonds you have forged whilst imprisoned will have been strengthened. Trust him, but no other. Your lives and that of George and Monica depend on it.

You must destroy this letter, the DVD and any other records, including any in your diary. Write an article about your experiences of being kidnapped. The Network will expect something from you to be published. Do not disappoint them.

Of the Network, what should I say? New Birth GmbH is the friendly face of the Network. It is the front company for the laundering of its currency – IVF progeny. The Network is the bagman of the Fourth Reich. Harry and Colin were part of the pilot experiment. As you now know, the pilot was brutally successful. Imagine a world populated by people like Harry and Colin. It is coming. As for the 600 Brigade, the Network seized upon the opportunity to test out how easy it would be to ignite chaos. The tinder you see is so very dry, so very thirsty. Flash mob violence and copycatting communities are so easy to inflame.

But as for now my darling Claire, I have one more letter to write. This one is also for you. It is one that the police will want to see. It will be my suicide note. Once again, forgive me. Plain language conveys a stark message horribly so I know.

I can imagine you have a jug full of emotions and confusion pouring through you right now. I wish I could be there to support you through it all, to hug you until your tears subsided and your breathing calmed and your mind settled into acceptance. Again, weak as the word is, I am sorry. I am truly sorry.

Please remember this. There is no other way, trust me in this. My silence buys you life. Look up Mother Teresa's poem, it starts off 'Life is an opportunity avail it.' I urge you to follow it with all your being, for time is short. Life is precious. This, at long last I now know.

And please my darling Claire, do not allow my mistakes to mar your future.

I love you more than words can ever say; I always will.

Dad xxx

A teardrop that fell from his eyes smudged the kisses. He picked up a tissue from the box by the side of his desk and quietly sobbed. What is done is done. It cannot be undone. Dreams are time travellers. Sadly, our bodies are not.

The silence of the night, of the house gave no succour. It never did. His one love had died here. He was the architect of her demise. Loyalty led to death. That should be the marching words for new recruits. Yet when death touches or threatens your own blood relations, what then? There would be no forgiveness for him now though he felt, although his mind, body and soul yearned for it. In that moment a memory flickered … a seminar lecture, he had attended as a young undergraduate. Where was it filed? It had been part of his extracurricular activities to understand ethical issues from different perspectives. The speaker had been a student from the Catholic Society – 'Cathsoc,' yes, that's right, and he had talked about forgiveness. Searching through reams of files and paperwork, he found the lecture note. Relief, he knew not, why then, but it was.

As he read and circled in ink sections which spoke to him, a light breeze fluttered in through the open window, almost as if a dove was landing on his desk.

Forgiveness Pathway

If you are ever, deep down, to find peace and joy, then the handmaid of this treasure lies in forgiveness and reconciliation with one another and God. This is the pathway you must tread.

Remember the antonyms of forgiveness: blame, censure, condemnation, find fault with, reproach and reprove. Know also the antonyms of reconciliation: alienation, antagonism, break-up, falling out and separation.

God seeks only that you come to him and seek forgiveness and reconciliation. He is waiting for you, to welcome you back into his arms, to follow his ways. Listen to Psalms 139 and 32 as God speaks to you.

You know me through and through, from having watched my bones take shape when I was being formed in secret, knitted together in the limbo of the womb... God examine me and know my heart, probe me and know my thoughts; make sure I do not follow pernicious ways and guide me in the way that is everlasting.

Happy the man whose fault is forgiven, whose sin is blotted out ... 'All the times I kept silent, my bones were wasting away with groans, day in and day out... At last, I admitted my guilt... And you, you have forgiven the wrong I did, have pardoned my sin.'

A sinner, who knows he has sinned, needs only forgiveness, to be loved without fear. Yet how often have you become deaf to the voice of love that calls you to be reconciled to God and to others and to forgive the sinner or be forgiven?

The difficulty is this, forgiving without holding something back, adding in your own conditions, ifs, and buts to the forgiveness, or being unable to forgive and reconcile at all.

Yet when you follow the pathway of forgiveness and reconciliation, you move out of darkness into light, from limiting love to unlimited love. You become filled with an all-embracing compassion. Forgiveness and reconciliation can become part of what you are and enable you to bring this gift to yourself and others. It is your choice. Live in peace, always.

Claire's father bowed his head and desperately asked God for forgiveness. When the pain of grief and letting go subsided, he penned a second letter, the suicide note. It was bleak, to the point. He had terminal cancer. He did not want his daughter to see him wither, suffer and die. He would rather pass away full of vigour and energy. That was how he wanted her to remember him. He mentioned that New Birth GmbH would need access to the house to remove all of his work files and IT equipment. He informed Claire that his Will was held at Barnaby and Graylings Solicitors – all of his assets, including the house had been left to her. He signed it, to my dearest beloved daughter Claire; I hope you find it in your heart to forgive me. I love you tremendously, but it is better this way, trust me. My love always, Dad xxx

Beth's ashes had been scattered amongst the roots and the soil of the tree. Both Claire and he had spent a quiet afternoon digging over the soil to make sure her ashes were mixed and blended. It had been exhausting in many ways, but conversely therapeutic. Beth was let go and released to live in Mother Earth. When they had finished, Claire had made some tea for them to drink under the dappled shade of the tree's branches. When settled in its strong embrace, he and Claire had shared and relived many vivid memories.

To ensure the tree remained in situ, Claire's father had had a covenant drawn up on the house and its curtilage, which he hoped, should prevent any future owner from removing his wife's beautiful garden creation. In his Will, he had asked that his body be cremated and allowed to mingle in the soil around it. Until then, he would join her by letting his blood merge with the earth. He could no sooner leave her or chop it down.

It was quiet outside. The tangerine segment of the moon barely cast a glimmer in the night sky. The air was pleasantly warm. He sat down on the grass with his back against Beth's tree. He felt closer to her this way. The scalpel cut easily into the veins across either wrist. The blood's warmth ebbed onto the grass, seeped into the soil and started immediately to do its job and nourish the tree's roots.

The morphine had served him well. A quiet stupor wrapped and nestled itself around him and in time overtook him. He drifted away upon a cloud venturing into the darkness and as yet for him, an unknown destination.

SEVENTY

07:18 hours, Tuesday, July 17, 2012 – Eaton Mews, Knightsbridge, London

Crowded thoughts had given sway to dream filled images. As the sunlight awakened Claire, the paper clipped sheaf of memories, so vivid and real in the night, dissolved into oblivion. She pulled back the side of the curtain, just enough to gain a view, leant forward near to the pane and looked around to gain a snapshot of the day. Crystal clear sky brushed its colours around the rooftops and trees. She glanced down into the garden. Her father was up early as usual. He was sitting on the grass with his back against the tree; soaking up the tranquillity of the day, she thought.

She breathed and sighed. How would she face her father this morning? Whatever was going on inside her father, she still loved him. It was all too easy to speculate and jump to wild scenarios. Last night was testimony. Her thoughts had had her riding wild mustangs of worries, which only sleep, it turned out, could tame.

The rain showerhead stormed her body with water. Invigorated, she dressed. The dark shadows under her eyes would disappear under a light foundation. To loosen her tight facial and shoulder muscles, she scrunched her face and moved her jaw in shape shifting angles as if toffee was stuck to her teeth and pulled her shoulders back, pushing both elbows inwards that caught knots in a pincer movement and squeezed an air pocket trapped in her backbone. Other stretching exercises and windmill arms helped to loosen the straightjacket feeling that strapped her body. It had been a rough night.

Downstairs, the simplicity of her father's house and its long sweeping curves designed to soothe stresses away through its quiet symphony of light and shadows failed miserably for Claire. Her mood for once had not been uplifted by water. She felt dishevelled inside.

No movement. No sound. The silence served tennis balls of nerves that bounced at odd angles in her stomach. As she made her way into the kitchen, the study's desk light was on, strange, she thought. Light from the ceiling window in the kitchen reflected in the stainless steel sink and draining board. When Claire looked at the surface, she squinted; such was the power of the sun's brightness. Yet the spotlights on the walls glowed brightly too.

All was not as it should be. She moved into the other living rooms, night lit illumination smouldered across internal walls and floors. Claire's footsteps kept pace with her rapidly increasing heart rate as she raced towards the sliding glazed doors that led into the garden.

Her feet were pulled up short; her body entangled itself in slow motion as the two white envelopes propped against the glass doors drew her attention. Claire's heart plummeted and blood rushed into her head as she stooped to pick them up and read in a blur their contents. The enormity of their message was impossible for her to take in on first reading. She let the letters flutter to the floor.

She slid the doors open and stepped back through the portal of time to her mother's death and burial. Collapsing onto her knees, she took her father into her arms and rocked his body back and forth. Immediately the grief buried fathoms deep within her blew all of its ballasts and erupted. The birds fell silent. Claire's distress call and sobbing, almost mutely beneath them, was impossible for their hearts to ignore.

Claire re-read the letters again. Gradually, it all sank in. The euphoria she had felt from the escape at Harry's had been short lived. One of life's illusions, it was good at that. She felt so very alone. Had she the stomach for any more of this she thought. Temptation to know more took over. She watched the DVD with a hand held to her mouth almost for the entire duration. As Mengele drowned the wretched woman in her own blood, Claire rushed to the bathroom and vomited. The DVD had continued playing and when Claire had returned to the living room to take up her seat again, Mengele was part way through a speech. His cheeks were flushed pink with excitement.

Saturday, March 16, 1974 - London

'… Initially no government, no statistician, no one, will notice the negligible change in the statistics of deaths at the hands of our foot soldiers. Yet I tell you, forty to fifty years from now, wave upon wave of our pre-determined serial killers will rampage across the world. Some of us may fall victims to their savagery. We must be willing sacrifices.

The world will be terrorised. Our genetically engineered storm troopers will be the vanguard leading to the emergence of a new world-order – the Fourth Reich's. They will be driven; they will be relentless; they will not stop. Their individual atrocities will stun the world. Blood relationships will be strained and severed.

The masses and the intelligentsia will clamour for an end to the carnage. They will demand that governments purge the human race, eradicate the viral spread of terror. When the time is right, when the carnage has reached its zenith, our leader will speak out. There will be willing ears. Others will follow. Until then, we must be as silent as a boa constrictor embracing our prey.

So, gentlemen, let us on this day, in this room, in this moment, raise our glasses filled with the still warm blood of the mother of our first soldiers... Long Live the Fourth Reich'

As one, they stood up, their heavy heels robustly snapping together, 'LONG LIVE THE FOURTH REICH.'

When the screen had gone blank, Claire sat on the edge of the settee in stunned silence. The sun was bright outside. Surreal feelings of having just emerged into the street from watching a horrific thriller film at a daytime cinema flooded her senses. Only the surreal did not leave her as she walked away from the screen. Everything was so difficult to take in. It was impossible to absorb in one sitting.

Naturally, Claire had not lived through the Second World War and all of its atrocities and hardships, so it had always been easy for her to look back at the antics of individuals involved in Nazism, dressed in their oversized baggy clothing, as being actors in a grim but dark comedy. It did not feel real; just stories or exaggerations made up to frighten future generations and justify the new versions of democracy marketed to the post-war public.

When people of the past die, she thought, experiential memories disappear too, no matter how much evidence exists. Maybe it is because there is too much information out there, people do not see any more. We need to remember and feel the past to understand, but how, she wondered? Watching the DVD had felt visceral enough. Something she would never forget. The imagery was now burned deeply into her.

Her thoughts turned and twisted to her father. Did the dark secret held by him for all of these decades loosen the grip of love she felt? She struggled and wrestled. It did not. How could it? Yet, it was impossible for her to comprehend the two realities of who he was. The one she had known and the one that had remained hidden. Was he two men in one? No, he was not. Nevertheless, why had he followed this cause? He never explained in his letter. The thoughts would stay with her wherever she went. The cause though, if she could call it that, was, as it had always been, a curse. Perhaps as her father had said, the exuberance of youth swept him along until the entrapment was complete. The cauldron of its spells had woven itself deeply into his life, so much so, her mother had died so that Claire might live. Had her father truly been the cause of her death? How could she forgive him? Yet her mother, seemingly so, went willingly into oblivion for Claire. Perhaps, both of her parents had made that choice. The realities could not readily be absorbed. More importantly, and perhaps for her own sanity, Claire's heart could not countenance the thought that her father might willingly have been the perpetrator of her mother's demise. Yes, denial felt better than the truth, well this time anyway.

Her mind raced around on a treadmill. She was like a dog chasing her tail. Further fruitless contemplations and her blood still ran cold. Three episodes from the DVD stood out: the clinical killing of that poor frightened woman; the toast in blood for the future of the Fourth Reich and; most of all, the young face of her father caught on camera, in what she could only see as insane euphoria of being in such 'exalted' company. Her eyes dropped to the unopened file her father had left out for her. If Claire wanted to know more, she need only read on. Had she not already suffered enough? She teased open the cover.

The story of how it all began. The point of return had been left on the stairs last night.

Monday, August 20, 1934 – Berlin, Germany

The window loomed from floor to ceiling. Its presence dominated the room. Light poured in. The shadow of Hitler's stature stretched across the dark wooden floor. The length it cast far exceeded his height. The long roads to power had been crushed under foot. Those in the way disposed of. His shadow now embraced the whole Nation. Today was tomorrow. He was president, chancellor and head of the army: the father, son and Holy Spirit of the Third Reich – the Führer.

He was looking forward to the meeting today; it might confirm his recent dream and gathering thoughts. The astrological readings a few weeks ago had continued to vex him. The Astrologer's final words had confused him. "You will conceive the future from offspring born of man's body yesteryear." The phrase made no sense. When he had invited the man to explain, he was unable to add anymore, other than a vague statement that had been banal in its utterance: "This is what the stars have foretold. The meaning has yet to be revealed to you."

Hitler's private secretary opened the office door and announced that Reich Leader – SS Himmler and Dr. Clauberg, a professor of gynaecology and a specialist in assisted reproductive techniques from the University of Konigsberg, were waiting in the anteroom.

'Good, please show them in.'

'Greetings Professor,' said Hitler, extending his hand to shake Clauberg's.

When Hitler spoke, his secretary took notes. 'Tell me Professor, how it might be possible to conceive offspring, let's

352

say, a hundred years from now, from a man who no longer lives?'

Clauberg adjusted his large round glasses further up the bridge on his substantial nose and cleared his throat. They were irritating habits, and all before he had set his somewhat round face into what he thought, Hitler imagined, was a square and determined jaw. His demeanour did not sit well with Hitler. Nevertheless, personalities must be put to one side for now, he thought.

'There may be a number of ways. This year in America, a Dr. Pincus demonstrated how eggs had been taken from a rabbit's ovaries and fertilised in a laboratory dish to create embryos. The embryos were successfully implanted into the rabbit's uterus. The offspring were born without problems. Despite his research being condemned in some quarters, some scientists in America are researching the viability of creating human embryos. It is only a matter of time before this process is perfected. With regard to offspring for birth one hundred years from now, we would need to understand how embryos, eggs and spermatozoa could be kept alive and healthy until they are needed… Freezing the materials might be a way.'

Hitler had one more question for Clauberg, 'Tell me, might it be possible to transfer a man's intellect and character into the embryos?'

'Indeed, that could be possible. Beneficial characteristics have been transferred into plants and animals by the interbreeding of similar species. Such practices have been carried out for many centuries mein Führer. This has been done to make them fitter, stronger, more productive.'

Himmler, a student of agriculture, nodded his agreement.

Clauberg continued. 'Of course, many mistakes have been made. It is a matter of trial and error…. And so, just as it is possible to produce good characteristics in people, ones which are not so desirable for the human race may also be created.'

353

Hitler stood up and pondered the possibilities as he walked slowly around the room. His dream had been confirmed. He made a snap decision. 'The Reich cannot, and must not have the Americans beat the Fatherland. This must become one of our highest priorities. Reichsführer, you will oversee the research. We need to increase the fertility of our purebred women. This will be the backbone for the Lebensborn strategy. Use whatever resources as necessary, at whatever the cost and... whatsoever the price in blood.'

Himmler spoke, 'Would you mind leaving us alone Professor? Please wait in the anteroom; I would like a private word with the Führer.'

'What is it Heinrich?'

'May I suggest an additional approach?'

'Go on,' said Hitler.

'The idea stems from what Clauberg said, "... just as it is possible to produce good characteristics, ones which are not so useful for the human race may also be created." Could we not look to create a breed of humans that when fully mature as adults might be drawn to kill purely for pleasure? Think how much fear and havoc that would create in local communities across the world when each individual starts their campaign of terror in the countries of our enemies.'

Hitler got up from his chair and stood in front of the massive window. He watched as a mother walked past the building, pushing a pram with two young babies sat either end. She was accompanied, he assumed, by her own parents and possibly a sister. How bonded they all looked, busy talking and absorbed in their own lives. Hitler turned on his heels and snapped his boot heels together. The thunderstorm clap, echoed in the room. 'I agree and I have just the name for it. You will like it Heinrich.'

Hitler sent a private letter to Himmler on the same day that Poland was invaded. The needs of Germany were paramount. In a few short weeks, a ready supply of women of childbearing age would be rounded up and transported for Clauberg's research.

```
Dear Heinrich,

I wish to build on our success in
disposing of disabled children under
the law for the prevention of
offspring with hereditary diseases. I
would like you to work with Wilhelm
from the Interior Ministry and assist
in extending the programme to adults.
I had previously asked him to
establish gassing facilities, and he
informed me recently, that these would
be established in Brandenburg,
Grafenck, Bernburg, Sonnestein and
Hadamar.
    I have asked my personal physician,
Dr Karl Brandt to lead the new
programme and direct a medical team
from Aktion T4. Those adult males
deemed to be fit and criminally insane
will be transported for Brigadeführer
Clauberg's use. These instructions
reflect Reich Executive Order
1035/20081934 and as such, the use and
disposal of the male organisms are for
his discretion.

    Adolf Hitler
```

Claire could almost feel Hitler's ghost hovering in the room. Still gloating, still smiling and still revelling in the fear his power emanated from the past. Only the past lived. She had touched it now, brought it back to life. Was she the daughter of a Nazi? The thought cruelly teased her. It was true. There was no escape from it. When she re-read the letter from her father a third time, emotion gave way to reason, German logic took command. No one knew yet that he was dead. No house window overlooked where he lay. Contrary to her father's wishes, she made a copy of the DVD and of the file too. Perhaps he had secretly wanted her to do it this way. Next, she called the police, Tom's parents and lastly, her father's PA at New Birth.

The wheels of change had begun.

The police officer who attended was understanding, gentle and professional. There was no reason to suspect anything other than a suicide. She arranged for a funeral director to attend and made Claire a pot of tea before recording a witness statement. Claire was subdued. Her face was drawn. The officer was reassured when she learned that relatives were on their way to support her. The officer stayed with Claire until the undertakers had been and gone. Despite the recommendation of the police, she had watched as her father was enclosed within the black plastic cocoon of the body bag. As the grey silver coloured zip was drawn up over his face, Claire noted a chapter closing in her life – forever. Her father's body was being taken to St. Thomas' Hospital mortuary where the bodies of Harry and Colin were still stored. Death had brought them together again, full circle.

Her father's employers, New Birth, had sent over office clearance staff with alacrity. Their arrival in the morning and so quickly, surpassed Claire's expectations of them coming over midweek. The shock on her face served to reinforce her grief-filled features. It also helped to mask anxieties igniting her heart when they worked to strip and box up her father's study. She gladly left them to it. Within an hour, they were gone.

Half an hour later, with remorseless efficiency, a large display of white stargazer lilies arrived. The note therein said, 'With our deepest condolences from all of the staff at New Birth.' The note even had a signature on it, below which was the title Chairman and Chief Executive. On closer inspection, the signature was not real. It was a copied and pasted digital version. To Claire it signified more. The reach of the Network was layered everywhere. Trust no one, she thought. How easy would that be? Her father's written words were the new mantra she and Tom must live by. However, how long can one survive without trust?

In the hazy days that followed, George and Monica were stalwarts. She allowed them to help her back into living the reality that they saw. Yet, that Monday and the following day, Tuesday, and like the many days yet to come, Claire remained detached, aloof; it stopped all from probing, asking questions, casting doubts and unravelling the façade her eyes desperately tried to convey to all she met.

Was the Network everywhere? The thought coursed through her veins. At times, she felt contaminated, part of the corruption seemed to seed its way into everyone's lives she imagined. How much she would now give not to know the truth. For despite her father's protective warnings, his unintended outcome had created an open prison for her. Were all future words and behaviour set to feel like small talk?

As colleagues and friends preoccupied themselves with the material concerns of their lives and the world responded to the ripple repercussions still being felt from 9/11 and the Arab Spring, she imagined her heart would slowly die inside. She was a bird no longer free. The cage door had been opened. The view outside of Harry's prison had looked beautiful, but now everywhere and virtually everyone seem corrupted. How far did the Network reach? Who was themselves and who was they? How many were sleepers? Were any active in her friendship circle? Maybe several were embedded as colleagues, she worked with.

Her Father was right. Stay low. Say nothing. The *real* outside world was frightening. She truly was a lonesome wanderer now without a home. The poem haunted her. She longed to tell all to Tom, but not yet. The time would come when he was well enough and they would be alone. And then, she knew, he'd be a rock. Until then she had to be determined. She had to force herself to carry on.

SEVENTY-ONE

14:30 hours, Wednesday, July 18, 2012 – St. Thomas' Hospital Mortuary Room, London

Sonita Paneshi stared at the DNA results with disbelief. These two men shared half of their DNA profile. They were siblings. Blood relations: two men, two murderers. She had been asked to type up the report and then e-mail it over to the investigating officer in the Metropolitan Police Service. Now that she had finished it, Sonita thought of Claire Yohanus and decided to make one discreet phone call first.

She thought her call might spark interest and appreciation. She was wrong. Sonita was met with a monotone reaction and a flat, perfunctory 'thank-you.'

Initially Sonita was nonplussed, until later, when she read the register of new arrivals and saw that Claire's father had been brought in on Monday. Sonita had been off on a day's leave. No wonder her reaction, then, she thought.

SEVENTY-TWO

Thursday, July 19 to Tuesday, August 28 2012 – Claire's Place, Iverna Gardens, London

Claire's work gave her a year's sabbatical. Although in the end, she never went back. She wrote an article as suggested by her father and left it at that. Following his funeral, Claire put the house in Eaton Mews up for sale. It fetched well over £7 million. It provided her and Tom with the freedom to choose another life. In time, they did.

Tom, following discussion with his monsignor and subsequent confirmation with the Church's hierarchy, was allowed to give up his duties and responsibilities and was released from clerical obligations. His monsignor blessed him. He wished him well in being fruitful in his new vocation; one he said Tom was more suited. They parted as firm friends.

Physical recovery for Tom was painfully slow, although eventually his strength did return. Before then, he would feel the snarling stitches rip at and chew into his skin every time he was audacious enough to walk faster.

"Not so very fast" – the stitches spoke to him, and he like a tenacious terrier, had been harshly reined to heel. His slowness doused him very quickly with the raw face of humility. One day, when a fine drizzle floated down from the heavens, Tom artfully dodged larger droplets dripping from awnings, as he daringly occupied the 'fast lane' on the outer side of the pavement. In so doing, he was 'sneered' past by a frail looking elderly woman, who with a cane in one hand, clicked her way around him on the inside, muttering and moaning to herself as she went by, "lane blockers".

Yet, the healing of the body is one thing. Healing of the mind, overcoming the nightmares and night sweats for both of them took time. Moreover, on top of this psychological mountain, Claire still had her story to tell.

SEVENTY-THREE

Wednesday, August 29, 2012 – Claire's Place, Iverna Gardens, London

Claire thrashed her way through the nightmare and the demon scouts melted away as if twinkling snowflakes caught in the emerging heat of the sunrise. Tom's sleeping pill still had hold of him. He slept undisturbed by her movement. The night sweat had left her and the bed linen wet. A stanza from a poem by William Blake, 'London,' stepped into her consciousness and added to the shiver that shook her body like a wet dog shaking its coat full of water. She rolled out of bed and curled the length of the duvet into a half sausage roll, tucking its edge under Tom's relaxed and prone body. Meanwhile, she was almost the opposite. Until they had shared everything she had been through, her state of readiness, the preparedness to fight stood sentinel over her like a bodyguard. Tom had sought to support her, but she had deflected him.

'I will talk about things Tom. But I'm okay right now. There will be time for that. Bucket loads. Until then, let us focus on getting you physically fit. Then, it will be my turn.''

The flight to water helped to clear her mind for landing on fresh perspectives and, too, enabled her to let go of tangled dreams. As her fingers curled around her scalp and she vigorously massaged the shampoo into her hair, the words from William Blake's poem reverberated in her mind's eye again.

I wander thro' each charter'd street,

362

Near where the charter'd Thames does flow,
And mark in every face I meet,
Marks of weakness, marks of woe ...

Yes, London felt contaminated to her senses right now. Until Claire got away, she knew any hope of cleansing her mind, body and soul would fail, like King Canute. Even yesterday on the Underground, yet another busker had followed her with more interest than she ever wanted, ever again. Men's eyes seemed everywhere. Her radar was constantly up and her nerves consequently, ragged. She studiously avoided looking up at the CCTV cameras. They were eyes on stalks prodding her insides.

When she came out of the bathroom, the tempting aroma of toast and coffee filtered into her senses. Tom must be awake. That was a first. As she entered the kitchen, his back to her buttering toast, she smiled warmly, her cares melting in unison. It was good to be with him. He was swathed in a crimson dressing gown, "pretentions to be a cardinal," he had said, "and now it represents me as a fallen man." His hair displayed the groomed qualities of a night's sleep, with one side flat and the other sticking out at odd angles, some strands were protruding like a bent metal coat hanger.

'Hi,' she said, wrapping her arms around his chest, touching his chest hair and resting the side of her head against his shoulders. He smelt good. Better than coffee and more moreish than the scent of Valrhona Noir Extra Amer chocolate. 'This is a lovely surprise. Just what I needed Tom. Thank-you.'

As they ate freshly warmed toast and marmalade and relished the cafetière made Columbian coffee, Tom's eyes showed their first signs of a sparkle that looked capable of being sustained. His face looked relaxed. She so loved him. Love was easily given to him and in doing so, she felt good inside, for she knew how much love, he was capable of reciprocating. And it was a love that enlivened, emboldened her to live life in the words gifted by Mother Teresa. Even the dark pupils of his eyes shone now. They had miraculously lost their flat matt appearance. The sun was returning and Tom was responding to its warmth at last. And when he said, 'What shall we do today?' the first signs of his returning Spring were a sure sign that new life was underway. She rejoiced.

'Let's go somewhere hot, close and romantic,' she said on impulse.

'A private health spa you mean?'

'I was thinking more of abroad, but within easy hopping distance.' She toyed with his mind. She knew where she wanted to go. He just did not know that he wanted to go there too. He would soon.

'Ah. You're thinking of Florence, perhaps?' His eyebrows were raised.

'Not quite. But I'll give you a clue. In Latin it might have been known as Sanctus, but in medieval Italian, it might have been pronounced another way.'

He humorously chided her, 'Call that a clue? I'd call it impossible.'

'Aw, come on Tom. You know you can do this.'

Claire's eyes twinkled. Her body had forgotten how in these past weeks. But its muscle amnesia soon evaporated in this gentle repartee with Tom. Laughter was not so very far away then, after all.

'Think of Greece,' she added.

'Well, that was helpful,' he retorted, his right elbow resting on the table, his hand and fingers poised in contemplation across his temple and brow, his eyes shooting a twinkle back at hers.

'Ah! One of the Greek islands, perhaps?'

364

'You're getting warmer ... Perhaps.' She could not stop herself then as a silent giggle shook her chest and a smile stretched like the Golden Gate Bridge across her face.

'All I can say, Madam, is that this tease is duly noted. Payback will be my pleasure – *entirely*.'

The infection burst out of him too, and a playful chuckle was music to both their ears.

'Now come on. I give up. Mercy, please,' he begged.

'You're almost there.' Here look at this map of the islands; I'll time you.'

'But there's over twenty of them'

'Five, six, seven ... and counting.'

'Got it,' he said triumphantly, 'Santorini.'

'Excellent. Fifteen seconds.'

'How is that easy to get to though?'

'You should listen to my words more closely darling.'

Teasing was such fun.

'I said, hot, close *and* romantic. There is a glorious romantic and luxurious hotel on the island, whitewashed walls, deep dark and spacious interiors and an outdoor restaurant set upon an outcrop on top of a cliff overlooking the crystal clear blue Aegean Sea. Other nearby islands appear as if they are floating across the water on the horizon.' She enthused, 'It looks heavenly.'

'It sounds magnificent. Let me see it.'

They fired up the laptop and before long both their hearts had grown wings, whose flight path followed the same compass direction – SSE. As it turned out, it was easier to fly to Santorini than they had both first thought, with connecting flights to the island from both Gatwick and Heathrow. There was a longish wait at Athens Airport, but it all seemed worth it. Next stop, Santorini. The desire to escape was in them. So much so, that a few phone calls later, a surprise vacant room, very expensive, but... what the heck... with Claire's now, undeniable wealth, saw them booked into a luxury suite, coupled with butler and maid service (if they wanted) for a two week holiday starting Friday 31 August 2012.

This time, heaven could not wait.

GREECE

SONNET 116:
'LET ME NOT TO THE MARRIAGE OF TRUE MINDS'

By William Shakespeare (1572-1631)

Let me not to the marriage of true minds
Admit impediments; love is not love
Which alters when it alteration finds,
Or bends with the remover to remove.
O no, it is an ever-fixed mark
That looks on tempests and is never shaken;
It is the star to every wandering bark,
Whose worth's unknown, although his height be taken.
Love's not Time's fool, though rosy lips and cheeks
Within his bending sickle's compass come;
Love alters not with his brief hours and weeks,
But bears it out even to the edge of doom.
If this is the error and upon me proved,
I never writ, nor no man ever loved.

SEVENTY-FOUR

Saturday, September 1, 2012 – Santorini, Greece

When they had booked the flights and hotel on the Wednesday, the journey had not seemed so long in their heads. However, a long journey brings the body down to below gravity quickly. They were tired as the airplane touched down at 6.15 am on the tarmac at Thira Airport.

Yet, unadulterated pampering awaited them. As they left arrivals, a chauffeur stood waiting for them with both their names typed and prominently displayed on a sign he carried. They looked at one another. This was another world and Claire, more than Tom knew at that moment, was hungry to step into a parallel universe and an alternative reality.

When they were closeted within the air-conditioned limousine, with chilled champagne for breakfast in their hands, they knew then that their collective shadows might fade in time. A few sun-drenched days recuperating by the pool in Oia, where they rested in the water, with their arms on its edge as they gazed out onto the Aegean, showed them the way.

Tuesday, September 4, 2012

Their car swept them along the spine of the island in a short fifteen-minute journey. They had hired a catamaran for the day. The captain greeted them warmly as they boarded. Provisions for their water borne private excursion were already on board. All Claire and Tom had to do was stretch out on the foredeck, relax in the ever present sun and let the crew do the rest. Water for them both was the cleansing spirit they needed. By 10:00 hours, the luxury yacht had anchored off a secluded bay and together with a hamper, snorkelling gear and large beach umbrellas they were ferried to shore in one of the boat's small landing craft.

'We shall be back for you at 19:00 hours,' said the crewmember in broken English, 'wishing you a blessed day.'

And with that he took off. They watched as the boat cut a surge through the calm sunlit sparkling water as it headed back to the mother ship, which was making ready to leave. It up anchored and left them to the much-vaunted privacy offered by the cruise company.

'I've no idea where we are, have you?' Tom asked.

'Nor me. It's part of the company's claimed mystique,' said Claire.

'Righty ho,' he said.

Tom made sure the yacht was well underway and then slipped off his clothes. 'Freedom. Come on, first things first, water'

As his progress was slower than Claire's was, although physio had helped a great deal, it did not take her long to catch up and overtake him. Not that Tom minded, of course.

She ran wading into the water and dived in when the depth increased. Up she came, spurting water like a whale, 'Wahoo,' she wailed.

Tom followed suit and dived in, coming up underneath her. She swam off like a dolphin, not so easily caught, and surfaced every so often along the small cove's coastline. Tom had no chance of keeping up and she knew it. Until he was fully fit, she was the master of the sea.

She found him shadow bathing under the umbrella, his naked body filling out nicely after the torture and virtual starvation he had been through she thought. Droplets of water dotted his body and clung to the hairs on his skin.

To forget everything, to securely wipe clean the unpleasant memories of the past month or so was a dream she wished could be engineered. Claire settled down next to him. She kissed him lightly on the lips and then laid back full length too. They held each other's hand, absorbing the silence around them. It was one devoid of man-made noise, and allowed nature's voice to sing to them: the lapping of the waves and the high distant calls of 'eee-yup' from the common terns that soared on the air vents above the cliff face behind. The voices of the birds almost mimicked the greetings made by people that hail from the north of England.

Tom squeezed her hand. 'Thank-you for this Claire, all of it, and for being there for me in all the long days and weeks since. In large part to you, I'm feeling much better and stronger. But we haven't talked about you yet. I know you haven't wanted to, putting my needs for recovery first and giving me time to heal, to cope. I'm ready now. I'm ready to be here for you if you want to talk.'

The warm, comforting air was soothing, and time on this beach, in this moment, with Tom, alone together, was as it should be, as it needed to be, just for her. As Claire approached the close proximity of those memories with Harry, her eyes welled with tears, her chest tightened and her body shuddered as the pain stuttered out. It belched out in fits and painful starts. At one stage, before she could even attempt to speak, Claire brought her hands to her mouth in a futile attempt to block the awfulness of the pain, which by its own force, had its way and burst out of her in discordant trumpet sounds that erupted through her trembling lips.

Tom moved his right leg, quietly towards her body until it was lightly touching her. She would know he was there for her, that he was prepared to love her through anything, to do anything, to help her survive and to be free from her pain. Minutes passed. Eventually, Claire was able to draw in enough breath to speak. But even as she did so the siren wail from deep within her drowned out all other sounds. The gravelly grief stricken groan stretched its sounds out across the bay. Claire brought both of her hands together and with her forearms covered her eyes. It was a futile attempt to block out the burning cinders of emotions seething inside of her – anger, sadness, shame, humiliation. But she beat them all down, and in a trembling voice, unleashed a ragged torrent.

'I want to cut it out of me Tom. But I can't,' her voice shrieked. 'I can't reach it or touch it, but it's there, his indelible stain.'

'Do you mean your father?' asked Tom hesitantly, wary of the erupting venom.

'No.' Claire stretched the word out in a wail to almost breaking point.

'Fucking Harry; that fucking evil bastard. He fucking raped me!'

Her arms flung outwards, one smashing into Tom's chest.

'He fucking raped me, do you hear me now?'

Claire's chest heaved as an earthquake of pain erupted and shook her body violently.

'My poor love. My poor, poor love.'

Claire reached down for his hand and held it tightly.

'I feel so humiliated. He took away my intimacy. He raped me of my independence, raped me when I was unconscious.' Her speech gathered pace. 'There was nothing I could do. The bastard invaded me. I wish I could kill him again and again and again.'

She screamed out the words, thrusting a knife deep within Harry's chest. That felt good; so very, very good. 'I'd cut his fucking heart out. Just like Colin did to others. That would be justice. That would be *my* justice.'

371

Claire's face was red with anger, swollen with tears.

'You made it through Claire. Don't forget that. You fought him back. You showed him – tooth and nail – how you would have tried to stop him. You showed him your spirit, your courage. He was no man. He could only face you when you *couldn't* fight back. You're right. He was a fucking bastard.'

Tom fell silent. Claire did not speak. Her hand felt warm. He gently stroked her skin with his thumb. And then he thought of something. He ventured.

'Now he's dead, is there anything you can do to erase the pain?

And immediately she responded.

'Yes an effigy. We could build a fucking effigy and burn the bastard at the stake.'

They were both silent again for a while. A half hour passed. The how was the question.

Claire spoke. 'There's some driftwood scattered here and there. With a bit of imagination that could work. Let's see if we can build a semblance of a body, my anger will do the rest.'

Sometimes small symbolic actions help the healing process. It gave Claire back power, control, and all the things Harry had taken from her. It was she who would be in control now. Not he. Not ever.

After forty minutes reverting back to their ancestors' roots by separating to search the cove as hunters and gatherers, they both returned to the spot, where Claire wanted to end it. She had chosen a shade covered area of the cove, sheltered by an overhang in the rock face.

From the darkness he came. To darkness, he belonged.

Tom took out the laces from his plimsolls and Claire used them to tie the monster together. The great pretence actually felt like it was working. She stood back. Tom spread dry leaves at its base, though in the intense and arid heat, none of them thought Harry would last long. Claire would use the gas from the camping stove stored in the hamper provided for their tea.

The yacht's steward had asked of them. 'You English, like your tea, yes?'

Tom and Claire had looked at one another and then naturally, they both agreed with him, what else could they do? It was so very sweet of the man.

Claire lit the stove. The noise from the flames gave off a very satisfying hiss. The sound made her feel venomous as she stayed in the roles of judge and executioner. Harry burst into flames. His face writhed in agony.

'Burn you fucking bastard, burn in hell,' shouted Claire, her anger given full vent under the sun.

And when Harry was all but blackened and grey ash, Claire jumped and stamped on his bones, burying them deep into the sand.

'You are gone Harry. Good fucking riddance.'

And with one final crushing stamp of her feet, Claire left her nemesis behind, this time for good.

When they walked away from the grave, she and Tom held hands. Claire breathed in and let out a deep satisfying sigh.

'Thank-you, I feel that I've purged myself, like a volcano erupting spewing out all my black ash and lava of hate, hurt and anger.'

Her face was red from the flames. Splodges of burnt debris splattered on her forehead and cheeks. Tom brushed the marks away with one of the hamper's napkins. She studied Tom's features as he methodically worked away. How good it felt to be so close to him. When he had finished, he leaned forward and gave her a gentle 1940s film star kiss. When he pulled away, he said, 'So how do you feel now?'

'Exhausted,' she replied, 'some food might help, not much though, my tummy feels tight.'

'Let's eat some treats first, see how you feel, perhaps leave the savoury for later. A little something, light and sweet, may just be what you need. What do you think?'

'Lead the way Sir Galahad,' her choice of words and tone signalling a step change in her mood.

'You honour me my Lady.'

Holding out his forearm, Claire ceremoniously entwined hers with his and together, with their eyes following the celestial wings of the terns as they flew in organic formation across the waves, they returned to sit under their beach umbrellas. Tom served up an array of sweet treats from the depth of the hamper and choosing between three chilled bottles, uncorked a Boutari Vinsanto noted, claimed Tom, 'As a sweet white wine, with a rich mixture of honey, crystallised fruit, raisins and sweet spices designed to complement dessert.'

'I'm impressed. I hadn't realised you were a sommelier.' She smiled. Tom the romantic lion-heart was well and truly back.

'The Catholic Church taught me a thing or two of course. It's all part of the preparation for Mass.' His eyes sparkled reflecting the luminosity of the sea. 'And naturally, a typewritten note in the hamper helped.'

She smiled, the redness lining her eyes diminishing. The treats, the wine and Tom, a perfect accompaniment to sweep away at least one shadow that haunted her.

Later they both lay back again to rest. Tom lying on his side using one arm to prop himself up, chatted about his wine tasting experiences whilst training in the priesthood and the different varieties available to pilgrims on the road to Santiago. Of course, being a faithful pilgrim to the last, he could not but help himself as he sampled the temptations of the grape. His voice blended into a background of white noise. He could see that Claire's breathing had slowed and her chest was rising and falling slowly. He continued, deliberately talking in a soporific tone. With her eyes closed, her arms by the side of her hips, she drifted off into the most sublime afternoon nap.

When she awoke, Tom was no longer by her side. She sat up and saw that he was by the water's edge skimming stones across the silky smooth surface. When Claire joined him, she said, 'How's it going?'

'The skimming was a bit of a struggle at first, not surprising with less fingers, but I found that if I imagined the missing ones are still there, then my brain somehow does the rest.'

Look,' he added.

With a lightening flick of his wrist, the stone skimmed lightly five or six times across the surface, before losing momentum and disappearing into the waters below.

'I'm pleased for you Tom. Your spirit of recovery is redoubtable. Fancy some snorkelling?'

He nodded.

'It'll slow me down and give you a chance to keep up with me,' she teased and poked him playfully in the ribs before running off along the beach to pick up the swimming gear.

SEVENTY-FIVE

Wednesday, September 5, 2012 – Claire and Tom's hotel room, Santorini

Claire walked back into the bedroom, her footsteps padding across the marble floor. Tom was asleep on top of the super king size bed. It was a blessing to have so much space. The ruby red coloured bedspread had crumpled here and there around the movement of his body. He looked so peaceful, she thought. His features, devoid of any worries were rested. All of his facial muscles appeared tranquil. His skin was taking on the silky smooth qualities acquired from sun-adorned hours.

She had looked at herself in the full length and wall width mirror and noticed too, that her body reflected the honeyed tones of a tan. Despite all, she looked calm. The dark shadows under her eyes, the underbelly of grief that had clearly been displayed since her father's death, had all but gone. The whole island, as an outcrop in the Aegean Sea, encouraged one, naturally, to relax, unwind, stretch out and allow the passing currents of life to flow unhindered. All of this though, Claire knew, was a mere bubble. A natural optimist, reality held the needle to burst their haven at any time. It was a safe place for Tom. He, as yet, remained oblivious to the deeper knowledge she possessed. She picked up the white sarong from the bed and with one swirling motion of her hands wrapped herself within its embrace. The light gust of air moved to and fro free flowing strands of Tom's hair, which for a short while, looked like underwater anemones in search of food.

She walked away from the bed and gradually moved through the fading shadows of the room and out onto the open expanse of the balcony. White washed walls abounded, necessitating that she wore sunglasses to dim the brightness of the outside world and help her eyes adjust to the light.

She and Tom had skipped breakfast and lunch today, opting to fast until the evening meal. It was part of their plan, twice over every seven days, to cleanse their bodies of the toxins built up from weeks of stress and to remove the residue of anaesthetics that resided in Tom's body following the operations he had undergone. So when Claire leaned out on the railings and looked down upon the houses, land and seascape, her senses, her desire to hunt and gather food, were heightened. The aromas from food being cooked far below in the houses reached out its tendrils and toyed with her nostrils. Added to which, the nearby sound of someone eating what sounded like an abundantly juicy melon, appeared to travel faster than light to reach her.

The bay's light and shadows danced together, proving how well nature allowed the two to coexist and yet through each day, diurnal combat ensued as they chased each other across the world, until at last, in the setting of the sun, the darkness had its way. Was that how it should be? Was that the natural order? Was that how it will be?

Thoughts, thoughts, she wished she could shut them all away. The phrase, 'ignorance is bliss,' must surely have been penned by someone who had faced the 'mirror of truth,' and now wished, they forever did not know. The truth can be ugly. Pandora's Box once released was never forgotten. The insight given into the evils that were coming to plague the world was a test of anyone's resolve to address the truth once revealed. Her father's warning in his letter was a constant. The consequences for her and for Tom and others would be fatal if she acted.

She was quite possibly the only person in the whole world of some seven billion people who knew what she knew and was, in this moment, on the side of the light. It was so tempting to walk in the dark: to pretend the world everyone sees is her life too; to allow the world to revolve and evolve into the destiny being shaped by the Fourth Reich's Network every second, every minute, every hour, every day, every year ... until ...

The weight of the pressure was enormous, especially when she brought it to consciousness, and ever more so when she was alone. Tom may be close at hand, but even if all her friends and extended family could surround her, she alone possessed the aloneness of someone on whose shoulders rested the fate of the world. And she was no leader of the free world was she? She longed to have the flexibility of a sea animal and be able to withstand the extraordinary pressures of great depth. Alone, she felt out of hers.

She sat back in a reclining chair and pressed the remote control on its arms. A canopy was activated and automatically lowered to provide partial shade for her to rest and reflect. Inbuilt sensors would slowly track the arc of the sun and adjust the canopy's angle and spread. Thus, ensuring, precious wealthy customers were pampered, naturally. Claire's eyes closed, but the dance between light and shadows continued unabated in her heart. She had raked over some embers. The far bigger fire was now waiting to engulf her conscience, body and soul.

Tom awoke an hour or so later, stretched and sat up. Framed in the light, he saw Claire reclined and apparently asleep. So, maybe after all she had joined him. She must have heard him yawning, probably the one that had involuntarily escaped and made him sound like a hungry lion cub. The thought reminded him of his fast too. He was never far behind Claire.

Her head turned in his direction and she smiled. The sea green beach towel lay discarded on the floor next to his side of the bed. He reached down to collect it. Wrapping the towel around him, the colour enhanced the healthy tone of his skin. The thought of an Ancient Grecian arose from within him, and although he was hardly a soldier of history, his body showed all the scars of battle. As he neared Claire and leant over to kiss her on the forehead, he noticed trails of moisture down her cheeks where the fault lines of tears had left their mark.

'How are you feeling?' she asked.

'Much better after the catnap,' Tom replied, 'I thought you'd followed suit and grabbed a snooze in the sun … What's the matter? Do you want to talk about things? Is Harry plaguing you?'

'No, it's not Harry. The volume of hurt is slowly being turned down on him. It will fade in time. I feel in control of him now, not him of me.'

'And so?'

'What's bothering me?'

She remained silent for several minutes. Tom eased himself into the chair next to hers. The outside world of life laughed onwards and upwards, carried by thermals let loose from the land.

Her voice sounded as if it was on the edge of a cliff of distress. 'I don't know where to start or even if it's wise to tell you?'

'You don't have to tell me anything,' Tom responded, 'but know this; I'm committed to you for the good and *the* bad times. We are a rare couple you know. We were pushed. We fell. We got up again. Not many go through what we have been through and survive. And perhaps some, many even, fall and drift apart, driven away by the inability to heal the scars and by default allow the seeing of one another to be a reminder of the pain. That's not us Claire. It never will be. We both know that.'

'Lovely words to hear, but ...'

'But even if the world was going to end, to be destroyed by some life extinguishing disaster, I would choose to be with you, to face it all head on, together,' Tom said. 'Even in the darkest of times we had with Harry, seeing you was and is a constant reminder that my life is worth living.'

'But what if, not only my life and your life were in jeopardy, but the lives of your parents, our extended families and that of our friends too? Would you risk all of those lives?'

'Those are big questions, he replied. 'Whatever you know, does my knowing put all of our lives at risk, is that what you're saying?'

'It's not by my knowing or in fact if you knew, it is what I or we choose to do with the knowledge that places ours and other lives at risk. Once you know, you will never ever forget. I wish I didn't know. It will haunt you as a shadow follows your day. A part of me rails against placing that burden on you.

'And if I do tell you and we choose to act upon it,' Claire continued, 'then yes, our lives will be at risk. As too will our family and friends, even the people we have come into contact with. All of our networks could be closed down, dead. At the moment, no one who conceivably might want to do something to me, knows that I know. I'm on the horns of a dilemma. The balance of lives of the people I know, care about and love, most importantly, you, they all rest on me ...' Claire's voice was trembling, 'and yet if I do nothing, then many more people, will ... will ...'

'Die ...' Tom said, and she looked up at him and nodded. Tom continued. 'So what do you do? I see now. You have a massive moral dilemma. It has infected you. The trouble is, the longer you leave the poison, the more it will dig in ... Look, I'm prepared to risk all for you. You know that. And I can't bear the thought of you carrying such a burden, whatever it is, on your own. Share it with me. Please. Tell me all. Then together we can decide what to do. Surely, that feels right, doesn't it?'

She looked over at him, her countenance uncertain.

Tom added, 'God will tell us what to do, and only God can then do what must be done. That is the strong advice of Mother Teresa. I say we go with that. What do you think?'

Memories of Patricia had flooded back to Claire. She had gone back to April 5th, 2010, it was 10.23 am. Claire had gone along with Pat to the radiology unit to provide support, a squeeze of the hand and a consoling shoulder. She had done all of that. But that didn't change the bleak facts. Lung cancer does what it says on the chest. Three months. Twelve weeks, oblivion. What does one do when faced with certain death?

After the first week of finding out, the fallout from fighting the truth, denying it was her name on the sickle list, the random bursts of fear masquerading as anger, Pat entered a sea change. She became the lynchpin, the stalwart, the steady as she goes ship. Claire had been there, playing a small part, but who in their two-way dynamic provided the real comfort? Pat was committed, hook, line and abyss. She had achieved what yogis must take years to master, serene within, serene without. Was facing death and accepting it the answer? Pat embraced the fact that her life was heading towards the end of a sentence and that the full stop at the end, would be just that. She lived life in those twelve weeks. Squeezed out the juices in the moments and rejoiced in the tangy zest they gave her.

In the end, Claire saw that Pat's life had been no full stop, no mere sentence, and no novella. She had been a trilogy. She had told her story and lived it.

But what was Claire when faced with the challenge of death? She was a small little comma hoping she would not be deleted off the page. But the push was coming to the shove. No terminal prognosis of the body. Yet to act meant extinction.

Was she the heroine who could climb over the ridge and face the flack? Would she even make it to the enemy's bunker to toss in a grenade? Had she the courage to cross the Rubicon? She could do it, but needed a helping hand. She needed Tom.

Tom listened to Claire without interruption as she recounted her journey of confusion and doubts. Her heart palpated all the time that she spoke. Her chest felt tight, her breathing shallow. If she did not know otherwise, she might have thought her heart was failing. In a sense it was, she was losing her optimism. She felt her life was being crushed, eliminated. Increasingly, the enormity of the challenge she faced had insidiously undermined and disempowered her will to act and to decide what to do.

When she had finished, thoughts puzzled Tom's face into a jigsaw of consternation. Still he said nothing. He watched the DVD of the birth in silence. His face aghast as the sounds of death trickled their way up through the earphones and into his mind and poured out the dying moans of the young mother, Ekaterina, all those many decades ago.

Claire was right. Pandora was not a box for the timid. The truth was hideous. The papers left by Colin, Tom assimilated in quiet contemplation. Claire's letter from her father moved him to wipe away the dampness welling in his eyes.

When Claire had sewn all things together as far as the pathway had taken her, Tom sat back and took a deep breath. He swallowed hard, the Adam's apple sticking in his throat. He then got up and went over to her. She stood up. They embraced one another and they howled. Oh, how they did. The tragedy of events overwhelmed them both. Emotions were run ragged and raw in the room as they held one another for as long as they both needed. It was a long time.

SEVENTY-SIX

Wednesday, September 5, 2012 – Claire and Tom's hotel room, Santorini

'It just beggars belief and yet ...' he shook his head as it hung down, his eyes staring unfocused onto the floor, 'and yet,' he looked up at her, 'my God ... how utterly terrifying. How on earth have you managed to carry this load Claire? You haven't buckled or divulged anything before. You are such a strong person. You truly are.'

Claire had not pictured herself in this way, far from it. Inside, she had been shaken to the core and kept going for his sake and for his recovery.

'So now you see the awful situation facing us both now,' said Claire, 'that's why I didn't want to tell you. Any thoughts on what to do?'

He did not answer her directly, but instead spoke about the way they might both discover a way forward.

'In my training for the priesthood, I was taught that in the very depths of our being we find our conscience, this is something we are called upon to obey. It is our moral compass, our guiding spirit that summons us, to first, love, to do what is right and good and to step away from the paths that lead us towards evil.

'Anarchists might argue that our innate conscience already endows us with the notion between what is right and wrong; hence why they consider we do not need laws to define what is good or bad, for we should, intrinsically, know.

'But I believe God whispers to us when it is the right time for us to hear and this will help us discern and decide upon what is the right or wrong path. If we are of sound mind and if we are honest with ourselves, all of us, to a person, knows deep down what is the right or wrong thing to do. When a person acts upon what he hears, and does good, he has chosen to listen to and respond to God's calling. That is our choice. That is our free will. The judgment on whether it is right or wrong is echoed in our conscience. Whatever the decision we take, it is something that will be with us night and day for the rest of our lives. That is, whilst our memory prevails. That will be our judgment.

'Therein, is a problem, particularly as life creates noisy distractions and endless temptations. It is all too easy to lose our hearing when listening to our conscience, to be pulled this way or that, and as a consequence, choose to do things which are not right. Hence, why meditation, plumbing the depths of our interior is absolutely necessary if we are to hear God's voice and act upon it. Many times, though, we know in and through our gut, what is the right thing to do, but we are frightened of the consequences. Fear is a powerful and sometimes paralysing force, as we both know. It can force us to act against our conscience and reason.

'As a result of the knowledge we both now have, we are faced with a situation that as you have already said, will have deadly implications for us and others. If we do nothing and carry on living as normal a life as possible, then we have made a good choice have we not? We have chosen to value our lives and the people we know and that is good. On the other hand, as you have already said, if we choose that path, then the Network's plan for humanity may well continue unhindered. But, we do not know enough yet to prove anything do we? Your father's letter and DVD, all of it could be ridiculed as the ranting of a dying man. The DVD could be just actors.

'So in the face of a known evil, do we do nothing? Is the challenge we face insurmountable? In other words, if we cannot stop it, perhaps it is better to do nothing, and let the world live as it is. Catholic teaching would say that if we are to remain faithful to God, then our choice is simple, to do what we know to be just and right. As for the outcome, that is beyond us or anyone to foretell. But as your dad's letter says, even if we do find out more and spread the news, who will listen? Will we be like Noah warning of the flood? Most likely, the Network will put up smoke screens, our efforts might dissipate and our lives and others we hold dear will be lost and the plan will still go ahead. However, these were your father's views and his beliefs. Are they ours?'

The sun was lower in the sky now. The sea sparkled as if it was teaming with life. The hubbub of chatter and laughter warmed the island's sense of community.

In the balance, she and Tom and those they loved, the people in Santorini, the population of the world, all mattered. Nevertheless, Claire was naturally drawn to the desire to provide a safe haven for those she cared for. The strangers across the world, how could she possibly care for them in the same way? It was not possible. But each of them, she knew, had their own loves and lives that they held dear too. Was it right, that their future should be placed in jeopardy, all for the sake of the time relative peace and sanctuary that she and Tom could attain?

It would be a false place to live. She knew so in her heart. To choose to do nothing would haunt her, always. But to do something, would likely have similar repercussions. The choice, as Tom had said, was simple. The greater good was for humanity's sake. But committing to the act of doing something with the knowledge they both now possessed was not easy.

Knowing you are on a mission with a one-way ticket is one for the brave hearted. Was she that brave?

She looked at Tom. 'Let's do it,' she said.

'Yes, and let's do it right,' he replied.

She would try to emulate Pam, accept her fate, embrace it, and be done with the fear of death. Meanwhile, she and Tom, before they stepped into the shoes that would take them on another path, would squeeze the last bits of fresh juice on the island of Santorini. The planning of what to do next could wait until this oasis, this sanctuary, had been left behind.

Cliff top restaurant overlooking the Aegean Sea, Oia, Santorini

The two Greek musicians wearing their traditional clothing of white shirts, black waistcoats, black flat hats, red cloth waist straps and black trousers played violin and guitar. The music's curling notes mingled with the aromas of the second course, lamb shank, which waited patiently to be eaten by the two lovers, engaged in each other's conversation and eyes. The food melted in their mouths, much like the feta cheese and mixed pepper salad drizzled in olive oil had done so for starters.

As they swirled the last residue of wine in their glasses, Claire and Tom declined dessert. Now they knew where their destinies lay, there was a lightness within them, which they didn't want to weigh down with gluttony and the inevitable consequence of over consumption.

The horse and carriage taxi was there waiting for them. A surprise Tom had arranged. The melodic clopping of hooves, the trundling of the wheels and the gentle swaying of the carriage, encouraged serenity to effervesce around them. Holding hands, the world they knew seemed a long way ahead of them. The view of the sea and the cliffs swept all thoughts aside of what had to be done. Claire looked at Tom. His eyes were warm. How easily she sank into them. He was her one true love.

Tom studied a tern as it soared on the thermals. How tempting to join its flight and cast one's life to the will of the wind. The bird tilted its body, like a spitfire and flew overhead. Tom's eyes arced across its path and followed its trajectory until it plunged downwards and out of sight. Claire's face came into focus. She was beautiful. They locked eyes with one another. Simultaneously, their minds moving in rhythm, each gently squeezed the other's hand. The warmth of shared intimacy spread over their mouths and eyes.

'Yes, Tom. I still want to. Let's arrange it and marry on Santorini,' said Claire, reading his mind.

A man in love needs no persuasion. What a woman in love wants … well that is for her to divulge on the wedding night, thought Claire. So they extended their stay on the island and moved into a luxury secluded villa. Claire's solicitor managed all the documentation and arrangements with their respective local authorities. The aim was to secure a letter of no impediment and have the details translated into Greek. Other documentation they had with them.

It came as no surprise to George and Monica. That is, all except the timing. That said, they acknowledged, impulsivity had been their lifeblood and had ensured a natural vibrancy and vitality had always resided well within their own marriage. As for the steep paths and steps of Oia, that would prove to be of no problem for Monica. The local marriage coordinator had arranged for a local carpenter to make a hand held litter, which would have suspended between the handles, a cane chair, with integral cushions of course, and an umbrella to ward off the sun if necessary. When Claire telephoned Monica with the news, she was delighted.

'At last, true recognition of my landed background has come to me. Did you hear that, George?' Monica called out, her voice echoing over the speakerphone in the villa.

Tom and Claire laughed, echoed by George in the background.

'Oh, and George, make sure you buy me an outlandish broad brim hat with a long plume of feathers.'

By mutual understanding, Claire and Tom did not invite friends to the wedding. They considered it best to keep them away from the radar of the Network if possible. Either way, the least contact they had with their past the better they thought.

They would hold the ceremony on the terrace of the villa, late in the afternoon. The local mayor would perform it. That was the tradition. Apart from the minimum number of two people required as witnesses, plus an interpreter for the Greek vows, the wedding itself would be small. Well, that was the intention.

Anastasoula, the marriage coordinator, said, 'No, I insist. A party is good. You must have one.'

Claire and Tom had so warmed to Anastasoula that on a wave of excitement, they invited her friends and relatives to the reception too.

The plan was to have traditional Greek dancing – people moving rhythmically to the music in a circle, holding arms and splitting off to perform in the centre of the ring. Such things reminded them of barn dances in Devon during their time at university, and what with the smashing of plaster plates on the wedding day, a unique atmosphere for them was assured.

'Yes, you leave things to me' said Anastasoula in her Greek accent, 'You no need to worry nothing. I will make this most special occasion. It will be a mark of good fortune.'

Tom and Claire had both agreed and then let his parents know they would have a Catholic blessing when they moved to live in Athens for several months. George and Monica accepted this without question. As voluntary part-time marriage guidance counsellors for the Church, they understood well the complications of getting a Catholic wedding arranged at such short notice. The story had been easy to fabricate. Indeed, half-truths always are. Although, things did not work out the way they had envisaged. Perhaps life is better that way. Not knowing what is around the corner.

The 2nd October had been chosen as the wedding day as it coincided with a Catholic memorial to Guardian Angels. They lived in hope that holy angels would watch over them. At 12 noon, Anastasoula had arrived, accompanied by a bustling bunch of helpers, who in concert with Monica, pampered, styled, made up and dressed Claire.

Tom had been booted out the night before to stay at the hotel with his father. That suited them both. It had been a while since they had been alone together. Some seven years. Tom treasured every minute, every moment of his dad's conversation and company.

Anastasoula's friends and family arrived early, in fact, in time for the wedding itself. Claire and Tom were not sure if that was by accident or design. Nevertheless, it was, in the end, the best outcome.

As Tom turned towards Claire when she walked out onto the terrace, escorted by Anastasoula's father, his breath was taken away by the aura surrounding her. She wore a Grecian wedding dress, the kind he imagined worn in Ancient Greece. It was simplicity itself: roped shaped shoulder straps, a plunging v-neck line and a waistband that gathered the dress's free falling pleated fabric. Her hair too was folded in layers above her head. If a woman could look more radiant than the sun, it was Claire. How he kept his heart in that day he never knew.

Once the Mayor had announced they were married, the crowd gathered in a circle and surrounded them, showering them with rice and Ta Koufeta, a traditional white candy. And in turn, first Tom's parents, then the Mayor, followed by Anastasoula and then everybody else, including the musicians, kissed them both and wished them a 'long life'. Then the dancing, the eating, and the drinking commenced. It carried on all night long.

As the evening jollied on, Tom and Claire said their goodbyes and made their way to a very private destination away from the villa and down to a luxury yacht, which was moored a little way off Amoudi Bay, below Oia. The yacht had been especially reserved for the night by Anastasoula, 'my gift to you,' she had said. It belonged to Iakov, a wealthy Russian billionaire, whom she had helped marry a few years earlier. He was only too pleased to be of service. And when she had moved to thank him, he had merely said in his smoke singed Russian accent, 'No problem, my pleasure.'

Tom miraculously, much to the uncertain, but excited screams of Claire, was able to carry her over the threshold of the state bedroom. They collapsed across the voluminous bed in laughter. The ice bucket and bottle of champagne lay invitingly near. But their eyes made contact first. Husband and wife, the realisation, the symbolism touched them deeply and the first deep kiss of many followed. Now was the time for a wife to tell her husband what she wanted. Claire leaned forwards and whispered in his ear.

REDEEM TIME PAST

By William Drummond (1585-1649)

That of my horrors thou right use might'st make,
And a more sacred path of living take:
Now still walk armed for my ruthless blow,
Trust nattering life no more, redeem time past,
And live each day as if it were thy last.

SEVENTY-SEVEN

14:27 hours, Tuesday, October 9, 2012 – Katerini, Greece

They had wanted to get away from Santorini not long after the sun was rising. A fresh start to the day they thought would make a clean break from this bubble in nirvana more bearable. Saying good-bye to the island was not the hard part. The parting from Tom's parents had been extraordinarily difficult, especially for Tom. Both Claire and Tom's emotions had felt shredded inside.

They had gone over to George and Monica's hotel the day after the wedding. Their limousine had waited for them in the shade outside the front of the building's white imposing structure ready to quietly hover off to the airport now that its suspension was raised.

Both George and Monica had been up, dressed and ready to see the newly-weds off. As promised, Monica was sitting on the bed to give each of them 'a proper hug,' as she had put it. Without a small degree of preparation, it had never been possible to give his mum a real deep body hug on impulse because of the physical barrier the wheelchair always presented.

Claire said her goodbyes to Tom's parents first and then it was his turn. He sat down next to his mum, who almost immediately embraced him the moment his body touched the bed's mattress.

'Now you have a wonderful honeymoon darling. You're an absolutely lovely son and I have no doubt you will be outstanding as a husband.'

'I love you Mum, thank-you. Now you go easy and enjoy the rest of your stay here and I'll see you soon, alright.' He hugged her tightly then. The kind of hug one never wants to end. A short while later he kissed her warmly on the side of the face and stood up to be with his father.

'That feels good Tom,' said his dad, who was patting his son on the back and enjoying the massive bear hug, 'you are coming back aren't you,' he ribbed.

'I just wanted to say thanks for all of the love and support you've given me Dad,' replied Tom, avoiding his father's humour, which might be too close to the mark. 'You have a good time on the island too. And make sure you both get out into the sea, the clarity of the water is magnificent; you'll love it.'

They had travelled to a pre-arranged rented flat, which was pretty much in the centre of Athens. The view of the Acropolis at night, despite the extensive scaffolding surrounding parts of it, had looked impressive when lit up. The flat itself had been simple and easy to live in, not that they intended staying long. The all in one living space had wall-to-wall bookshelves and was stacked full of fiction and non-fiction. Most of it in Greek, so even if they had been inclined to read, the offer in the flat was of no use. However, the books by their presence served one purpose. They imbued the room with stillness; this was an ingredient both of them had relished in the busier urban environment, which was somewhat opposite to what they had left behind.

The stopover in Athens had just been long enough for them to track down a second hand car dealer in the southeast suburb of the city and purchase a vehicle paying by cash. Following a short debate, they had both agreed to find a Land Rover Discovery. It had become an easy preference for the both of them in the end. In comparison to many other vehicles on the market it wasn't the most fuel efficient, but as they were unsure of all the road conditions that they might encounter, transport that was solid, reliable and all terrain would be their best bet, they thought, and as Claire had said, 'it's a vehicular athlete with plenty of muscle power and comfort too.'

They had left the flat just after nine in the morning and followed the largely eastern coastline of Greece. Their last breakfast on the veranda had been spent watching the workmen on the Acropolis, who since 7 am, had been like monkeys and ants, swinging from ropes and swarming over the structure in a surge of work that was well underway before the noise of the city hushed their activity to more dulcet levels. After some four hours or so on the road, they had both been ready for some lunch. Katerini was chosen as the pit stop, primarily because the last two syllables in the word reminded them of their island holiday.

'The feta and olive salad was lovely, thank-you,' said Claire as the waiter cleared away the plates and served coffee. 'I'm ready to go after this. What about you?' she asked Tom, who was sat opposite her.

Tom, caught in the act of sipping the hot liquid and savouring the aroma, whilst lost in this simple pleasure, made a guttural sound of agreement.

A short while later, after they had climbed back into the Discovery and were on their way again, Tom who was driving, spoke first.

'Impulse is one thing, but naivety is another. How on earth did we imagine Katerini would live up to Santorini in charm and ambience?'

'We imagined? Hold on Thomas. I recall you waxing lyrical about the possibility of unearthing a hidden treasure in the side streets of this mysterious town.'

Claire motioned with her fingers to post invisible quotation marks, 'I was sold on the imagery your words conveyed mate.'

'So in other words, you agreed with my sentiments.' He smiled triumphantly.

'Yes, but – '

'Yes, but nothing,' said Tom.

MACEDONIA

SEVENTY-EIGHT

Tuesday October 9, 2012 – Hotel, Esperanto Street, Kumanovo, Macedonia

At journey's end for the day, they found a quiet hotel in a street called Esperanto. The choice was purely down to the street sign being linked to a language created to engender peace and understanding amongst nations.

'A ray of hope,' Claire wistfully said.

'Excellent. That's what we need,' replied Tom, pointing to the hotel sign promoting in large letters – Free Wi-Fi.

The room was basic but gave them the essentials they required: desk, chair, double bed and en suite. Tom commenced his task of hacking into sites and network computers, whilst Claire went out in search of a takeaway.

As midnight approached, Claire spoke. 'Come on Tom, call it a day now. I'm whacked and you look done in.'

He looked up.

Claire's prompting reminded him of how tired his body was. Without her saying something, he would have carried on well into the early hours, not conscious of time. What he had found had solidly kept his attention. He knew when Claire read it that she would see, as he had, just how much the jigsaw of history had been pieced together.

He sat up and stretched his arms towards the ceiling.

'You're right,' he said as a yawn reached out from nowhere and took him unawares, elongating his words unnaturally and giving them a cavernous sound in the room. He yawned again and shook his head in an effort to shake off the feeling and put his eyes back into focus.

Claire asked, 'How was progress?'

'Better than I dared hope. I've downloaded an exchange of letters between Himmler and Clauberg when the professor was working in Auschwitz. I've also traced an extract from Mengele's personal notes. Over 3,000 pages had been auctioned in Connecticut in July 2011; an anonymous Jewish buyer had bought them. What I found is an extract that had been donated to a Jewish library in America, but archived for some reason.'

'And?'

'You'll need to read it all. It will come across to you better that way. The letters are a bit arid, of their time I guess, but once you accept that, you'll see just how cold, brutal and systematic they were in carrying out their research.'

```
January 18, 1943 - Auschwitz

    Dear Reichsführer,

    I understand from the December meeting
    of the Reich Working Group that you are
    unenthusiastic about Reichsaerzteführer
    Conti's desire to see the artificial
    insemination of high quality German
    women.
        The enclosed book, reviews techniques
    in this field. With hundreds of
    thousands of our soldiers now dead, the
    availability of good male stock is in
    short supply.
        However, with access to the best Aryan
    semen it would be possible for example,
    for just one donor's sperm to inseminate
```

as many as 150 women without risk of cross contamination.

In the meantime, as the initial phases of my research in the Auschwitz insemination programme are using male organisms supplied by Aktion T4, I assume continuation of this work is still acceptable.

Heil Hitler.

SS - Brigadeführer Clauberg

January 30, 1943 - Berlin

Dear Brigadeführer Clauberg,

The book by Herr Rohleder was illuminating. I will give this more consideration and discuss the merits with the Führer. Confirmation from you over the telephone that freezing and re-use of sperm may soon be possible will inspire him and assist the Reich's long-term plans.

Continue to press ahead with the insemination programme using males supplied by Aktion T4. However, I also expect you to assess the efficacy of conventional means too, which in my view is in keeping with the natural order of procreation.

One last thing Brigadeführer, would you confirm the name of the individual who mentioned my concerns regarding artificial insemination, I would like to show my appreciation.

In the meantime, do keep up the good work on the sterilisation programme.

Heil Hitler.

Reichsführer Himmler

June 7, 1943 – Auschwitz

Dear Reichsführer,

Today I am fulfilling my obligation to report to you from time to time about the state of my research and that of my medical team's recent collaboration with Hauptsturmführer Mengele and his work on twins.

The work to sterilise male and female organisms deemed unworthy of reproduction has made substantial progress. With one sufficiently trained doctor, supported by 10 SS-Unterscharführers, the Reich could sterilise 1,000 females per day. This I hope satisfactorily addresses the question you asked me a year ago. The programme can now be implemented at your discretion.

As a matter for your records, you may wish to add to the list the 400 males and 250 females used in the experiments. They are of course redundant and will be transferred to cleansing facilities shortly.

Heil Hitler.

SS – Brigadeführer Clauberg

September 20, 1943 - Auschwitz

Dear Reichsführer,

We have removed brains from a selection
of males provided by the Aktion T4 Unit
and also from normal males we used as a
control group. They were selected at
random from the train transport-
arrivals. Observable differences in grey
matter volume were recorded in Brodmann
Areas 10, 20 and 38. The brains of males
supplied from Aktion T4 possessed
noticeably less grey matter.
Neurologists in the research team
believe lower volumes may inhibit an
individual from expressing empathy and
may even indicate a preference towards
violent behaviour. The first batch of
male foetuses produced will be examined
for variation in volumes of grey matter.
All female foetuses are destroyed at
birth, as women are less likely to
display the same capacity towards
violence.
   Healthy, fertile female specimens aged
between 20 to 35 years are used for
reproduction experiments. Postmenopausal
women are held alive whilst we perfect
the extraction of gonadotropins from
their urine. This, when injected into
fertile females should help to increase
the production of ova when we progress
onto IVF experiments.
   We always assess the quality and
health of semen produced. To increase
the volumes of sperm available for
sexual intercourse or extraction for

insemination, we have regimented ejaculation to occur every 5 days. Prostate gland stimulation hitherto used in the sterilisation programme to secure ejaculate for insemination has not been used. This can result in a loss of semen into the male urethra. Instead, males are constrained face down along the length of a table, underneath which a hole in the surface allows their genitals to protrude. Females not required for fertilisation are forced to stimulate males and ensure ejaculate is deposited onto petri dishes. Each semen sample is used immediately by medical staff to inseminate females who are restrained on adjacent tables. The effectiveness of sexual intercourse and artificial insemination procedures are described below.

The most violent of males from Aktion T4 were used for sexual intercourse. Three unterscharführers are assigned for each insemination procedure. Their role is to prevent injury to females during or post coition. We found this necessary, as two unterscharführers were unable to prevent a female from having her eyes gouged and throat torn out during coition.

Whilst I understand your preferences Reichsführer, we have found the sexual intercourse procedure to be inefficient. Conceptions are low, only a 17 per cent success rate has been achieved. Only five mothers went to full term, despite the intravenous usage of drugs to mimic the follicle hormone and lower the risks of early births. Four births arose from the control group and only one from males supplied by Aktion T4. The lone male baby sired by the Aktion T4 participant proved worthless. The brain when examined contained more fluid than grey matter.

The artificial insemination programme is more efficacious. We do not impregnate direct into the uterus as this can result in genital infections and miscarriages. The vaginal method is used. A long tube attached to a syringe deposits fresh semen as near as possible to the cervix. The conception success rate has varied between 22 per cent from Aktion T4 supplied males and 33 per cent from the control group.

To counter lower rates we are now only using spermatozoa that display the strongest and healthiest capabilities. Separate research is underway to determine which spermatozoa produce male and female offspring. However, this may take some time to bear fruit.

To date we have produced 100 male foetuses from artificial insemination. Their brains have been examined; some 18 per cent displayed less volumes of grey matter in the Brodmann Areas mentioned. These offspring are the product of four males supplied by Aktion T4. We will increase the number of females artificially inseminated by them.

We will also continue to observe the maturing offspring for signs of psychopathic behaviour seen so clearly in their fathers. Naturally, in the meantime, we will search for additional male organisms to increase the gene pool for our procreation programme.

Heil Hitler.

SS – Brigadeführer Clauberg

July 16, 1944 – Auschwitz

Dear Reichsführer,

I am pleased to report solid progress regarding artificial insemination and in-vitro fertilisation.

Using liquid nitrogen, we have frozen and thawed healthy semen from the most malevolent males available using glycerol as a protective layer for the spermatozoa and fertilised dozens of females.

In addition, we have overcome technical problems in the maturation of human ova to be ready for in-vitro fertilisation. After much trial and error, we have identified the most effective timing for successful transplantation of the embryo into the uterus. The transfer must be done when the cells have divided into the blastocysts stage, some 37 hours after conception in the petri dish.

Unfortunately, two technical obstacles to be overcome remain. To build up a steady supply of human embryos in-vitro for transplantation into receptive uteruses, it would be more efficient if the ova and also the embryos could be frozen for future use, much like the

storage of semen. We have attempted
freezing procedures. However, when we
have retrieved eggs from females in the
sterilisation programme, we have found
that ova as well as IVF created embryos
contain a high proportion of water and
the ice formation damages viability. We
have yet to resolve how to dehydrate
these components without destroying them
in the process.

   The second obstacle, identifying the
DNA responsible for psychopathic
behaviour and sterility, currently lies
beyond our technical capabilities. Our
research focus has determined that if we
are to create embryos with these genetic
defects then germline modification is
required at the zygote stage. With more
time, solutions will undoubtedly be
found. Until then, the process of
artificial insemination and IVF, without
genetic modification, holds out the best
prospects for the creation of hybrid
male organisms from the mixture of
malign semen stock we have in cold
storage for the future.

   Heil Hitler.

   SS - Brigadeführer Clauberg

October 2, 1944 - Auschwitz

Dear Reichsführer,

Thank you for accelerating the
construction of the new block at

Auschwitz. With the two gynaecological clinics in Silesia, which already house 800 pregnant females and 200 offspring, we now have the means to transform the efficiency of the programme. We are in a position to produce 3,400 pregnancies per year and achieve a production line of some 1,100 offspring.

Heil Hitler.

SS - Brigadeführer Clauberg

December 1, 1944 - Upper Rhine High Command

Dear Brigadeführer Clauberg,

My apologies for the lack of regular contact; I know you have tried to reach me by telephone on several occasions; however, other demands from the war have required my dedication. As you can see, I have been transferred to the Upper Rhine to defend the Fatherland from approaching American and French Forces.
It is good to read that our genetic research has made such good progress. Unfortunately, you will have to end the work forthwith. The Führer has commanded me to ensure the future of the research programme. He has asked me to arrange with the utmost urgency night flights for all of the male and female participants and progeny of the programme and transport them to a clinic in Switzerland, which has been established by the Reich Main Security Office. In addition, he expects all

evidence relating to the research and findings are readied for transport and stored in secure containers.

I have instructed senior personnel and security staff from the Reich Main Security Office together with a specially selected field medical team to accompany the evidence, participants and progeny.

With the exclusion of yourself and Hauptsturmführer Mengele, all witnesses to the programme will be executed.

I have ordered the commandant to prepare a landing strip for the aircraft and have it ready by December 12th. An advance party from the Reich Main Security Office will arrive at midnight December 13th. They will carry out the execution order.

The aircraft for the evacuation will arrive at 2200 hours December 14th and take off at 2330 hours. The night should be particularly dark; the moon will be in its waxing crescent phase. It should be perfect for the evacuation.

Good Luck and Heil Hitler!

Reichsführer Himmler,
Commander of the Upper Rhine High
Command

Private diary extract of Josef Mengele

Thursday, December 14, 1944 – Temporary airfield, Auschwitz

The lanterns were gradually lit and the lines of the airstrip, which had been hastily covered in asphalt atop the crushed bones of the dead used as hardcore, stretched into view as little by little the runway was illuminated. As twenty-two hundred hours approached, the inspiring throaty roar of multiple engines chanted out the impending arrival of aircraft at Auschwitz. Although initially unseen from the ground, one by one the distinctive shapes of thirty Junkers 52 aircraft, each powered by three BMW engines, swooped gracefully down to land one by one. The Führer had dispatched thirty of his fifty personal air fleet, which had been converted into air ambulances. Since the 1930s, these had been the solid workhorse of the Luftwaffe, and I knew from first-hand experience they were often a welcome sight for soldiers injured on the battlefield. We called them our beloved 'Auntie Ju'. They had rescued many and transported the wounded, me included, in 1942, to medical facilities over the war years.

Brigadeführer Clauberg and I were both dressed in long black military overcoats. Clauberg turned to me and smiled.

'Well, Josef you see now; our way out of this godforsaken hell is arriving. You and I can carry on the research without fear of capture hey,' he said. The vapour from his breath ballooning and then vanishing as quickly as it had arrived.

'Indeed, Carl. Indeed. I wanted to say one thing, about last night…when our colleagues and assistants ...' I changed my mind mid sentence and finished off by saying, 'Well, it is done now.'

Last night had taken me by surprise. Not all things were divulged to me, I now realised. All who had assisted in the research, bar one, my assistant orderly, had been garrotted in their sleep. I had always insisted the man's support had been vital to my motivation to save some and dispose of others.

"Secrets die with the dead Josef, you know that," Clauberg had said, when he and I had sat down to breakfast this morning.

"The male and female guinea pigs that we no longer required, I sent them off for a shower at 0800 hours."

Clauberg had laughed, "The damn fools. You would have thought after all of this time they would have known what awaited them. Yet even those who were compos mentis went like cattle, just dully walking to their deaths. Quite amazing don't you think?"

The aircraft, as they landed, were directed by the advance party into side bays to embark their cargo. The soothing growls of the engines simmered and stopped and the propellers slowed down to a standstill. As they did so, Waffen – SS paratroopers quickly disembarked from the first two of the craft and spread out to form a protective defence perimeter. The commanding officer from the Reich Ministry's Security Office called out.

'May I have your attention please?'

An unnecessary request I thought, as lines of men and women and those with babies stood in rows looking at him anyway. The men and women were shackled, even those females that were pregnant.

'We have enough space to carry 336 passengers. No more will be allowed on. Is that clear? These are the absolute orders from Reichsführer Himmler. Priority for space will be allocated to the participants and the progeny of the research programme.'

The Jewish inmates dressed in their striped pyjamas, more rags than stripes, obediently and silently helped in the loading of the passengers and of the containers carrying the research findings. When all were boarded in seats or litters on the adapted aircraft, Clauberg and I with our luggage and personal files walked towards the last in line. The paratrooper's commanding officer stood in our way.

'There is no more room on the aircraft.' He barked, 'Stand back.'

'What is the meaning of this?' exclaimed Clauberg. His rounded height tried to expand with the sound of his raised voice. 'I have led the programme since 1934 under the direct orders of the Führer himself. Hauptsturmführer Mengele has assisted me since 1943. You must let us both on. I insist.'

The Waffen – SS commanding officer drew his pistol and pointed it at Clauberg's head.

'And I insist too. I am in command here, not the Führer or the Reichsführer. You will stand back or I will shoot you.'

The shimmering landing strip lights were insufficient to illuminate Clauberg's bulging face and inflamed eyes, but I knew him of old. There was no way out. The paratrooper's eyes betrayed no intention of standing down, only survival and stress powered his decisions now. Near anarchy was breaking out, I thought. Clauberg stepped back, his head down, his body resigned.

Before the Waffen – SS paratroopers mounted the aircraft, they made the Jewish inmates line up against one of Auschwitz's buildings, three rows deep. The near skeletal men shivered from the cold, not fear; that emotion I am sure had run out of them a long while ago. Death's familiarity, as common as one's heartbeat in this place had seen to that I expect. I watched their faces for any trace. However, there was none. Fear had been banished.

They must have listened to the knowing 'clock' as the machine guns were readied. Release at last, they may have thought and welcomed the end. The Waffen – SS Commanding Officer sharply lowered his pistol and the echoes of machine gun fire reverberated until silence finally shouted out to stop.

I learnt later from Clauberg that the research programme participants were being taken to Davos in Switzerland. Some years later, one of the SS-paratroopers gave an account of the journey when by chance he spotted me in Montevideo as I was taking coffee in a bar and reading the morning paper. For

410

posterity's sake, I have written up a version of his words below; well, as far as I remember them that is.

Friday, December 15, 1944 – Samedan, Switzerland

Some 789 kilometres away from Auschwitz lay the airfield at Engadin. It is over 1,700 metres above sea level and occupies a secluded spot in a valley amidst the Alps. At just after three in the morning, two of the Ju 52s carrying our troops arrived and as before, we spread out to protect the cargo. There was no need. The protégé successor of Wilhelm Gustloff, the founder of the Swiss Nazi Party for Germans abroad who had been assassinated in 1936, was waiting with a convoy of trucks to greet us.

I watched as the remaining aircraft circled and in turn took up a place on the airfield. The cargo was quickly disembarked. Within the hour, all of the aircraft took off again. Talking to one of the pilots on the way over, he said the aircrew were looking forward to the return trip to the Fatherland. The Führer had released them from his service. Some people were lucky, I remembered thinking at the time, their war was over. My commanding officer gave the order and the convoy moved off. It would be an hour or more before we reached our destination and the pleasantries of a warm soft bed to sleep in. That was all that was keeping me going at the time. We had had some very long days.

Tuesday, January 30, 1945 – Gross-Rosen Concentration Camp, Prussia

I had transferred to Gross-Rosen, three hours away from Auschwitz. I was glad to be away from the sounds of multiple explosions and massacres mainly because the stench had been overpowering and I had run out of perfumed handkerchiefs.

Clauberg in his fear of the Red Army had sought sanctuary in the forced march of the Auschwitz inmates to Ravensbruck and hopefully, he thought, safety, deeper into the lands of Germany. To protect his self-interests, he had stuffed a suitcase with thousands of photographic files, evidence of the sterilisation programme. Such information might save his skin, or so he thought. He was probably right.

It had not taken me long to settle into a daily routine at Gross-Rosen. The camp was run much the same as Auschwitz, only smaller in scale. As usual, early in the morning, I was sitting at my desk signing orders, this time for a series of dissection experiments, when the radio operator handed me a coded message from the Führer.

BLOOD RELATIONSHIPS

I read the words quietly to myself. I, Josef Rudolph Mengele had been selected by the Führer to be the Fatherland's Angel of Death. I read on.

```
You are hereby charged with a holy duty:
to ensure, above all else, at whatever
cost, that the Reich's resurrection is
complete. From the ashes, we must reign
supreme. The following Swiss numbered
bank account has been established. The
bank will only recognise the following
name as authorisation to access the
account and enact transactions: Wolfgang
Gerhard.
```

Later, when sat alone in my office, I listened to the radio. The Führer was speaking. It was, as it turned out, his final speech. I was listening for confirmation of the order I had received. And there it was, in his closing sentences.

> "However great the crisis of the moment may be, we will master it in the end through our unbreakable will, through our willingness to sacrifice, and through our abilities. We will survive this misery."

So this is the end, I thought. The Reich was about to fall. The nightmares of the past several nights were coming to pass. Scouts had told me the Red Army's boots were not far away. I could almost hear them crunching on the bones of the German army. No sanctuary, no forgiveness. Those thoughts drove me onwards. Efficiency as is my way kicked in. I looked around the office and decided which of my belongings I could safely take with me. Not much, but enough for the long roads ahead.

Friday, August 9, 1957 – Nuremberg, Germany

This date gave me some cause to be joyful. Clauberg the hunted, as I liked to think of him now, stooped as low as a rat under a doorway to escape the Red Army's grip. He had hastily abandoned Ravensbruck to its fate, fearful of revenge from Russian soldiers, and sought refuge in Schleswig-Holstein located in the uppermost reaches of Germany. Here he joined the other sewer inhabitants who had raced to abandon their Nazi heritage, the traitors. The topmost of which, which stunned me at the time, was Reichsführer Himmler. As the net drew in and inexorably tightened the noose around the last remnants of the SS, Himmler was captured and committed suicide whilst in custody. Clauberg, I heard, had grabbed his case full of images, and scrambled as fast as his short legs would carry him away from the Soviet's snatching at his heels. However, by June 8 1945, the hunt was over and they captured him. Instead of impalement and death, he was imprisoned and

413

abandoned in a gulag of his own making. However, that was not the end of his story.

The reach of the Network had continued to expand. At the end of the war, our influence hidden behind the frontage of others had negotiated Clauberg's repatriation back to Germany in 1955. He was, to my frustration, a free man, or so he would have been. Yet when he returned in October, he behaved as if the world had not changed. He set about boasting of the success of his work for the Reich and in particular, of using guinea pigs in the sterilisation programme. His mouth was getting too wide. The Network stirred up protests and Clauberg within a month of his return was arrested. He was later charged with war crimes. I knew as the Network did, that he should never be allowed to give evidence in court. The day before he was due to stand trial, we sent him a visitor in the early hours of Friday morning. He was a new member of the prison's medical team, summoned to treat Clauberg's asthma. Even now, I smile. I can imagine the surprise in Clauberg's eyes after he had inhaled the spray filled with gas derived from a crushed cyanide ampoule. News coverage at the time reported he had died of a heart attack. The Network made sure of that.

Wednesday, October 10, 2012 – hotel, Esperanto Street, Kumanovo, Macedonia

The early hours had fallen asleep unnoticed. Claire closed the laptop's lid and the whirring sounds emitted from the computer told her it was automatically closing down. There was no end to Nazism was there? Dedication and determination defined the Network's relentless drive to destroy life.

'Will the sites you've hacked into help the Network to track us here do you think?' Claire asked.

'I've been accessing data via a proxy server. This has provided me with a secure and hidden pathway, a tunnel if you like, between your laptop and the computers and sites I've been connecting with, all the data transferred back and forth has been encrypted,' said Tom.

Claire looked bemused.

Tom continued, 'I'm using another internet server as a middleman between where we are and the sites I've been hacking. Basically, it hides my presence and slows down traceability.'

'I hope so,' said Claire, 'but surely the Network is bound to know we've left Santorini? It won't take them long to conclude it's us searching will it? Who else will be looking for the evidence we're after? It would be a magnificent coincidence, wouldn't it?'

'That's true, but they'll not know where we are. So if we keep ourselves below the radar, we might avoid contact.'

'If, might, and the world of unknowns. Now we're actually doing it ...' Claire's body shivered.

Tom went over to her and they hugged, Claire's head rested on his chest. 'Aye, we're two pawns in play now. I'm apprehensive too. We can only do our best and leave the rest to events. It never was going to be easy was it? But as the saying goes, whatever happens next, all the pieces will end up in the same box. Let's hope they take a while to make their move,' said Tom.

SERBIA

SEVENTY-NINE

Wednesday, October 10, 2012 – Smederevo, Serbia

It was just over half an hour past midday when Claire and Tom stopped for lunch in Smederevo, an ancient city that once held the crown as capital of Serbia. The early hours were now paying them back, they were tired and edgy. Belgrade is some thirty miles away. If they really had been on a road trip, Claire and Tom would have taken a detour and a slower route along the tempting highway, which hugs more or less the banks of the River Danube and tracks north-west to reach Serbia's capital.

The Discovery's rooftop slid comfortably under the barrier, which prevents access by high-sided vehicles into Smederevo's first and only underground car park. The parking bays were wide, unlike the sometimes excessively snug fit provided in many of the UK's parking venues. Steps from the underground levels led to a hotel, which to Claire and Tom's relief allowed non-guests to order food in the restaurant. They learnt from their waiter, who possessed a voluminous bushy moustache that Smederevo's fifteenth century iron fortress was nearby. They chose a hot lunch recommended as a traditional local meal, one that used cabbage as a main ingredient. Feeling somewhat solid afterwards, they both decided a stroll along the winding pathway upwards to the fortress's ramparts would be a good idea.

Since leaving Santorini, there had been an autumnal feel in the air, and although not cold, they both slipped on a thin woolly layer under their rucksacks. It kept them from feeling

417

any chill. Pausing halfway along one of the ramparts, Claire slid her bag to the ground and Tom stood behind her. He slipped one arm around her waist and the other across her shoulder and chest, and nuzzled his mouth into her nape.

'The views across the river and up and down stream are wonderful aren't they? How I wish we could be here and just be idle minded tourists' said Claire as she half twisted her head towards Tom's.

Tom pulled Claire's waist closer still. 'I know,' he said, 'a touch of heaven. We could hire a boat and slide slowly along the currents again. Remember?'

She nodded, his breathing, warming her neck as his eyes arched upwards and looked out across the expanse of water.

'Thanks for driving this morning Hon, my head's busting,' said Gil, as his wife was turning into the car park. 'My whole neck is on lockdown.' Looking at the sat nav, he added, 'the nearest drug store is ten minutes walk away in a downtown pedestrian precinct. Sure hope they stock some powerful medicine,' he added.

'I'm sure they will,' said his wife, Jackie, 'hey look, there's one of those Land Rover's we've been after, I'll park next to it, let's look inside.'

'Let's look on the way back. Do you mind Hon? I'm desperate.'

Five hours on the road from Budapest, the Network's operative gratefully set the side stand to the floor and left his BMW 1250 RT on a nearby side street. The CCTV cameras in Kumanovo had picked up their images and digital facial recognition software had tied the targets together and even showed them getting out of their vehicle the previous night. Thereafter, it was a simple matter of targeting a satellite to track their car.

He walked swiftly into the car park and down the slopes that led to the underground spaces. All was quiet. The Land Rover was easy to find. From the pouches around his waist, he removed a magnetic car bomb, placed it under the front driver's mudguard, and lodged a spring loaded pressure detonator between the inner rim of the door and the vehicle's jamb. Several minutes later, he was sitting comfortably on the sidesaddle of his bike. He had a good view of the pedestrian entrance and took a long draw on his cigarette. It eased the tightness in his chest. The exhalation of the smoke plume was slow and satisfying. He relaxed.

No matter how much lighting underground car parks have, they always seem dim and uninviting. Smederevo's was no different. Illuminated backlit concrete walls do not draw the eye in pleasure. Colourful graffiti, unfortunately not aesthetic, festooned the wall space and served only to add to the gloom in the bunker like structure.

A mother pushing her twins in a double-seated pram, her six year old, Javor, at her side, walked down the slope's entrance first. Gil and Jackie followed her. Gil's brain was still flashing lights across his eyes. He longed for the relief to kick in and kill this blinder of a migraine.

Javor ran ahead of his mother. No cars were moving. It was safe. He turned round and looked at her, a cheeky grin passed across his eyes. She knew that look and shouted out, her voice echoing across the space.

'Javor don't. Whatever you're thinking of, it's no!'

Sometimes when people speak in a foreign language, translation is not necessary. Jackie looked at Gil, and despite him feeling so unwell, he was able to raise a knowing smile with her. Children across the world were the same and their son, Will, when he was that age, had tested their patience on

419

many careworn occasions. Easy to look back now with fondness, but at the time, well …

Javor's mother cried out again. Lost in his own plans, Javor darted off sideways and headed towards Claire and Tom's car. Javor got to their vehicle before anyone else. He reached up and put his hand around the driver's door handle. He looked around. His mum had not caught up with him yet.

'Javor, behave yourself. No,' his mother shouted as the pram careered around the rear end of the Discovery, 'Javor!'

Unperturbed, Javor pulled on the door. The hinges must have been slightly loose. Such can be the case with less than new vehicles. The detonator connection was broken. The flash was fractionally ahead of the large sounding explosion. Instinct had seen both Gil and his wife Jackie fall forward to the floor. Nevertheless, the blast swept them, the mother, and her pram containing her two young children viciously into the air. Crashing metal pieces and chunks of body splayed out across the now blood red surface of the car park, its ceiling and walls. The bomb had been unforgiving in the pressure cooker confines of this sub-surface space.

Smoke rolled across the ceiling in great balls and billowed out of the car park's entrance. Sirens wailed in the distance, panic cast its pall in the air. High pitch shouting competed to be heard. People who had rushed for their lives or from the hotel gathered in a morass of uncertainty. Smoke, heat and fear kept them at bay. Fire appliances arrived. Faces became streaked from the detritus of the disaster. People were pushed back. Other explosions were possible. Deep in the crowds, Claire and Tom jostled for space. They turned away and fought their way to a fragment of clear pavement outside the hotel entrance. The hotel waiter who had served them earlier stood outside, calm amidst the chaos, and dragged deeply on a cigarette, his moustache like his white tea towel stained since the start of the day.

'Do you know what has happened?' Claire asked.

The waiter nodded. 'Big boom, I heard it from in kitchen. Gas tank exploded, someone say. But I says, it bomb. I heard before. During war, you understand, yes?'

'A bomb,' said Tom, his voice sounding doubtful.

'Yes. Bomb-bings still happen here. Old wounds not heal. Always keep eye open,' he replied. His voice was heavy with sombre conviction.

'Have you seen any strangers around today?' asked Claire.

'Strangers a plenty,' he said. 'Now only you ...' he pulled on his cigarette and the rapid inrush of smoke and air inflated his lungs like a balloon, almost as if his chest was about to burst. He inclined his head and raised his eyebrows and looked surreptitiously across the street, 'and him. He looks trouble. Turn round and look, but slowly.'

They obeyed. Reality had been a brick in the face and they were still reeling. A biker sat on a large motorbike, his helmet on, sunglasses masking his eyes against the now overcast sky. He could have been looking in their direction. They were not sure. But no sooner had they turned towards him, his bike rumbled into life and he was gone.

'Why did you say he looks like trouble?' asked Tom.

'He not interested in fire and smoke. He stay away. Me thinks not natural.'

He stubbed the cigarette butt out on the ground, adding to the circle flattened by his shoe from previous smoking excursions.

He turned to go and added before leaving, 'Be like me. Keep eye open, yes?'

The man's eyes held war ravaged stories within. He knew intimately the depths of human brutality. The leviathan never slept for long.

Mutely, they both nodded their heads. Their mood hung heavy across the pavement.

'My God,' whispered Claire, her face was smeared with soot and stretched in shock.

'We shouldn't jump to conclusions … should we?' Tom's rhetorical question spiralled off into the plumes of steam and ash as the fire lost its battle.

Tom pulled a handkerchief from one of his pockets and dampening it with saliva wiped Claire's face clean. She reciprocated. As the crowds filtered back into the hotel, Claire and Tom mingled with them and took the stairs upwards into the lobby. Some of the guests returned to their rooms. Others had stayed outside lingering to see if a view could be gained from the road. Claire and Tom, shaking inwardly, made their way to the bar, along with a few other guests. They kept themselves apart. After ordering drinks, they took up the only table that had a wooden alcove with curved overhanging eaves. The alcove was designed for those seeking intimacy and was normally occupied, but not today. It was sheltered, like a dog's kennel, and gave Claire and Tom a sense of security when they sat down. No matter how false the reality, they needed it right now.

The arrival of armoured vehicles and personnel from Serbia's Special Anti-Terrorist Unit, and later, confirmation on the news wires, heavily underpinned the waiter's warning – a car bomb had been planted, the main damage was to their Discovery Land Rover. Human body parts had been found. That left them in no doubt. They had been the target but unfortunates had been caught in the crossfire.

The Rakia alcohol shot recommended by their moustached waiter steadied their nerves, but burned their throats. The distraction helped. They talked. No internet. Avoid attention and survive long enough to gather evidence, for the tunnel they had entered had no light at the end.

They found a local newspaper lying discarded in the bar. They searched car ads and found a Peugeot 406 sedan, dark blue, over two hundred and forty thousand kilometres on the clock, two thousand Euros. They are a favourite car for taxi drivers, 'it must be reliable,' so their logic told them. Cash only.

Sometimes the light shines in unforeseen places.

With a bottle of Rakia from the bar as a gift and a thousand Euros for his trouble, the waiter bought it for them. No questions asked. No papers exchanged. With a bit more persuasion, the waiter also went out, bought them hair dye, scissors and two sets of clothes in their size, and secured them use of a vacant room for several hours.

The haircuts and hair colouring had altered their immediate appearances; her hair was now a red colour shaped into a short elfish cut. The styling had been started by Claire and finished by Tom. He had found the handling of the scissors more difficult than he had first thought. It was all too easy to forget when doing the familiar, until one did it, that his missing fingers might be a problem. Tom's conversion to blonde had made him look pale and washed out, but it threw an illusion that it wasn't him. The clothes bought added to visible first impressions of them being local. Tom even looked a bit on the rough side of life. It was the dark blue hoodie crumpled up above his jeans, and a lightweight beanie to hide his reconstructed ear that did it. She had done a pretty good job of converting him.

As for Claire, the floppy hat she put on, they thought, would mask her head from any skyward prying by satellites, but the denim dungarees, although definitely a novelty, were a bit of a task, as she soon discovered when using the bathroom.

Their phones were now fully charged. Unplugging them, and turning them both onto silent mode, Claire hid them behind the back of the room's radiator. Their GPS signals would continue pinging back and forth to the internet sounding off their location. With luck, the phones would remain undetected, at least for several days, and convince those who aimed to harm them regardless of the collateral damage that might be caused, that they were staying at the hotel.

Branislav, the waiter, 'their very welcome friend,' came back into the room.

'You two … good!' His moustache stretched wide across his mouth as he smiled. 'Very big difference. Here. Your money. I no need. You go see my cousin, Dejana. Her name means, to take action. She take good care of you, yes. Please. Give her note. Is letter from me. I say you friends, need help and place to stay. She understand. Trust me. She very good woman. She speak Serbian and Romanian like me. English much better.'

Claire and Tom tried to refuse the return of the money and at one point Branislav's face almost looked on the verge of being offended. Defeat accepted, they gratefully received his kindness. As they left, he gave them a hearty hug.

'Remember. Keep head down' he said, 'not forget'.

They promised not to.

Branislav had filled the car up with fuel and parked it in the staff parking bays at the rear of the hotel. It was nearly twenty minutes past nine in the evening; it was time to be on their way.

OXFORD – ENGLAND

EIGHTY

Thursday, October 11, 2012 – George and Monica's Place, Banbury Road, Oxford

The rain fell like lead crashing from the eaves, such was the downpour. Monica's sleeping pill and George's deep slumber left them unaware of the storm.

Other ambient sounds lost existence that night.

The circle cut from the glass door panel at the rear of the house was neat. The suction cups on the glass enabled its quiet removal. The intruder's entry was easy and silent. The bedroom of the targets was above the kitchen. It was an easy job. The intruder checked the gas boiler; it was timed to ignite at 7 am. At the stove, the intruder turned on all of the gas outlets on the hob and in the oven. In the living room, the gas from the unlit fire was vented into the room. Doors were closed.

The intruder left the way he came. He passed a snail making its way upwards across the glass. Its trail thinning out as the residue stretched from the rim on the doorframe's base. The grass impressions left in the garden by the intruder soon faded. The egress from the house and its curtilage had posed no problem.

The driver of the 4x4 parked in a nearby street started the car when the pager vibrated. A few moments later, the intruder opened the passenger door and got in. No words were exchanged, just a nod, the deed was done. As the rear lights from the car faded and were lost to view, it was not long before the veil of rain was the only movement in the neighbourhood. The silent assassins were gone.

At 06:57 hours, George's circadian clock awoke him as usual. His bear like mouth opened in a large yawn. He stretched and then rolled one of his arms over Monica's waist and snuggled his paw around and underneath her. Monica opened her eyes and a sleepy smile creased them as she looked into her husband's loving eyes. He leaned forward and rubbed his nose gently on hers. Her body relaxed into his.

'I'll make us some tea soon. I just want to listen to the news headlines first,' said George.

'No hurry darling. I'm so very sleepy this morning.'

LONDON

EIGHTY-ONE

Thursday, October 11, 2012 – Royal Street, near St Thomas' Hospital, London

Sonita Paneshi, anatomical pathology technologist at St Thomas' hospital had had a busy week. It was nearly 8 am, the start of her shift. This was the last day of twelve hours of work, her thoughts were on Friday, and the long weekend she had planned for her visit to see her parents and Leonia, an old childhood friend in Leicester.

The cycle to work was lousy as the heavy rain had been non-stop. The drains were overflowing. The water rushed off the sides of offices which stood on concrete stilts, almost as if their skirts had been pulled up to avoid the floods. The lights on her bike shone brightly, although even with the best of windscreen wipers flipping back and forth rapidly on vehicles, she still appeared a blurry smudge for drivers who passed by closely despite her bright yellow reflective jacket and trousers.

One 4x4, containing two occupants, followed Sonita to the end of the road. As she turned left, the driver nudged the vehicle's bumper against the bicycle's rear wheel and pulled to a stop. Sonita's bike slid from beneath her legs and she fell sideways onto the wet glistening tarmac. As she rolled onto her side facing the vehicle, her eyes just had time to take in the laughing faces of the occupants.

The driver accelerated hard. The wheels slipped and spun, before gaining grip and propelling the chassis forward, crunching over Sonita's bicycle and dragging her body underneath. The vehicle made its way rapidly over the rough terrain as if it were a mere sleeping policeman. The tread marks left a tattooed pattern across Sonita's squashed and extended face and embedded her cheekbone into the road's surface. To the sound of raucous laughter in the 4x4's cabin space, the vehicle sped off along Lambeth Palace Road, over Lambeth Bridge and beyond the distant sound of sirens heralding help that was already too late to save her.

ROMANIA

EIGHTY-TWO

Friday, October 12, 2012 – Timisoara, Romania

They had taken the long way round to get to Timisoara, travelling along the E75 towards Belgrade and then cutting up north and later east into Romania. It had taken over five hours to find their way, arriving in the outskirts at nearly two in the morning on Thursday. Eventually they found the dead end road off Strada Martir Hernan Sporer, which led to a rectangular shaped open space in between several blocks of flats. It was parking for residents.

With some relief on their faces, Claire and Tom could see there were some spaces available. They had parked the Peugeot at the far end. It was partially hidden by some trees growing in the spartan cityscape. In one of the flats, lived Branislav's cousin. They would look for her in the morning. In the pale map light before they had curled up to sleep in the car, Claire and Tom had both looked dishevelled.

When Claire awoke, it was 8.30 am. Tom was still asleep in the passenger seat, his midriff showing his stomach hair. His clothing had ridden up, having been caught on the car's velour cloth as he wrestled with his dreams in the confined space. She looked through the windscreen and immediately realised why this space had been vacant. Bird droppings were splattered across the glass and bonnet.

Outside, people were on their way to work, by foot, car, bicycle or scooter. There was a stream of them flooding out from the surrounding flats. Everyone kept themselves within their own world. Interaction was avoided. Those on foot kept their eyes cast down; it appeared to be the norm. That would suit her and Tom fine. Claire leaned into the back seat, grabbed a water bottle and a roll of toilet paper, and got on with the messy task in hand. Tom stirred as the breeze from outside caught his midriff unawares.

Their escape from the clutches of death in Smederevo had been narrow, and others tragically had lost their lives. The awful nature of their decision to act weighed heavily on Claire and Tom and even after exhausting their feelings about the blast and its repercussions, it had occupied the silent spaces in the car. Being vigilant, better than they had been, leaving no footprints to follow were the watchwords of the lives they had to live. However, they were amateurs at it. It had been all too easy, too seductive to live in the world of hope and to imagine they alone amongst all others could avoid detection by the Network.

The silent spaces of contemplation had multiplied after Tom expanded on the other files he had accessed behind the walls of intelligence agency networks.

The information when pieced together had demonstrated the distortions to freedom engineered by the Reich's network. He thought that the type of freedom sought by the Fourth Reich mirrored the violence of Ancient Greece and the hegemony achieved by Sparta. The Reich has endowed itself with the freedom to oppress all and everything that stands in its way.

Since the Second World War, the Network had honed the art of sophistry to nurture terrorism and the fear of it as a global threat. Consequently, they had encouraged the adoption and acceptance of an ever-expanding surveillance culture. A culture, all but a few voices in the wilderness around the world, now accepts.

Step by incremental step, the use of satellites, nano-size drones, CCTV, room, telephone and computer surveillance and bugs have come to be the accepted tools of democracy. The foundations of control are in place.

'It is one of the pivotal building blocks for the establishment of the Fourth Reich's version of freedom,' Tom had said.

Claire got back in, Tom was wide-awake.

'Hi. I'll move the car to the space over there,' she said, 'away from the bird nests. And then let's see if we can find Dejana.'

Tom leant over and kissed her before opening up the folded letter from Branislav and re-examining the address.

'Block 1, Apt 36, 012645, Timisoara, Sector 3, Romania, I never thought we'd find this place in the dark, but we made it. Thanks for driving last night. I was beat,' he said.

The four blocks of flats surrounding the communal car park were in sequential order, so finding Block 1 was easy. The lift was not working, so they made their way up the bare concrete stairwell plastered in largely black painted graffiti. Three floors up, they pushed open the fire door and three doors along the bleak looking corridor, they found themselves standing outside a matt grey painted wooden door. A small glass circular security spy hole was located in the upper middle of its surface. The hallway either side was quiet, apart from the sound of a baby crying in a flat some two doors further along.

Claire knocked on the door. Tom stood to her side and slightly behind. A few moments later, the door opened. A security chain hung in place and a pale young woman, in her early twenties, peered out. She was tall, slim, with high cheekbones, had Slavic eyes and long waist length black hair; she was wearing a long woollen dark brown dress.

Claire smiled, and said, 'Dejana?'

The young woman nodded. Claire said nothing and instead handed over the letter from Branislav. The young woman read its content, and then looked at both Claire and Tom for a few moments before unlatching the door and silently, with her hand, beckoned them forwards and let them in.

Breathing out a sigh of relief when the door closed behind them, Claire and Tom walked from the narrow entrance straight into the all in one room. A small cubicle with a spring door to the left, served as a toilet, sink and shower room. Most of the walls were exposed brickwork covered in an off-white gloss. One wall, which angled L shaped above and around the electric cooker and sink in the kitchen alcove, was turquoise. The gloss painted brickwork underneath looked almost like tiles. Brown grease clung to the wall behind the cooker. A wooden crucifix hung above it and a prominent icon of Mary stood on the windowsill in the living area. Grey white net curtains covered the window's expanse, which overlooked the car park and the trees below. A few posters of Hollywood film stars from the 1950s hung on the wall and an acoustic guitar rested on a stand by the red settee, which they later discovered doubled up as a bed when the cushions were spread across the floor. This was covered in a red and blue floral pattern rug, which seemed to cover most of the floor space.

'It helps to keep cold out in winter,' said Dejana when seeing Claire and Tom cast their eyes over it. 'My cousin Branislav says, "I must help you as much I can," he also says, "People may want to hurt you and I must help to keep you safe." This I will try to do. You may stay here for as long as you need.'

'This is really far too much to ask of you,' said Claire.

'Absolutely, I agree,' said Tom, 'we can't possibly ask this of you.'

'It is my cousin, he has asked. He is my blood relation. This I have to do. It is no problem. I am happy. I can stay with my boyfriend.'

'This seems so unfair,' said Claire.

'My boyfriend, Eugen, he think it very fair. I think he like a lot.' Dejana smiled awkwardly as the inference dawned on her.

'This is so very kind of you,' said Claire.

'It is,' chimed Tom, adding, as much to change the subject and to overcome the stilting embarrassment of the moment, 'Do you and your boyfriend work?'

'He study at University Timisoara, like me. We both want to be engineer. Now, please, tell me, what can I do for you?'

SERBIA

EIGHTY-THREE

Friday, October 12, 2012 – Smederevo, Serbia

Branislav was exhausted when he finished his day shift at 9 pm that night. He lobbed yet another stained and smoke impregnated waiter's apron into the wash basket in the staff changing room; he should have taken up basketball, and slipped on his black plastic bomber jacket over his white shirt and zipped it up.

Stepping out of the rear hotel door, he struck a match and lit up his twentieth cigarette of the day. Breathing in the smoke so deeply felt so very good. He rotated his shoulders back, tense after a day carrying food and waste back and forth from the kitchen, weaving around the tables serving customers and cleaning tables. Some days it did not let up. And this day had been one of them. He arched his head backwards and blew the smoke high into the night air. Boy that felt good.

He walked to the end of the car park. His Nissan Juke's warning lights flashed a few times when he pressed the door lock release button on his car keys. With the high point security light out, the short flashes of orange were magnified in intensity against the side of the black van parked next to his. So much so, it looked as if the large blinking eye of a hungry, ravenous ogre was alive in its surface. Branislav shrugged his shoulders – must be Goran's. As he reached his car, the van's sliding door slammed open and men far stronger than Branislav grabbed his shoulders and yanked him fiercely back off his feet and into the vehicle. When he tried to shout out, the butt of a special operations Glock pistol smashed against his head and he lost consciousness.

One of the small lakes north-east of Smederevo, Serbia

A clenched fist smashed into his cheekbone. His head reeled sideways from the shock, blurry vision returned as he regained consciousness. The back of his skull was bulging and in pain. He was strapped to a solitary chair bolted to the floor of the van. He was naked. Two bouncer-sized men wearing silk balaclavas stood either side of him. One started speaking in Serbian, although from his accent, it was clear it was not his native tongue.

'Where are the couple you spoke to outside of the hotel after the vehicle fire in the car park?'

'Who? ... What? ... I've no idea ... What the fuck is going on?' Branislav's raised voice was loud inside the van's cramped space full of three large men including him.

The man's voice scraped the base of his vocal chords. 'You can make as much noise as you like. No one will hear. You are on your own. Now, tell me ... where are they?'

'I've told you. I don't fucking know who or what you're talking about.'

'I think you do. We found their mobile phones hidden in one of the staff rooms. Now how would they get in there without any outside help, huh?'

The interrogator nodded to his accomplice who moved in quickly with a pair of bolt cutters. With one incisive bite, three and a bit fingers on Branislav's right hand were carelessly severed. They momentarily stuck to the tool's metal surface before the butcher shook them off and they fell to the floor. With one scuffing kick from his boot, the fingers landed upside down and came to a lopsided standstill against the van's outer panelling.

439

Branislav raged in agony, 'You piece of shit,' he shouted, his eyes bulging, the veins virtually popping on his forehead.

'We can make this quick or slow; it's your choice.' The interrogator's voice lingered in the smoke as he lit two cigarettes and shoved one into Branislav's mouth.

'Go fuck yourself,' said Branislav hoarsely, the cigarette bobbing on his lips.

The interrogator inhaled deeply, the glow from the burning tobacco blazed red. He studied the ember and then jammed it hard into Branislav's left eyeball. The fingernails of hell scratched painfully down his skull. The cigarette in Branislav's mouth fell somersaulting onto his genitals and slowly burnt its way deeper into his skin. His head hung forward, unanswerable pain defining fractures across his face. The brutality and torture of the civil war had taught him one thing, there was no way back. Do not speak and they kill you slowly. Speak, and they kill you slowly.

Thirty slow minutes passed. In the few moments before he would draw his last breath, and ahead of the heavenly seconds when he would drift into delusion as his mind skewed inwards away from the agony, the interrogator leaned over and whispered into what was left of Branislav's last ear.

'You could have saved your family from all of this you know.'

Branislav shattered and broken, looked down at the bare floor through the swelling of his one remaining eye, his tongue lay partially squashed underneath one of the butcher's boots, its pink furry surface covered in dirt.

'We'll start with your parents, your brothers and then your cousins. And if you have women in your family, we'll fuck them before they die.' The interrogator's vocal chords purred with salacious pleasure.

Branislav groaned aloud the guttural protest of the dumb and spat into the man's eyes before his body shuddered, and his bowels opened.

Heavy chain link was wrapped around Branislav's body and the two men loaded it onto a nearby rowing boat. Butcher laboured with the oars. The interrogator leaned back against the stern and drew on another satisfying cigarette. When they reached the square pontoon, which was anchored almost dead centre across the lake's waters, the interrogator lashed the boat to the metal berthing cleats. He used his hands to hold onto the pontoon's structure and steady the rocking of the boat. The butcher used his muscles, which bulged and contorted as he rolled the weighted and soon to be bottom dweller up and over the gunnels and pushed the discarded body into the cold dark depths.

The interrogator shone a torch onto the surface. Both men watched the last of the bubbles rise to the surface. The boat's hull gently bobbed on the fading ripples, before momentary silence returned to the lake. The return row was easier, but slower. The butcher was in no hurry. At the water's edge, they returned the boat to its resting place on the stones.

The rapid crunch of the butcher's boots on the gravel heralded the start of the final task. He ferried buckets of water back to the van. If there was one job he hated, it was slopping out. He always got that task. He detested it as much as the stench when it crawled into his lungs. The smell never left his nostrils for hours afterwards. It was times like these that he wished he was the driver, but his skills from the abattoir were always in demand.

ROMANIA

EIGHTY-FOUR

Sunday, October 14, 2012 – Dejana's flat, Timisoara, Romania

When Dejana had warned them their visitor might call early, it was now apparent what she had precisely meant. He had arrived at 5.15 am. The alarm clock set for 6.30 am was redundant. The evidence of their slumber, cut short, was arrayed around the small room, cushions, a quilt and pillows still lay across the floor as Tom let the elderly man in. He waited patiently standing beneath one of the posters, whilst Claire and Tom restored order to the small living space.

The newcomer was at best five feet six inches tall and by the look of him, not overweight. Age weary bones had taken their toll on his spine though, the upper reaches showed early signs of curvature, as if a bowyer was just starting to pull the sinew taut between the two ends of his creation. His grey hair, brushed back behind his ears, was wavy and full of life. Around his neck, curled and flipped back across his shoulders, was a thick woollen scarf, emerald green. Underneath he wore a brown long overcoat, green corduroy trousers and polished brown brogues. Age had not diminished his sense of self-care and grooming. Yet his face, aged as it was, also betrayed a weight that had grown heavier in him. It bore his features downward. However, when he looked at you, his eyes, which were deep and dark brown, penetrated and held – no demanded – your attention.

When they were ready, he placed his attorney-sized briefcase on the floor, sat on the small stool that had been stored behind the settee and looked at the lens of the digital camcorder resting on a stand in the corner of the room. It was one of the many things that Claire and Tom had asked Dejana to buy for them.

'I am Doru. My name means longing. I am nearly 80 years old. I wait for very long time to see you,' he said. 'I pray, many, many years now, and you here,' his tears flowed freely down the crevices of his craggy and careworn face. 'It is miracle. I am Ekaterina's father. I never know what happened to her after she taken. Please. Tell me.'

There are some things the heart and mind cannot absorb. The detail of how Ekaterina had died occupied central territory, which was navigated around in the telling: her Father learned that she had died in childbirth; her children, two twin boys had grown into strong men.

'She would have been proud of them,' said Claire, 'but sadly, they had fallen ill and died this summer.'

'I never get to see my grandchildren.' His shoulders slumped. He said nothing for a few moments and sat as still as a living statue. Eventually, in a voice heavy with grief's resonance, he said, 'that is God's will.'

Claire and Tom looked at each other and realised that in one way it was. The secrets of the dead rested safely away from this man's heart and left him in peace. What he had most surely suspected was true. His daughter was dead. In his dreams, she had come to him nightly, unchanged, but always out of reach. Now, he could mourn her loss and find solace in the knowing. No longer would his eyes forever search for images and chase after the fleeting ghosts on a trail, which melted as soon as his footsteps drew near.

Ekaterina had not come home one night in late January 1973. His daughter's kidnapping and disappearance was never recognised under Ceausescu's communist regime. He recounted a memory of those from the State.

"It not possible," 'Securitate would say, "No one can leave Romania without permission." Then they laugh. Every day in 1973, I protested at Securitate headquarters in Timisoara. I carry stick with picture of Ekaterina. Stand on street. Securitate still no listen. Instead, at three in morning on Sunday, 26 January 1974 they imprison me; say I am "threat to State." It was Ceausescu's birthday,' Doru spat out the phrase in disgust.

'I kept in prison for over fifteen year. Only when revolution in Timisoara in 1989 was I let go. Doors open, Securitate gone. I celebrate when Ceausescu shot.'

For the first time that morning, Doru laughed, although the hoarse sound echoing from his throat was absent of any real mirth.

'I need drink. Water please. I not want anything else.'

Tom poured Doru another glass as the first was downed in one. Doru nodded appreciatively, took another sip, and then placed the glass on the windowsill. He looked down at the birds, which were still nesting in the trees. They were waking up and fluffing their feathers, making ready for the hunt for food. Like humans, they had a daily routine that only ended upon death or incapacity.

Doru continued, 'I go straight away to Securitate headquarters and with others, we look for secret files. Everyone look for files on themselves. Me, I look for Ekaterina.' His eyes suddenly flashed and opened wide, 'There I find papers marked "Female Transport Cargo." My Ekaterina, her photograph and name with her medical records was inside. And big red Securitate stamp across page, it say, "Shipping Approved!" I scream in anger and grief. You understand? I throw lamps in office against wall. I smash windows. I break many things. Pain, it not goes. And then I sit on floor against wall and stare at Ekaterina's face and cry. I cry … I…'

History's veil of tears touched the room they all shared in the flat. Claire, Tom and Doru stood together and hugged. Words were superfluous.

Doru stepped back from them both, took a handkerchief from his trouser pocket, and blew his nose before downing the second glass of water. After washing his face in the bathroom, he returned to continue, his eyes swollen and red from the unlocking of yet more grief. The chasm of pain was thirty-nine years deep.

'Ekaterina's file, it say, she shipped to Odessa in Ukraine. I know not where to look. She remain lost to me. I then search other files in office of Securitate. I learn Securitate agents had been placed in Timisoara gynaecological wards. Mass propaganda say, "to monitor pregnancy tests, to stop abortion." But I then see long list of women who were pregnant. It says each one artificially made pregnant for experimental purposes. Each one spontaneously aborted except one. On bottom of list, I see Ekaterina's name. She is marked as success. I have all files here. I show you.' Doru clicked open his briefcase and removed a large wad of faded manila folders, which had been creased and marked over the years.

With his face showing hesitation, Doru spoke solemnly.

'I will give you them, but promise me this: do not stop until the whole world knows. No, until the whole world believes. In Romania, no one listen. In European Parliament, no one wish to hear. I lost hope of seeing Ekaterina again. Instead, I work with others in my Catholic Cathedral in Timisoara. It is St George. Like England, no?' He looked at them both before continuing. 'We set up organisation to stop trafficking of women – STOP NOW we call it. We do our best, we provide safe houses, but Timisoara is place where many women go missing. It is capital for such things. It is holding place for women taken from elsewhere. I read reports; they say many go for prostitution, but some I think, like my Ekaterina, taken to be baby factories.'

When Doru handed over the files, Claire recorded their contents page by page on the camera, the first of which was Ekaterina's medical record. Her file showed her young and innocent face. She was hauntingly beautiful. Emotive in the facial shadows cast in the black and white photograph, her frightened eyes called out to be saved. Tom took the completed files from her and slid them into the back of her rucksack. They slotted neatly into the compartment next to the laptop and the other grizzly evidence, which, if seen by Doru, would surely shake his faith and break his resolve to keep on living.

When Doru learned of Tom's training for the priesthood, he insisted they must come with him to Mass, 'You must come with me. It start in hour time.'

They looked at their watches, it was 10 am.

'We light candle in memory of Ekaterina. Come you pray with me. Also, you must meet friends who lead STOP NOW. I not work when reach seventy-seven. Cathedral of St George is beautiful. Mother Mary she watches over you. This I know.'

Claire and Tom's faith in supernatural protection was a pale shadow to Doru's conviction, but perhaps the battle between good and evil, was as it may have been in the beginning, was now and always will be, played out through the choices humans made.`

The square surrounding the cathedral is in itself vastly impressive, dwarfing an individual's presence with its gargantuan size. The proximity of its baroque architecture drew the eyes of all. Claire and Tom craned their necks to survey the upper reaches of its beauty. The sound from the bells occupied the spaces between thought. They pounded out every second, repeating the call to the faithful to attend Mass. Doru told them that the building could hold some three thousand people. Claire and Tom looked around them, seemingly in their thousands they were streaming into all four corners of the square.

Inside the building, the architecture was embellished with layers of gold leaf. The vaulted ceiling naturally led one to feel awe and created a sense of something sacred regardless of one's faith or none at all. The three of them slowly made their way to the left hand side of the Cathedral. At the end, adjacent to the backdrop of the altar, Mary stood holding Christ in her arms. They joined a nun who was dressed in a sky blue habit and skirt and white blouse and lit a candle for Ekaterina. The background sounds of people gathering and shuffling into the pews faded for a while as they bowed their heads in prayer.

During Mass, one of the people reading passages from the bible whilst very ably projecting her voice from the lectern happened to look up at Claire and Tom when she read out the first response to the Psalm. Later, Tom asked Doru which Psalm it was.

Doru replied, 'Psalm 39, 'Here I am Lord! I come to do your will.'

Come what may, they knew they would.

EIGHTY-FIVE

10:23 hours, Sunday, October 14, 2012 – Dejana's boyfriend Eugen's flat, Timisoara, Romania

The adhesive tape was snatched away from Dejana's mouth, stretching her lips painfully.

'Your flat's fucking empty. So where the fuck are they?' The interrogator's ringed fingers slashed heavily across her face.

'They should be there. I don't know.'

Dejana's eyes darted around in panic. The pain had been unbearable. And the butcher's breath smelt ungodly when he'd breathed heavily into her face when he had raped her.

Eugen, in his stupid ignorance and in his broken promises, had responded to the Facebook message that purported to be from the British Police, sent to people in Timisoara, asking if anyone was aware of the whereabouts of an English couple who might be in the city, there was some important news for them regarding their relatives. A reward had been offered.

Dejana had told him not to. It was dangerous. Unbeknown to her, Eugen had agreed to meet the originator of the message to collect his reward and hand over the information for the cash. When they had asked to meet him in a dead end road, far off Strada Grigore Alexandescru away from the city centre, he should have listened to his sixth sense warning him. Greed had consumed his sanity. The money was enough for him and Dejana to live on for a whole year. When he got out of his car to greet them, they had bundled him into their black van and very quickly found out that his girlfriend, Dejana knew the address. In his shock, burnt into him from their brutality, his mind had frozen blank.

Back at Eugen's flat, they had found Dejana. She had been determined to say nothing, but when she had refused, the butcher slashed Eugen's throat with a long slim bladed knife. Blood gushed and glugged from him. As he lay dying, the butcher had sliced apart her dress with the blade and raped her. In addition, as she had lay sliding in Eugen's blood, the light in her boyfriend's eyes had died.

'And now', the interrogator spoke as he nodded to the butcher who picked her up off the floor and put the knife to her other ear. Dejana's sinews screamed to pull away.

'No, wait. Please. I know. I know. They must be at Mass with Doru.'

In her flight from terror it was too late she realised, she had blurted out even more information.

'Doru?' The interrogator's breath, expelled from his mouth, licked the side of her face.

When she could tell no more, they always knew when that moment had been reached; the butcher was allowed a final taste of her. During the final thrust, his hands tightened mercilessly around Dejana's throat and squeezed her life away until her body slumped raggedly across the floor.

The interrogator made a concise call from his mobile. 'We need a cleaner, yes, now,' and he gave the address before they left.

Strada Eugeniu de Savoya, Timisoara, Romania

The sun was still out. The Faithful had scattered to their homes. A few cars were dotted along the one-way street, made up of shops, doorways and street signs. One building on the opposite side of the road had a skip positioned outside. It was partially filled with debris from a building being renovated. A couple of planks lay side by side from the road to the lip of the skip and provided a gangway for the labourers to dispose of the waste by lumbering up their length with a wheelbarrow and tipping the debris away into its hold. There were no builders in sight, on a lunch break or enjoying a day of rest, who could say.

Claire and Tom's Peugeot 406 was still some way off. They were walking arm in arm, aware of the risk, alert, but pacing slowly, not wanting to get too far ahead of Doru. He was a few metres behind them, walking with his neighbour, Anca.

She was an elderly woman, similar age to him; possibly, it was difficult to tell, as Anca's face was wizened from years in the sun and perhaps smoking too. She was of a similar height to Doru, but seemingly, all elderly people of that generation were. She was wearing a black netted shawl over her head and shoulders and wore a grey and black heavy cotton dress, which fell to a fair way below her knees.

Anca had been an amiable companion to Doru they had learned. The friendship had come about not long after Luminita, his wife, had died in 2007. It was good that he had such company. Life had been tough for him. The small morsel of goodness that Anca was, allowed Doru to smile a little again, and that was good, thought Claire and Tom.

Traffic was quiet and infrequent. In the distance, the sound of a vehicle unhurriedly trundling along the road at the speed of a gulley-sucker could be heard. As it drew closer, the vehicle's engine shrieked as if full of angry horses. Claire span around, she was more agile than Tom since his injuries and immediately saw the looming killer whale of a black van descend at terminal velocity towards them.

Claire reached into the power of her lungs and shouted one of the few words Dejana had taught them, 'Pericol,' it meant danger.

Doru and Anca looked up, surprise clear on their faces. Simultaneously, Claire pulled Tom sideways towards her and they fell headlong into a gap between some concrete pillars that held up the storefront of a department store.

The van mounted the pavement, its bumper, acting like a cattle catcher on the front of a railway engine, scooped the two docile puppets – Doru and Anca upwards and over – their bodies split open and broke upon impact with the van's hard, unforgiving surface. The driver, in an effort to smash into the bodies of Claire and Tom, accidentally collided into one of the columns catching the nearside front of the van and knocking clumps of concrete away from the pillar. From then on, physics took over, the driver lost control of the wheel and in those moments, with the accelerator still pushed hard to the floor, the van bounced violently sideways, its offside wheels mounted the wooden planks of the skip. The vehicle twisted and turned into the air before smashing roof down on the road and sliding to a gut wrenching and grinding stop as it came up against another building and lay embedded in the shop frontage.

It was too late for Doru and Anca, even though their lifeless bodies still dribbled blood. Tom had landed on top of Claire and he hauled her upright. The few people that were witnesses to the carnage still cowered, overtaken by shock. Claire and Tom walked slowly. Their bodies screamed out for them to run. They could not afford to be wrapped up in police investigations. They would never be allowed to leave alive. As they passed the upturned vehicle, they saw that the side panel of the van was gashed open and two men lay upended on the van's crumpled roof, their legs and heads twisted, bones protruding, their eyes glared wide. The driver was dead or dying also. The cabin space of the roof had concaved so much that his body resembled a concertina; his intestines had burst out through his shirt.

Their Peugeot, a car but one away, remained unaffected. Shaking and trembling Claire and Tom walked towards it. Swinging their rucksacks off their backs, Claire and Tom dropped neatly, with utter relief, into the car's seats. Tom turned to Claire, 'Thank God for your nine lives.' He switched the ignition on and the engine started. Before any of the onlookers had gathered their senses, they drove quietly away. 'Where do we go now?'

'I guess there's only one way,' she replied and pointed to a place on the map.

He nodded his head in unspoken agreement. And with that, he pointed the car in the direction of the E70. They headed out of the city as the first signs of mizzle paved the way for oncoming sheets later.

Remetea Mare, Romania

Fifteen minutes out of Timisoara the mizzle by progressive amounts had metamorphosed into a torrential downpour. They had not spoken. Their minds, dislocating from what they had just seen and experienced, were numb. The one massive adrenaline rush that had slammed into their bodies had now evaporated; shock had set in and impounded their brains. As everyday Claire and Tom, they had ceased to function on any level other than survival mode. Conversation, other than for directions, was beyond them.

The swish swash, back and forth, of the windscreen wipers, especially when the sensors automatically increased speed in response to more rain was oddly therapeutic and mesmerising. It distracted them from dwelling on any lingering feelings of panic that awaited them if they looked at their reflections in the mirror, or the windows, or one another, and allowed their subconscious minds to collect thoughts and ideas, which fizz popped and bubbled slowly to the surface. Eventually, it was Claire, who spoke first.

'Branislav and Dejana are probably dead. They must have got Doru's name from her.'

'Yes, I agree. It wasn't by chance the black van went for him and us. They've probably run a check on him too by now.'

'Check? In what way?'

The rain relented slightly, the momentum of the wipers slowed. Towering in the opposite direction a lorry's headlights dazzled Tom. Its offside wheels seemed closer, were closer, edging the colossus to their side of the carriageway. Tom swerved the car inwards. Claire swept off her balance stopped herself from smashing into Tom by grabbing hold of the passenger door's handrail. The lorry veered to its nearside, the tail end of its trailer sliding past them a hairsbreadth away.

Whoever drove, from then onwards, made sure the car was kept out of harm's way and close to the right hand verge, just in case other oncoming drivers straddled the invisible central boundary of the highway.

Tom looked across at Claire. 'Sorry about that. Who Doru was, I mean, and what he'd been up to over the years. It won't take long for their database to cross reference that he was Ekaterina's father, the mother of the Fourth Reich's first born offspring. He was the man they could afford to ignore in the past; no one ever believed his story. But why kill him off and give his campaign the potential for credence? He never knew about the Network's existence.

'Doru's campaigning was years ago,' replied Claire, her knowledge coming to the fore, 'Other than the local press, the media probably won't even pick up that he's died. I doubt his death will draw any focus the Network's way.'

'You're probably right, but,' added Tom, 'the Network will know Doru hit a dead end at Odessa. They must have guessed by now that we probably have his evidence. They've probably ransacked his home and Dejana's flat by now, just to make doubly sure.'

'And Odessa could be a killing ground if we go there.'

They looked at one another and silence engaged them both once more. The rain's veil gradually retracted and dwindled to mizzle again before petering out of existence. A hesitant sun poked out from behind the grey clouds and cast oil patterned rainbows on the tarmac. The scenery, revealed in the twists and turns of the road, became their new distraction and put a distance between them and the dark thoughts of what lay ahead.

An hour or so later they passed through the city of Deva; as far as their memory served them, it seemed to be about half the size of Exeter. The road they were on had been tracking on its left the meandering course of a fairly large river and with clearer skies the views beyond into the rolling hills had become extensive.

'Isn't the water down there beautiful,' said Tom, 'I wonder what the river is called,' doing his best to brighten the cabin mood and reflect the changed weather pattern.

Claire unfolded the road atlas and ran her fingers along the river's course until she found the name, 'the River Mureş.'

'How is that spelt?'

'M-U-R-E S; the S has a cedilla underneath it.'

Tom mouthed the word over several times, his thoughts clicking each letter into place, like a combination lock.

'The name has a familiar ring to it. I have a feeling a chap I met at a training seminar last year or so, either lives around here or is in a parish somewhere nearby. He's a priest, Hungarian or Romanian, I'm not sure. He was giving a lecture on the logic of celibacy, I remember that.'

'What was his name?'

'Mi ... Mihály,' said Tom, 'that's it, I'm sure of it. Father Mihály. Are there any towns or cities that have the word Mureş in it?'

Casting a finger in ever increasing concentric circles across the map's flat two-dimensional topography Claire spotted the city of Târgu Mureş. Using a pencil as a rough guide rule, she said, 'As the crow flies, it's about 100 miles from where we are now. Not exactly near?'

'Shall we?' Tom looked at her sideways and raised his eyebrows.

'What do we do if he is there, seek sanctuary?' asked Claire, doubt tinged in her voice.

They talked then and eventually worked out a plan of action, if Father Mihály was there and if, he was prepared to help. If not, well, there remained the seemingly enduring conundrum of what and where next. Setting out on their course of action had been one thing, but knowing where it would end and how they would get there... the irreconcilability of it all had pressed the atmosphere downwards in the car's cabin space again. They were just two little people fighting an invisible Goliath.

Shortly after passing Deva they changed over driving, stopping briefly on the outskirts of a smallish town called Simeria. Ever since meeting Branislav in Smederevo they had gotten into the habit of having in their rucksacks an emergency supply of food and drink too. Do not buy anything, other than fuel. Do not speak to anyone. Leave nothing behind. No trace. They could not afford to stop and have their English voices overheard or have a CCTV camera identify their faces. In these ways, they had hoped detection would be avoided.

EIGHTY-SIX

18:17 hours, Sunday, October 14, 2012 – St. John the Baptist
Church, Târgu Mureş, Romania

The six pm Mass had already started by the time they arrived.
The church appeared to be just over half full; mainly middle
aged to elderly people filled the pews, although several
teenagers and young adults were there too, and possibly, at
best, two or three families with young children. Most probably
many other parents with youngsters were home having supper
and getting their charges ready for bed as they ran through the
tried and tested sleep routine. Every parent's dream when it
works.

Claire and Tom sat in the side aisle of the church, their view
of the altar partially obscured by one of the pillars. Father
Mihály was washing his hands, an act of symbolism portraying
his desire to secure purification. He dried his hands, and then
extended his arms to the congregation and invited all to join
him in prayer over the gifts of bread, wine and their offerings.
Part of Tom longed to be alongside Mihály, sharing in the
celebration of Mass. He felt strangely awkward playing a more
passive role as a member of the Faithful. Claire took hold of his
hand. The simple touch reminded him that love had found its
home in their hearts. The rush to be somewhere else in life no
longer endured.

Mihály gave the concluding rite and reminded everyone to
go and serve the Lord. And with that, he blessed everyone with
the sign of the cross. Most people left the church then. Some

hovered to chat to each other, before silent eyes ushered them to leave. About a dozen or so of the congregation had moved to the right hand side and centre of the church and knelt down in prayer. Claire whispered to Tom, 'What's going on?'

'You see Father Mihály; he's walking down the side aisle. I think he's taking confessions. I'll join the queue.'

The priest entered one of the confessionals and one by one, each entered the adjoining cubicle to seek forgiveness and guidance. Tom was the last to go in. Familiar surroundings welcomed him. He could see Mihály through the closed slatted cover separating them; he was sitting on a stool, facing forwards, the left side of his face close to the divide enabling him to hear each confession clearly. When Tom was seated, Mihály said a welcoming prayer in Romanian and, Tom, assumed, invited him to confess his sins.

'Father Mihály,' Tom said, and immediately he could see the priest's body posture change from looking relaxed to sitting upright, taken aback by the sound of an English voice. He so very rarely heard the language nowadays unless he listened to the BBC's World News, which he did when events appeared to be more unsettled and divisive than normal. 'It's me, Tom Abimelech, I am, was training to be a Catholic priest. We met briefly when you came to my seminary in Spain to talk about...'

'I remember you Tom. It is strange to hear English spoken first hand again. Tell me, what is it that is troubling you?'

'I'm not here for confession,' said Tom, 'I need your help.'

Mihály slid the partition open and looked at Tom. He absorbed how different his appearance was from when he had seen him in Spain. How very distant from the look he expected of a priest. He said nothing and looked at Tom expectantly.

'In July I was kidnapped whilst in London. I was tortured. The man who did this to me also kidnapped an old friend,' he corrected himself, 'a girlfriend I had known before I went into training. We were rescued and were lucky to escape with our lives. The Church has released me and we are now married.

'After being held captive we uncovered things, not of our choosing, that had remained hidden for decades. Plans that the world needs to know about. We have been hunted across Europe. People have been murdered in efforts to find and kill us. We have evidence of it all. We have to get the information to someone we know and who we hope can and will do something with it and make people believe.'

'How can I help you?' enquired Mihály calmly, as if he was helping a passing stranger who was about to ask for directions.

'We need to make copies of everything we have and ask you to arrange for it to be couriered. If it's sent by us, it will never reach its destination. We need access to a photocopier, blank CDs and DVDs, a DVD player, a TV and a white screen. We need it all tonight. And no one must know we have been here or seen you, or it will fail and they will kill you Father.'

Mihály pondered this most strange of requests. He knew this man, Tom. He was a good person. He would have been a powerful priest. But God works in mysterious ways. Father Mihály's role, as Christ's advocate, as always, was to work for the good of God.

'I will help,' he said.

The Presbytery, St. John the Baptist Church, Târgu Mureş, Romania

Father Mihály put the pot of coffee and doorstep sized sandwiches to the side of the large dark brown mahogany oval table and quietly left the room. Claire had finished her letter and was now busily working her way through the papers using the office copier, and stacking and stapling them into files as they rolled out, hot to the touch, from the machine. Tom, meanwhile parcelled up each file, and all of the documents they had gathered since July. What was keeping both he and Claire going was impossible now to fathom. Both felt as if they were burning up inside. Sure signs of exhaustion and adrenal gland depletion. Their bodies ached. Even their brains felt sore as if their dried and curling edges were being scraped along the sides of their skull.

When the copying work was done, they both stopped to eat. Tension had made their facial muscles tight, so much so, that stretching their mouths wide to take a bite out of a sandwich hurt. Almost simultaneously, they had responded with an 'Ouch,' and instinctively, to relieve the pain, had rubbed the side of their jaws just beneath the lower ear lobes.

Replenished, they continued. Claire wrapped more files. Tom set up the DVD player, the TV, the digital camcorder and positioned a chair in front of the flat white screen, which was attached to the wall. Lastly, he pulled across a small desk in front of the chair.

'It's nearly twenty past nine,' said Tom, 'shall we start?'

Claire looked up from the large table where she had just wrapped the last item of documentation. She nodded and gave Tom a weak, exhausted smile. He walked over and kissed her on the forehead.

'We're nearly there,' he said. 'We've done our best. God couldn't have asked more of us, could he?'

Claire wrapped her arms around Tom's waist and held him close. 'No Tom, he couldn't.'

She looked up into his eyes and squeezed him three times.

'I love you too,' he said and they kissed.

Claire settled herself onto the chair behind the desk. Tom turned on the camcorder.

'Ready?' He asked.

She nodded and took a deep breath.

'My name is Claire Juliette Yohanus. I read English at the University of Exeter. I formerly lived in Iverna Gardens,

London. Up until the summer of 2012, I was a lead reporter for one of the surviving broadsheets in the United Kingdom. I was responsible for the North American Continent. Since 2008, I have covered the presidential race for the White House. The nature of events that unfolded in 2012 prevented me from returning to the USA for the 57th presidential election on November 6 2012 … What you are about to find out is true. It is a foretaste of things to come.'

She stood up went out of camera shot and operated the camcorder. Tom walked into view and took up the seat.

'My name is Tom Peter Abimelech. I read Computer Science at the University of Exeter. I formerly lived in Banbury Road, Oxford. Up until the summer of 2012, I lived in Spain, where I attended a Roman Catholic Seminary to prepare me for the priesthood. The nature of events that unfolded in 2012 prevented me from resuming my vocation … What you are about to learn is the truth…' He paused before allowing his eyes to bore deep into the camera's lens, trying desperately to reach those who might see. 'God help us all.'

Claire switched the camcorder off.

They looked at one another. It was over.

ODESSA – UKRAINE

EIGHTY-SEVEN

Monday, October 15, 2012 – Roundabout Kil'teseva and Ob'izna Rds., Odessa, Ukraine

The Militsiya police officer looked at his watch; it was six minutes past seven in the morning. Another fifty-four lousy minutes and his night shift would have been over.

The half-metre deep concrete gulley gaping at the side of the road held the Peugeot 406 saloon car it had swallowed. The car was lying on its side, trapped in a tight embrace against the gulley's hard unforgiving walls. The car's metal surface was crumpled. Its paintwork was scarred by the impact of collision. The exposed rear wheel had spun for a while, but as is the want of things, the law of thermodynamics had its way, and the burst tyre had eventually come to a natural dead stop.

The officer looked around casually, vaguely, anything to hand in looking for a reason to write this one off. Something big, an articulated lorry carrying heavy cargo containers, most likely, he thought, must have ploughed across the roundabout at one hell of a speed, smashed, and scraped the car clean off the road. No witnesses either, despite it being the start of a busy day. He might get home sooner rather than later then. The whole chassis was smashed up. It had a Romanian number plate. That might provide some leads. He could pass on the file for them to investigate. Things were looking up.

There was no baggage in the car or the boot. Their bodies carried no identification. They had not moved since he had arrived. No wonder, they were dead, he thought. Just as well, less paperwork. Only a breakdown truck to arrange, with lifting gear he guessed and he would be done for the day.

Funny though, perhaps at the last moment they had seen the crash coming and that had given them the chance to hold each other's hand tightly before the impact. He shrugged his shoulders. The choices people make, he thought.

EIGHTY-EIGHT

23:53 hours, Saturday, April 4, 2015 – USA, location withheld

SOJOURN

By Tom Abimelech (1983-2012)

Let us go on a sojourn along pathways never trod,
Apart from those beyond our touch
Who are given the gift of immortal life by God.

Let our imaginings guide all our ways.
Let us touch love with gentle affection
And be unhurried by senseless reflection.

Let us go beyond the gift of life,
Allow ourselves to float in mystery,
And rest unsullied by painful histories, come, follow me.

Dear Reader

Claire's letter enclosed with the parcel sent by Father Mihály – he'd kept his promise and waived his right to anonymity, "whatever is God's will," he'd said – reminded me that I'd met her in 2012, and also, both her Tom, when I was a guest speaker at a moot in 2003 on the right to self defense and gun control, hosted at the University of Exeter when they were undergraduates and she was Chair of the Debating Society.

I am sorry that you have had to learn that they are both dead. I was not sure how and when it was best to tell you. You may have realised somewhere along the journey they might not make it. However, I wanted you to have an intimate insight into their world and gain a taste of the one, which co-exists and ultimately overwhelmed them. Sometimes we cannot run away can we? They occupied a small corner of the planet and just got on with it. Until that is… I know I did ... Not now.

You see, in America, when people died, it used to feel like a numbers game. If it did not involve my family or friends, I was removed from it all. I did not apply any emotions to humans dying, just another bead to move on the abacus, my secondary multi-task thinking sweeping away such thoughts into the recycling bin of my head.

I focused on my life. However, all that changed on Sunday, July 6 2014. My wife, Kate, Billy, our twelve year old and Annie, our six year old, were killed when a front tire burst on our station wagon. The vehicle had rolled into a ball as it twisted and turned over several times across the turnpike lanes. I had backed out of the journey to the beach at the last minute.

I had taken a call on my cell despite Kate's eyes urging me to leave it. It had been Jack Delgary, Chair of AGL – the American Gun Lobby.

I had put the mic on mute and said to Kate as she looked on, 'Something big.'

She gave me a knowing look – on her own again.

'I'll follow on, be with you all soon,' I said.

Prompted by her eyes, I added, 'Promise.'

How I regret now not asking her to hang on for me, even though I knew she would have insisted on going on ahead anyway. I might have persuaded her. I was hardly looking up when she blew me a kiss goodbye. How I wish I had given her my full attention as she left or not taken the call. At what point

466

should I have pressed rewind? Would that have changed the outcome?

I learnt from the police that a bullet gash in and out of the rubber had been found in the burst tire. It seems a random sniper, or so they thought, had been taking pot shots on the highway. Other vehicles had been hit too.

Of course, I knew differently. Claire and Tom, they'd warned me, and I'd done nothing.

In the days and weeks that followed, I'd looked for anything to salve my conscience. Nothing worked. Instead, on that day, unaware of my family's impending deaths, I had turned my full attention to the call.

'Hi Jack, sorry about that, just seeing Kate and the kids off.'

His Texan drawl stuck to my phone as he spoke and glued his words into my mind.

'Making a speech tomorrow son, you best make your way there. Shooting pigeons, them vermin just gotta be the way forwa' now. You unner'stand wha I mean?'

'What?' I stumbled out, trying to make sense of his words, '… you talking about people? That's tantamount to murder.' The derision in my voice lost in translation.

'You've seen the deaths, son. Somethin's up, I'd bet my steak on it and it's boys like you stirring up the dung heap and got 'em lunatics out there jumping on the wagon trail. We've gotta put a stop to it. The way I sees it son, it don't seem like there's a dime of difference between what I'm sayin' and what the U… nited States' policy has been since 2005 on pre-emptive strikes. See wha I'm sayin'?

'If someone poses a potential threat, we take 'em out! Clean kill. And I'm betting my boys and gals is a damn sight more accurate than them drones used abroad. There ain't gonna be no collateral damage. You know what I'm sayin' son?'

He hung up the phone.

I was hooked and booked a seat on an early flight for the next morning out of Jacksonville to Austin, courtesy of Delta Airlines and left a voicemail on Kate's cell to say I was on my way.

Of course, she never got my message and I never caught that plane to Texas. I had escaped death twice. Who would have thought the Chair of the AGL would turn a loaded automatic rifle on the gathered media and kill everyone, but he did. We were the vermin. The itch had gotten to him I guess. Seems the maturation process is switching people on early, or maybe they are just more of the vanguard, with many thousands turning later across the globe.

Either way, back then, I did not feel good about escaping death, nor do I now. But whether it was an ethereal influence or nothing at all, just coincidence, the fact remains I've lived to publish this story and all of the supporting evidence I'm going to upload on the Net shortly.

Perhaps now, though, whilst there is still time, it is fitting that Claire and Tom have the last say. It is the final entry in his diary and signed by them both...

Sunday, October 14, 2012

Silence, nothingness and wholeness wedded together by light, asleep in the warm comfort of the womb. Blind, yet able to feel the light within, without, beyond the beyond and still further yet.

Listen, the truth has to be told.

You are a bearer of the truth. You are from the light. It pervades your whole being. Like others before you, like others now, like others yet to come, you have the chance to remain part of the light. Will you be a bearer of the light, a truth teller, or will you choose to be eternally blind, to be drawn into the coming darkness and in the balance, remain forever locked in its embrace?

Some though, have no choice, do they?

You, the lucky ones, always have a choice. How will you choose? Each moment weighs in the balance. Right or wrong, this or that, do, or don't. Each moment you can restore the balance. It's your choice. Make sure, you choose right, right?

Tom Abimelech   Claire Yohanus

EPILOGUE

VISION

By John Clare (1793-1864)

In every language upon earth,
On every shore, o'er every sea,
I gave my name immortal birth
And kept my spirit with the free.

23:53 hours Saturday April 4 – USA, location withheld

Dear Reader

You should know that I have met some of the people in this story. Innocent people like many of us; they had their own issues; competing and confused dreams can sometimes pull apart the bonds of love and commitment. For Claire Yohanus and Tom Abimelech, the only way forward was back. This book would not have been possible without their courage and testimony.

Those history dubbed as vanquished never gave in. London witnessed their first experiments bear fruit. The past is not dead. It has a heartbeat.

To understand the present, you must know the past. Cast your mind back to the previous decade, better still, research it, recall if you will the rise of computer worms, such as Stuxnet, designed to sit hidden within IT networks, slowly but surely infiltrating and infecting them, subverting systems and taking control. Did you know that viral variants of Stuxnet were allegedly planted into the IT network of Iran's uranium enrichment infrastructure in 2010? Eventually, it is claimed, they sent the reactor centrifuges spinning out of control.

Since then, the world has also seen Flame, Duqu and Gauss – all believed to be state sponsored, all designed to steal and monitor data. Take that technological know-how, and imagine how it must have required vast resources to engineer. It's often claimed that it was only achievable with Nation State resources.

It is the access to such resources, which lies behind what has already happened and the plans that have been set in motion. I have presented research in the form of a story. The evidence gathered underpins this book's narrative. It is based upon many lines of investigation undertaken by me and by those that came before me. I have pieced together facts wherever possible, used hidden records unearthed by others and have had access to private diaries.

I have merged these fragmented pictures of events over time and space and sewn them all together with the first-hand accounts of people herein. I will upload all of the documents and the video files as soon as I can. However, I warn you now, some of the reading and the viewing may turn your stomach. So be it. The truth must be told. There is a conspiracy. It is real.

When I first received Claire and Tom's account, I was struck with astonishment and disbelief. In my ignorance, I continued my small life, blessed, so I thought, by the company of good friends and family. My work was busy, challenging and their claims sunk back into the filing cabinet of my mind. Blood relations and 'blood brother and sister relations,' I thought, are bonds we should do our utmost not to sever. But sometimes in the mists of the chaos, blood relationships can be our downfall. In time, you'll see.

It was not until later, after the wrecking ball of chaos smashed into my reality that I researched some of the victims in this story – the real heroes – and verified their accounts.

Sometimes the impossible, the implausible, is the reality. It was the tipping point that threw me into action. I just hope it's not too late. Of course, I regret not acting sooner, yet even if this action right now is in itself but a small glimmer of hope; it might make all the difference, give all of us – you out there – time to prepare.

Planning is complete. The Network – the Fourth Reich is on the verge. Their evil tide of history has been rolling in for over seven decades now. We all know deep down, sense this truth, that the fear of it happening is real. Fear about the far-right, Nazism, has never really left our consciousness has it? For good reason, the Fourth Reich has no intention of ebbing. Not now.

Those in the Network are masters of manipulation and fake news. Look to what went before. They had good teachers. Nazi Germany gave rise to extreme and violent behaviour and a collective reign of terror. Some historians have long argued that many individuals willingly filled themselves with the propaganda of mythologized heroes and believed in the need to destroy imagined demons – neologised as sub-humans. Such a war over thoughts engendered an acceptance of brutality. An enthusiasm for barbarism was unleashed. Rape, stabbing, hacking, battering, bayoneting, shooting, burying alive, gassing, hanging on meat hooks, and experimenting and torturing sub-humans were just some of the tools sharpened through use. These and many other atrocities were carried out to cleanse the human race.

However, unintended outcomes happened. The more the Third Reich cleansed and stretched its governance across nation states, the more it needed to import foreign workers into Germany's heartland to ensure the engine of its war machine was sustained. Despite the Propaganda Ministry's attempts to prevent unholy liaisons through the meting out of harsh punishments, sexual relations between sub-humans and the master race were commonplace. Aryan fertile waters were muddied. The dreams of the Third Reich withered. Yet that which was born and conjured never faded from the mind of the Führer.

There have been many myths and rumours since. Seeds of truth talk of a dark underbelly. Those seeds, scattered in the cross winds of history, whisper of the Odessa Network, Die Spinne and the Bilderberg Group. Indeed these whispers are the stuff of fiction and the banter of conspiracy theorists.

Do not be fooled into disbelief. What history has shown us is this. Power rarely goes quietly to its own grave. In fact, real power never dies. When the Second World War drew to a close, handmaids of the Third Reich gave safe passage to Nazis seeking safe haven and anonymity in return for know-how.

Herein lies the foundation of the research uncovered – the insidious manipulation and use of reproductive technologies.

We all know that Frankenstein is the stuff of legend. He fascinates and abhors us. Yet his rebirth mirrors the dark corners of humanity. Humankind has long been inquisitive and tempted to modify and create life. How long, may surprise you. History lays a dubious crown upon Cleopatra's head, who during her reign in first century BC authorised the impregnation of handmaids who were later opened up to study the development of the foetus. The words of Coleridge's stanza from Frankenstein, twisted in time, play well here for I can imagine the rapid heartbeats of the women as they lay upon the *lonesome road* of death and felt its clammy tendrils wrap around their wombs as they listened to the footsteps of the 'doctor,' *a frightful fiend close behind* their heads *tread* ever closer bringing *fear and dread*. Such thoughts may have been riveted into many women held in concentration camps run by Nazi Germany.

Nevertheless, following Cleopatra's death, the next 1,800 years has shadows of mysterious history covering up what went on. Perhaps eugenics was the glacier. A veil of silence seems to have blanked out, or should I say, redacted, the myriad of experiments for the creation and manipulation of human life that must have been conducted in such a vast period of time. I imagine the reason might lie in the fact that as with many experiments carried out on humans they have not always been consensual.

It was not until 1790 when history's lantern was relit for all to see. Dr. J. Hunter, a Scottish surgeon published the first account of how he artificially inseminated a woman using her husband's sperm, and which resulted in a live birth. Thereafter, successes around the world have been widespread and countless babies have been born via artificial means.

In 1866, Dr. P. Montegazza stated 'a man dying ... may beget ... an heir with his semen frozen and stored at home.' Aldous Huxley's 1932 novel, *Brave New World*, described a global society run by one world government in which all babies are created by artificial insemination and gestated in bottles within hatcheries. Each destined for different roles in the economy. This influential book unsettled people. Some might say, and rightly so. It was, after all, a timely addition to Nazi Germany's thinking during their rise to power in the 1930s.

However, ideas about what ifs are one thing; studies and research are legion too. Towards the end of this book, I have put together a selection of verifiable events and facts on genetics dating from 1869, including reference to the book by Dr. H. Rohleder published in the 1920s, the title of which begins with the opening words *Test Tube Babies*. Yes, that's right; the term is not a late twentieth century invention. It surprised me too. The purpose of the selection, I should add, is to demonstrate that even without access to nation state resources, research ideas and achievements were phenomenal.

It all paints a picture of the progresses made to enhance reproductive capabilities, drive forward technologies for the manipulation of our DNA and change the means of human procreation. In all it left me with one unending feeling. The desire for scientists to tamper evermore is never long resisted. The envelope of genetics is forever being stretched. Our genome is the battlefield. Some say for our good, others...

Each person's genetic makeup, known as their genome, contains up to 25,000 genes, which is mapped out as their DNA sequence. The majority of a person's DNA comes parcelled in 46 chromosomes, half of which comes from the mother's egg and the rest from the father's sperm. As soon as the egg is fertilized, the human embryonic cell, known as a zygote, starts to divide and grow. Each time the embryonic cells divide and multiply, the same chromosomes are replicated within the growing body. The 0.1% difference in an individual's genome makes them unique and sets each person apart from the 99.9% of similarity each of us shares. Importantly, some aberrations in a person's DNA – their genes or the nucleotide within a single gene – can determine if an individual will have a genetic mutation and develop a disease or possess enhanced capabilities.

Today, advances in technology, use of CRISPR/Cas9 for the editing of genomes, have outpaced our ability to forecast the real consequences if used.

Once genetic markers have been identified and located in a particular gene, 'healthy,' 'enhanced,' or 'defective,' genes can be introduced into the petri dish at or shortly after the zygote stage. Thereafter, these transgenes create genetically modified individuals. The alteration is known as germline genetic modification. Changes genetically modified may only become apparent and switch on when an individual matures into adulthood. If not rendered infertile, the genetic modifications will be passed on in their offspring.

The world you and I now live in runs the risk of redefining what is human. Fundamentally, because of uses now applied from the field of reproductive technologies, the survival of our species is in jeopardy. Not all man-made things dangerous to the world are stored in underground bunkers or held in laboratory isolation facilities. Not all seemingly innocuous activities are safe. As always, the hand that holds the instrument seals the fate of its innocent subject. For good or evil intent, for reckless or determined action, all of life can pivot on one decision, one act and one successful experiment.

Unseen powers may try to dismiss these claims that the world you are about to read about exists. They dismiss worldwide conspiracies out of hand. Most of us do too, don't we? But I urge you; look always for those grains of truth. They are dotted out there, trapped behind firewalls, hidden in war archives and blended into everyday structures of society.

My biggest fear though is this. Out of the rampant chaos to come, the only alternative the populace of the world will demand, if their change is to be delivered, is the vehicle dreamed of by the Fourth Reich. It should be a fear that you, and all sound people should share: the emergence of the Fourth Reich as our saviour. If that disaster comes to fruition, then compassion, the lighted candle of democracy, our freedoms, our very lives, will be extinguished.

History will not be repeated. It will be achieved. Occupied territories will be home for only one people. The removal of local inhabitants – literally billions, underpins the goal of the Network's strategic plan. Overpopulation will be a redundant debate trashed in the dustbin of history. Anarchic historians, if they exist in the future, may attempt to unveil the machinations through the telescope of time. However, by then, if we have not acted, it will be too late. Winners make history. They erode truth. They scar what really happened. They are the glaciers of the human race.

Now as I sit here at my computer about to push the button to publish on the Net, I feel trepidation and hope. I *hope* that hope prevails. I hope like the Arab Spring of 2011, social media networks erupt into frenzy, but this time people act together with one voice, one vision and overwhelm powerful plans to see the Network's status quo, the status quo.

We must be strong. You must be strong. Do not be drawn into the zeitgeist, the clamour for change when it arrives. Like me, if you survive, we may be the world's only hope, truth tellers, and people of the light. We the people of humanity must fight back. And fight we must. We have to act together. I am talking about the real will of the people, for the people. We have to smash the powers that will squeeze away our democratic lifeblood – forever. We must somehow, seize the day and say aloud, as one voice: 'This world is *ours*. We will *not* be extinguished.'

There is a storm coming. I warn you. Be prepared.

HISTORY USED

The lists of discoveries under the heading of genetic research are to the best of my knowledge and belief, accurate. References made to other medical discoveries within the main body of the story are also, as far as is possible, factual within the boundless ties of fiction. Readers wishing to explore in more detail the background to discoveries, procedures or drugs mentioned, or indeed expand their own research, would do well to start their journey by searching the myriad of documents available through Google Scholar.

From the years 1934 to 1979 an eclectic range of facts and points of historical note were woven into the fabric of the story. I have not recounted the minute detail below, but instead opted to provide you with a flavour. I am sure those with an avid interest will know more or be motivated to explore the detail further.

On August 20, 1934 when in the story the Führer waits in his office to meet Himmler and Clauberg, this is the day after the German public voted overwhelmingly for Hitler to become the Leader and the Chancellor of the Reich. Earlier in that year in June, known as the 'Night of the Long Knives,' Hitler and his Nazi supporters carried out a range of planned political murders, mass beatings and imprisonment of those standing in the way of the National Socialists' rise to power. Hence why, and understandably so, Professor Clauberg, if he had met Hitler would have been somewhat nervous in his company and conscious no doubt that his life and prestigious career could be ended at the flick of a pen.

The occult held a fascination for the Nazis. For a while, even the German's Propaganda Ministry fell under the spell of astrology's power to seemingly predict the future. It is indeed true, especially in the early years of the Reich, and up until a purging of occultists ordered by Hitler in the early 1940s, that some of the top Nazis consulted astrologists, including Rudolph Hess and Heinrich Himmler. Forecasts were apparently, also drawn up for high-ranking generals up against Allied Commanders in military campaigns.

Many readers will be well aware that September 1, 1939 marked the day when Germany invaded Poland in a brief alliance with the Soviet Union. One fact, not so many readers may realise was that on this day, Hitler secretly authorised the extension of the euthanasia programme to adults, one which had been successfully run and had been disposing of disabled children since the mid 1930s. The actual law was referred to in the story as portrayed in the memo dictated by and signed by Hitler. To assist in the disposal of the adults and mentally impaired individuals, the Aktion T4 Board, led by Hitler's personal physician did actually assess those deemed fit to die by gassing; the six facilities as listed in the exchange of memos in the story were actually built and used.

Whilst history widely records in tragic detail the Final Solution and the mass sterilisation programme, which heavily involved SS – Brigadeführer Carl Clauberg, less evidence is available on the Third Reich's other key population control policy, namely its aim to increase the birth-rate/fecundity of those individuals deemed worthy of reproduction. The Lebensborn Strategy mentioned in Hitler's memo formed a public facing major part of this approach. Mengele's widely reported experimentation on twins also aimed to crack the code on how to increase Aryan stock.

The Nazis pursued artificial insemination as an approach. There was, as mentioned in the memos within the story from

Clauberg, a Reich Working Group that was set up to address support for childless marriages and sterility. The Working Group's brief did include the task of examining the efficacy of artificial insemination. It is true that Himmler did not view favourably artificial insemination as a practice for human beings, but for a variety of reasons grudgingly supported further work into its capability.

Surprisingly, there appears to be little information on what was undertaken in Nazi Germany in terms of artificial insemination programmes and research. Given the fact artificial insemination, or impregnation as it was generally known in those days, was widely practiced throughout Europe and the United States of America, it seems strange that no apparent records of Nazi activity appears to be available. That said, I have not sought to translate the vast array of Nazi research papers which recorded their medical experiments and have relied upon translation available in English and which is publicly available on the internet. If readers have more information on the activities of the Nazis in the use of artificial insemination, I would be very happy to hear from them.

In the meantime, I would refer readers to an interesting paper by Heidrun Kaupen-Haas, who published a paper in *Reproductive and Genetic Engineering,* Vol. 1, No 2, pp 127-132, 1988. This paper provides a stimulating insight and an example of Himmler and Clauberg's impact into 'the way in which population control in Nazi Germany – to promote those "worthy of reproduction" and to eliminate those "unworthy of reproduction" – influenced the international research in genetic and reproductive technology.'

Clauberg and others to conduct their experiments used Block 10 at Auschwitz. Clauberg led the sterilisation experiments. In one of his memos to Himmler, I drew on the actual writing style used by him to reflect, in a small way, a degree of authenticity from history.

Clauberg was in many ways a geneticist; he was a practising gynaecologist and infertility expert of his time. Medical papers today still use the eponym Clauberg when referring to his then groundbreaking work in the 1930s onwards. Unfortunately, not all medical papers that I came across make mention of his infamy, even in a footnote, which I believe as a consequence, avoids the memory of the insidious impact some people have made in history.

Other activities mentioned in the story, such as men held in the camps being forced to ejaculate by stimulation of their prostate gland and freezing experiments on survival of the human body were conducted at Auschwitz. There were two hospitals nearby to the network of the Auschwitz camps as mentioned, which were used to house concentration camp mothers and their offspring; the numbers that could be accommodated in those hospitals were mentioned in the last memo from Clauberg in the story. Within this memo, it was also mentioned that a new block was constructed and could contain more people for experiments, this is factually correct. However, Auschwitz was closed not long after its completion.

Brains were also removed from some of the people experimented on in Block 10 and these were sent from the Nazi death camps for dissection and analysis.

Himmler was transferred to the Upper Rhine Command as his last letter to Clauberg mentions. The ensuing conflict between the Germans and the Allies – the Americans and the French is perhaps better known as the *Battle of the Bulge*.

As far as I am aware, a landing strip was not built at Auschwitz. However, Hitler did indeed have his own private air fleet. His fleet used more modern planes at the time, but held in reserve fifty aircraft – Junkers 52, which were known as 'Auntie Ju', and which did often operate as air ambulances when and if they were transformed. The story describes how a flight of 30 Junkers 52s flew to Engadin Airfield, Switzerland from Auschwitz. Their fuel tanks were capable of such a round trip. Engadin airfield exists. It was also used as a setting for the film, 'Where Eagles Dare.'

The Swiss Nazi party leader, Wilhelm Gustloff was assassinated and the Swiss Nazi headquarters were based in Davos, Switzerland. The Germans did have a sanatorium in Davos before and during the war.

The dates in the story where I have indicated Clauberg and Mengele were at Auschwitz are factually correct. When the Red Army was near, Mengele did go to Gross Rosen; he was later detained by the Americans and inadvertently released by them or so history tells us.

The account of Clauberg's escape and capture and that of Himmler's death are also broadly factual. Clauberg was captured by the Red Army, imprisoned by them and later released back to Germany. Upon his return, he did boast about his sterilisation work during the war and referred to the victims as guinea pigs. He was arrested in Germany and was due to stand trial. However, the night before he was due in court, he apparently died of a heart attack.

The quotes from Hitler's last speech on January 30, 1945 and the one from Goebbels at the beginning of the story are accurate.

Over the past decade salvage hunters have searched the bottom of lakes in Austria and Germany for the gold, worth billions of pounds that the Nazis are widely reported to have stolen during the war. The alias Hitler gives Mengele in the story is one of the many names he actually used during his life on the run. The date and location of his death in the story is also factual and he did live, amongst other places, in Bertioga, Brazil. Reports in the media have also claimed that Mengele may have influenced the cluster of twins being born in a town in Brazil. Arguments abound about the causes and also whether he was involved or not.

In terms of more recent history, the following facts were mentioned in the story:

Burundanga or devil's breath is recounted in popular culture and media reports as causing people to obey instructions without question and to lose their memory of the event. The articles and research I came across hail from stories describing burundanga as a favoured drug of use by criminals in many South American countries.

The story mentions the death of Tom's childhood friend Jim, whose mother later died in a train accident in Germany in 1988. That year did witness a tragic train accident in Lower Saxony, not far from Hannover. It was one of the worst train disasters of all time, one hundred and one people died. Fatigue in the metal of one of the wheels apparently resulted in a failure to its structural integrity and the train, travelling at high-speed, derailed.

The statistics on missing people in London are broadly accurate and reflect also the nature of bodies and parts found. I have referred to the Missing Persons Bureau, which in fact covers the whole of the UK. In order for them to record a missing person, the individual has to be registered as missing by the police. In the story, this essential action was missing, as DS Raven, readers may recall would not have Tom recorded thus so. I would like to add, that I have not made contact with the Bureau for the purposes of writing this book, however, I imagine they must do a great job in supporting and assisting people and providing an outlet to voice awareness of a loved one to be found.

Following the tragic events in Norway in July 2011 when seventy-six young people and adults lost their lives to a lone individual who expressed far right beliefs, the UK Home Office did indeed inject additional resources into security services' activities. The story describes a secret intelligence report prepared for the Home Secretary. Therein it mentions several aspects, which have actually been cited in the media as having happened, namely: the *Winter of Terror* in the 1950s in which a series of avalanches killed hundreds of people in Austria and Switzerland and; the destruction of evidence on neo-Nazis by German domestic intelligent services as reported in the press on 29 June, 2012.

The book refers to Davos in Switzerland. The geographical statistics are broadly accurate as too, are mention that it is home to research facilities, hospitals and conferences. The annual World Economic Forum (WEF) is also held in Davos.

In the book, Doru talks about his daughter Ekaterina. A vast array of research is publicly available which presents data and discusses what is known about the activities and flows of people forced around the world. Timisoara is viewed as being one of several European hubs for the inward and outward distribution of people against their will. Sadly, human trafficking of millions of women, girls, boys and men for slavery, sex, begging and organ transplants, amongst other uses and abuses, is an on-going global evil.

Three further points, which, although not directly linked to history, may be of interest for some. The story makes frequent references to travel, by sea, by train, by road and by air. I have tried to be as accurate as possible in terms of the method of travel and the time it might take to use each mode to reach particular destinations mentioned in the story. The GPS tracking device used by Harry can be bought, worryingly, over the internet. References to parks, streets, towns and cities and indeed most of the buildings, apart from the pubs, hotels, the 201 Club and some organisations mentioned, are factual, all of which can still be seen today.

The poems in the book, *Truth, Fallen Angel, The Orphaned Asked Equation* and *Sojourn,* were written by me. On a more personal note, with regard to two of these poems, I named my maternal grandparents, Ethel Bedford and George Henry Smedley, as the poets.

My grandfather died, was killed in action during the First World War on October 8, 1917 and some five weeks after the birth of my mother. I had not planned to assign their names to the poems, but in the last few days of writing the story, I felt the calling to do so. On the actual day I decided to include my grandfather's name, I discovered that it was the exact day he died. Some might say coincidence. I feel it is more than that. And that makes me smile. So, some ninety-six years after my grandmother and grandfather parted, perhaps in a very small way, this book has brought them back together. Love had found a way.

Finally, as a human being, and as far as I know not genetically modified, I apologise in advance for any errors or omissions, which may have crept into the story, or the historical note; they are entirely my responsibility.

GENETIC RESEARCH

1869: DNA was first discovered by Dr. F. Miescher.

1883: Liquid nitrogen was first produced by Polish scientists, Z. Wróblewski and K. Olszewski.

1891: Professor W. Heape reported the successful transplantation of embryos from one breed of rabbit to another.

1921: Dr. H. Rohleder published his book, 'Test Tube Babies: A History of Artificial Impregnation of Human Beings.'

1928: Dr. A. Butenandt's research resulted in the capability to extract sex hormones from women's urine for subsequent use in the stimulation of the ovaries and the production of multiple eggs during ovulation.

1934: Dr. G. Pincus reported the first successful in-vitro-fertilisation (IVF) transfer and subsequent live birth of rabbits.

1938: Scientists observed sperm could survive freezing and storage at temperatures as low as - 321° F/-196° C.

1942: Dr. J. Scott first discovered the DNA genes MOA – A and MOA – B, which are associated with aggressive and violent behaviour.

1944: Drs. J. Rock and M. Menkin reported that between the years 1938 and 1944 they had collected 800 human ova by laparotomy and successfully fertilised 138 eggs in-vitro.

1949: Drs. C. Polge, A. Smith and A. Parkes reported on the protective properties of glycerol when freezing spermatozoa.

1953: Dr. J. Sherman used glycerol to protect sperm during freezing and thawing to fertilise human ova in-vitro. That year he opened the world's first sperm bank.

1957: The DNA gene COMT, which is associated with extreme violence, was discovered by the biochemist J. Axelrod.

1957: The DNA gene DAT-1 was discovered by Dr. A. Carlsson, subsequent studies suggest there is an association with schizophrenia.

1962: Dr. J. Lederberg, a leading geneticist speculates the use of gene therapy.

1973: Professors C. Wood and J. Leeton reported the world's first successful IVF pregnancy in a woman.

1978: Professors P. Steptoe and R. Edwards reported the world's first successful live human IVF birth. That year, Drs. S. Mukherjee, S. Mukherji and S. Bhattacharya reported the world's first live human IVF birth using a frozen embryo.

More than 5 million IVF babies have been born worldwide since, an average of 166,000 year on year.

Philip A. Oldfield – October 2013

Printed in Great Britain
by Amazon